The Secret of the Dragon's Scale

Steven Eisenberg

Copyright © 2025 Steven Eisenberg

All rights reserved. No part of this book may be reproduced or transmitted in any form or by any means, electronic or mechanical, including photocopying, recording or by any information storage and retrieval system without permission in writing from the publisher.

ISBN: 979-8-218-74141-9
Title: The Secret of the Dragon's Scale
Author: Steven Eisenberg
Digital distribution | 2025
Paperback | 2025

For Xiaoping

献给我的妻子,
她是我有生以来最珍贵的财富,
她的爱是指引我航向的星辰,
是鼓起我风帆的风,
是让每一次旅程都值得的奇迹。

Contents

	Preface	v
1.	Where Ye've Been, and Where Ye're Goin'	1
2.	Where the Sun Kisses the Sea	24
3.	Bella	44
4.	The Stone that Sings	73
5.	Fresh Beginnings and Salt-Kissed Endings	99
6.	Where the Serpent Dons a Feathered Guise	134
7.	Lullabies	173
8.	Where Light and Darkness Dance and Twirl	205
9.	A Radiant Tear	220
10.	Redemption	261
	About the Author	292

Preface

When Robert Louis Stevenson introduced the world to *Treasure Island,* he didn't just craft a story—he redrew the map of adventure literature itself. The names of its characters, the allure of its treasures, and the thrill of its adventures have echoed through time, inspiring countless tales of high seas and hidden riches. *The Secret of the Dragon's Scale* was born from that same legacy.

Originally envisioned to be part of a series inspired by *Treasure Island*, readers will recognize echoes of Stevenson's classic in the names that populate this story, Billy Bones, Ben Gunn, and others, as well as the fabled ship, the Admiral Benbow. But here, these names take on new life, anchoring a tale that ventures into uncharted waters. The Admiral Benbow, once a humble inn in *Treasure Island*, becomes a legendary ship at the heart of this story—a vessel shrouded in mystery, rumored to have vanished with a treasure so vast it could rival the wealth of empires. And yet, as with all great legends, the truth is far more extraordinary than anyone dared to imagine.

What sets *The Secret of the Dragon's Scale* apart is its depth. It is not your traditional swashbuckling pirate story. It is a tale of destiny and sacrifice, of the choices that define us and the truths we uncover about ourselves. It explores the cost of obsession, the power of love, and the realization that the greatest treasures are not found in chests of gold but in the bonds we forge and the lives we choose to lead.

So, prepare to set sail. The journey ahead is one of danger, wonder, and discovery. And as you turn the pages, remember: the true secret of the Dragon's Scale lies not in its legend, but in the lessons it teaches about what truly matters.

Also by Steven Eisenberg

Can You Rape a Robot? Morality, Rights, and the Rise of Conscious Machines

Fifteen Men: The Curse of the Aztec Treasure

Connect with Steven

Web site: StevenEisenbergAuthor.com
Facebook: StevenEisenbergAuthor
YouTube: @steveneisenbergauthor

The Secret of the Dragon's Scale

Where Ye've Been, and Where Ye're Goin'

It was nearly a year ago, in a dimly lit corner of the Sea Serpent's Den, that Jim Allardyce sat, his eyes reflecting the dancing flames of the hearth.

Buried in the heart of Nassau, where the air was heavy with the scent of salt and the echoes of a thousand tales of piracy and battle, this old tavern sat—hidden from prying eyes by a labyrinth of winding alleyways. Built from the bones of shipwrecks and the grit of rough quarried stone, its low ceilings and thick-timbered pillars gave the space a cozy, if slightly claustrophobic, feel. Upon pushing open the creaking door, one would be engulfed by a cloud of warm, smoky air that carried the tang of brine, the musk of damp wood, the sweetness of aged rum, and the faintest hint of gunpowder. The flickering glow of oil lamps cast dancing shadows on the rough-hewn tables and benches, while the crackling fire in the stone hearth added a comforting warmth to the otherwise cold, dim room. The taste of grog, a fiery concoction of rum, water, and a hint of lime, lingered on the tongue—a harsh yet comforting reminder of the lawless life that thrived within these walls. The tavern was always alive with the raucous laughter of grizzled seafarers, their faces weathered by sea and sun, their eyes sparkling with tales of high-seas adventures. The clinking of tankards and the low hum of hushed conversations filled the air, creating a cacophony of sounds as intoxicating as the strong spirits served here.

Bathed in the flickering light of a lone lantern sat a gaggle of motley buccaneers and freebooters, each bearing a tale in their scars and salt-matted hair. Their eyes glimmered with emotions too raw to hide—fear that shadowed their bravado, greed that sharpened their gazes, and the wild gleam of hunger for fortunes yet unseen. They huddled over a tattered map, its edges curling with age, their calloused hands tracing lines with reverence and calculation. Their voices, rough as the creak of old rigging, dropped to conspiratorial murmurs, each word laced with the intrigue of schemes laid in the dark.

Jim's ears tuned in to the tales that spilled from the ale-stained lips of these roughened seafarers. Their words carried the weight of legend, hushed with awe and edged with foreboding. They spoke of the Admiral Benbow, a ship that sailed under the banner of a captain as ruthless as he was cunning, carrying a treasure so immense it was said to put a king's ransom to shame. But the ship, like a specter, had vanished, leaving behind nothing but whispers and rumors. Some said it was taken by a monstrous sea creature, its jaws large enough to swallow a ship whole. Others whispered of curses laid thick as fog—vengeance wrought upon the crew for crimes too vile to be spoken. Then there were those who claimed the treasure was still out there—that the captain had tricked fate itself, hiding it in some uncharted abyss, waiting for a worthy soul both daring and damned enough to uncover it.

These tales of grandeur and intrigue ignited a spark deep within him, a flame fueled by ambition and an insatiable thirst for adventure. Although still young, Jim was no stranger to the sea, having spent countless days chasing dreams of gold and glory across the endless expanse of the ocean. Yet, the Admiral Benbow stood apart—a prize unlike any he'd ever imagined. This wasn't just treasure; it was legend. The ship's allure, cloaked in shadow and secrecy, called to him like a siren's song, its mysteries more enticing than its hoarded wealth. The promise of riches was intoxicating, but it was the story that truly held him captive—its beauty lay in the unknown, its value in its elusiveness. It waited, a riddle begging to be solved, a chapter yearning to be written by daring hands.

The Secret of the Dragon's Scale

As the tales crescendoed into a climax, a bold decision took root in Jim's heart—a terrifying yet thrilling prospect. He would find the Admiral Benbow himself, claim its riches, and etch his name into the annals of pirate legend. He understood his journey would be fraught with danger and treachery, but the reward promised to outweigh the risks.

Stepping out of the tavern, Jim tilted his head toward the star-studded sky. The salt air filled his lungs, and the sea's rhythm filled his ears. He made his way out of the narrow alleyway, his boots echoing softly against the cobblestones, and toward the wharf, a sense of purpose surging within him as he looked out at the moonlit waves.

His only problem . . . where to begin?

A moment later Jim heard shuffling coming from the alleyway. The group of old scallywags Jim had overheard were getting too drunk to even see the map let alone follow anything on it, so they had decided to get some sleep. As the first one dragged himself out of the alleyway, Jim seized his chance. Swallowing hard, he summoned up his bravado and sidled up to the man.

"Friend!" Jim cried out, slapping him on the back with feigned camaraderie.

The man glanced at him briefly, his eyes glassy with intoxication.

"Let's get ye home, ye've had a few too many tonight," Jim said.

His balance unsteady, the man peered at Jim, trying to anchor his gaze.

"Who're ye?" he slurred.

"Jim, your old chum, remember?" Jim responded quickly, inventing a backstory on the spot. "We've shared many a rum and tale." His words hung in the air, as deceptive as a mirage, but the man was too lost in drink to notice the lie.

He blinked at Jim, his eyes, bloodshot and heavy-lidded, struggled to maintain focus. "Jim, eh?" he echoed, the name seeming to stir some vague recognition. "Must've been some good times. I don't remember a thing!" With that, he let out a hearty laugh, swaying dangerously.

Jim felt a strange mix of relief and guilt. His ruse was working, but the deception left a bitter taste in his mouth.

As they stumbled along, Jim chattered about their supposed past adventures. His goal was to confuse the sailor into spilling secrets about the ship and the old map, but he wasn't getting anywhere. Frustration mounting, Jim abandoned subtlety and asked directly about the map.

"And that map ye was jabberin' 'bout the other night . . . Did anyone figure if it be real or not?"

A spark of confusion darted across the sailor's face as his brow twitched and his eyes widened momentarily. "A map?" he muttered, his mind wading through the foggy marsh of his memories.

He squinted at Jim, his focus wavering. Then, in a sudden burst of rage, his eyes blazed with a wild fire as he unsheathed a knife from his side, thrusting it menacingly toward Jim's face! "THERE BE NO MAP!" he bellowed, his voice a thunderous roar. "AIN'T NOBODY KNOWS NOTHIN' 'BOUT NO MAP!"

Jim was taken by surprise and staggered back, his heart pounding as he put his hands up. It was then he noticed the "B.B." engraved on the knife.

"Now . . . c-calm down . . . Buh, Buh . . . Ben! We's old friends, ain't we?"

"Name's Billy! Billy Bones! And I don't know ye from Adam's off ox! So if I was ye, I'd forget ever knowin' anythin' 'bout any map! GOT IT!?"

Jim, trying to calm Billy down, stuttered, "Uh, r-right, absolutely . . . I know nothin'."

Although now wide-eyed and seething at the thought of the secret of the map being known to anyone else, in his still inebriated state Billy unintentionally spilled a clue. "Besides, the map be worthless anyway," he divulged. "Don't say nothin' 'bout findin' no ship. Only has some scribble on it 'bout some dragon's scale, or somethin' like that."

Lowering his knife, head now held low, feeling cheated and depressed, Billy turned and began to stagger back to his ship to sleep off the grog.

But now, Jim was back to square one. All he knew was that the map mentioned something about a dragon's scale. That made no sense and meant nothing to him.

As dawn broke the next morning, Jim found himself strolling along the wharf, the sea breeze tugging at his worn-out clothes. The air was heavy with the briny kiss of the sea and the whispered tales of the many majestic sailing ships docked there. Flanking him on either side, their massive hulls, scarred by time and countless voyages, creaked softly as they swayed to the rhythm of the waves, their masts reaching up toward the sky. The sharp cries of gulls, wheeling overhead, echoed across the water. The occasional bell tolled from the ships, marking the passage of time in this timeless place. At the dockside, barrels and crates were stacked high, filled with goods from all corners of the Earth. The scent of tobacco, rum, and exotic spices from distant lands, created a heady blend that was both intoxicating and invigorating. Dockworkers toiled under the weight of these goods, their muscles straining, their faces glistening with sweat, their curses and laughter mingling with the soundscape of the wharf.

The previous night's events still lingered in Jim's mind, especially Billy's drunken confession about the dragon's scale. Jim didn't put much stock in it; he'd never heard mention of such a thing in any seafaring lore, yet something about it gnawed at his curiosity.

Lost in his thoughts, he nearly walked into a grizzled old sailor, the man's face a map of deep lines and sun-darkened creases, each one a tale of storms braved and horizons chased. Apologizing, Jim's gaze fell to the man's arm, where a faded tattoo came to life beneath bronzed skin. It was a jagged shape that called to mind the scale of some great serpent. With an astonished look on his face, he couldn't help but stare at it—an echo of the strange confession that now would not leave him be.

The old sailor, a twinkle of madness dancing in his sea-blue eyes, noticed Jim's gaze trailing to the tattoo. With a knowing glance, he looked down at his arm, then back up at Jim. He traced the tattoo with a gnarled finger. He chuckled, a sound that was half a cackle and half a sigh.

"Ah, the Dragon's Scale," he said slowly, his voice carrying the weight of a thousand lost tales. "A riddle drowned in the depths of the sea, its truth hidden where men dare not wander."

"What be the Dragon's Scale?" asked Jim. "What does it mean?"

His eyes distant, lost in a labyrinth of legend, he tells the tale. "No one really knows what it is, or what it means, boy. But us sailors . . . we've been chasing after it for centuries, like a ship pursuing the endless horizon. The Dragon's Scale, a mystery as elusive as the ocean's deepest secrets, has held a different meaning for each soul. Most believe it leads the way to a vast hidden treasure, that to find this treasure you must first find the Dragon's Scale. Others believe it's a charm protecting us from the sea's wrath. But there are those who believe it's a curse, a harbinger of doom."

His laughter filled the air again—a chilling, unhinged cackle that sent shivers down Jim's spine. "But be warned, boy. The Dragon's Scale . . . It's a siren's call, luring you into a dance with madness." Then his gaze turned serious, his words heavy with an unspeakable dread. "I've seen the strongest men, those who feared neither storm nor cannon, unravel before my very eyes. I've seen the bravest sailors lose not just their way, but their very minds, torn apart by the endless riddle of the Scale. It devours them, boy—consumes their thoughts, their dreams, their souls—'til there's nothing left but hollow shells, haunted by what they could never grasp. That be why, for many a year, no man has dared speak of it, for fear of returning to an abyss of insanity."

He leaned in closer to Jim, his voice now a mere whisper, yet it carried the weight of a storm. "So listen well, boy. Many a foolhardy soul, their lust for riches unbound, have spent their whole lives searching, yearning, for the Dragon's Scale. But what they find . . . is a descent into madness. The sea, she keeps her secrets deeper than the bones of drowned ships. And those fool enough to dig 'em up? . . . They pay the price."

With a final, eerie chuckle, the old sailor turned and walked away, leaving Jim adrift in a sea of bewilderment. With the cryptic tale of the Dragon's Scale swirling in his mind, he was no closer to understanding its meaning than he was before, and its connection to the Admiral Benbow was as elusive as the ship itself. However, the whispers of danger, the descent into madness—they became to Jim not cautionary tales meant to instill fear, but rather a call to the wild spirit that had always dwelled within him. In the ghostly echo left by the old sailor's departing laughter, Jim found his resolve hardening. The Admiral Benbow, a specter shrouded in myth and mystery, called out to him.

His head still in a bit of a fog, Jim continued ambling along the wharf, admiring the fine vessels moored to the docks. He had found himself drinking away the time at the Sea Serpent's Den after his own ship, the Mermaid's Fury, had barely limped into port. It had once been among these majestic vessels. But now, it was a crippled hulk, its hull eaten away by relentless shipworms and scarred by too many brushes with the cannons of the Royal Navy, a hollow echo of her former glory. With his ship no longer seaworthy, Jim, along with his crewmates, was adrift on the vast ocean of uncertainty, searching for a new ship to call home.

With his steps slow and deliberate, his head down as if weighed by the depth of his reflections, Jim didn't notice the familiar figure approaching him. It was Ben Gunn, a crewmate and young pirate like himself, their shared dreams of riches and adventure woven into the very fabric of their being. Ben, ever resourceful, had managed to find himself another ship. He had always possessed a silver tongue, and wielded charisma and cunning like twin swords. He was a master storyteller, able to spin a tale so captivating, so compelling, that it was almost impossible not to be drawn in. And with this innate flair for persuasion, Ben had deftly maneuvered his way to become the first mate on a grand new vessel.

"Jim!" Ben hollered, his voice echoing over the din of clattering crates and squawking gulls.

Jim turned, his youthful face breaking into a grin at the sight of his friend. "Ben!" he called out, his voice cutting through the clatter of the dock. His eyes took in Ben's new attire—a crisp officer's coat and polished boots. With a teasing grin tugging at his lips, Jim quipped, "I see ye've moved up in the world."

Ben chuckled, running a hand through his unruly hair. "Aye, that I have. Sweet-talked me way into the first mate post on a new ship."

Jim raised an eyebrow. "That so? And what trickery did ye use for that, eh?"

"Charm and guile, Jimmy boy," Ben replied with a wink, "Charm and guile . . . And a bit of luck, of course."

They shared a laugh before Ben's expression turned serious. "So Jim, this ship's still in need of a few good hands. Reliable men who know their way 'round a ship."

Jim crossed his arms, leaning against a barrel. "Oh? I'm all ears, Ben."

"I can get ye on board," Ben said earnestly. "We need strong, experienced hands. I've already got John Silver signed up." John was a young friend and shipmate of theirs from the Mermaid's Fury.

For a moment, Jim was silent, his gaze distant as he looked out to the sea. Then, he turned back to Ben, his eyes twinkling with the old, familiar spark of adventure. "Ye've got yourself a deal."

The Secret of the Dragon's Scale

"Come," Ben said, "I'll take ye to 'er."

As the last echoes of their pact faded into the salty air, Jim and Ben began their ramble down the long, weathered pier that stretched out from the furthest end of the wharf. The wood beneath their boots, worn smooth by countless footsteps and the relentless lapping of the sea, creaked softly in protest with each step they took.

At the end of the pier, their destination loomed—a majestic ship moored securely, its sails furled tightly to the yards and its masts standing tall and proud against the bright blue sky. As they approached, the ship revealed its splendor. The hull gleamed with a rich, dark luster, its wooden planks carved from aged oak that bore the marks of its many voyages. Its surface showed hues of deep mahogany, weathered by brine and sun, with streaks of salt kissed white into the wood's grain. Barnacles clung to its lower reaches like ancient armor, testaments to countless journeys through tumultuous seas. The timbers, though scarred with the ghosts of cannon fire and the battering of waves, held firm with the stoicism of an enduring legend. At the prow, the carved figurehead of a youthful maiden emerged, her visage captured in an eternal, enchanting melody, her flowing hair and delicate features evoking a haunting beauty that seemed to breathe life into the very wood itself.

Coming nearer, Jim's eyes became drawn to the ship's stern, where its name was elegantly painted. His pace slowed, each footfall lighter than the last, as the words came into focus. Then he froze, his boots rooted to the dock as if the wooden planks had suddenly fused with his soles. The color fled from his face, his eyes wide and unblinking; his jaw slackened, the usually firm set of his mouth replaced by a slight gape.

"Siren's Call," he read aloud, his voice scarcely more than a breath. He just stared at the name, his wide eyes reflecting both disbelief and a creeping dread. A chilling echo of the old sailor's ominous warning coiled around his thoughts—*The Dragon's Scale . . . It's a siren's call, luring you into a dance with madness.*

As the words swirled in his head, Jim could almost hear the phantom strains of siren songs. And just as the songs of mythical sirens, laced with honeyed deceit, lured sailors to their doom, the Dragon's Scale hypnotized men with its seductive promise of riches beyond mortal imagining. Those who heeded its call were caught in an endless chase, a pursuit that unraveled their sanity thread by thread, until all that remained was the hollowed husk of what they once were. Even the most hardened mariners found their resolve splintered, drawn by their obsession into a fevered descent, as if the Scale itself drank deeply from their souls.

A hand clapped on his shoulder, making him jump. "Jim, ye look like ye've seen a ghost," Ben said, a tinge of concern in his voice.

Jim turned to face him, a haunted look in his eyes. He opened his mouth, trying to articulate the sense of foreboding that was washing over him, but he found himself unable to form the words. Instead, he simply nodded toward the ship, his gaze lingering on its haunting name. Then he spoke. "Siren's Call . . . I've got a bad feelin' 'bout this. It be a bad omen, Ben."

Ben followed his gaze, his brows furrowing. "It just be a name, mate," he replied, a note of dismissal in his tone. The omen was still there, whispering its eerie song, but Jim swallowed his fear and made his choice—he would join the crew of the Siren's Call, ready to brave the dance with madness, ready to face whatever the fates had in store. With that, they strode up the gangplank and boarded the ship.

The ship was a masterpiece of maritime craftsmanship. Its deck's lustrous wood gleamed under the sun like polished bronze; the planks, seasoned by countless voyages, bore the faint grooves and scars of hard-fought battles, yet their seamless alignment spoke of meticulous care and unwavering pride. The three main masts soared skyward, carrying massive folded sails rippling subtly in the breeze, their intricate lattice of rigging crisscrossing with the precision of a masterful tapestry. The ship's wheel stood proudly at the stern, an impressive arc of mahogany encircled by iron, its spokes tipped with smooth, dark caps polished to a shine. Cannons, sleek and menacing, lined the gunports to the sides, their barrels braced like guardians, each paired with neatly coiled ropes and stacks of cannonballs. Even moored and motionless, the ship radiated a quiet grandeur, a promise of adventure and distant, uncharted waters waiting just beyond the horizon.

Jim stood amidst it all, taking in the commanding view of the deck and the men who called it home. The crew was a daunting assembly of hardened seafarers, their strength apparent in the confidence of their movements and the precision of their tasks. Faces bronzed by unrelenting sun and sea glinted with beads of sweat, the lines etched into their features telling stories of distant horizons and perilous exploits. Tattoos snaked along muscled arms, telling tales of battles fought and victories claimed, while calloused hands worked tirelessly, knotting ropes and repairing sails with an efficiency born of years at sea.

Despite being the freshest face among the ranks of the crew, young Jim was fully aware of his many responsibilities. His tasks were both humble and important—swabbing the salt-stained planks to keep the ship ready for action, mending the lofty sails that propelled them through uncharted waters, and threading the tangle of rigging with practiced hands.

Here, skill and toil would pave the way to survival, but respect would be earned only in the crucible of combat. During battle, Jim was expected to defend the ship alongside his comrades, though, as a seasoned pirate himself, he was no stranger to the weight of a cutlass in his hand or the heft of a pistol at his side. These were not mere tools, but extensions of his own being, honed through countless skirmishes and duels. On board this new ship, his courage and competence would need to be tested in combat, a trial by fire that would either earn him his crewmates' respect or lead to his demise.

Soon after he had settled into his berth and the ship set sail, Jim was on his hands and knees, a coarse brush in hand, scrubbing the planks of the deck, when he heard the clomping of boots coming toward him. They stopped directly in front of him. He slowly raised his gaze from the wet wood, trailing upward past a pair of tall boots to meet the formidable figure looming over him, and found himself in the towering presence of the captain of the ship.

It was none other than Billy Bones!

Staring down at Jim, the skin around the captain's eyes tightened, his eyelids narrowing to thin slits from under which he glared with an intensity that could set the deck ablaze! His weather-beaten face, a map of countless battles and storms endured, twitched slightly in surprise; a flicker of recognition then darted across his steely gaze, igniting his fury!

"YOU!" roared Billy, his voice thundering across the ship with the power of a cannon's blast! His arm shot out, and his finger jabbed accusingly at Jim! His other hand clenched the hilt of his cutlass, his grip tightening around it like a vice! Standing tall, his presence blotted out the world around him, while his stare, as sharp as a dagger's edge, burned into Jim with a ferocity that rivaled the wildest of tempests. Every line of his body, every ripple of tension in his muscles, spoke of a brewing storm, one that promised devastation. Billy Bones was not a man known for his mercy, nor one to forgive easily. His reputation for fierce justice and zero leniency preceded him, and those who dared cross him often felt the cut of his blade.

Billy lunged downward, his arm, as thick and sturdy as an oak tree, shot out with a speed that belied his imposing size! His hand, calloused and scarred from years of sword fights and hard labor, clamped onto Jim's collar with an iron grip. With a single, swift movement that was as fluid as it was forceful, he hoisted Jim off the deck!

"Look at me, boy!" he growled, his voice a low rumble that echoed ominously across the deck, shaking the deathly silence surrounding them. Jim's feet flailed helplessly in the air as Billy lifted him, bringing him face to face with his rage. The captain's hot breath washed over him as he was brought inches away from that furious glare. The veins on Billy's forehead bulged like twisted rigging against the weathered canvas of his face, his eyes two blazing coals in the hearth of his anger, burning with a wrath that was as terrifying as it was mesmerizing. "What're ye doin' on me ship!?" he shouted with a booming ferocity that caused even the seagulls overhead to scatter, the storm in his eyes never leaving Jim's face. His grip on Jim's collar didn't waver, his fingers digging into the fabric as if he intended to wring the life out of the man; his other hand clenched into a rock-like fist, every tendon and sinew visible against the tanned skin of his forearm, shaking slightly with the effort to contain the full brunt of his anger.

With no intention of waiting for an answer, Billy stormed toward the ship's railing, the timbers shuddering beneath his wrathful stride, echoing his fury with dreadful groans. His grip upon young Jim was as unyielding as iron shackles, holding the lad aloft with an ease that bore testament to his formidable strength. The muscles in his arm flexed as he prepared to hurl Jim into the merciless arms of the sea, his intentions as clear as the rage etched on his face.

Shocked at what he was witnessing, Ben's voice suddenly rang out, sharp and desperate, "Avast, Captain! What in God's name are ye doin'!?"

Billy's head whipped around, his wild eyes blazing like a fire trapped beneath his brow. "This pox-ridden bilge rat's a lyin' thief!" Billy yelled back, each word a hammer blow of accusation, the veins in his neck straining with the force of his shout.

Turning his sights back to Jim, Billy growled, "Prepare to dance with Davy Jones, boy!" his grip tightening around Jim's collar. The words hung heavy in the air as the crew watched in horror, the fate of their shipmate hanging precariously in the balance.

Ben launched himself across the ship's deck with a fearful urgency, each stride striking the planks with a thud matching the wild pounding of his heart. "He's no thief!" cried Ben. At the moment he reached them, panting heavily, he explained, "He's me friend. We were shipmates on the Mermaid's Fury! I swear by it—he's no thief! He's no thief!" His eyes, wide with terror and blazing with sincerity, locked onto Billy's, searching for a glimmer of mercy.

Fearing for his life, Jim's mind raced, grasping frantically for a lifeline to save himself, his heart pounding, a wild drumbeat echoing his fear and desperation. Just then, the words of the old sailor on the wharf echoed in his mind. He swallowed hard, his throat dry as sand, and stammered, "Th . . . the Dragon's Scale . . . I know 'bout the Dragon's Scale." His voice cracked, trembling under the weight of the captain's searing glare. "Find the D-Dragon's Scale and it will l-lead ye t-to the Admiral B-Benbow."

The words had barely left Jim's lips before the world seemed to slow. Billy froze in his tracks, his eyes becoming as wide as the moon. His thick brows, normally furrowed in a perpetual scowl, shot up, carving deep crevices in his forehead. His rugged features softened momentarily, his usually stern lips parting in a silent gasp of disbelief. Jim could feel the captain's grip slacken. His words, though stumbling and shaky, had found their mark.

"The Dragon's Scale?" Billy muttered, his gravelly voice barely a whisper against the wind. "Ye be speakin' old tales, lad. Fairy stories spun by drunken sailors and fools." Yet, his voice lacked conviction, and his gaze bore into Jim with an intensity that belied his dismissive words.

With a suddenness that made Jim flinch, Billy released him.

Still simmering with anger and mistrust, the captain asked, "What be yer name, lad?"

"Uh . . . Jim, Captain . . . sir. Jim Allardyce."

"He's on the list of new crew I gave ye before we set sail, Captain," Ben tried to explain.

Pointing at both of them, the captain commanded, "You and you. To me cabin."

The map that Billy Bones and his fellow pirates had been poring over in the tavern was in fact in his possession. He rolled it out onto the map table in his cabin. "Aye, I saw through the lad and his little game," Billy said, pointing to the map, a knowing smirk playing on his lips. "Clever as a fox, ye were." Looking at Ben while pointing at Jim, Billy explained what happened. "I found meself in the depths of drink, as loaded as a cannon ready to fire. But even in such a state, I kept a tight hold on me senses. Upon leavin' the tavern, there was young Jim, claimin' we was old friends, weavin' tales of our past exploits, his words flowin' as freely as the spirits from me bottle. He hoped to befuddle me, pry secrets from me rum-soaked brain about this here map, eyein' to find and steal the treasure before anyone else, I'm guessin'. Bold, indeed, for such a young whelp. But audacity's a trait I can respect. It be the same trait that separates a seasoned pirate from a common sailor." Billy then turned and stared straight into Jim's face, his eyes steely and cold, his brow knit tightly. And with a low, threatening growl, he delivered his words like a blade pressed to Jim's throat. "Now listen well, ye scurvy dog. Ye'll stay alive on this ship as long as ye work. Work 'til yer bones ache and yer fingers bleed. Ye'll work 'til the sun sets, and then ye'll work some more under the cold stare of the moon. The sea's got no time for laggards, and nor does this ship." Then, leaning into Jim's face an inch from his nose, he warned, "But most importantly . . . if ever a word were to slip from yer lips, if even a whisper of the map or the Admiral Benbow reaches unfriendly ears,"—his eyes flashing with a menace as chilling as the icy depths of the sea— "I'll draw and quarter ye with me bare hands, and feed each rottin' piece to the sharks! GOT IT!?"

Summoning a facade of bravery so as not to betray any hint of weakness to the formidable captain, even though his heart pounded in his chest, Jim squared his shoulders, steeled his gaze, and locked eyes with Billy, refusing to flinch under the weight of

Billy's piercing stare. His chin lifted, a subtle defiance in the set of his jaw as he fought to rein in the trembling that threatened to betray him, and he responded with a steady and firm, "Aye, Captain."

"Then we's all in agreement, are we?" Billy continued, looking at both men. The tension in the room began to ebb as Billy's rigid posture relaxed; the hard lines of his face softened as he let out a measured breath, his clenched jaw gradually relaxing. A small, genuine smile tugged at the corners of Billy's mouth as he looked back at Jim. "Ye held yer ground well, lad," he acknowledged, his voice now carrying a note of respect rather than its earlier menace. He gave Jim a hearty clap on the shoulder, a friendly gesture that further broke down the wall of tension between them. "It ain't easy, standin' up to the likes of me," he admitted, a gravelly chuckle rumbling deep in his throat. The captain turned, stepping toward a shelf where mugs and a bottle of rum waited. He poured generously and handed one to Jim and then to Ben.

"Here's to fair winds and full sails," he toasted, lifting his mug in salute.

After emptying their drinks, the captain looked back down at the map, then at Jim. "Now tell me ol' Jim. Ye really know nothin' 'bout the Dragon's Scale, do ye?"

Realizing the captain would see through even the slightest deception, which would surely lead to his demise, he repeated what the old sailor had told him. "From what I been hearin', most believe it leads the way to a great hidden treasure, and that to find this treasure ye must first find the Dragon's Scale. Others believe it's a charm protectin' us from the sea's anger. But there are those who believe it's a curse, a harbinger of doom." Then he admitted, "I overheard ye and the others in the Sea Serpent's Den talkin', and I just put two-and-two together and figured the Dragon's Scale must be havin' somethin' to do with findin' the Admiral Benbow."

Billy leaned heavily on the worn wooden table, his eyes locked onto the parchment spread out before him. He ran a roughened finger over the lines and curves, eyes narrowing as he traced the contours on the map. "That be the problem with this here map," Billy said, his voice echoing softly in the dim light of the cabin. "Ye see, a proper treasure map, it'd have markin's, clues, maybe even a riddle or two. It'd guide ye, show ye a path to follow, a place to start, a destination to reach." He shook his head, a wry smile tugging at the corners of his mouth. "But this? Nothin'. Just the land and sea, some stars and constellations decoratin' the top here, and some scratches there, lookin' like a drunken crab stepped on it." He shook his head, his face a mixture of frustration and intrigue.

"Then why do ye think it be havin' anythin' to do with the Admiral Benbow?" Ben asked.

In a hushed tone, Billy painted the tale of the Admiral Benbow with the colors of legend. "Among seafarin' folk, tales be told of the Admiral Benbow, a vessel of great splendor that vanished into the sea's embrace scores ago—gone, with nary a trace left behind. No wreckage, no cries, not even a ripple to mark her passin'. One moment she was there, proud as a queen, and the next—she was nothin' but a hush on the waves, leavin' naught but rumors and whispers in her wake."

Billy's words had cast a spell, pulling the two younger men into the web of his story.

"And what she carried! Her holds groaned under the weight of treasures so vast, they'd make a king's ransom look like a pauper's change—her riches claimed from battles so fierce, the skies themselves wept for the fallen."

Billy leaned forward, his hands mimicking the cascade of treasure, his low voice steeped in awe. "It be overflowin' with a sea of gold, glitterin' so fiercely it'd blind even the boldest soul. Coins stacked high as the masts, spillin' over like golden waterfalls, the colors richer than the sunrise on a summer's morn. Then there be chests packed to the beams, filled with jewels!

Great, glitterin' gems, lads, some the size of yer fist! Emeralds green as a mermaid's eyes, sapphires blue as the open sea, rubies as red as dragon's fire, and diamonds that catch the light like shards of stars fallen to earth. Even more, from bow to stern, every shadow and crevice gleamed with statues, jewelry, crowns, and goblets of such unmatched beauty they were somethin' divine, as though the gods descended from the heavens, their hands guidin' the tools that forged such wonderous objects."

Billy paused, a glint of mystery in his eyes. "But the ship . . . she be veiled in riddles, her secrets guarded by Father Time himself. Yet, in every tale told, in every hushed whisper, one story has remained the same—the key to findin' 'er be bound to somethin' known only as the Dragon's Scale. Find the Dragon's Scale they'd say, and it'll lead ye to the Admiral Benbow."

As the tale flowed from Billy's lips, Ben and Jim stood enthralled, their minds filled with visions of the Admiral Benbow and its legendary treasure, eager to cast their gaze into the sea's belly, to search for this phantom ship.

"Now, consider this map we've got, taken durin' a raid on a fearsome Spanish galleon," Billy continued. "She be as useful as a peg leg on a mermaid, 'cept she's got those same words scrawled on 'er in a faded hand—Dragon's Scale. Aye, it be the first thing anyone has seen since the Admiral Benbow vanished that gives even the barest glimmer of a link between the riddles of the sea and the secret of the Dragon's Scale." His fingers hovered just above the faded words, hesitant, as if touching them might stir some ancient spirit from its slumber. "She's achin' to tell us somethin', beggin' us to listen. I can't rightly explain it, lads, but this . . . this scrap of parchment—she holds the key. I feel it in me very bones. What we's havin' to do is figure out what that somethin' be. And no more dawdlin'—it be time we get to it."

Despite wracking their brains of maritime lore and countless hours spent scouring whatever seafaring texts and other old maps were stored on the ship, the significance of the Dragon's Scale

The Secret of the Dragon's Scale

remained beyond their grasp, just as it had for every other seafarer daring to discover its secrets.

Compelled by a gnawing thirst for answers, Billy plotted a new course for a harbor he knew well—a notorious refuge known for its motley inhabitants, each a wellspring of myths and legends.

Beneath a vault of endless azure, Billy stood firm on the quarterdeck, his silhouette sharp against the horizon, his keen eyes scanning the outline of a distant shore, while the wind, brisk and salted with the breath of the sea, teased the edges of his well-worn coat.

"Ben!" Billy called out, his voice booming over the sound of crashing waves against the hull. "We be nearin' our port o' call!"

A figure emerged from the bustling crew below. His eyes met Billy's, and he nodded, understanding the unspoken message in his captain's gaze.

"Ready yourselves, lads!" Ben's command thundered across the ship, his booming voice easily reaching the farthest corners of the vessel. The crew sprang into action. The sails were expertly furled, snapping briskly as they were secured, while others manned the ropes, their hands deftly guiding the thick lines through the blocks. The rhythmic clanking of the anchor chain joined the symphony of sounds, mingling with the gentle slap of water against the hull as the ship gradually slowed its pace. Eyes were keenly fixed on the approaching dock, ensuring alignment and a smooth arrival.

And with one final effort, the Siren's Call drifted gracefully into place, its movement stilled as mooring lines were secured with practiced hands.

Billy, Ben, Jim, and a handful of the other crew disembarked, and made their way through the bustling harbor, their boots echoing on the old cracked and faded planks. Ships of all shapes and sizes were docked, their flags fluttering in the gentle sea breeze. The air was thick with the scent of salt and fish, mixed with the tang of spices from distant lands. Seagulls circled overhead, their calls adding to the symphony of the harbor. Jim's and Ben's eyes sparkled with curiosity, darting from sight to sight, lingering one moment on the colorful banners rippling in the wind, and the next on the crates of exotic goods being hefted onto the dock by sweat-soaked workers.

"And where, pray tell, are we to go, Captain?" asked Ben.

A subtle crease formed at the corner of Billy's eyes as he squinted toward the nearby settlement. "We're to seek out an old friend of mine," he replied, a hint of nostalgia in his voice.

Billy trusted a seemingly ordinary old fisherman he had known since his younger sailing days. This old man had spent his life listening to the whispers of the sea, and was said to carry an ocean of secrets in his heart. If anyone could reveal the truth behind the Dragon's Scale, it would be him.

"Ahh ha ha ha ha ha!" The old fisherman's laughter boomed out—a deep, hearty sound that echoed against the rustic walls of his seaside shack. "Ah, Billy boy," he chuckled, leaning back in his chair. "That's the same tale that's been spun for decades." He wiped a tear from his eye, still chuckling. "Avast there, Billy Bones," the old fisherman warned, his voice as deep and rumbling as a stormy sea. "You know this story as well as any man, and you know as well as I you be only chasin' phantoms if you pursue it. Every sailor worth his salt knows the legend of the Dragon's Scale, but no man alive or dead has ever discerned its true meanin'."

Billy met the fisherman's gaze with a defiant spark in his eyes. "I reckon I might just have more to go on now, old man. The legends speak of . . . "

The fisherman cut him off with a dismissive wave of his hand. "Legends! Fairy tales and fables, nothin' more! Many a good man has lost himself to this obsession, Billy. It be as the haunt of the Lorelei, her song as deadly as it is enchantin', enticin' ya to yer doom."

"The difference now," Billy insisted, "be a map."

"What map?" asked the fisherman.

The Secret of the Dragon's Scale

Ben, Jim, and the others had been quiet, standing behind Billy as he spoke to his old friend. But Jim now chimed in, tracing an imaginary line in the air as he spoke, mimicking the shape of the land on the map. "The land, it's there. The sea, it stretches far and wide, unmarked by any ship's path." Finally, he pointed upward, toward the sky. "And the stars, they're etched across the top."

"There's more," Billy added, his voice dropping to a low and deliberate whisper. "And there, scrawled at its heart, writ in a hand long faded, be the words 'Dragon's Scale.' I'd wager me very soul this holds the way to the Admiral Benbow." His eyes lingered on some far-off vision only he could see, his gaze haunting, as if he'd caught a glimpse of a puzzle piece never meant to be found. "I not be able to explain why . . . I just feel it in me bones."

"Ah, Billy, my recollection is yer bones have led ya astray many times," the fisherman said sarcastically. Leaning back in his chair, he took out his old worn pipe. "Ya see, Billy, that ain't a map that'll lead ya straight to yer prize. Not to the Dragon's Scale nor to the Admiral Benbow. No, that there be a map of a different kind."

Just as Jim had done, the fisherman's leathery finger traced out in the air the depiction of the land on the parchment. "This here represents where ye've been, the ground ye've tread and the battles ye've fought. It's yer past, Billy, and it's just as important as where ye're goin'." Then his finger moved to the vast expanse of the ocean, tracing invisible circles. "And this, this is yer present. The sea is rough and unpredictable, just like life. Ya never know what lies beneath its surface or what the next wave will bring." He struck a match, its flame dancing in the dim light before he guided it to the bowl of his pipe, drawing in a deep breath as it came to life. His gaze shifted upward, a look of distant contemplation painting his weathered features, gesturing side to side as he envisioned the stars scattered across the top of the map. "And the stars, these are yer future, lad. They're distant and

21

untouchable, but they guide us all the same. Follow them, Billy, and they'll lead ya to the Dragon's Scale."

"Heh, heh, heh," Billy chuckled. "Old man, you're still as daft as ever," he said in a mocking but affectionate way toward his old friend. In Billy's mind, as it was with so many other seafarers, the Dragon's Scale had to be a physical object of some kind—a type of compass, a puzzle piece, or perhaps a tablet inscribed with instructions that explained where to find the Admiral Benbow—and that the purpose of the map was to show the location of the Dragon's Scale, but for some reason, he assumed, the map was never completed. The old fisherman's words, to Billy, made the Dragon's Scale sound mystical, more like a spiritual quest than anything tangible.

"Yer words be like the mornin' fog," Billy continued. "What I seek be not a ghost to chase but a prize to claim."

Standing to return to his ship, Billy said to the fisherman, "It was good to see ye again, old friend."

The old fisherman nodded, his eyes twinkling like distant lighthouses guiding weary sailors home. "May the winds be ever in your favor, Billy boy," he replied, his voice as soft and soothing as the ocean's lullaby.

One by one, the crew followed suit, each offering their own parting farewells. With a final nod, they turned away from the old fisherman, their figures receding into the late day sun. But each was silent, contemplating in their own minds the meaning of the old fisherman's puzzle. The soft creaking of the planks of the wharf under their weight slowly faded, replaced by the gentle lapping of waves against the hull of their ship. The sails unfurled, catching the evening breeze, and the anchor was hoisted with a chorus of synchronized heaves.

As the Siren's Call slowly pulled away from the dock, Ben went up to the captain on the quarterdeck.

"Captain," he said, his voice carrying over the sound of whistling wind and creaking ropes. "That old man . . . his words have been playin' on me mind."

Billy turned to him, a questioning eyebrow raised. "Aye, and mine, too. He weren't as much help as I was hopin', though. Question now be, where to next?"

Ben nodded, leaning against the ship's wheel. "He said, 'This here represents where ye've been, the ground ye've tread and the battles ye've fought. It's yer past, and it's just as important as where ye're goin'.' What if . . . what if he meant ye need to revisit yer past? Maybe there be clues there."

At first, Billy was dismissive, shaking his head with a chuckle. "Ye're makin' less sense than the old man."

Billy's gaze then fell upon the timeworn planks of the ship, his eyes tracing the grain as if it held the answers he sought. The chuckle that danced on his lips began to fade, replaced by a thoughtful silence. The sea whispered tales of old around him, the rhythmic lullaby of waves against the hull setting a rhythm for his thoughts, a steady beat that helped him organize the chaos in his mind.

Billy looked up, his eyes reflecting the vast ocean before them. He muttered, "He said, 'This here represents where ye've been . . . It's just as important as where ye're goin' . . . '" his voice barely audible over the sound of the waves. "Where ye've been . . . "

His mind began to wander to the places he and his past shipmates had been, the ports where they'd docked, the treasures they'd unearthed. He thought about the battles they'd fought, the storms they'd weathered, the camaraderie they'd forged. Each memory pulsed with purpose. They spoke of something unfinished, a truth waiting to be unearthed, a destiny waiting to be charted.

"Ye know, there was this island . . . " he started, his voice carrying the weight of memories. "An island we stumbled upon years ago, when we was just landlubbers."

He turned to Ben. "Ben. Set course, south by southwest."

"Aye, Captain."

Steven Eisenberg

Where the Sun Kisses the Sea

The Siren's Call turned her prow toward the memory of her captain's youth, still well over the horizon. The ship was a living entity, her wooden skeleton groaning with the weight of countless voyages. Her sails, vast and windswept, fluttered in the sea breeze; like great white birds, her wings stretched wide against the azure expanse, a sight that never failed to stir the soul. The crew of the Siren's Call were as much a part of her as the timbers that held her together—men hardened by salt and sun, their laughter as raucous as gulls, their hearts as deep as the ocean. They moved about her decks with a familiarity born of countless sunrises and sunsets spent at her mercy.

Days melted into nights and nights into days as they sailed toward the island. The rhythm of life aboard the ship was a dance of duty and rest. From the crack of dawn, when the deck was swabbed and sails were tied, to the hushed twilight hours, when tales of the mythical Dragon's Scale were whispered under the blanket of stars, each day a step closer to uncovering its mystery.

As the first rays of dawn pierced the charcoal sky, a hush fell over the crew. All eyes turned to the horizon. The sight that unfolded before them was breathtaking. Ben and Jim were watching at the bow together, leaning on the railing, as the island, little known to the world, rose majestically from the ocean depths, its emerald peaks wreathed in tendrils of mist. Above them, the jib sails billowed out, catching the morning wind; the rigging ropes quivered and groaned in a steady rhythm, singing in harmony with the sounds of the sea, the bowsprit pointing steadfastly ahead.

Wondering about the significance of this destination, Jim asked, "Why this place?"

"The captain," Ben said, "is trustin' his instincts. Settin' course for this island ain't no decision born of rhyme or reason." He pointed toward the island, its vague outline growing clearer with each passing moment. "It be a gut feelin'."

Jim peered toward the island. "But that seems to be the way every sailor has tried to figure out the secret of the Dragon's Scale, with nothin' to show for it, 'cept for surrenderin' to the ravages of madness."

Ben, unfazed, simply nodded. "Somethin' in that old man's words struck a chord with the captain. He may not reveal his reasons, but I'm trustin' the method to his seemin' madness, for now. I reckon this island's a first step."

"Prepare a longboat," the captain called out, his voice cutting through the gentle crash of waves and the subtle whisper of the wind dancing through the rustling palms in the distance.

Billy, Ben, Jim, and a handful of the other crew descended into the waiting boat. The island loomed closer with each stroke, its lush greenery and towering cliffs a stark contrast to the endless blue that had been surrounded them for weeks. The air was filled with the calls of unseen birds, and the scent of earth and foliage was a welcome change from the briny tang of ocean air.

As they approached the island, the raw beauty of the place unfolded. Cascades of verdant foliage spilled down the hillsides to meet the golden sands. Vibrant parrots and resplendent toucans, their feathers a kaleidoscope of iridescent hues, darted joyfully between the swaying palm fronds, while unseen creatures rustled through the undergrowth. The air was thick with the perfume of hibiscus and wild orchids, tantalizing their senses with the promise of discovery.

The boat scraped against the shore and the men disembarked, their boots sinking into the soft sand warmed by the tropical sun. A stone's throw from the shoreline, they discovered the remnants of long-abandoned encampments—

ghostly echoes of European settlers who had once sought temporary respite here along their voyage to the New World. Weathered, tattered canvas flapped in the sea breeze, tethered to rotting wooden poles, while crumbling fire pits were filled with the ashes of long-extinguished flames.

The men moved around the encampment, their gazes sweeping over the scene. Billy ran his fingers over the frayed edge of the remnants of a tent. Jim prodded at the extinguished embers in one of the fire pits, his mind conjuring images of weary sailors, their faces illuminated by the flickering firelight as they traded stories of their old world and their hopes for the new. Ben, ever watchful, stood still, his eyes keen on the encampment, the forest, and the sea that stretched out behind them. His gaze was distant, as if he could see past the physical remains and past the expanse of time, straight into the heart of the stories these fragments held.

Continuing to explore, Ben and Jim followed close behind the captain, while their shipmates took the opportunity to gather fresh water and provisions as they traversed the island.

As Billy's boots crunched on the familiar shore, memories of his early days as a sailor came flooding back. He saw himself as he once was—a young deckhand, green to the ways of the world, plying these same waters with no inkling of the pirate life that awaited him. His eyes swept across the forest's edge, his breath catching as it landed on a solitary, gnarled tree, standing defiant against the horizon. The sight halted him mid-step—he recalled the first time he laid eyes upon it, so many years ago, its odd, contorted form unlike anything he had seen before. Now it stood before him again, strangely unchanged, its presence tugging at the threads of his past.

Rising no taller than a man, the tree's twisted branches reached out like ancient arms. The bark was rough and scarred, a testament to the centuries it had silently witnessed. But if one were to look closely, with a creative mind and an open heart, the shape of a dragon could be discerned in its contorted form. The

The Secret of the Dragon's Scale

wide, sturdy trunk served as the body of the mythical creature, its texture akin to the scaled hide of a serpent. Twisted ridges and valleys, shaped by the ceaseless push of wind and weather, mimicked the rippling muscles beneath the beast's skin. Halfway up the trunk, two large branches stretched out at an angle, resembling the powerful wings of a dragon poised for flight. Above, the wood twisted and turned to form the beast's head, with deep-set knots casting dark pits—the fearsome gaze of watchful eyes. A jagged break in the bark hinted at a snarling maw, its shadows deepened by the shifting sunlight to suggest teeth lying in wait. And a series of smaller branches sprouting from the top zigzagged into a ridge of fearsome horns and spines running down the dragon's back. Then, as the breeze stirred, the dragon-tree seemed to come alive—the wind rustled through the leaves, and one could almost hear the beating of dragon wings, with the creaking of the branches echoing like a low, resonant, growl.

His eyes moved slowly over the tree's every curve and knot. And as he stood there, studying it with a pirate's keen scrutiny, there was a softness to his expression, as if staring into the face of an old friend. "Well, I'll be . . . It still be here!" he whispered to himself. He took a hesitant step forward, and the air seemed to thicken around him. "What devilry keeps ye standin' all this time?" His widened eyes stayed fixed, unable to look away. The coincidence to Billy was nothing less than a marvel woven by fate's unseen hand; his intuition had led him to this remote place, finding himself in the presence of an emblem that reflected the very essence of their quest.

Billy approached the tree with a sense of reverence. He reached out a trembling hand to touch the aged bark, and a flood of memories came washing over him. Running his fingers over the rough wood, he searched for a gold coin he remembered placing in the mouth of the dragon figure so long ago.

At that time, Billy had carried a single gold coin around with him, a lucky charm passed down from his father. It was a piece of his family's legacy, a symbol of adventures undertaken and fortunes won. In a symbolic gesture to appease the spirit of the dragon, the youthful sailor decided to offer his gold coin, honoring the dragon's dominion over land and sea, and in turn, seeking its favor. Such blessings, he believed, could turn the tides of fate, imbuing him with the strength and courage needed to navigate treacherous waters and return home laden with prosperity. As he lodged the coin in the tree, he whispered an old sailor's prayer he'd learned from his father, asking for fair winds and calm seas. Upon stepping back, he felt a gust of wind ruffle his hair and rustle the leaves around him, as if the dragon-tree was acknowledging his humble offering. From that day forward, Billy's voyages unfolded like tales of legend, each journey marked by luck and fortune.

Standing before the tree now, a thought fluttered in Billy's mind, a glimmer of hope that the coin might hold a clue to their next destination in their search for the Dragon's Scale. He reached into the mouth of the tree, his fingers grazing over the rough wood until they met the smooth coolness of the coin. He gasped! It was still there, after all these years! Carefully, he twisted and tugged, the coin stubbornly resisting before it finally came free. He held it up to the sunlight, his eyes narrowing as it burst into a dazzling gleam, its surface etched with intricate symbols whose meanings were lost to time. He turned it over in his hands, studying each symbol, each scratch and imperfection. But as he tried to glean whatever clues he could from it, it became clear that the coin held no secrets, offered no guidance.

However, he felt the coin would be a token that would herald the auspicious beginning of their voyage; it shimmered with promise—a harbinger of fortune yet to unfold. Tucking it into his pocket, the captain felt a surge of optimism. Accepting the coin back, he believed, would serve as a silent affirmation that their path was blessed from the start, a concrete sign of the adventure and riches that awaited them beyond the horizon.

As the coin fell into his pocket, a gust of wind ruffled his hair and rustled the leaves around him. And at that moment, the once still, blue waters started becoming restless. In the distance, a storm was just beginning to assemble, its faint outline becoming more discernible as the colors of the day gradually turned to shades of gray, and the comforting warmth of the sun was replaced by a biting chill.

Billy redirected his gaze back toward the distant silhouette of their ship, its masts jutting up like skeletal fingers against the dimming sky. He stood there, framed by the island's landscape, before turning to speak to Ben and Jim. His voice, usually vibrant with the thrill of exploration, now carried a muted tone of disappointment.

"There be nothin' here," he admitted.

He paused for a moment, gathering his thoughts.

"I not be able to really explain it, lads," he said, his look drifting back to the enigmatic tree that had lured him here. "There was this . . . this pull. A force I don't rightly understand. It was like somethin' tugged at me very soul. Like it guided me here, as sure as the tide knows the shore." Billy's hand gestured toward the tree, its dragon-like shape stark against the fading light. It was as if some ancient spirit resided within it, whispering cryptic riddles and teasing him with secrets it wasn't willing to share.

Hiking back toward the longboat, Jim kicked up some sand; a glint of something unusual then caught his eye. He bent down, curiosity piqued, and carefully unearthed a delicate seashell necklace, half-hidden beneath the grains—two small shells with one large shell in the middle, laced together with a leather cord. They were intricately patterned, each with a unique combination of hues—creamy whites, soft pinks, and splashes of blues and greens. Jim picked up the necklace, somewhat surprised that it was still intact after so many years of exposure to the elements. He showed it to Ben and the captain.

Billy leaned in, squinting closely at it. "Hmmm, looks strangely familiar," he remarked. It looked strikingly similar to a necklace he had gifted Molly, his first love back when he was a young man. He could still picture the delicate smile on her lips as he placed it around her neck, just days before he set sail on his maiden voyage as a sailor. The sight of it also triggered a long-buried memory, a memory of the promise he had made to her—a vow whispered under the stars—that he would return soon, that their parting was only temporary. But life had charted a different course for Billy. The lure of the sea and the seductive chaos of piracy had consumed him, pulling him far from the shores of home and the woman he had loved. A sharp pang struck him as another memory pushed its way through—the day he learned of her fate. It had been years later, shared in low, solemn tones by friends he hadn't seen in ages. Molly had died of yellow fever, her life cut short while he had been chasing fortune and danger across the waves. Regret now washed over him, the weight of that broken promise pressing down as he stood there, the ghost of a necklace forcing him to confront what he had lost.

Upon closer inspection, Jim noticed a small inscription carved into the back of the large shell:

Where the sun kisses the sea
Where your heart yearns to be

Not really thinking much of the words, Jim placed it in his satchel to bring back to the ship.

Back on board, the captain stood on the deck, his eyes fixed on the brooding sky, watching the storm gathering strength. Dark, ominous clouds swirled and twisted, their underbellies lit up intermittently by flashes of lightning. The air was thick with tension, carrying the faint scent of rain and a heavy sense of foreboding. The storm was heading toward the island, and Billy judged it was better to dodge the storm than to stay anchored and risk the ship being blown up onto the rocky shoreline.

"Ben!" he called out. "Weigh anchor and make haste!"

"Aye, Captain!"

With a sense of urgency, Ben relayed the captain's orders. "Weigh anchor, lads!" he bellowed.

The previously quiet deck erupted into activity. Men scurried about, pulling up ropes and securing loose items. The clattering of boots against the wooden deck mingled with the creaking of ropes and pulleys, as the anchor was hauled up and the sails unfurled.

The ship pulled away from the island to escape the onslaught of the storm, the increasing distance from it bringing cautious relief to the crew. With the immediate threat behind them, they could finally ease their minds, and Billy made his way to his cabin. With a weary sigh, he pushed open the door, entering his personal sanctuary amidst the vast and unforgiving ocean. The room was dimly lit, a single flickering lantern casting long shadows that danced across the cramped space, imbuing it with a sense of warmth and familiarity. He kicked off his boots, letting them drop carelessly to the floor. Going through his pockets, he felt the gold coin retrieved from the dragon-tree's mouth. Billy looked down and stared at it, feeling a strange mix of nostalgia, bewilderment, and disappointment in that it could offer no guidance in their quest. For now, it was just another fragment of his past, weighted by meaning he could not decipher, and utterly useless against the endless questions ahead.

With a sigh, he tossed the coin onto the table where the Dragon's Scale map had been sitting. The coin was sent spiraling into the air, its golden surface winking under the warm glow of the lantern light. It fell onto the parchment with a soft clank, then spun and wobbled, gradually coming to a rest next to some scratch marks on the map. Billy grabbed a bottle, and sank into an old chair that bore the weight of countless sea voyages, the worn fabric yielding beneath him. He closed his eyes and tilted his head back.

Ben, Jim, and the other hands were on deck, guiding the ship safely away from the approaching storm. The sails billowed gently, filled by a playful breeze, as the ship cruised at a leisurely pace, the rhythmic lapping of the waves against the hull a soothing serenade.

Amidst the sounds of creaking timbers and the gentle snap of canvas, the helmsman stood at the wheel, eyes on the endless horizon. Others grappled with rigging, muscles coiling as they maneuvered the massive sails to seize the capricious wind. High above, the lookout scanned the expansive sea from the crow's nest, a solitary figure against the vast sky. As they navigated the ship toward safer waters, the storm, for now, remained a distant threat.

"Now where be our course, Ben?" inquired Jim, as his eyes scanned the sprawling canvas of the sea ahead, a soft breeze playing with his hair.

Ben shrugged. "I've not been given any orders from the captain."

Just then, John Silver approached Ben. "Any new orders, sir?"

Jim exchanged a look with Ben, an unspoken understanding passing between them. They were sailors in need of direction, a crew adrift.

"The captain still be in his cabin," Ben responds. "For now, I say we stay the course, steady as she goes. When the captain's ready, he'll let us know."

"Aye, sir," acknowledged John.

But just as Ben was giving his order, the sea turned mad! The storm had suddenly changed course! The placid ocean roared to life, its surface marred by angry waves that grew larger with each passing second!

Chaos erupted on deck! Orders were shouted over the roar of the storm; the crew, once chattering with laughter and spinning tales of distant shores, now moved with grim resolve, their voices drowned by the tempest's wrath. The wind screamed like a banshee, twisting through the rigging in frenzied gusts, while waves now crashed against the hull with a bone-rattling ferocity. The sails strained against the power of the wind, the ropes snapping taut like the lash of a giant's whip! Rain pelted down, each drop a sharp sting against the skin! Peals of thunder exploded above them—sharp, guttural cracks that split the heavens, their echoes rolling endlessly across the tumultuous sea. Lightning tore through the sky, its blinding flashes a stark contrast to the ominous darkness, illuminating the faces of men wrestling with their fate!

The ship groaned in protest, its timbers straining and creaking as it was thrashed about by the merciless waves! It was tossed like a mere toy, each rise a moment of breathless anticipation, each fall a stomach-churning drop into the watery depths!

The first blast of the storm struck without warning! Billy, in the midst of savoring the last drops of his rum, was thrown violently from his chair, his body meeting the wooden floor with a painful thud that reverberated through his bones. Objects once securely fastened were now airborne projectiles—books, maps, and bottles flew around, their trajectories as unpredictable as the ship's movements! Billy dodged and weaved, his every step a gamble against the storm's relentless assault. With a grunt, he lunged toward the door, his hand reaching out for the cold metal handle. But the ship gave a violent jerk, and he was flung aside! Summoning every ounce of his strength, he clawed his way back, gripping the handle just as another wave struck. His knuckles turned white, his grip unwavering even as the ship bucked again beneath him. And then, with a roar that matched the fierceness of the storm, he wrenched the door open!

The captain was immediately assaulted by the storm's rage! The wind, a tempestuous demon, howled in his ears and whipped his face, its icy fingers clawing through his clothes. Rain, driven by the gale, lashed against him in torrents, soaking him to the bone in seconds and turning the deck into a treacherous nightmare.

"Steady, men!" Billy yelled, his voice slicing through the ferocity of the storm. He fought his way to the helm, his hands closing around the wheel with a furious resolve. His body leaned into the wind, every sinew straining as he wrestled for control of his vessel.

With speed born of urgency, the crew set about reefing the sails, shrinking their expanse to resist the wind's brutal assault. It was a task fraught with peril, demanding they ascend the storm-tossed masts slick with rain. To secure objects on deck, ropes were swiftly fastened, loose gear stowed away, and cannons lashed tight. Below deck, the rest of the crew scurried, binding barrels and battening down hatches.

The Siren's Call waged an epic battle against the sea's unbridled rage! The tranquil ocean had morphed into a monstrous beast, its waves, reared up like giants, crashed into the hull with a force that echoed in the marrow of the ship. Deep, bone-rattling thuds would resound as the towering swells slammed into the timbers, followed immediately by the sharp, splintering crash of seawater surging over the deck. The spray hissed with venom as it ricocheted off the surfaces, mingling with the guttural gurgle of churning water that seeped into every crevice. Between each collision, the sea growled and snarled, the echoes of its wrath vibrating through every brace and mast.

The deck became a battlefield, with men thrown around like ragdolls in the storm's relentless game. Amidst this chaos, intervals of suspense arose—the eerie silence before each wave a cruel prelude to the next impending assault. One moment, the men were gripping onto ropes, the next they were airborne, hurled by the violent force of the waves. Shouts and orders were ripped from their throats, only to be swallowed by the storm's deafening roar. "Hold fast!" one would yell, just before being swept off his feet. "Brace!" cried another, his warning coming too late as another wall of water crashed over them.

The storm's fury spilled into each wave—a legion of snarling, frothing monsters clawing hungrily at the vessel! Suddenly, a colossal wall of water loomed before the ship, its crest vanishing into the churning sky above. The sailors on deck froze, their eyes wide as they stared up at the behemoth wave—

their faces ghastly masks of horror, lit up by the sporadic flashes of lightning! It was as if time itself had paused, allowing them a moment to take in the chilling spectacle. Then, with the sound of a massive beast exhaling its rage, the wave lunged across the deck, striking with the ruthless precision of a skilled executioner! Everything in its path was obliterated—barrels, cannons, and men alike hurled aside as if they weighed nothing! And at the heart of its merciless wrath stood John Silver. The wave seized him, lifting him off his feet with terrifying ease, catapulting him into the air like a toy tossed by a petulant child! He arced through the stormy sky, a human missile flung by the sea's giant hand, before disappearing into its tumultuous depths. The sea had claimed him, swallowed him whole, leaving behind nothing but shock and dread in its wake.

A collective gasp echoed across the ship, the crew frozen in horror. The agonizing image of John, flung into sea by the monstrous wave, was seared into their minds. Ben stood rooted to the spot, his heart pounding against his ribs. His eyes were locked on the roiling sea that had taken his friend. A cold dread washed over him, replacing the sea spray that drenched his face. Jim ran over to the railing, his hands clenching and unclenching at his side, his face ashen. His throat tightened, the weight of a deep sadness pressing heavily on him. He swallowed hard and set his jaw, his gaze sharpening as it fixed onto the restless waves. Billy was aghast! As captain, every soul aboard was his responsibility, and the loss of John landed like a blow to his very sense of duty. His shoulders slumped under the weight of guilt, a heavy anchor dragging him into a pit of self-reproach. A captain was supposed to guide, to protect, to weather every storm alongside his crew. But this storm had stolen a life under his watch, a loss that would weigh on him forever.

Then, as if spent by the sheer energy of its cruel act, the wave receded, its fury dimming. It was as though the storm had poured all its remaining strength into that last horrible blow, and now, exhausted, it began to retreat. The tempestuous wind that had howled relentlessly through the rigging began to die down, its fierce roars dwindled into feeble sighs. Lightning that had once split the sky with terrifying brilliance now flickered weakly, its fire fading into feeble remnants. The sea, which had been a churning cauldron, gradually stilled. Towering waves that had loomed like the walls of a watery prison now collapsed into gentle swells, their edges softening as they cradled the ship in a soothing, rhythmic embrace. Above them, the thunderous clouds began to dissipate, their dark forms fragmenting into wisps of gray, revealing the blueness of the sky.

As calm returned to the sea and the ship, Billy, his face etched with the harsh lines of grief and responsibility, rallied his crew. "The sea has claimed our brother," he began, his voice rough and solemn. "But we press on, for that is the way of the seafarer. We mourn, but we also survive."

In the days that followed, the crew worked tirelessly to repair the damage inflicted by the storm. Ropes were spliced, sails mended, and the fractured mast reinforced. Every task was underpinned by a solemn silence, a quiet testament to their loss.

While repairs were underway, the ship wandered aimlessly, guided solely by the whims of the current and wind. The decision by the captain to let the ship drift was a calculated risk, born from necessity rather than choice. The Siren's Call was a battered shadow of its former self, its hull scarred, its sails torn, and its rudder unreliable. Attempting to steer such a crippled vessel would have risked further damage. And with the ship in dire need of repair, the crew needed calm waters and time to mend what the storm had broken.

Twilight descended, the last day's labor drew to a close, and the crew looked upon their handiwork with a sense of satisfaction. Their bodies were weary, muscles aching from the strain of the day, but their spirits were buoyed by the sight of their ship, standing strong and ready to brave the seas once more. With a final nod of approval to his crew, the captain turned toward his cabin, and surrendered to the call of sleep.

The Secret of the Dragon's Scale

Ben returned to his quarters and sank into his bunk, the gentle sway of the ship soothing his tired muscles. Meanwhile, Jim, along with the other hands, headed toward the crew's quarters. His berth was a hammock slung between beams, nestled among those of his fellow sailors, the familiar sight of it offering the promise of rest and rejuvenation. But as he approached, he noticed something out of place. The satchel he had carried with him on the island lay haphazardly on his place of respite. He had tossed it there earlier, in the rush of returning to the ship and diving into the repairs. As Jim stood there, his weary eyes fixated on the satchel, he felt a tinge of irritation. He was tired, his muscles ached from the day's labor, and all he wanted was to collapse into the comfort of his bedding. With a grunt, he reached over and shoved the satchel aside, sending it rolling into a crumpled heap as its contents shifted with a soft rustle. He hoisted himself onto the hammock, letting out a contented sigh as his body sank into the netting. But his relief was short-lived as he shifted to find a comfortable position only to feel the satchel jab into his side. With a resigned sigh, Jim looked over and grabbed it, deciding to check what was left inside. His fingers fumbled with the buckle, finally managing to pry it open, the dim light from the lantern hanging nearby illuminating the contents. He rummaged through the satchel, his fingers brushing against various objects—a rolled-up map, a small leather journal, a piece of flint, and something smooth and cool to the touch. He paused, curious despite his exhaustion, and pulled out the object. It was the seashell necklace he had kicked up from the sand. Although his eyelids were heavy, his body begging for sleep, the necklace held his attention. He turned it over in his hands, his fingers tracing the imperfect edges of the shells. Noticing the inscription again, he squinted, bringing the shell closer to his face. The lantern light flickered, casting dancing shadows around him, but illuminating just enough for him to make out the words he had read back on the island—*Where the sun kisses the sea, Where your heart yearns to be.*

With the words still echoing in his head, Jim's grip on the necklace loosened. He was too tired to ponder their meaning now, his body demanding rest. The necklace slipped from his fingers, landing softly on his chest, the shells cool against his skin. As the gentle sway of the ship rocked him, Jim succumbed to sleep. His last conscious thought was of the seashell necklace and the inscription, a riddle to be solved in the morning.

Ben, being second in command, bore the same sense of responsibility for the ship and its crew as the captain. But he felt this loss especially hard since John Silver had been a good friend, and it was he himself who had signed John up to serve on the Siren's Call. As he lay in his bunk, the ship creaked gently around him, and sleep eluded him. His mind was a whirlpool of guilt and regret, the loss of John gnawing at him like a relentless tide. Eventually, though, exhaustion took over. His body, worn out from the physical labor and the emotional toll, demanded rest.

As the first light of the next dawn pierced through the inky canvas of the night, the crew of the Siren's Call stirred from their deep slumber. The ship, still carrying the fresh scars from the storm, swayed gently on the calm, forgiving sea—a serene contrast to the chaos that had sought to claim her just days before. Crew members slowly emerged from the belly of the ship, blinking sleep from their eyes and stretching muscles stiffened by hard labor and the cold night.

"Ben," Jim called out, as Ben emerged from his quarters into the morning sun. "The ship be fit to sail. But where does our compass point?"

"Well, we be needin' orders," Ben responded as Jim walked up to him. "I should go see the captain."

Billy was just stirring in his cabin when Ben, with Jim following behind him, knocked on the door.

"Aye?" Billy answered, still groggy.

With a groan that echoed around the silent cabin, he pushed himself out of his bed and shuffled his way toward the small washbasin in the corner as the two entered. Uncorking a clay jug, he poured water into the washbasin and cupped his hands into it. The chill of the water hit him like a sharp slap, jolting his senses awake. While Billy patted himself dry with a towel, Ben broke the silence.

"Never seen the likes of it in me life," he said of the storm, running a hand through his disheveled hair. " No warnin', no nothin'."

Billy looked around his cabin and started picking up all the objects that had been thrown around by the violence of the storm. Anything that wasn't tied down—books, charts, bottles of rum, quills and ink wells, lanterns, his spyglass and sextant—all had been strewn across the floor.

"Aye," Billy agreed, as he's going around the cabin. "Sometimes, lads," he said, looking around the floor, "the sea don't give ye warnin's. She's a fickle mistress, she is. One moment calm, next moment a ragin' beast."

Billy eyed his sextant on the floor. Sighing, he bent to retrieve it. As he rose, his eyes fell upon the table where he had placed the Dragon's Scale map and the gold coin he had tossed onto it. The sight stopped him cold!

"Impossible," he breathed, the word barely more than a whisper in the silent cabin.

The storm had nearly ripped the ship apart, tossing everything in its path with reckless abandon—yet, these two objects remained undisturbed, as if the Devil himself had held them in place. A chill ran down Billy's spine. The cabin was deathly silent, save for the ticking of an old clock affixed to the wall. He leaned closer to the table, his hand trembling as he extended it toward the coin, unable to shake the feeling that the map and coin were more than mere relics. Were they a bad omen, warning of impending danger? Or perhaps they were sending a message of some sort? Could they be a beacon, guiding him toward a great prize, or a sinister signal of a curse awakened? As these possibilities swirled in his mind, the clock seemed to grow louder with each tick—a reminder of the mysteries and perils intertwined with their quest.

Billy Bones wore the wisdom of the sea like an invisible mantle. The sea had been his teacher, and its lessons were unforgiving but simple—survival depended on skill, grit, and a sharp mind, not fanciful tales or unseen forces. It was the kind of wisdom no book could teach—a deep understanding of the world that came only from living in it. His life had no room for the supernatural. Ghost stories were, in his eyes, nothing more than drivel concocted to pass the time in dark taverns and restless bunks. He had rolled his eyes through countless tales of phantom ships, enchanted artifacts, and vengeful sea gods. Billy measured his world in knots and leagues, in charts and stars—not in omens or spectral whispers. He scoffed at tales of apparitions, dismissed curses as old wives' tales, and regarded evil spirits as nothing more than figments of overactive imaginations. But now, as he stared at the coin and map held steadfast on the table, something within him stirred.

"Captain. Ye look as if ye've crossed eyes with Davy Jones himself! What be wrong?" asked Ben. His gaze followed the captain's to the untouched coin and map on the table, their calm presence a stark contrast to the chaos wrought by the ravages of the storm.

Billy's hand hovered over the table, hesitant, as though the objects might spring to life at his touch. The coin glinted faintly in the dim cabin light; the map, it felt alive, pulsing with a strange energy, as if its secrets were whispering into the stale air of the cabin. Billy shuddered, an involuntary chill running down his spine.

"The coin and map," he said, pointing to them on the table, his voice carrying a hint of uneasiness he rarely showed. "The storm nearly cast us all overboard . . . But look ye here. These things didn't move. Not by so much as a hair's breadth."

With a mix of apprehension and curiosity, Billy, Ben, and Jim found themselves huddled together, squinting down at the mysterious coin. The jagged lines etched around it, which to Billy had been just random scratches, now revealed themselves to be a mirror image of the seemingly meaningless squiggles on the parchment. It was as if an invisible hand had guided the coin to its current position, aligning it perfectly with the "scratches of a drunken crab," like a puzzle piece finding its long-lost match.

Ben gasped, his eyes wide as the moon. "Blimey," he managed to mutter. His eyes darted between the coin and the map, the gears in his mind visibly turning as he struggled to make sense of the eerie alignment. Jim blinked rapidly, his mouth agape in stunned silence as he processed the sight before him. The cabin air grew heavier, colder. A prickle ran up Billy's neck, and he swore he felt the faintest presence, something unseen and not entirely of this world, circling them.

The scratches on the map intertwined seamlessly with those etched into the coin, coming together to form the silhouette of a fiery sun, its rays just grazing the rim of a distant horizon. The coin itself seemed to transform, glowing softly as it took on the semblance of a golden orb—its surface gleaming with an ethereal light. But appearing to hover at the edge of the world, it left an unsettling question hanging in the air—did it herald the beginning of a bold new journey with the promise of dawn, or the end of one in the tranquility of dusk?

The three of them stood in awe and amazement as they began to realize what they were witnessing.

"The coin . . . " Jim said, a slow smile spreading across his face. "It be the sun!"

Ben bent low over the map, his brows knitted with quiet intensity as his fingers hovered near the coin, careful not to disturb its placement on the faded parchment. Suddenly, his eyes brightened with clarity!

"And the line under it—don't you see? It looks like it be sittin' square on the horizon!"

The picture of the sun resting on the horizon held their gazes captive. Yet, it remained a riddle, its meaning shrouded in veils of gold and parchment.

Jim leaned closer, his breath quickening as his finger traced the sun's fiery arc. "Could it be tryin' to tell us somethin'?" he wondered aloud.

Just then, like a rogue wave crashing over them, realization struck! The horizon, a timeless symbol in nautical tradition, spoke of new beginnings and endless possibilities—a place where dreams were forged and destinies written. To these men, this image was a beacon, a call to adventure, urging them to follow the light and uncover whatever treasures and truths awaited.

"It not be just a sun on the horizon," Ben mused, " It be callin' us—tellin' us to go in that direction!"

Billy, wide-eyed and sober, wondered, "But be it a risin' sun or a settin' sun?" He paused, glancing from the map to the faces of Ben and Jim. "If it be risin', we be lookin' eastward. But if it be settin', that'd mean westward."

In that moment, Jim's thoughts drifted back to the seashell necklace and the rhyme etched into it. Deep within him, a gut feeling stirred—a whisper of intuition that refused to be silenced. He couldn't shake the sense that the coin and the necklace, found together on the island, were bound by more than mere chance. Perhaps it was superstition, the kind that sailors clung to in the face of the unknown, or perhaps it was something deeper, an instinct honed by years of navigating the unpredictable seas. His lips moved silently, whispering the words to himself, "Where the sun kisses the sea, where your heart yearns to be." His brow furrowed as he turned the phrase over in his mind, a sense of revelation slowly dawning on him. He blinked rapidly, as if to clear his thoughts, then looked up at Billy and Ben.

"West! West!" Jim yelled out. "The necklace from the island spoke of where the sun kisses the sea! The sun kisses the sea at sunset! In the west! It said that's where your heart yearns to be! That's where we must be!"

The inscription's poetic allure resonated with Billy's own sense of adventure, but with eyes that mirrored the depth and mystery of the ocean itself, he was not one to accept intuition on a whim. Yet, deep down, Billy felt a gnawing pull he couldn't explain—a whisper, as soft and insistent as the play of ripples against a hull, was telling him this was right. Every rational part of him rebelled, and yet, beneath the fight, he couldn't shake the sense that something far bigger than himself was calling him, waiting for him to listen.

"Westward," he muttered, tasting the word like salt on his tongue. It didn't feel like it came from within him; it carried the gravity of something ancient, something as vast as the ocean and as persistent as the tides, urging him toward the western horizon. Thus, with a resolve as steady as the stars that guided their path, Billy set his sights west, ready to embrace the unknown that awaited them just beyond the edge of the world.

Slapping his hand on the table, Billy blurted out a hearty command. "Ben! Set course, due west!"

Ben ran out of the captain's cabin and called up to the helmsman at the wheel, "Mr. Pew! Head course, due west!"

"Aye, sir!"

Bella

The Siren's Call sailed smoothly across the calm sea, its course set due west, her destination as mysterious and elusive as the prize they sought. Overhead, the sky was a canvas of soft pastels, painted with delicate strokes of orange and pink, a parting gift from the sun as it bled its final light of day into the heavens. The journey was quiet as the ocean cradled the ship in its gentle rhythm, the silence broken only by the harmonious chorus of the waves caressing the ship's hull and the sailors' mutterings as they went about their duties. The map, once a baffling mystery, now held the promise of discovery, unveiling a fresh clue in their pursuit of the Dragon's Scale. This revelation spurred a surge of hope that coursed through their veins, warming their spirits for the journey that stretched before them.

Undeterred by her scars, the ship bore her crew onward. And after many sunrises and sunsets, there, on the horizon, a silhouette emerged—a small village nestled at the edge of the coast where the untamed emerald jungle met the cerulean sea. The sight was a promise of rest, of human interaction, and the comfort of dry land.

A longboat emerged from the soft morning mist, the rhythmic creaking and splashing of the oars filling the air as it moved closer to the shore. The village slowly came into view, appearing like a watercolor painting illuminated by the rising sun. Pastel-colored houses stood huddled together, their terracotta rooftops glowing in the morning light. Beyond them, the dense jungle added a vibrant splash of green, giving the village an aura of an idyllic oasis. Down on the shoreline, the village's docks were modest—a few rickety wooden structures extending into the water, teeming with small fishing boats that bobbed gently with the waves. The fishermen were busy at work, mending nets and hoisting up woven baskets from their boats, filled to the brim with the abundance of the sea.

As it neared the dock, the rowing ceased and the craft glided smoothly in. The locals, going about their morning routines, paused to watch the spectacle. Though such visits from sailing ships were routine, there was always a sense of curiosity and mild interest in newcomers. They watched as ropes were tossed from the boat onto the dock, landing with a muffled thud on the gray and worn wood. Conversations soon resumed as the fishermen worked, the murmur of voices blending with the creak of ropes and the cry of gulls overhead.

Billy, Ben, Jim, and a handful of the other crew disembarked one-by-one, each landing on the dock with a solid thud of boots. As the last of the ropes were secured, they turned to face the curious gazes of the fishermen—their faces friendly, their eyes sparkling with tales of the sea. Leaving the dock behind and heading toward the village, they were met with the faint scent of salt air mingling with the sweet, earthy aroma of the surrounding jungle. Gentle breezes carried the sounds of chatter and laughter, which grew louder with every step, pulling them into the warm, inviting heart of this humble settlement. A quiet anticipation settled over the men as they strode further in; they may not know their exact path yet, for the map gave them no more answers, but as the gentle warmth of the village embraced them, intuition whispered that they were exactly where they needed to be.

The men's eyes were full with curiosity, scanning their surroundings with keen interest. As they strolled along the gravel path, they were drawn to the vibrant tapestry of colors that painted the landscape. The path itself, a mosaic of soft grays and ruddy browns, meandered through a corridor of towering palm trees, their fronds gently swaying in the breeze. Dappled sunlight played across the ground, creating shifting patterns of light and shadow. Along the edges of the path, wildflowers bloomed in vivid colors—yellows, pinks, and purples—each petal seeming to dance in the gentle wind, adding a lively contrast to the lush greenery that enveloped them.

They soon found themselves walking through the market, a bustling open area on the edge of the village. It was a tranquil buzz of villagers—a riot of color and sound, of haggling voices and laughing children. Small carts, adorned with wildflowers or brightly colored cloth, stood side by side with makeshift stalls, their hand-built frames draped in patchwork fabrics. Tables crafted from rough-hewn wood displayed an abundance of exotic fruits—mangoes, papayas, and guavas—their golden and orange hues looking as though they had captured the morning light. The air was thick with a medley of scents—the comforting aroma of freshly baked bread intertwined with the saltiness of fish just hauled from the sea, while the sweet, lush perfume of the tropical fruits lingered in the breeze.

The visitors from the Siren's Call fanned out to explore the offerings and meet the people at the market. Captivated by the scene, the men moved with an eager curiosity. But it was the fruit in particular that caught their eyes. Billy ambled toward an elderly woman's quaint little cart, adorned with garlands of dried flowers and vibrant hand-woven cloths, and laden with a rainbow of fruits. He was entranced by the pile of sun-kissed mangoes, their skins smooth and glowing in the morning light. The woman, her face creased with years of laughter and age, handed him one to sample. The taste was an explosion of sweetness, the juice dribbling down his beard. Chuckling, he handed over some coins and selected a few of the ripest ones. Meanwhile, Ben found himself drawn to a man's table laden with unusual cherimoya. The villager, with a broad smile and twinkling eyes, cut one open, revealing the creamy flesh within. Taking a bite, Ben was met with a refreshing, subtly sweet taste—a perfect balance to the heat of the day. He happily exchanged coins for an armful of the enticing fruit.

The Secret of the Dragon's Scale

Above the hum of conversation, the clucking of chickens, and the footfalls of the villagers meandering around the market, a soft melody wafted through the air. It was a soothing tune that seemed to cut through the clamor, drawing Jim to the other side of the market. Following the music, he found himself standing before a merchant's cart, with fruits piled high in a display of colors so bright it rivaled the most vivid rainbow. Beside the cart sat a woman on a high wooden stool, young and beautiful, her fingers gracefully plucking the strings of a lute. Her lips curved into a small smile as she lost herself in her music. Her long chestnut hair fell in loose waves around her shoulders, and her eyes sparkled with a joy that seemed to mirror the beautiful notes she was producing. Jim stood transfixed, caught in the spell woven by this beautiful musician. His heart pounded in his chest, matching the rhythm of the melody that flowed from her lute. His eyes took in every detail, from the gentle sway of her dress to the way her fingers caressed the strings, creating a symphony of feelings that left him utterly captivated.

Being a young sailor, Jim was naturally gregarious and confident. But with this attraction came a wave of nervousness. He was shy, awkward even, and the thought of engaging in small talk filled him with dread. But gathering a smattering of courage, he approached the woman, clearing his throat a little too loudly.

"Um, these are . . . uh . . . nice fruits," he said, pointing at the cart, his voice barely above a whisper.

She looked up, her emerald green eyes meeting his. A rush of intrigue swept over her. His hair, the color of midnight, was tousled just enough to hint at a carefree spirit. His eyes were a mesmerizing blend of sea and sky, holding a depth that whispered of unspoken stories and hidden secrets. He was broad-shouldered, his frame lean and sinewy. Ruggedly handsome, with a jawline that could have been chiseled by the gods themselves, he exuded charisma and confidence. Yet, there was a warmth in his face, and a gentleness in his demeanor. His steady gaze reflected an inner fortitude that resonated deeply with her.

She had an immediate attraction to him—a complex blend of visceral allure and intuitive connection, drawing her in with an irresistible pull.

A smile played on her lips. "Just picked them this morning," she replied, her voice as melodious as the lute she played. "Would you like to try one?"

Jim nodded and reached for a papaya, his fingers clumsy as he nearly dropped it in his nervousness. He caught it just in time, managing a weak laugh as a flush crept up his cheeks. "I'm not really good with fruits," he said, cringing slightly as he realized how silly he sounded.

She let out a soft giggle, a sound of sweet delight that reflected her kind-hearted nature.

Her gentle laugh helped calm Jim's nervousness. "What be yer name, miss?" Jim asked.

"Bella. I'm Bella," she said, her voice soft, accompanied by a warm, albeit slightly shy smile.

"I'm Jim."

Just then, Jim heard the sound of the captain's voice thundering through the marketplace. "Crew, assemble!"

"Oh, my captain be orderin' us back to the ship. I need to be goin'," Jim explained. "But I'm sure I'll be returnin'." Jim grabbed a handful of fruit and paid Bella with some coins.

Bella offered another shy smile as Jim turned to leave.

Each of the crew had bought a fair amount of fruit and fish at the market to add to the ship's provisions, and gathered together to return to the ship.

The map had whispered a secret into their ears, to go westward, and had brought them to this small, unassuming village. It was as though they were destined to find it, and in finding it, they were one step closer to uncovering the secrets of the Dragon's Scale. Yet what they have only found so far is themselves at a standstill. The map had only told them to head west, but now that they were here, the path forward was nowhere in sight. The parchment fell silent, offering no more signs, no more riddles.

Billy, Jim, and Ben gathered with the others on the deck of their ship as it rocked gently with the rhythm of the waves, the sea stretching endlessly around them, its surface shimmering under the golden light of the afternoon sun.

Billy leaned against the ship's railing, his fingers tapping idly against the smooth wood as he spoke, his voice firm and resolute. "The map got us here, but it won't take us any further," Billy declared. Slowly, he straightened, his broad shoulders stiffening as the wind ruffled his hair. "We need to know this village, its people. There's a story here that we're missin', a clue hidden in plain sight."

Ben was usually a steady force, the kind of man whose calm presence could ease a storm. His voice carried a natural authority, measured and unwavering, while his body language often radiated quiet confidence. But now, subtle cracks in his composure began to show. When he spoke, his tone held a brisk edge that wasn't typically there. Words came a bit faster, his usual thoughtful pauses replaced by a clipped urgency.

At hearing Billy's decision, Ben blurted out with impatience, "But we don't even know what we be lookin' for! We don't know what the Dragon's Scale is! What is it, eh!? How would we be knowin' if it's even here!? Blimey, this be nothin' but a fool's errand! We be wastin' precious time in this blasted village! I say we weigh anchor and be gone, lest we rot here like barnacles on a sunken ship!"

He was starting to show signs of an unsettling transformation. The recent loss of his friend, swallowed by the storm, had left an indelible mark on his spirit. His usually bright eyes began to flicker with an eerie light, reflecting a turmoil that was simmering within him. The changes unfurled slowly, almost too quietly to notice at first, like the faint rustling of leaves before the wind picks up. His quiet confidence began to waver; the calm resolve that had always defined him started to fray at the edges.

Patience, once his greatest ally, now scattered like ashes in the breeze, and he found himself increasingly irritable, snapping at the slightest provocation, his tolerance dwindling to a mere thread. The shadows of madness were beginning to creep into Ben's resilient spirit, gnawing at the edges of his mind—a storm brewing inside him that threatened to consume the man he once was.

Billy's eyes narrowed, the weight of his irritation sharp and unmistakable as he fixed Ben with a cold stare. "Hold your tongue, Ben," he said, his voice low but edged with steel. He took a measured breath, his tone calm, deliberate, and brooking no argument. "Listen well. Me orders be clear—we stay at the village. And that, me boy, is exactly what we're gonna do." He paused, letting the weight of his words sink in before continuing. His gaze hardened, a silent warning in his eyes. "So, I suggest ye buckle down, and follow orders like the first mate ye're supposed to be."

The next morning dawned with a brilliance that set the sky ablaze in hues of crimson and gold, casting a warm glow over the village. The crew strode back into its heart, their steps sure and deliberate, as the village stirred to life, its streets filling with the quiet buzz of a new day. The air carried the tantalizing aroma of freshly baked bread, mingling with the rhythmic clang of a blacksmith's hammer in the distance. Children darted through the cobbled streets, their laughter ringing out like a melody, weaving joy into the morning. The chatter of villagers rose and fell, harmonious with the gentle rustle of leaves in the soft breeze.

With his charismatic charm and razor-sharp wit, Billy sauntered into the tavern, where he effortlessly wove himself into the fabric of village life, coaxing out tales and legends from the lips of those who had indulged a bit too freely in ale, each story a potential treasure map to hidden truths. Meanwhile, Ben and the others ventured through the bustling streets of the market, weaving through stalls and striking up conversations, their ears keen for whispers of untold secrets. They moved with purpose, their eyes ever-watchful, as they sifted through stories and trinkets alike, hoping to unearth any missing piece of their puzzle. At first, the villagers viewed these strangers with a hint of suspicion, but Ben and his crew put on their best friendliness, and with their disarming smiles and genuine interest, soon won them over.

Jim, however, had a different mission. His mind was preoccupied with thoughts of Bella, the enchanting village woman he had met the day before. The market was bustling with activity, yet a sense of quiet disappointment enveloped him as he scanned the crowd. He expected the spot where he had met Bella to be vibrant with color and music, only to find it empty.

He looked to his left, settling on a group of women huddled around a fabric stall, their laughter ringing in his ears. Then he turned his head to the right, eyeing a couple strolling leisurely past a fruit vendor, their hands entwined. But Bella was nowhere in sight. Standing at the market's edge, Jim's eyes traced the dusty path weaving into the heart of the quaint village. Resolute, he decided to follow it. The further he walked, the more the cheerful noise of the market faded, replaced by the tranquil sounds of the village—a distant church bell tolling the hour, the soft rustle of leaves swaying in the breeze, the occasional clip-clop of a lone horse trotting down the streets. The scent of the market gave way to the sweet fragrance of blooming flowers and the earthy smell of freshly tilled soil. He passed by quaint adobe houses, men adorned in simple cotton tunics and wide-brimmed straw hats working diligently at their crafts, women dressed in traditional hand-woven skirts and blouses, and children playing around a majestic fountain in the town square. Yet, every place he visited seemed empty without Bella's presence.

As he moved deeper into the village, he found himself on an old stone bridge, its graceful arch casting a shadow over the river below, the calm waters reflecting the lush foliage of the trees lining the banks. The river was the lifeblood of the village, winding its way lazily around the outskirts and disappearing into the dense forest beyond. Amidst this peaceful backdrop, Jim's eyes caught the sight of Bella, standing in the water, her figure bathed in the warm glow of the morning sun. A rush of relief washed over him.

She was knee-deep in the gentle current, her simple cotton skirt hitched up and secured around her waist to keep it dry, and her hair was pulled back into a loose bun, a few tendrils escaping to frame her face. Around her, neatly piled on the grassy bank, were baskets filled with freshly washed clothes, their colors as vibrant as the wildflowers dotting the landscape.

"Mornin', Miss Bella," he called out, a hint of nervousness in his voice.

"Jim! Mornin'," she responded as she watched Jim come down off the bridge, surprised at seeing him there.

"Didn't see ya at the market today."

"I . . . I have chores to do."

A moment of awkward silence hung between them as they both fumbled for words, their nervous attraction making conversation tricky.

"Chores, aye? Same as me duties aboard ship. They be never-endin'."

Bella, looking down shyly and wringing out a cloth, replied, "Yes, there's always something that needs doing. But it's not so bad. It keeps me busy."

In the serene setting of the river, their words stumbled and tripped over each other. Their glances were fleeting and shy, their laughter forced, echoing awkwardly against the rustling reeds. But as the morning sun climbed higher, casting long shadows and bathing the world in a golden hue, a subtle transformation unfolded. Slowly, like the steady current of the river beside them, their banter began to find its rhythm—gentle, unhurried, and natural. The nervous energy that had initially hung heavy between them began to evaporate, replaced by a soft blanket of soothing comfort that settled like sunlight on their shoulders. Laughter now came easily, its sound carrying across the river and intertwining with the soft rustle of the trees. Their smiles lingered longer, reflecting the warmth that had begun to kindle between them.

Meanwhile, the tavern was a whirlwind of drink and jocularity, filled with the boisterous mirth and spirited chatter of the villagers. Aromas of spiced rum, sea salt, and smoky wood from the hearth filled the air. In the heart of this lively chaos sat the captain, a figure of intrigue with his weather-beaten tricorn hat and gleaming cutlass, his hearty laughter harmonizing with the locals' merriment.

"Friends," he began, his voice jovial and warm. "I've crossed the seven seas, seen sights that would make your heart skip a beat. But the real treasure, I tell ye, lies not in exotic lands, but in the heart of humble abodes like this village. For what gives a village its soul be not its fields or houses, but its people and their tales. Tales of love, of loss, of victories and defeats. Them be the lifeblood of this place." A murmur rippled through the tavern, the clinking of tankards momentarily stilled as curiosity bubbled among the gathered villagers. His voice softened, dipping into a tone as inviting as a warm hearthfire. "Yer lives, yer history, yer struggles, yer joys—them be the real adventures. Would ye share them with an old sea dog?" he beseeched the small group in there. His smile deepened as his eyes fell upon an elderly villager whose features bore the marks of time, his face a roadmap of life's many journeys. The captain leaned toward him, his tone turning softer, becoming a gentle plea. "Sir," he said with earnest respect, "would ye grace me with a story of yer village? Not as a stranger, but as a friend who wishes to understand the soul of this wonderful place?"

The aged villager leaned in, his voice raspy as he shared the story of the Ancient Whispers. "Ages past, 'fore European folks made this their home, native tribes were masters here," he began, his eyes distant as if peering into the past. "Their ancient ruins still stand, silent watchers of a time long gone. At first light, when the world is still caught 'twixt dreams and day, you can hear it—

the whispers of the natives' ancestors. 'Tis the sound of ancient prayers, chants that once filled the air, now trapped within this village." His eyes sparkled with a mix of mystery and mischief as he spoke. "And at twilight, when the sun bows out for the day, the whispers change. They become the songs of celebration, the laughter of the spirits, the pounding of hands against ancient drum skins." His voice dropping to a near-whisper, he added, "And on some nights, when the moon is full and the sea's at peace, you can even hear in the distance the soft lullabies sung by mothers to their children."

Then, a spirited woman, her dark hair adorned with vibrant beads, wove a tale about how their lives were intertwined with the sea. "Sir," she started, her words simple but full of heart. "Our little village here, we live by the sea's heartbeat." Her hands moved gently, mimicking the rise and fall of the ocean's tides. "Our days, they follow the sea's lead. We get up when the tide comes in, and rest when it goes out. The sun guides us through the day, and at night, the moon lights our way." She spoke of their fishing customs with a certain reverence in her eyes. "When the moon is round and full, that's when we cast our nets into the glittering sea. That is our Moonlit Harvest." She painted a scene with her words that was as vivid as the night sky. "Our people, stepping into the moon-kissed sea, cast their nets under a canopy of twinkling stars. The waters, quiet as a hushed whisper, mirror the sky above, makin' it seem like we're walkin' among those stars." As she continued speaking, her eyes held a twinkle that rivaled the stars themselves. "But the real magic isn't in the harvest itself. It's up there, hidden among the stars. They speak to us, whisperin' secrets, tellin' where the fish are plenty, guidin' our nets." Leaning back with a wistful smile, she let the weight of her tale hang in the air before adding, "We dance with the sea under a sky ablaze with stars, where the secrets of the heavens are etched in the constellations above, leadin' us to the bounty we seek."

The Secret of the Dragon's Scale

The hours slipped away unnoticed, measured only by the soft crackle of logs dwindling in the hearth and the steady emptying of tankards. The captain's voice, rich and captivating, filled the room as he spun tales of perilous journeys, fierce storms, and encounters with mythical creatures. Each story was punctuated with roars of laughter or collective gasps, his audience hanging on his every word. Other villagers, too, shared their own anecdotes. A fisherman talked about his biggest catch, a farmer shared memories of a year of bountiful harvest, and a young lady shyly recounted her first journey outside the village. Billy's eyes glimmered with interest, drawn to the rich history and traditions embedded in these tales.

The tavern door creaked open, piercing the boisterous laughter and chatter. Ben and his shipmates, weary from their exploring in the village and market, trod inside. The room was a simmering pot of stories, swirls of pipe smoke, and the warm glow of candlelight dancing on worn wooden tables.

"Ah, me hearties!" the captain bellowed to them. "Speak of yer wanderin'. How did ye fare under today's sun?"

A collective sigh ran through the crew. Every glance, every word, every shadow, was scrutinized for even the faintest trace of clues that might reveal the Dragon's Scale. Yet, despite their efforts, they uncovered nothing.

"Captain," Ben said, choosing his words carefully among the prying ears. "The sea seems calm . . . too calm."

A knowing glint sparked in Billy's eyes. He understood Ben's coded message—their search so far had been fruitless. "Aye, sometimes the greatest storms brew beneath the calmest waters . . . We must be patient," he said. "We must watch, wait, and be ready. For when the storm comes, it will bring what we seek." His words hung in the air, being both a promise and a prophecy. "Now, where be Jim?"

As dusk descended, the world around Jim and Bella was cloaked in a gentle twilight, the lingering warmth of the day melding with the cool whisper of evening. Their conversation ebbed and flowed, revealing layers of shared dreams and unspoken yearnings. Bella's laughter, once restrained, now filled the air with its melodious charm. Their conversation, once stuttering, now evolved into a comfortable rhythm, their words intertwining and dancing in the evening air. Bella's eyes sparkled as she described the mornings spent in her orchard, picking fruit to sell at the village market, and of evenings in the village square, where elders wove ancient tales into the heart of their community. She painted vivid portraits of autumn festivals where lanterns glowed like a thousand captured stars, and music and merriment filled the night. Jim shared tales of his seafaring life, of distant lands and stormy seas. He carried her to bustling foreign ports fragrant with exotic spices, and to lonely stretches of ocean where the horizon seemed endless. She could see the spray of saltwater, hear the creaking of wooden decks, and feel the boundless freedom of staring into a world so vast and wild—making her feel as though she was there with him, amidst the roaring waves and underneath the vast, open sky. Between them, their words crafted a bridge between two distant worlds, drawing them closer with each shared story, each a glimmering thread of a life the other could almost touch.

But as the stars began to twinkle in the evening sky, a sense of urgency washed over Jim. His shipmates would be waiting, his duty calling him back to his ship. Looking up at the darkening sky, he realized the others would be looking for him by now. "I must return to me ship," he said to Bella, the words tasting bitter on his lips. His gaze lingered on her, drinking in the sight of her under the light of the setting sun.

"So, you'll be leaving the village then?" she asked, a hint of sadness in her eyes.

"Can't say just yet. I wish I could tell ye that we'll be stayin' here longer," he explained, uncertain about what will happen until he knows more from the captain. "The ship, the crew, we's all at the mercy of the captain's orders. If he decides to sail at first light, we must go."

He felt a tug in his chest, a longing to stay rooted to this spot, to remain in this moment. But the call of his duty could not be ignored. With a final glance at Bella, whose image was now etched into his memory, he turned away, leaving behind the comforting sound of her laughter, the inviting warmth of her smile, and a piece of his heart by the riverside. He left with the promise of tomorrow, a new day to continue their story.

The village was quiet, save for the distant laughter and music coming from the tavern. As he walked, Jim could see the warm glow of light spilling from the tavern's windows. He could hear the raucous laughter of his shipmates, their voices carrying tales of adventures and sea monsters to entertain the villagers. Just as he reached it, the door swung open and out stepped Billy and Ben, followed by the rest of the crew. They were all laughing, their faces flushed with drink and merriment.

Billy spotted Jim. "Jim, me boy! There ye be, lad!"

Jim forced a smile onto his face and approached them, though his mind was elsewhere. "Aye, Captain," he replied, nodding his head in greeting. He cast one last look toward the river—toward Bella—before joining his shipmates, ready to return to the ship for the night.

As they gathered aboard ship at the end of the day, they shared their experiences, attempting to piece together the puzzle they hoped would lead to the Dragon's Scale. The village, with its unique charm and intriguing tales, was rich in possibilities, though so far yielded nothing they could hang their hats on. Their individual pursuits, though, had set the foundation for their collective journey. Billy, ensconced in the local tavern, had his ears tuned to the chorus of tales spun by the villagers. Each word from their mouths was like a breadcrumb on the path to the elusive prize. Ben and the other crew had immersed themselves in the village's vibrant culture. They explored the streets and alleyways, tasted exotic dishes, and bantered with merchants at the market. It was their camaraderie with the villagers that brought to them intriguing insights into local lore. Jim, however, had been distracted by tugs on the heart. He was captivated by Bella, the village beauty with entrancing stories and eyes as deep as the ocean.

In the morning, up on deck, there was much chatter among the men. Huddled around the captain, they wanted to know what to expect. What were their next orders?

Billy leaned against the ship's railing, his determined voice carrying over the faint whisper of the sails as the breeze teased their edges. "We've not been here long, men" he said, as he looked out toward the village. "We be stayin' 'til we find somethin'—a clue, a hint, anythin' that'll set us on course or reward us with the prize we seek. Mark me words, we won't be leavin' empty-handed."

Ben scoffed, his impatience evident as he threw up his hands. "We've heard enough tales, Captain! They've led us nowhere!"

Billy met Ben's challenging stare, his voice firm but calm. "Every tale, every word, be a potential clue, Ben. We must be patient."

"But Captain," Jim interjected, "we not be knowin' what the Dragon's Scale even is or what it looks like. Ye talk of tales and clues. But have ye considered that we might not even recognize the Dragon's Scale if it were right before our eyes?"

"We'll know it when we see it, lad," he answered, his voice carrying a note of finality. But his eyes, usually so confident, betrayed a flicker of doubt.

Ben grumbled in frustration. "We be wastin' time, Captain. We've heard a hundred tales and none be leadin' us any closer to the Scale."

Billy, in a low growl, snapped back. "And we'll listen to a hundred more if we must!"

Ben was continuing to grow edgy. The quest for the Dragon's Scale, and the promises of untold wealth when it revealed the Admiral Benbow, had lit a spark in him. Of course, all the crew were alight, but for Ben it was a flame that had begun to burn a touch too brightly. This mythical treasure, that had long been relegated to tales spun on drunken nights, was becoming an obsession threatening to fray the seams of his mind.

Billy, on the other hand, found comfort in the villagers' stories. To him, each tale was a potential map leading to their coveted prize. As they delved deeper into the village's life and lore, their quest became more than a simple treasure hunt. It was a journey into a world steeped in riddles and mysteries, where the words of the villagers were but lanterns casting light on their winding path.

They had their orders. The men of the Siren's Call were to become a part of village life for as long as it took. It was decided that the crew would offer their services for whatever work needed to be done around the village or in the fields in order to further ingratiate themselves and coax forth whatever secrets may lay nestled within the heart of the village and its people. For now, at least, they were no longer pirates but laborers, fishermen, and carpenters. Every morning they would rise with the sun and head to shore, their hands taking up tools instead of swords, their voices raised in work songs rather than battle cries.

Billy spent his days either at the tavern, sharing drinks and laughter with the villagers, or wandering the market. His boisterous personality and captivating tales of life on the high seas endeared him to the villagers—with each story, he transported his audience to the boundless ocean and to mysterious islands shrouded in mist. The villagers began to see him not as an outsider, but as a part of their community. More and more they opened up, sharing bits of folklore about the village and its traditions.

Ben found himself working alongside the local blacksmith—his strong arms accustomed to hoisting sails now hammering red-hot metal into shape. He wore his new role well, his easy smile and helpful nature quickly winning over the usually reserved smith. In between the ringing of the hammer and

59

the hiss of quenched steel, stories were exchanged, and Ben came to understand the rhythm and pulse of this community.

Other crew members found their place within the village, too. They helped with the harvest, repaired roofs, and even played with the village children, all the while listening and learning. Others mended nets with the fishermen, their nimble fingers weaving stories along with cord. Each day brought them closer to the villagers, their shared labor a bridge that connected two very different worlds.

Every dawn, as the sun painted the sky with hues of gold and crimson, the men came ashore, spreading out to their respective tasks. Jim, however, found a way for his responsibilities to lead him to Bella. Their paths crossed often, each meeting a chance for them to steal moments in each other's company. Bella, with her fiery spirit and gentle heart, would either be at the bustling market, or performing her chores with a grace that made even the mundane seem enchanting. Whether she was selling fruit, washing clothes, tending to livestock, or helping the village elders, she did so with an infectious joy that warmed Jim's heart. He was coming to realize that this place, with Bella, was where his heart yearned to be.

Their companionship evolved naturally, like a melody that flows effortlessly from a well-tuned instrument. They found comfort in their shared silences and laughter, their stories weaving a tapestry of a deepening bond. Jim shared more of his life at sea, of distant lands, and of thrilling exploits. Bella, in turn, brought the village to life for him, painting it with vibrant colors as she told of its customs, its people, and her yearning to see the world beyond. Tales of past adventures and dreams of future ones were exchanged, each word pulling them closer, intertwining their lives in ways they had never imagined.

With each passing day, their conversations, once light and carefree, became more intimate and personal. They found themselves lingering in each other's company, their eye contact holding for a moment longer, their bodies leaning in slightly closer. When Bella's fingers danced over the strings of her lute, serenading Jim with melodies as sweet as summer wine, every other concern faded away. The world blurred into insignificance when they were together, their focus solely on each other.

The signs of their growing affection were as subtle as they were profound. A nervous excitement washed over them whenever they saw each other, a feeling of comfort spread like a gentle wave at the melody of the other's laughter. With time, the physical space between them dissolved away. A light touch on the arm while passing a bread basket, an accidental brush of hands while washing clothes—each lit a surge of warmth in them. These small moments soon gave way to full-blown embraces—a comforting hug after a long day, a playful lift during a dance at the village festival. Each caress was a whispered promise, an affirmation of their blossoming love. The longing in their eyes when they bid goodbye each day spoke volumes of their desire to spend every waking moment together.

"Come," Bella entreated Jim as she took hold of his hand. "I want you to meet someone."

She walked with him to her home. "Father!" she called out. Stepping into her humble cottage, Jim saw a very old man entering the front room, leaning heavily on his well-worn cane. His back was bent with the weight of years, and his movements were slow and deliberate, each step taken with a patience born of age and infirmity. Encircling his bare head were long, wispy threads spun from silver. His face was a tapestry of time, each wrinkle a testament to years lived and experiences gathered. His eyes, once bright and full of life, were now clouded over. The cane, gnarled and cracked like its owner, seemed to be an extension of him.

Despite his failing sight, the old man moved with a certain assurance, his other senses heightened to compensate for his diminished vision. He paused at the doorway, his head tilted slightly as if listening to the room's heartbeat. Then, with a nod to himself, he ventured further in, his cane tapping rhythmically on the wooden floor.

Jim's eyes widened in surprise as he took in the sight of the elderly man. He turned to Bella, his voice barely above a whisper. "This be your father?" His mind struggled to reconcile the image of the man before him—so ancient and frail—with the vibrant, youthful Bella standing beside him. "Your grandfather?" he couldn't help asking.

Bella glanced at the elderly man, a soft smile gracing her features, before turning back to Jim. "Well, not true father as you might think, though he did raise me since I was a child," she explained. "This is Father Ignatius. He's our village priest."

"Oh, uh, Padre. It be an honor, sir," Jim greeted the priest.

Although the most he could still see were dim, ghostly figures, Father Ignatius knew Bella was there with a young man. He leaned heavily on his knotty cane, each step slow and measured as he moved toward them.

"Welcome, young man. May God's grace be with you," he said, extending a hand toward where he sensed Jim to be. He used what limited sight he had to take in the young man before him. His gaze was slow and deliberate, moving from Jim's tousled hair down to his weather-beaten boots. He leaned forward slightly and remarked, "You've travelled a long way. A great voyage across the sea. Come. Sit."

Bella's life in the village was simple, yet filled with responsibilities. Her days were spent helping in the village and tending to her duties at home. But amidst all the chores, Bella found solace in her blossoming bond with Jim, the young sailor who had drifted into her life. Their relationship was an unexpected surprise, like a wildflower blooming in a barren field. Their connection was undeniable, and Bella found herself powerfully drawn to him. Jim was different from anyone she had known—brimming with tales of the sea, adventures, and a spirit as free as the wind. He embodied a world beyond her small village, a world that was exciting and filled with possibilities. So introducing Jim to her guardian was a significant step for Bella. She valued Father Ignatius' opinion and was eager for his blessing. She sought validation for her feelings, understanding for her choices, and acceptance for the man who had lit a flame in her heart. It was her way of acknowledging the new-found importance of Jim in her life, and that what she felt for him was more than just a fleeting infatuation. She was coming to see in Jim a companion, a partner, someone with whom she could envision a future.

Ultimately, Bella brought Jim to meet the man who had been like a true father to her because she was standing at a crossroad. It represented Bella's readiness to embrace a new chapter in her life, marking her transition from a young girl bound by the confines of her village to a woman willing to venture into the unknown, hand-in-hand with the man she was growing to love.

Surprise washed over Jim's face as he looked upon the priest. "It be true. It has been a long journey to find meself here," he admitted. "Bella has been speakin' kindly of me, I hope," Jim jested light-heartedly with a smile, assuming Bella had already told the priest much about him.

But Bella confessed, a little sheepishly, "Oh . . . ummm . . . no. I haven't spoken a word about you to Father."

"But how could ye know of me travels, Padre?" he inquired, his voice carrying a mix of bemusement and curiosity.

Father Ignatius chuckled softly, his sightless eyes sparkling with an inner light as he began to speak. "Ah. A river does not question the journey of a single drop," he began, his words weaving an intricate tapestry of riddles. "It flows from the mountain peak, dances through valleys, and kisses the ocean's cheek. Yet, it is still part of the river, carrying stories of distant lands." He paused, letting his words hang in the air. "Just as the river knows its drop, the Earth knows its child. It hears your footsteps, feels your heartbeat, tastes the salt of your tears. It silently tells these tales to those who listen with more than just their ears."

Jim turned to Bella, a confused expression on his face. He didn't understand a word of what the priest said. Bella tried to explain. "We carry our stories with us, and just like a mother knows her child, the Earth knows us. It feels us, every step we take, every beat of our heart, every tear we shed. Father listens with his heart to the unspoken stories of our lives. That's how he knew you've travelled far, even without anyone telling him."

Then Bella felt it was time to reveal more about the bond forming between her and Jim. "Father," she began, her voice as gentle as the morning breeze, "I need to share something with you."

"Ah, my child," the priest interrupted. "The morning dew greets the Earth at dawn, sharing tales of the night, of silent promises made under the watchful eyes of the stars. The river that wanders through the valley has witnessed stolen glances, gentle touches, and secret smiles. The wind carries laughter, whispered words, the sighs that float in the air. The Earth herself feels the weight of shared steps, the warmth of shared embraces, the rhythm of shared heartbeats. I know, my child, I know."

Bella, deeply moved by his words, now understood that Father Ignatius already knew of the deepening love between her and Jim, and gave it his full blessing.

Then the priest slowly turned to Jim. His faded eyes appeared to hold no sight but looked toward something unseen, gleaming with a knowing light. "And you, my son." His lips curved into a gentle smile, speaking in a voice that echoed with the resonance of ancient lore. "When dreams greet the edge of dawn, a dewdrop will fall where shadows stand still. It will flow passed the stone that sings to the sky, etched with the wisdom of the ancients, their whispers echoing with prayers and sacred chants. It will flow through the heart of the forest, where the whispers become songs of celebration, and the laughter of spirits dancing in the twilight to the rhythm of ancient drums. Then, under the moon's silvery disc, to its ears come soft lullabies, putting the world to sleep."

As the priest spoke, the strain of his age began to show. His voice, once steady, wavered, the words coming slower, more deliberate. Though each sentence seemed to drain him, leaving his breaths shallow and labored, he continued, "And when the drop finally feels the ocean's embrace, it transforms into a radiant tear, entreating the daughters of the sea to reveal their secrets."

And with that, his voice fell silent, his energy spent.

With a nurturing instinct, Bella rose from her chair and approached the weary old priest. "Father," she said, her words gentle yet firm, "you should rest." With an appreciative nod, he allowed Bella to guide him toward his room, where a soft bed awaited him.

"Come," Bella said to Jim. "We should go walk, and let Father sleep."

Walking through the village, Jim looked at Bella with confusion and some embarrassment in his voice. "I . . . I couldn't make head nor tail of the padre's talk. I've sailed to many a land, but he speaks in a language more puzzlin' than any foreign tongue I've heard."

Bella laughed softly. "In his age, his mind has grown faint. 'Tis now such a time that when he speaks, it seems only in riddles. Since he's cared for me from a young girl, I'm the only soul who can understand his tangled thoughts, and even that be far from a simple task."

"Ye said ye was raised by him?"

"Yes. My true father died in war when I was a tiny thing, back in England," she explained. "And years later Mother died of sickness. Father Ignatius took me in and raised me. When he heard the calling to be a missionary in the Americas, he took me with him, so I am here."

"Can ye say what he was speakin' of in there?"

"Though I never spoke to Father of us, he knew of the feelings growing in our hearts. The river has watched us, the wind has heard us, the earth has felt us. They whisper their stories to those who listen with more than just their ears," she tried to explain. "Then he spoke of your journey. 'Tis the drop carried by the river. Father's words, they were much more than riddles. Think of them as a map, a guide, a prophecy. He told of the place where your journey begins. And as the river flows, the signs that guide you to each next place will be revealed. You will see, hear, and feel these signs, but only if you listen with your heart. And at journey's end, just as a river empties into the sea, the secrets you seek . . . they will be revealed to you here."

Jim froze in his tracks. His jaw fell slack, his lips parted, dropping open in a silent gasp. His eyebrows shot up, his eyes suddenly transforming into wide pools of astonishment. The words—*map, journey, prophecy, secrets*—echoed in his mind. Jim grabbed hold of Bella's hand and yanked her with him as he bolted forward. "I've got to find the captain!" he exclaimed to her.

Running through the village, Jim saw the captain and some of the other crew near the market. He ran up, Bella in tow, panting, "Captain . . . Captain!"

"Jim, me boy! What news bring ye?" Billy responded. His gaze then shifted to Bella, a twinkle in his eye. "Ah. Word's been gettin' 'round ye've been keepin' the company o' this lovely lass. Can't say I blame ye, lad."

"Oh, uh, well . . . aye," Jim admitted, somewhat sheepishly. His words came out tumbling and confused as he tried to catch his breath and calm his thoughts. "Bella's father . . . I mean, not true father . . . her father, the priest father . . . spoke in riddles, prophecies, of me journey . . . and secrets that will be revealed to me. I think it means somethin' important. I think it be what we're lookin' for."

"Jim," the captain said, with a skeptical arch of his brow and a mix of doubt and curiosity in his voice. "We've been docked in this village for many days now. Heard hundreds of tales from the locals. So, tell me, lad, what makes these stories from a priest any different?"

The Secret of the Dragon's Scale

"Well . . . I, uh . . . I can feel it in me bones," Jim insisted. "First, he be talkin' 'bout me journey bein' like a river, carrying me to many places. It will start where dreams greet the edge of dawn, and shadows stand still. There will be a stone that sings to the sky, carved by the ancients, and, umm, I will hear whispers echoing with prayers and sacred chants . . . ummm, ummm . . . "

Trying to remember what the priest had said, he turned to Bella, his eyes showing forgetfulness. Bella, understanding his silent plea, responded, "He spoke of the journey going through a forest, and that at night the whispers will turn to songs of celebrations and the laughter of spirits dancing to the beating of ancient drums."

"Aye . . . Aye!" Jim exclaimed. "And when the moon is full, we will hear the songs of soft lullabies."

A remarkable transformation began to take hold on the captain's face. His initial skepticism started to give way; his sharp, hawkish eyes, which had been narrowed in suspicion, widened slightly, a spark of intrigue igniting within them.

He recalled what he heard in the tavern, his voice low and tinged with incredulity. "A tale was told to me of ancient ruins that still stood. At first light, when the world is still between dreams and day, you can hear the whispers of the native's ancestors, the sound of ancient prayers and chants. At twilight, those whispers become songs of joy and the laughter of spirits, and the rhythmic beating of hands against age-old drum skins. And under the full moon's glow, when the sea is calm, you can hear the soft lullabies sung by mothers to their children."

Billy fell silent and just stood there, his face reflecting the growing feeling that these tales and prophecies were more than just shared remnants of folklore. Something about the priest's words and the villager's story resonated in a way he couldn't ignore—they carried a purpose that seemed far too deliberate to dismiss. It was as though an unseen hand was threading these stories together into a pattern only he was meant to see. And deep within, he felt it—a pull as old as the stars, a whisper tugging at the corners of his mind, urging him to listen, to believe. After all, he sensed, the map had brought them to this village, not by chance but by design, and he couldn't help but feel that these stories were the reason for this, to guide them toward a truth waiting to be revealed.

Bella then finished what Jim was trying to recall. "Father also said when his journey is at an end, the daughters of the sea will reveal their secrets."

"The daughters of the sea?" Billy mused. Trying to think of what that could mean, he mumbled it over and over to himself. "Daughters of the sea . . . daughters of the sea . . . will reveal their secrets." His rugged face lit up as the answer dawned on him. "Mermaids! Mermaids!" he blurted out.

Billy knew well the legends of the mermaids. Spun amidst the scent of salt air, tarred ropes, and aged rum, the tales of mermaids were among the most cherished pieces of lore for pirates and sailors alike. Seafarers would speak of them as magical beings who could calm the stormiest seas or summon tempests at will. These fabled sea maidens, they'd say, were as beautiful as they were mysterious, their hypnotic songs echoing over the waves in the still of the night. Their long, flowing hair shimmered with a kaleidoscope of colors, their skin gleamed like polished pearls, and their iridescent tails sparkled like moonlight on the water's surface. Their eyes, the deepest pools of amethyst and sapphire, flecked with glittering gold, held a wisdom that transcended the ages. They were said to speak the language of every sea creature, feel the ebb and flow of every tide, and know the hiding places of every ship that sunk into the watery depths. They were the silent witnesses to the sea's untold stories, privy to the secrets that lay missing in the vastness of the ocean.

Billy had always dismissed such fanciful tales. To him, the priest's words weren't a literal vision of mythical creatures unveiling hidden truths, but merely a metaphor. Yet, as he pondered, an unshakable gut instinct settled over him. Only by pressing forward, by continuing their difficult and uncertain voyage, could they hope to unravel the true meaning hidden within those words. Somewhere ahead, cloaked in mystery, lay the answers they sought—secrets waiting to surface, guiding them to the prize that had remained elusive for so long.

"Where be Ben!?" Billy bellowed, his voice reverberating through the tranquil village. Ben came running from nearby, answering the captain's call. "Ben! Rally the crew with haste! We be settin' sail this hour!"

Bella turned to look at Jim, her heart pounding, her eyes brimming with unshed tears. Her face was a canvas of emotions—a mix of fear, sadness, and an undeniable love that had taken root in her heart. "You're leaving then?"

Their eyes met and held. It was a silent conversation, their fears reflected in each other's gaze. "Aye," he had to respond.

Jim's breath quickened. His face grew pale at the thought of leaving Bella, not knowing when or if he would see her again. Staring at the radiant beauty he had come to love, a sudden wave of determination came over Jim. Clasping her hands in his, he entreated, "Bell—Bella . . . Please, come with me."

Bella's eyes widened in sheer astonishment. "What?"

"Aye . . . Come with me . . . I love you. Be with me," Jim pleads.

Bella looked around at the village, her home—a confused and frightened look on her face as the thought of leaving tightened its grip on her heart. The small cottages, the familiar faces, the winding paths she had walked a thousand times—all of it anchored her like roots sunk deep into the earth. But those walls, those paths, had always felt too small, too confining for the restless soul stirring within her.

She turned back to Jim, standing there with hope and longing etched in every line of his face. Her eyes softened, and a sudden warmth flowed through her, chasing away the cold grip of fear. At that moment, Bella realized this would be an opportunity to be with the man she loved, to escape the provincial confines of the village, and to finally free her adventurous spirit. She looked at Jim with a broad smile, and with love and eager anticipation in her eyes, nodded, "Yes."

Billy, witnessing their impassioned exchange, declared, "Nay. Me ship be no place for a woman."

"But Captain," Jim implored. "Now, we're all here, scratchin' our heads, tryin' to figure out what we're missin', tryin' to unearth those secrets we be searchin' for. The priest spoke the prophecy of me journey. But I could not make head nor tail of it 'cause he only be speakin' in riddles. Bella, she's grown up hearin' thousands of his riddles, and she's the only one who can know their meanin'. I be certain there's so much more wisdom he has uttered, and her understandin' would be our compass. We need her, Captain. I need her. So, I'm askin' ye, please, let Bella come with us."

Billy watched as Jim, a fine young sailor with fire in his eyes, pleaded with Bella to join him on his ship. The earnestness in Jim's voice, and the desperation in his plea, were emotions Billy had not witnessed since his youth. He saw the surprise in Bella's eyes, the fear, and then the resolve. He watched as she looked around at the village she called home, her gaze lingering on familiar paths and houses—a silent farewell to a life she had known for so long. And then her eyes met Jim's again, filled with love and anticipation, and Billy knew that she had made her decision.

Billy felt a strange sensation in his chest, a mix of admiration and concern, but also an intense hopefulness that Bella might truly be key to their quest. He watched the two before him, the way Jim held her hands as if she were an anchor in the storm, the way Bella's eyes shone with both love and the quiet courage of someone ready to leap into the unknown. And then, a memory, soft and bittersweet, came back to him. In the place where Jim and Bella stood were the ghostly shapes of another pair—younger versions of himself and the woman he'd once loved more than life itself. Her laugh, bright and musical as sunlight on the waves, echoed in his mind. He remembered the warmth of her touch, the way her fingers had fit perfectly between his, and the dreams they had once spun together under endless star-filled skies.

It was a moment that echoed deep within Billy's soul. His old heart softened, and he found himself nodding in approval. "Oh . . . aye," he said reluctantly, shoulders sagging as he let out a breath of resignation. He pulled off his captain's hat and rubbed the back of his neck, a soft, almost wistful smile playing on his lips. "Agreed," he grumbled. "I suppose we be carvin' out a spot for one more soul aboard ship."

"Father!" Bella gasped out. She felt a sudden panic, with tears welling up in her eyes. "I, I must tell Father." She turned and ran back to her cottage, a whirlwind of emotions churning within her—fear, guilt, sorrow—at the thought of leaving him alone.

As she came to the cottage, she could see Father Ignatius standing in the doorway. She stopped right in front of him. "Father," she began, her voice choked with emotion. "I—"

He lifted a hand, hushing her. A gentle smile curved his lips. "I know, my child, I know. I have heard the whispers of your soul. You have a restless heart, a longing for something more than this place can give. God has chosen a different path for you, a path of love. Your new journey is all part of His plan."

"But you . . . " Bella worries. "I don't know when I'll return."

"I will be fine. The Lord, and my flock, will watch over me," the old priest reassured her. "Now, go. Follow your heart."

Bella ran past him into the cottage, wrapped together as much clothing as she could carry, and hurriedly threw a shawl around her shoulders. Then her eyes fell upon her beloved lute, resting in the corner. Her arms now filled with her hastily packed belongings and the lute, she returned to Father Ignatius still standing in the doorway. They embraced, a long, lingering hug that spoke volumes of the bond between them. Tears welled up in Bella's eyes. The farewell was silent, their emotions too deep for words. But in that hug, in those tears, Bella conveyed her love for the man who was as true a father as any, and her promise to return. And the priest, in his quiet strength, gave her his blessings for the journey ahead.

The Stone That Sings

The sun hung low on the horizon, the fading light spilling across the sea. Bella stood at the base of the gangplank, her hands gripping the fabric of her shawl, knuckles white with uncertainty. The wind caught her hair, as though even the breeze was trying to pull her forward, away from everything she had known. She cast a glance back at the village she had called home for most of her life. Her heart pounded like a drum, filling the silence of the evening.

Jim extended his hand to help her aboard, his eyes holding a promise of adventure and a trace of apprehension.

Now on the ship, she couldn't help but marvel at the expanse of it all—the vastness of the ocean, the towering masts, the billowing sails, and the enormity of the journey she had embarked upon. The ship creaked beneath her feet, an unfamiliar sound that made her stomach flutter with both fear and excitement.

Jim led her to a small cabin below deck. "This will be yer quarters," he said, his voice echoing slightly in the confined space. "I know it not be much, but . . . "

"I'm glad for it," Bella interrupted. She looked around the room, from the small hammock that would serve as her bed to the tiny porthole that offered a view of the ocean. It was a far cry from her cottage back in the village, but this was her choice, her new life.

Ben called down to them, "Jim, and the girl, the captain wants ye in his cabin."

In his cabin, filled with the soft glow of oil lamps, Billy paced. His hands brushed over maps and charts, his mind wrestling with the riddles they'd heard in the village. The prophecy that Jim said was told to him by the priest, in particular, held his attention. The words seemed to dance around his head, elusive yet promising.

A knock at the door interrupted his concentration. Ben, Jim, and Bella gathered with Billy in his cabin. The four of them stood huddled around the map table, the creak of the ship beneath their feet a constant reminder of the restless sea outside. The walls seemed to lean in, as though the cabin itself was straining to hear what would be said next.

"Now," Billy said to the group. "Let's see if these tales and prophecies be worth their salt. The first thing we need, be knowin' where to set our course."

Jim rested his hands on the edge of the table, his fingers brushing the rough grain of the wood as his gaze lingered on the shifting lines of the maps. "When dreams greet the edge of dawn," he recalled, "seemed to be where everythin' started. We're bein' told to be somewhere just before the first rays of light come over the horizon."

"Well, that tells us when. But where?" Ben asked.

"I'm guessin' where shadows stand still. That be what the old priest was sayin'. But what does that mean?" Jim asked.

The captain, stoic and contemplative, stroked his beard, his expression unreadable as his eyes scanned all the maps strewn on the table. His fingers hovered over the markings of distant isles and uncharted waters as if he could divine the truth from the labyrinth of inked lines. Having lived his life by the sun and the stars, his mind began to churn through his treasure trove of navigational knowledge, trying to decipher the cryptic phrase.

"Where shadows stand still," he muttered to himself. Shadows. Cast by light's obstruction. Always shifting as the sun prowled across the sky. Never constant, never still. His brows furrowed as he traced the thought, his mind feeling its way

The Secret of the Dragon's Scale

through the idea. But what did it mean for a shadow to stand still? Could such a thing even happen?

"Of course!" he exclaimed, slapping a hand on the table. He realized shadows would appear to move the least at a place on the Earth where the sun was more directly overhead than anywhere else. A place like . . . the equator!

A satisfied grin spread across Billy's face as he traced his finger along the imaginary line on a map that cut the world into halves. But something was still missing. Shadows at the equator didn't stand still every day. Then it struck him—the equinoxes! He knew that on these two specific days of the year the sun would be exactly above the equator, causing shadows to stand still longer than at any other time or place on Earth.

The only problem was, where on the equator? The Siren's Call found herself in a region where the equator traced its invisible path across both an expansive stretch of mainland and through a constellation of islands. Their destination could lie anywhere along the equator's length.

Keeping silent while the others poured over the maps and charts, bantering about ideas, Bella found herself lost in a sea of thought. She heard many of Father Ignatius' riddles in her mind, his wisdom hidden beneath layers of metaphor and imagery. And his favorite topic? Destiny—the unseen force that steers the course of our lives with a wisdom that transcends our understanding.

Often, Bella would see the priest standing outside at night, the stars winking down at him. He would point to them. "Lift your gaze up to the heavens, child," he would softly intone to her, his voice a gentle murmur amidst the night's quiet. "See how the stars sprinkle the sky like diamonds strewn across the firmament? Each one tells a tale of our future, guiding us with their timeless, twinkling light through the varied and mysterious journeys of our lives." He would talk about how the stars represented our dreams and aspirations, shimmering in the vast canvas of our existence like distant beacons of hope. He'd say God put them there to be our guides, but beneath them, it is for us to choose our path, to make our own decisions that shape our destiny.

Drawing in a deep breath, Bella broke her silence. "Umm, Father would often speak about destiny. He used to say that the stars were like a map, each one representing a different path that our lives could take. Each star, he said, was a possibility, a potential life that we could lead." Her voice softened as she continued, "But he would often say of my destiny, 'Beneath the star that never moves, lies a path that you must choose.'"

The men exchanged glances, a spark of realization flickering in their eyes. "The star that never moves . . . " Ben pondered. "The North Star! It be always in the same place, no matter where you are!"

Jim folded his arms, staring hard at the floorboards as if the pieces of a puzzle were shifting into place in his mind. "Maybe that be what it means . . . A path to be chosen. Like . . . maybe our course ought to head that way?"

Billy turned his attention to a map sprawled across the table, his finger tracing a line directly northward from their current position to the equator. He huffed out a breath, loud and sharp, shaking his head as a bitter chuckle escaped his lips. "Prophecies, riddles . . . " he muttered, his voice low and cutting. "They be nothin' but fool's games, if you ask me. Stories spun by old men with idle tongues and heads full o' smoke."

Then he turned his gaze to Bella. Something about her presence unsettled him. She didn't belong here—not among the salt-worn planks of the Siren's Call or the hardened men who knew its every creak and groan. And yet, there she stood, her voice quiet but steady, speaking of stars and destiny as if the sea and sky themselves had conspired to place her here. Her words, the North Star, the priest's prophecy . . . it all seemed to draw a thread between them, tying Bella's sense of destiny to the Siren's Call in a way that made his chest tighten with reluctant conviction. Against every instinct telling him to turn away, Billy found himself interpreting the priest's words not as meaningless ramblings, but as the quiet herald of a new journey—Bella's, yes, but also the ship's.

He exhaled slowly, the resistance in his posture softening just enough to reveal the tug-of-war raging inside him. But what choice did they have? Whatever skepticism burned in his gut was overshadowed by the truth of their situation. They had no clear destination, no solid lead. The priest might as well been selling madness. But madness was better than aimless wandering. Right now, it was all they had.

So that was where they would start. His finger tapped on the equator like a final punctuation to his wavering resolve. He straightened fully now, his voice harder, more deliberate, as he turned his decision into a command.

"The North Star . . . " The words came steadily now, his tone solidifying with each one. "Hmmm . . . north. Aye, then. North. If these tales and prophecies be in any way the words that guide us, then I say we trust in their wisdom for now." Snapping his gaze to Ben, he barked his next order, confidence hardening his tone. "Ben. Set course north. And make bloody haste!" He jabbed the map with a decisive hand, the faint urgency in his earlier words now breaking into full force. "The next equinox be nearly upon us, and if there be any sense in that priest's mad ramblin's, then we must reach the equator before dawn that day."

"But Captain," Ben responded. "If we go due north from here, aiming for the equator . . . " He paused, tapping his finger on the blank expanse of sea at the equator. "None of these charts or maps be showin' any land there. Nothin' but open sea."

As the men and Bella wrestled with interpreting the tales and prophecies, every word spoken, every argument made, seemed to amplify an echo in Billy's mind, an echo of the conversation with his friend the old fisherman weeks before—*The sea is rough and unpredictable, just like life. Ya never know what lies beneath its surface or what the next wave will bring.* His words were as profound and mysterious as the ocean itself, bearing a hidden message that gnawed incessantly at the edges of the captain's thoughts.

"I just feel this be right, Ben. I feel it in me bones," he said. "We never truly know what fate awaits us beyond the horizon."

Ben studied the captain, the silence in the room amplifying the strength of his words. Finally, with a slow nod, he agreed, "Then we set our course north, Captain."

The sun began to dip below the horizon, its departure leaving a trail of vibrant oranges and purples that bled into the canvas of the sky, casting a gentle spell over Bella as she stood at the ship's bow, eager to experience the sights and sounds of the vessel slicing through the water. The ocean seemed to stretch out into infinity, its surface glittering with the reflection of the night's first stars. The wind whispered tales of the sea, carrying the salty tang that would soon become as much a part of her as they were of any sailor. The cool spray of the mist on her face made her feel alive in a way she had never felt before.

Jim joined her, his presence a comforting warmth against the evening chill. They stood there, two souls intertwined by love, embarking on an adventure under the banner of the Jolly Roger. Fear and excitement danced in Bella's heart, but as she looked up at Jim, his smile told her that whatever lay ahead, they would face it together.

This had all been a whirlwind for Bella. One moment she was a simple village girl, the next she was sailing aboard a pirate ship, the salty air teasing her hair as she sailed to destinations unknown. And having no understanding of seafaring life, everything around her was strange and new—the creak of the wooden planks beneath her feet, the constant sway of the ship, the shouted commands that sounded more like their own language than any words she'd known. She felt a mix of anxiety, intimidation, and caution, afraid to say much or ask any questions, just naturally assuming there was both rhyme and reason to all the events that had been taking place.

The Secret of the Dragon's Scale

Now with Jim by her side, Bella felt a sense of calm wash over her. The anxiety that had been knotting her stomach began to loosen its grip, letting her breathe a little easier for the first time since stepping aboard. Jim was a beacon of comfort in this unfamiliar environment; his presence made the unknown a little less daunting.

She glanced at Jim, taking a moment to study his profile. His eyes were focused on the vast ocean ahead, their depths holding flecks of silvery light, and there was a quiet confidence about him that she found reassuring. In the way he stood, balanced easily on the rocking deck, one hand resting lightly on the railing, he looked as though he belonged here, as if the sea recognized him as one of its own. Watching him, Bella felt that same connection, as though the sea's timeless rhythm had quietly made room for her too.

At ease in his presence, Bella finally had to satisfy her curiosity with the simplest of questions. "Jim. Where are we going?"

Jim turned to look at her, the light of the rising moon highlighting the contours of his face. "We've been chasin' dreams," he replied, his gaze returning to the ocean ahead. There was a moment's hesitation as he grappled with how much to reveal. The secret of the Dragon's Scale wasn't one to be shared lightly. It was a legend that had lured many to their doom—and yet, in its glittering promise lay the power to transform their lives beyond imagination.

Bella felt a chill run down her spine at the thought, but there was also a strange pull, an irresistible draw toward the unknown. "What dreams? What are we looking for?"

"A secret so powerful, it has lured many a brave soul into its unforgivin' depths." Jim paused for a moment, his eyes now more distant, drifting toward the horizon. "Legend has it that scores of years ago, a ship, called the Admiral Benbow, laden with vast treasures, had gone missin'. Sailors and pirates be searchin' for it ever since. But the legend also says that in order to find this ship, ye must first find somethin' called the Dragon's Scale, and it will lead ye to the Admiral Benbow. But no one knows what the Dragon's Scale even be, or what it means. We've been travellin' place to place, tryin' to figure this out. Each place has given us new hints where to look next. That be what brought us to yer village . . . Now, the captain has a feelin' that the tales and prophecies we've heard in the village be guidin' us to the next place we must go."

"I see," Bella responded simply, her voice tinged with an unmistakable undertone of exhilaration.

The thought was intimidating, but Bella felt a stirring of excitement, the promise of an adventure unlike any she could have imagined in her quiet village life. She looked back at the waters in front of them, the reflections of the stars shimmering on the rhythmic ripples, and took a deep, steadying breath, her eyes wide and full of awe at the seemingly boundless sea, and journey, that lay before them.

Ben had retired to his quarters. The room was sparse, decorated only with the necessities of a seafaring life. It was his calm and quiet refuge. But tonight, the room echoed with an unfamiliar restlessness. He lay on his cot, his usually calm eyes now stormy with a whirlwind of thoughts. The legend of the Dragon's Scale had been relentlessly weaving its way into every corner of his mind. His fingers clenched and unclenched on the rough blanket, mirroring the turmoil within him. The wooden beams overhead stared back at him, indifferent to his inner struggle.

His captain, once a figure of unwavering certainty, now seemed like a puppet dancing to the tune of fanciful folklore and cryptic prophecies. The thought of chasing after what Ben believed to be mere fairy tales had begun to chafe at his reason. He could almost hear the echo of laughter in the wind, mocking their pursuit of the elusive Dragon's Scale.

The ship was now sailing on a course charted by gut instincts and whispered legends, venturing into regions where maps showed only vast expanses of empty ocean. It felt as if they were chasing shadows, moving farther away from solid reality and closer to the nebulous realm of myths. Each creak of the ship, each lap of the waves against the hull, seemed to underscore Ben's growing unease. The captain's self-confidence and common sense, once a source of reassurance, now felt like a blindfold leading them all toward an uncertain fate.

Ben tossed restlessly on his cot, unable to shake off the haunting vision of the Dragon's Scale. For all his doubts about their journey, its allure continued to gnaw at the edges of his sanity. Once, his dreams were alive with the roar of the sea and the exhilaration of their pirate adventures. Now, they were invaded by the gleaming specter of this mythical treasure, glinting seductively in the shadows of his closed eyes, promising untold riches and glory. Alone in his quarters, Ben was undergoing a transformation. A man known for his resilience and fortitude was now precariously balanced on the brink of obsession, gradually descending into the dark abyss of madness. All the while, the Siren's Call sailed on, oblivious to the storm brewing within him.

The voyage carried them steadily closer to the equator, the air growing warmer, the sea calmer. Each day was a vibrant tableau, painted with the brilliant hues of azure skies stretching endlessly above, mirrored by the shimmering seas below. The sun stood high and bright, its golden rays dancing playfully upon the waves, creating a dazzling spectacle of light and motion. The crew, their skin bronzed by the sun's embrace, moved with purpose through their daily tasks, their spirits buoyed by the steady rhythm of progress. And as the sun would begin to dip toward the horizon, the world would burst into a spectacular display of colors. Hues of orange, pink, and purple painted the canvas of the sky, reflecting off the calm waters. The nights, however, held a charm all their own. The fiery hues of the sunset would fade, leaving the sky draped in a velvety black. Overhead, a thousand stars sparkled, scattered like a fistful of diamonds tossed carelessly across the heavens. They shimmered with cold brilliance, their patterns forming ancient constellations—a celestial map etched into the vault of night, guiding those bold enough to chart a course through these distant, untamed waters. Their twinkling forms danced upon the still surface of the sea, turning the water into a mirror of the heavens. The ship seemed to float not on waves, but among the stars themselves, as though it were adrift in the vastness of the cosmos. It was during these tranquil hours that the ship glided effortlessly through the water, its sails filled with a soft breeze, as if drawn not by wind but by some unseen hand of the universe, leading it along a path written in starlight. And the closer they got to the equator, the more balanced these day and night cycles became. This predictable pattern was an important navigational aid, signaling the crew that they were nearing their goal.

By a stroke of fortune and skilled navigation, they had arrived at the equator well before dawn, the world around them still swathed in the midnight blue of the nighttime hours. The moon hung high in the star-studded sky, casting a silver sheen over the ocean's surface, the ship's sails billowing gently in the night breeze. Jim and Bella were forward by the bow, while up on the quarterdeck, Billy and Ben stood, with Mr. Pew at the wheel, their figures silhouetted against the celestial backdrop. The captain with his sextant, and Ben with his astrolabe, checked and rechecked their location, using the dazzling array of stars as their guide.

A look of understanding passed between them. They nodded at each other, a wordless confirmation that they were indeed where they were supposed to be—right on the equator.

Their eyes, now accustomed to the darkness, scanned the horizon with great curiosity. Each squint, each turn of the head, was a silent question posed to the vast expanse around them: *Is there land?* From the crow's nest, the lookout peered into the distance, his spyglass cutting through the darkness. Every ripple, every wave that caught a sliver of moonlight, was scrutinized with anxious anticipation. But each time, the sea would laugh back at them, her surface empty but for the playful dance of the waves. The crew of the Siren's Call, under the watchful eyes of a thousand stars, waited patiently.

"When dreams greet the edge of dawn," Jim softly spoke to Bella, his gaze peering in one direction, then another. He kept repeating, "When dreams greet the edge of dawn . . . When dreams greet the edge of dawn," mulling over the words of the priest.

As the crew watched on deck, the air now seemed to hold its breath, the sea seaming to grow more calm. The darkness of night still held dominion, but its reign was slowly fading. The stars began to dim, their brilliant sparkle slowly yielding to the impending light. The moon, once radiant and full, was now pale and waning. The horizon was the first to hint at the transformation underway. A thin, almost imperceptible line of mauve began to etch itself against the obsidian expanse, deepening gradually into a band of rich amethyst, the color bleeding upward into the sky like ink in water. As moments passed, the purple gave way to a softer palette—blush pink and peach tones infused the skyline, their delicate colors reflected in the mirror-like surface of the sea below.

Jim, Bella, and the others continued to stand watch, their faces etched with anticipation and a touch of apprehension, hoping their faith in the tales and prophecies wasn't sending them on a fool's errand. As they stood there, waiting, they knew that the coming dawn would bring either validation or disappointment. But they didn't know what to expect. And so, with bated breath, they watched, expecting the first rays of sunlight to soon pierce the horizon. But all was quiet. No sign of land. No nothing.

The Siren's Call hung in a moment of profound stillness in the equatorial waters, a silhouette against the pre-dawn sky. Her once billowing sails now hung limp and lifeless on the masts, awaiting the morning breeze. The ship bobbed gently in the calm sea, her movements rhythmic and soothing, the only sound being the soft lapping of water against the hull, the creaking of timbers, and the quiet whispers of anticipation from the crew.

Then, without warning, the silence of the pre-dawn moments was suddenly shattered by an ominous rumble—a low growl that seemed to originate from the belly of the ocean itself! It was a deep, resonant sound, more felt than heard, vibrating through the hull of the Siren's Call and into the soles of the crew's feet. Abruptly, a mysterious sensation gripped the ship—a feeling of being tugged downward, like the unseen hand of a giant pulling at her keel! The crew stumbled, their eyes wide with surprise as the ship groaned under the sudden strain!

"Aaaaaaah!" screamed Bella, a piercing siren in the quiet of the morning.

The ocean around them began to churn, frothing white at the edges, as if the sea itself was awakening from a deep slumber.

Then came the hiss, a sharp contrast to the earlier rumble! It was the sound of water on the move, a sibilant whisper that quickly grew to a loud roar. Soon, an insistent, rushing noise surrounded them as the waters began to recede, pulling away from the Siren's Call in a swift, relentless retreat. This was a spectacle that defied belief—the mighty ocean yielding, revealing its hidden secrets! The crew clung to the railing, their hearts pounding in their chests as they watched the sea surrender to this mysterious force!

Bella flung her arms tightly around Jim, her slender form trembling against his sturdy one. Not understanding anything that was happening, her mind was a whirl of fear and confusion.

It was as if the sea had suddenly been summoned by some mystical presence, its waters heeding a call that resonated from the fiery sphere ascending in the east. The crew could hear the slap and splash of water against the hull becoming increasingly frantic, interspersed with the grating sound of sea-creatures hastily retreating with the water! The ship creaked and groaned in protest as the water level dropped, the sound echoing the unease of the men! As the water receded further, new sounds joined the symphony—the grumble of rocks and sand being dragged along by the withdrawing tide, the intermittent clatter of shells and pebbles colliding, and the sharp crack of releasing pressure as the ocean floor was exposed to the open air.

"The tide!" the captain's voice rang out over the ship, filled with a mix of astonishment and excitement. "Look sharp, lads! The tide's makin' a run for it faster'n a rat desertin' a sinkin' ship!"

Around them, a landscape began to reveal itself, stretching out in all directions, as the water was pulled eastward—land, where there should have been nothing but endless ocean!

The sight stole their breath away, a testament to the power of nature and the truth of the prophecy they had followed. The crew stood in shocked wonder, their eyes wide in disbelief as they took in the unearthly scene. The Siren's Call, once a proud vessel cutting through the waves, now sat as a solitary sentinel on a newly revealed land, the first rays of dawn casting long shadows around her.

The captain had anchored his trust in the wisdom of the priest. Now, despite his doubts, the prophecy seemed to be unveiling its mysteries. At the time and place foretold, the ocean had receded, exposing hidden land, and the Siren's Call had been there to witness it. Then, slowly, the eastern horizon started to burn with a fiery intensity. The sun was announcing its imminent arrival, casting long, glowing fingers across the expanse of the early morning ocean, turning the water's surface into a rolling field of molten gold. And as the sun began to rise, they knew they were not on a fool's errand. They had been right to believe, to hope.

As more land was exposed, in the distance appeared what seemed to be a rocky hill. This stone monument emerged as if rising from the depths, its rugged contours etched against the backdrop of the sky. Sunlight kissed the exposed rock face, casting shadows that danced over its crevices and crags.

Then, with a gentle shudder, the ship came to a halt, its imposing hull nestling into the seabed. The once deep cerulean ocean had receded, surrendering to the sandy bottom that now cradled the vessel like a mother's loving arms. The ship seemed to sigh as it settled, its timbers creaking in soft protest after the abrupt descent. It now rested mere feet away from the shore of the newly revealed land, casting a long, imposing shadow over the sunlit sand. Its masts, proud and tall, reached toward the clear azure sky, their riggings humming softly in the sea breeze. The sails, which had thrashed violently only moments ago, now hung limp and exhausted, mirroring the stunned silence that had fallen over the crew.

Bella and the men stood shoulder to shoulder on the deck, their faces etched with disbelief as they beheld the landscape unfolding around them, their eyes wide with wonder. Their gazes swept across this impossible vista, drinking in the surreal spectacle. Their lips parted, but words failed them. The landscape that stretched out was beyond anything any seafaring lore had prepared them for. For Bella, the sight was unlike anything she had ever experienced in her simple village life—it was overwhelming, breathtaking, and terrifying all at once.

The captain and Ben, regaining their wits, came down from the quarterdeck. Billy looked down over the side of the ship, his eyes scanning the virgin landscape that stretched out before them, his face a study in concentration and curiosity.

"We be goin' ashore. Lower the ladders," he ordered, his gaze never leaving the newly revealed island.

The crew burst into action without hesitation. Rope ladders were pulled from their hooks, quickly unrolled, and thrown over the side, their ends dangling just above the few inches of shallow water still encircling the ship.

The sunlit seabed spread out like a patchwork quilt of muted tones, the sand interspersed with scattered pebbles in shades of grey and brown, each glinting faintly under the light. Here and there, the motionless forms of stranded sea creatures lay as silent remnants of the ocean's retreat. Billy, Ben, Jim, Bella, and the rest of the crew stood on the damp sand, their figures etched against the receding sea behind them, while ahead, the barren landscape stretched into an uncertain horizon. A cool breeze whispered across the exposed shore, carrying the briny sharpness of the ocean mingled with the raw, earthy aroma of freshly uncovered land.

Their attention inevitably drifted toward the sole remarkable feature in this barren panorama—the rocky hill standing in the distance. It rose from the flat seabed like a lone monument, its craggy silhouette etched sharply against the backdrop of the surrounding land and sea. Billy examined the hill intently. His sharp eyes traced its uneven outline, taking in the jutting rocks and shadowy crevices. He took a step forward, his boots squelching in the wet sand, his mind already mapping out a path forward. Jim scanned the surroundings warily before his curiosity turned to the hill. His eyes narrowed, picking out patterns that seemed to weave a story of ages past. Next to him, Ben leaned forward slightly, peering into the distance, his hands shielding his eyes as he too studied the formation, picking out the distinct layers of rock. The rest of the crew stood quietly, their faces reflecting a mix of curiosity and apprehension.

Bella stood rooted to the damp sand, her heart thudding with a mixture of wonder and unease as the exposed world stretched endlessly before her. This was a land reborn, stripped bare of its aquatic cloak and exposed to the open sky for the first time in centuries. She crouched down, scooping up a handful of the wet sand, letting it sift through her fingers, feeling its cool grittiness against her skin. Then, as with the others, her focus shifted to the distant hill. It seemed to rise from the seabed with quiet defiance. Bella tilted her head, her youthful curiosity piqued. From this distance, she could see the play of shadows over the rocks, lending the hill an air of mystery. She found herself drawn to it, a pull that seemed to resonate with the adventurous spirit within her.

"We head there," declared Billy, his voice cutting through the hushed air. He pointed toward the rocky hill that loomed in the distance like a guardian of secrets long buried. He couldn't help but feel an insistent tug deep within his chest urging him toward it; it felt alive, as if some ancient force was entwining itself with his being. "Mark me words, there be more to that thing than meets the eye. It could hold the secrets of this place."

As they drew closer to the hill, they were astonished to make out that it was not a natural formation, but the remnants of an enormous, towering structure—an ancient temple, long swallowed by the sea. For what from the distance had seemed to be the haphazard scattering of rocks and boulders, were in fact blocks of chiseled stone—the straight lines and precise angles hinted at the work of skilled masons—tumbled and worn smooth by centuries of relentless currents, laying strewn about like the forgotten playthings of giant children.

"By the seven seas," Billy breathed out, almost speechless, his incredulous gaze locked onto the ruins. His chest rose and fell rapidly, his hands grasping by his sides, as if reaching for something unseen to steady himself.

Ben opened his mouth to speak, but no words came out. He simply shook his head, completely dumbfounded.

"It . . . it not be possible," Jim whispered.

"What is it?" Bella wondered.

The stones bore the proud scars of time. Encrusted with algae in hues of emerald and turquoise, and adorned with vibrant coral formations like jeweled ornaments, they were more than mere rocks—they were remnants of an ancient civilization, each one holding stories waiting to be told. Intricate carvings, though softened by the caress of relentless tides, whispered tales of sacred rituals and celestial dances.

But from the heart of this tumbled chaos, one stone stood apart—a towering spire, rising from the ruins with an air of defiance and grandeur; a lone sentinel reaching skyward, its silhouette cutting a striking figure against the first blush of dawn.

The Secret of the Dragon's Scale

The crew stared, transfixed at the revealed marvel, a silence falling upon them, a reverent hush that spoke volumes more than words ever could. It was a hallowed stillness, a sacred pause that seemed to stretch time itself, allowing each of them to absorb the magnitude of the moment. Emotions surged within them, a tidal wave of astonishment and awe, mixed with an inexplicable bond to the ancient stones. Bella and the men moved among the scattered ruins, their hands gently tracing the worn surfaces, feeling the echoes of the past etched into each one.

Billy, looking up at the remains of the grand temple, answered to Bella, "It be ancient ruins, lass. Long lost to the sea."

The tall spire, standing defiant against the ravages of time, drew them irresistibly. As they approached, they could see it was a meticulously crafted work of art. Each side was covered in intricate carvings peeking out from the encrusting algae and coral, symbols that danced and twisted under the caress of the morning sun. Also carved into the spire were a labyrinth of holes and grooves that seemed to be both random and purposeful. The holes, each of different size and depth, were positioned with mysterious precision. The grooves snaked their way around the spire, connecting the numerous holes that punctuated the stone, creating an intricate pattern reminiscent of constellations mapped onto it. Each hole was a star in this stony sky, and the grooves were the invisible threads connecting the universe.

Just then, they felt the wind kicking up, rising from its slumber, gathering strength from the vast expanse of the sea and sweeping across the new island. It rushed over the worn stones, whistling softly through the gaps and cracks. As it reached the towering spire, it swirled into the labyrinth of holes and spiraled up through the intricate network of grooves, causing a resonant sound to be produced. Each hole sang a different note, the grooves acting as guides, directing the wind's path upward along the length of the spire to each hole. The grooves themselves whistled softly as the wind danced through them, adding a rhythmic undertone to the spire's voice. Together, they created a melody of haunting beauty that blossomed from the spire's summit. It was as if the stone itself had come alive, to call forth the spirits of the ancients, stirring them from their eternal rest.

Staring up and marveling at the sight and the sound of the wonderous music emanating from the spire, his voice filled with awe and wonder, Jim remarked simply, "The stone that sings to the sky."

Bella, for whom music was a language of the soul, felt an immediate connection with the sound. It was a melody unlike any she had ever heard—haunting and ethereal, a song that seemed to emanate from the heavens. The music flowed around her, through her, its rhythm pulsing within her veins, echoing in her heartbeat. A wave of emotion washed over her—melancholy and joy, longing and fulfillment, all intertwined.

"It's . . . it's beautiful," she said, as she closed her eyes, surrendering herself to the music, her head tilting upward as if to drink in the melody from the sky.

Her face, usually lively and animated, took on a serene expression, the soft glow of the morning sun highlighting the tear that traced a path down the curve of her cheek. Her body swayed gently, moving instinctively to the rhythm of the song. She felt a sense of peace, a gentle mist of tranquility descending upon her.

The spire erupted into brilliance as the rays of the morning sun danced upon it, draping it in liquid gold. Its surface, rough and timeworn, awoke under the light, each jagged edge catching the warmth and throwing it back in dazzling bursts. The stone seemed alive, its once-muted tones now shimmering with an otherworldly radiance, as though some ancient fire had been reignited within its core.

Then, standing before the ancient ruins, they began to hear a ghostly concert of soft, haunting voices unfolding around them. It was as if the very stones had learned to speak, their timeworn tales breathed into existence by the wind. The whispers, faint and airy, echoed off the crumbling blocks, filling the air with a serpentine hiss that seemed to come from everywhere and nowhere, a symphony of a thousand voices speaking as one. The sound ebbed and flowed, each surge bringing a new tide of indecipherable murmurs.

They stood there, listening, entranced, as the whispers wrapped around them, the sound touching something deep within their souls.

At first, the voices came as faint echoes, drifting in and out like breaths of wind barely brushing the edges of their awareness. But slowly, almost imperceptibly, the sound began to swell, its timbre resonating within the depths of their beings. Each of them began to hear different voices, speaking to their innermost thoughts, feelings, and desires.

Billy had found himself drawn to the intricate carvings on the stones, his fingers brushing over them, his touch light as a feather. He saw faces of ancient deities, etched with reverence, staring back at him, their eyes seeming to hold secrets from an age-old civilization. It was then that he realized he was hearing the voices speaking to him—the voices of ancient spirits, their words echoing in his head as if they were right next to his ear.

"Leader of men," the spirits began. "Your heart beats with the rhythm of the endless sea, your soul echoes the cries of the gulls, yet your destiny lies not beneath the waves but above the firmament. Your desires are not for gold or glory, but for a haven amidst the chaos. Your quest is a journey not just across the waters but within yourself. The dragon, like your desires, is elusive. It breathes fire, yet guards a treasure, much like your own fiery spirit that guards your inner peace." The voices ebbed and flowed like the tides. "Seek the land of emerald and jade, where the serpent dons a feathered guise. Here, you must embrace the unknown, dance with the spirits, listen to the songs of the people. For only then will you truly understand the path that you must follow."

Nearby, in the shadow of the towering ancient ruins, stood Ben, his body rigid with tension. His usually steady gaze now darted around, his eyes wide as the voices of the spirits filled his ears, weaving a tapestry of sound that seemed to echo from every direction. His head swiveled sharply from side to side, lines of confusion and fear were etched deeply into his forehead, his brows knitted tightly together in a futile attempt to locate the source of the mysterious voices.

"Your thoughts," they said. "Once serene pools of tranquility, now roil and churn like a tempest. The prize you covet is but a phantom quarry, its chase a voracious beast that grows with each feed, casting long and dark shadows over the landscape of reason. Its growls echo in the hollows of your mind, its eyes gleam in the shadows of your thoughts. Do not feed the beast with your relentless pursuit," they warned. "For once the beast is sated, all that will remain in its wake is the desolate landscape of madness." The voices ebbed, then returned. "The richest treasures lie not in a dragon's hoard, but in the hearts of men. Gold and jewels may shine like stars, but they are as fleeting as a comet's tail. They burn bright, only to flicker into oblivion, leaving darkness in their wake. Beware, lest you become lost in the labyrinth of your own desires, for a soul shackled by greed bears only a blackened heart, where no light can dwell."

Jim just stood there, his gaze locked onto the stone, a growing fascination uncoiling within him. The playful spark usually shining in his eyes was replaced by a mesmerizing gleam that shimmered with profound intensity and unspoken mysteries. His stare was unyielding, riveted to the stone as if it held some ancient truth that only he could see. His body swayed gently, his movements echoing the rhythm of an unseen force, like a tree leaning into the soft coaxing of the wind. His lips, usually curved in a cheerful grin, were parted slightly, as though he were trying to taste the music in the air. At his sides, his fingers twitched and flexed, subtle movements that betrayed the storm of emotions surging beneath his calm exterior. Awe, curiosity, and a flicker of something almost sacred rippled through him, each wave sharpening the lines of his usually carefree face. In this moment, the normally mirthful Jim had disappeared, replaced by someone caught in the grip of an otherworldly trance.

The voices Billy and Ben each heard spoke in perfect harmony, as a singular, ethereal chorus that rose and fell like a celestial hymn. But for Jim, it was different. The voices were not in unison. Instead, they seeped into his consciousness one by one, each spectral tone distinct and deliberate, a slow and steady procession of whispers meant solely for him. Each voice felt intimate, carrying within it a fragment of something ancient, something vast—a wisdom drawn from the endless river of time.

"I am the Spirit of the Sea," spoke the first one. "Your courage is the relentless fury of the tempests, an unstoppable force that tests the heavens and reshapes the earth. Your laughter is the thunderous crash of waves against the shore, a sound both powerful and joyful. Your dreams, wild and untamed, speak of grand adventures and fellowship stronger than any storm. Your quest is more than a mere voyage across land and sea—it is a journey of transformation, a confluence of fresh beginnings and salt-kissed endings, revealing the strength of your spirit and the resilience of your heart."

"I am the Spirit of the Sun," declared the second. "I am reborn each day, stirred from slumber by your love's radiant spirit. Her presence has kindled dreams in you of a life flourishing in the warmth of shared sunlight, vibrant and illuminating like the brightest summer day. Inside you, I see a radiance that pulsates with the rhythm of your heart, a passion as warm and inviting as morning's first light. And just as the great eagle casts a mighty shadow while soaring under the sun, her love casts a powerful influence over your life. Hold firm where the eagle's shadow falls, for it is there that your hearts' desires and destinies will intertwine."

"And I am the Spirit of the Moonlit Tide," said the third. "Hidden within your rugged shell is a gentleness as smooth as a tranquil lagoon under the moon's affectionate glow. It shines in your gaze, resonates in your voice, trembles in your touch. Your yearnings, quiet yet profound, whisper tales of understanding, acceptance, and a love as soothing as a calm sea. The path you seek is one of tranquility amid chaos. And as the tide recedes and advances, so do your joys and sorrows, your victories and setbacks. But just like the sea that never ceases its dance with the shore, you too will continue your journey, undeterred, unyielding, and filled with life. Your voyage now brings you to new realms, where the rhythm of the sea gives way to the heartbeat of the earth. Here, let the jewel of the forest be your guide, for her song embodies the spirit of your quest."

The wind suddenly softened, shedding its earlier urgency and settling into a tender breeze that rippled across the water's surface, its touch light and unhurried. It slipped past them, brushing their faces with the cool, salty kiss of the sea and carrying with it the final notes of the spire's haunting melody. As the ethereal music ebbed away, Bella's eyes fluttered open, a peaceful smile gracing her lips, the serenity of her expression mirroring the stillness around them. The voices, before a harmonious chorus echoing through the air, dwindled to faint whispers before fading into the ether.

There they stood, silent and still, looking around at each other. Each face bore an expression of quiet introspection, as they struggled to comprehend what they just experienced; a sense of awe settled upon them, a tangible testament to the mystical and magical event that had touched them all.

As the morning sun rose higher, its golden warmth spilling over the horizon, they remained in a profound stillness. The ocean lay quiet, its surface smooth and glasslike, reflecting the soft hues of the morning sky—it was though the world had taken a deep breath and held it, suspended in timeless tranquility.

But then, the silence fractured! From the farthest reaches of the horizon, a low primal rumble rolled across the water, deep and resonant, like the growl of something ancient stirring to life! Growing steadily in volume, it echoed across the barren landscape. The ground shook beneath their feet! Their eyes darted in every direction, wide with astonishment, their brows arched in a portrait of confusion and surprise. Suddenly, the horizon erupted in a surge of churning water! At the island's edge, the sea responded with a subtle yet perceptible dance. What was once a tranquil surface began to ripple in anticipation, mimicking the rhythm of an anxious heartbeat. The waves, no longer gentle, began to lap against the shore with greater rhythm, each one a soft sigh that washed over the sand before retreating back. It was as if the sea was pulling at the shore, beckoning it to brace for an imminent attack.

The Siren's Call, her timbers keenly attuned to the ocean's ominous rumblings, sensed the shifting temperament of the waves. Once gentle and languid, they now lapped against the ship with a sense of urgency. The sound of water against wood grew louder, more insistent, each wave a rhythmic slap against the hull, a playful percussion that hinted at the thunder yet to come.

The movement on the distant sea now drew everyone's rapt attention, their gazes locked onto the vast expanse of the ocean. There was a palpable tension in the air as they watched the once tranquil water begin to transform into a tempestuous beast. Suddenly, a collective gasp echoed among them as realization dawned!

"The tide's comin' back in!" yelled Billy. "Make for the ship!"

Everyone was jolted into action by the captain's command. They charged toward the ship, their movements frantic but focused, each footfall shifting and sliding in the wet sand as they struggled to reach safety. But as Bella hurried, her foot slipped, and she went down. Her scream cut through the air! Jim whirled around. Reaching her, his hand closed around Bella's trembling one, and with a burst of strength, he lifted her off the ground and hoisted her onto his shoulder. Her slender body felt almost weightless against his sturdy frame as he pivoted back toward the ship.

A wall of frothing waves now raced toward the land! The sound was deafening—a thunderous roar that drowned out all other noise! Soon, the first waves began to crash onto the shore, the foamy tendrils reaching out, grasping at their heels! The ship bobbed and swayed in the turbulent water, its hull creaking under the strain, the rope ladders swinging wildly across the side!

And as the sea grew bolder, the lapping against the ship became more insistent, each surge a pounding of a drum, its beats growing faster and faster, stronger and stronger! Then, the first mighty swells collided with the vessel, exploding against its wooden flanks with a deafening reverberation that shattered the air—a cacophony of splintering wood and roiling foam! Rushing around the ship, the water swirled and eddied, creating a turbulent chorus of high-pitched whistles and low, guttural growls. The ship creaked and groaned in protest, its timbers straining under the onslaught! Above the chaos, the wind howled through the rigging, adding its mournful wail to the orchestra of sound.

With surging waves grasping at their feet, threatening to pull them back into the ocean's depths, they leapt for the swinging ladders. The salty spray stung their eyes and whipped against their faces, a harsh reminder of the merciless sea that threatened to claim them. Bella, jumping down from Jim's shoulder, was the first to reach a ladder. At first lunge her fingers slipped, then found their grip on a rung. A breathless gasp escaped her lips as she began to climb, her body shaking with fear and exertion! Jim was right behind, his hand reaching out to steady her. Ben and the rest of the crew followed, their faces etched with grim determination. Billy, bringing up the rear, watched as all the crew climbed the ladders. He glanced back at the churning ocean around him, then made his way up last.

Suddenly, with a resounding concussion, the ocean surged forward and reclaimed its domain, drowning every grain of sand, every shell and pebble, and every ancient stone deep within its depths. The ship shuddered as the sea slammed into it, its icy fingers clawing hungrily at the battered hull, an anguished symphony of creaks, moans, and splintering wood echoing from its straining frame. Water surged around it, swirling and gurgling as it hissed and spat against every plank, leaping skyward in frothy bursts as if determined to pry the vessel apart and drag it beneath the waves.

The once immobile vessel began to stir, its timbers groaning as they were lifted from the seabed. And as the ship began its ascent, the sounds of the sea intensified—the deafening crash of the waves, the guttural growl of the water swirling around the hull, the sharp crack of straining wood, and the high-pitched whistle of the wind through the rigging.

With a final surge, the ship was freed from the sand's grasp, rising majestically as the water lifted it. The creaking timbers settled into a rhythmic rocking, swaying in harmony with the rippling surface. The sails billowed out with a soft rustle, capturing the fresh, salty breeze that now promised a peaceful voyage ahead.

Bathed in the warmth of the late morning sun, the Siren's Call swayed gently upon the now calm sea. The crew, drenched and shivering, huddled together on the deck, their eyes reflecting a kaleidoscope of emotions—fear, relief, uncertainty. Their breaths came in ragged gasps, their hearts pounding in time with the rhythmic rocking of the ship.

The air was heavy with the echo of the mysterious voices they had heard. The ancient spirits had whispered their cryptic riddles to Billy, Ben, and Jim, wrapping around them like an enigmatic fog. The puzzling words filled their minds, their meanings as elusive as the wind that carried them. Yet a wave of fatigue was washing over the crew, their bodies echoing the ship's groans of weariness. So, while the riddles of the ancients tugged at their thoughts, the irresistible call of rest beckoned with a gentle hand. They found comfort in the sun's warmth, their bodies sprawled across the deck, lulled into a brief respite by the ship's gentle rocking. Their next course of action was hidden within the puzzles of the spirits' messages, but for now, rest was their sanctuary.

Fresh Beginnings and Salt-Kissed Endings

Billy was the first to stir, woken by the gentle rocking of the ship. He blinked, his eyes adjusting to the late afternoon light that danced playfully on the undulating surface of the water. His gaze fell upon the empty helm, a silent reminder of their task at hand. The ship was rudderless, wandering aimlessly without direction. With a grunt, he pushed himself up, the rough texture of the wooden planks pressing against his palms. Making his way up onto the quarterdeck, his hand reached out, gripping the cold, worn wheel, the familiar grooves under his fingertips sparking a sense of purpose within him. With a deep breath, the captain took control of the helm, his eyes focused on the endless expanse of blue ahead.

Ben and the others each began to rise from their respite as well. With heavy limbs, Ben retreated to his quarters, washing off the grime and salt at a basin. The cool water splashed against his sun-beaten skin, droplets cascading down his cheeks, tracing the contours of his face, cutting rivulets through the grime before falling into the basin with hollow plinks that echoed unsettlingly in the silence. Peering down, his reflection stared back at him—but what he saw was a stranger's face, the expression hollow, holding a hint of desperation that was as chilling as the water on his skin. His eyes, once bright with purpose and resolve, now held a far-off look. They were the windows to a mind grappling with confusion, where the voices of ancient spirits whispered warnings that twisted like spectral vines around his thoughts. In his mind echoed their words of a phantom quarry, the relentless pursuit of which fed the beast within him. They spoke of a dangerous path, of a heart blackened by greed and a man blinded by his desires, teetering on the edge of a precipice he could not see. But their words were akin to wisps of fog, vanishing through his fingers just as he tried to grasp their meaning. For now, at least, Ben remained steady, anchored by a determination that had seen him through many a storm. He washed away the remnants of his unease with another handful of water, his eyes never leaving the stranger in the reflection.

Up on deck, the ship was coming to life with activity, the crewmen stretching and yawning as they shook off the remnants of sleep. Jim's eyes fluttered open to take in the boundless expanse of sea and sky that stretched out before them. Beside him, Bella also began to stir, her wavy chestnut hair fanning out across the wooden deck, her emerald eyes wide and searching, as a mix of surprise and bewilderment played across her face. She turned to see the others beginning to rise, and instinctively, her hand sought Jim's. His fingers curled warmly around hers, offering a small comfort amidst the uncertainty, their shared confusion hanging in the air. Rising to their feet, they moved as one, their hands still entwined. The wind whipped around them, tugging at their clothes, and tossing her hair across her eyes and cheeks in soft, fleeting moments.

The day drifted into evening, and the sun was soon painting the heavens with hues of fiery reds and oranges, casting long shadows that stretched languidly across the deck. Bella and Jim, still entranced by the haunting melodies and voices that lingered in their minds, each retreated to their own quarters to cleanse themselves. Bella moved about her cabin as if suspended in a waking dream, her mind still foggy from the stone's influence, the sounds from it blurring the lines between her reality and the mystical world it had revealed. She approached the basin, her trembling fingers reaching for the cool water. Drops splashed onto her face, breaking the stillness. But each one seemed to pulse with a sound that only she could hear, faint echoes of the stone's melody rippling through her skin. Meanwhile, Jim was in his spartan berth. The rough wooden planks under his feet felt different though, each creak seeming to whisper the ancient words he had heard. As he washed himself, the cool touch of water felt like a balm on his skin, momentarily driving away the confusion. Yet this surreal experience, while baffling, had ignited a spark of curiosity in him. The riddles of the ancients, the stone, the inexplicable connection he felt—they were all pieces of a puzzle that he yearned to solve.

Once cleaned and changed, Jim felt drawn to Bella's cabin. He knocked lightly and called to her, his voice barely a whisper against the wooden door. He wasn't sure what he sought from her though—an answer, a sign, a shared glance that might confirm she felt it too. The wonder. The strangeness. He hoped to see reflected in her eyes the same confusion that rattled within him, and, perhaps together, they could make sense of this extraordinary experience.

She opened the door, her eyes meeting his in a silent exchange of shared understanding, her hand reaching out in silent invitation. With her heart still enraptured by the mesmerizing music from the stone, she looked at him, her face a whirlpool of wonder and bewilderment. The music had stirred something primordial within her, a connection to the universe that words could not express. Jim, his ears still filled with the haunting voices, returned her look with equal intensity. His normally steady eyes were clouded with questions, the cryptic messages of the spirits still whispering in his mind.

"I . . . I heard voices," Jim began softly, the words tumbling out hesitantly. "Spirits spoke to me," he said softer still, as if confiding a secret. "They . . . they spoke in riddles, like yer padre back in the village." He paused, dragging a hand through his hair, fingers tangling as if he could comb some sense out of the chaos in his mind. His eyes searched the floorboards, finding no answers there. "I can't—" His voice caught, and he rubbed the back of his neck, a flicker of frustration seeping through. "I can't make head nor tail of them, Bella." His eyes lifted to hers, searching, his voice now laced with a subtle plea for understanding. "I don't know what it means."

Bella sought to offer some words of comfort in a gentle effort to soothe his troubled mind. She stepped closer, her voice soft, her gaze steady, filled with quiet understanding. "Father spoke of your journey. I think this is all part of that journey. And to know the signs that guide you, you must hear with more than just your ears," she reminded him. "You must listen with your heart." She tilted her head gently, her tone carrying a promise. "Tell me what the spirits said. I will help you."

"Well, I heard three of them," Jim explained. "The first spirit called itself the Spirit of the Sea. It said my courage was the relentless fury of the tempests that tested the heavens and reshaped the earth. My laughter be like the thunderous crash of waves against the shore, a sound both powerful and joyful. Then it talked about me dreams bein' wild and untamed, that spoke of grand adventures and fellowship stronger than any storm. And me quest was more than a voyage across land and sea, it be a journey of transformation, a confluence of fresh beginnings and salt-kissed endings, revealing the strength of me spirit and the resilience of me heart."

Listening to Jim, Bella found herself transported back to her small village, caring for Father Ignatius as his mind grew more and more worn by the relentless march of time. His wisdom, wrapped in the guise of riddles, echoed in her memories. The lessons she learned from having to interpret the convoluted utterances of the old man were not just about deciphering words but understanding their essence and finding the deeper truths hidden within.

Calling upon the wisdom of the priest, Bella tried to explain. "The spirits speak in this way because they see in you who you truly are. They see into your soul."

"But the padre said this is all part of me journey. We be at the first place. Are the spirits telling me where to go next?"

"'Tis your own spirit, what's inside you, that guides you to your destiny," she answered. "That's what they were saying to you. Along your journey, your courage will give you the strength to face dangers, your laughter is the spark of joy that will keep the darkness at bay, your dreams speak of a path that is not about finding a prize but of the journey itself. And a change will happen to you along the way."

Jim's look was distant as he pondered Bella's words, his mind swirling with the images painted by the Spirit of the Sea. He understood the metaphors of courage, laughter, and dreams, but it was the final part that had him stumped.

He gazed out the portal toward the horizon, as dusk bathed the world in shades of deep indigo and soft gold, the sounds of the water lapping gently against the side of the ship providing a soothing calm. He listened to the voices again, this time not with his ears but with the his heart. Then, like the light of day breaking through a fading storm, a realization slowly unfolded before him, stirring something deep within.

"A journey of transformation . . . a confluence of fresh beginnings and salt-kissed endings," Jim spoke softly, the words taking on a new meaning. His eyes widened as the pieces fell into place. "It be where the river meets the sea . . . That's the transformation! It's not just 'bout me own changes! The spirit be speakin' of a place, Bella!" he exclaimed, his voice dancing with excitement. "Water begins fresh in the river, mixing with the salty sea in the end. That's the confluence! That's where we must be! I feel it in me heart!"

Jim ran out of Bella's cabin and up to the quarterdeck to the captain, with Bella in chase. Billy had just handed the wheel over to Mr. Pew.

"Captain!" Jim called out as he leapt up the steps. "On the island! The spirits spoke to me! The spirits spoke to me! I think I be knowin' where they want us to go!"

"Aye. Somethin' there been speakin' to me too, but spirits . . . that I can't say," Billy admitted, still a bit perplexed and uncertain about what to make of the experience. He ran his hand through his thick beard and shook his head slowly. "But I'll be damned if I can make heads or tails of their mumblin's. It be like tryin' to catch smoke with bare hands, it is. I don't know if they be leadin' us astray or pointin' us right." A heavy sigh escaped him as he confessed, "We be in uncharted waters here, lad. We be sailin' blind, and I don't much care for it."

The captain's eyes, normally as clear and steady as the horizon, now betrayed a flicker of unease. A lifetime at sea had made him a man of unwavering confidence—his self-assurance was his compass, guiding him even when the stars were hidden behind shrouded skies. It was this quiet, unshakable belief in himself that had been the anchor for his crew. But now, Billy found himself grappling with a new and unsettling feeling; the fearless sailor had been replaced by a man haunted by whispers of the unknown.

The voices of the spirits had jolted the very foundations of his beliefs. He had always been a man of the sea, not the church. He found his solace in the ebb and flow of the tides, not in the verses of holy books. His religion was the sea, his prayers were for fair winds, and his angels were his loyal crew. His faith was placed in the sturdiness of his ship, the strength of the men under his command, and his own skills as a mariner. To Billy, spirits, ghosts, and supernatural beings belonged in the realm of fantasy, in the stories told to scare greenhorn sailors on dark nights. But the mystical whispers that echoed in his mind had cast a shadow of doubt over his indomitable heart, making him question his instincts as a sailor and the sureness of his senses. The uncharted waters and hidden corners of the world had always been his playground, his arena. But now, it was a landscape filled with shadows and uncertainty, transformed by the mysterious voices on the island.

"But Captain," Jim tried to explain. "I think the spirits was givin' me hints. The first one talked about a change in me, that it'd be like the confluence of fresh beginnings and salt-kissed endings. But they wasn't just talkin' 'bout me. It be at the mouth of a river where fresh water mixes with the salt, where two worlds meet and create somethin' new. I be certain, Captain, that's where we're meant to be headin' next. The spirit be guidin' us there. I feel it in me heart."

Billy stared at Jim, his eyes narrowing slightly as he took in the young sailor's words.

"River's mouth, ye say?" he mused aloud, his voice tinged with skepticism.

He leaned back against the ship's wheel, peering out to the horizon where the ocean melded with the evening sky. So far, he had been willing to trust in tales and prophecies, but this . . . this was a realm of spirits and premonitions, a world as unfamiliar to him as the uncharted territories they sought.

Turning back to Jim, Billy's expression softened. "In all me years sailin' the seven seas, I've trusted naught but me sword and savvy, for no phantom has ever kept me ship afloat nor filled me hold with treasure," he said, "so I can't say I've ever put much stock in the spirit world. Still . . . " He trailed off, the silence hanging heavy between them. "I can't pretend to understand it all, lad. This spirit talk be as foreign to me as the stars be to a fish. But, these words ye say the spirits gave ye . . . well, we be havin' no other maps to follow."

Billy yelled down, "Ben! Ben!" Not seeing Ben on deck, he called to John Hawkins. "Hawkins! Find Ben and tell him to bring up the chart in me cabin!"

The captain's orders, relayed by Mr. Hawkins, broke through the fog in Ben's mind. He lingered a moment longer in this quarters, his hands gripping the edges of the basin as if it could steady him against the storm raging in his mind. Finally, with a deep breath, he straightened, shoulders squared in defiance of the weight pressing on his chest. He toweled off his face, the cool droplets giving way to the roughness of the cloth. He donned a fresh shirt, the fabric stiff against his raw, sun-bruised skin, and ran a hand through his damp hair, slicking it back out of his eyes.

He then sprang into motion, each step swift and decisive as he darted out of his quarters and ran to Billy's cabin; he crossed the room in two strides, grabbed the chart, and brought it up to the captain.

Billy laid the chart out on a bench in front of the wheel. He traced the outline of the coast nearest to their location with his finger. "There be many rivers drainin' into the sea along here," he pointed out. His voice dripping with a heavy dose of skepticism, he asked Jim, "Which river ye suppose be the right one?"

"Well . . . umm . . . " Jim hesitated.

The captain, willing to listen but still wary that the voices were even real and not figments of their imaginations, then asked, "What else did these spirits whisper to ye? What other secrets do they hold for us?"

"That's what we're still trying to figure out, Captain," Bella interjected.

Billy studied Bella and Jim for a moment. Then, intuitively putting his trust in Jim's instincts once more, he turned to Mr. Pew.

"Change course, Pew! We be headin' for the coast!"

"Aye, Captain," Mr. Pew acknowledged.

He gave Jim a firm nod, his decision made. "Right then, lad. We be settin' our course for now. Let's see what tricks these specters be havin' in store for us."

Mr. Pew, a helmsman with eyes sharp as a storm's edge and hands rough as the ship's timbers, commanded the wheel with a masterful touch, guiding the Siren's Call as if the ship were an extension of his own will. With a determined look, he began to turn, coaxing the grand vessel to change her course. The Siren's Call, as if a living entity, headed her helmsman's silent command; her majestic bow began to shift, slicing through the dark cobalt waters with newfound purpose. Above, the sails billowed out, catching the sea breeze like giant lungs drawing breath, propelling the ship forward with renewed vigor. At the

The Secret of the Dragon's Scale

prow, the ship's figurehead, a masterfully carved siren, seemed to come alive, her eyes watching vigilantly across the shimmering canvas of the ocean that stretched before them.

Before Jim could reflect on the other cryptic riddles spoken by the spirits, Ben, throwing his hands in the air, burst out in a sudden display of impatience. "All this jabber 'bout spirits and specters! What if the Dragon's Scale were on that island!?" His voice ricocheted off the ship's timbers, a piercing note of exasperation in the otherwise steady rhythm of the Siren's Call sailing through the night.

Ben gestured wildly back at the now-invisible land, swallowed whole by the power of the sea. Then he turned to Jim, the soft glow of lanterns lighting up his stern features. "What if it was there, Jim? What if the Dragon's Scale was lyin' there, waitin' for us, and we just sailed away?" His voice was a jagged edge, laced with irritation and impatience. "What if, Jim? What if?" Ben threw his head back, laughing bitterly. "And we . . . we just sailed away, didn't we? Sailed away from the treasure of a lifetime because of some ghostly gibberish!"

Ben's frustration was then directed at Billy. " We ain't be chasin' ghosts, Captain! We be chasin' treasure!" His words were delivered in a rapid-fire manner, each sentence punctuated with a huff of annoyance.

But before Billy could rouse his ire, with a dismissive wave of his hand, Ben turned away and went down below, leaving his words to ring in their ears.

The dawn broke over the horizon the next day, casting long, golden beams of light across the deck. The ship creaked and groaned as it cut through the calm sea, its sails billowing gently in the soft breeze. Bella rose, her chestnut curls catching the morning light, and knocked lightly on Jim's door. When he emerged she grabbed his hand, and with a mischievous smile, pulled him along with her. Jim, still rubbing the sleep from his eyes, allowed himself to be led, chuckling softly at Bella's enthusiasm. As they came out onto the open deck, a gentle sea breeze greeted them, carrying the fresh scent of the ocean and setting wisps of Bella's hair into a delicate dance around her face. They just stood there, side by side, their hands entwined, as they soaked in the beauty of the morning. And closing their eyes, they let the sun warm their faces and the wind whisper in their ears.

Ben stepped out shortly after, his demeanor noticeably more composed than the night before. His eyes, though still carrying a trace of frustration, were softer, the edges of his anger smoothed over by a night's rest. As Bella and Jim were soaking in the morning sun, they heard the soft tapping of footsteps behind them. Turning around, they saw Ben approaching, a sheepish look on his face. His eyes were downcast, his usual confidence replaced with a hint of regret.

"Ye not seem to be yerself these days, Ben," Jim said, with a note of concern.

"Oh, no need to fret. There ain't nothin' amiss with me," Ben tried to assure him.

"Jim and the captain said they heard the voices of spirits," Bella said to Ben. "Did you hear anything?"

The voices still lingered in Ben's mind, weaving riddles of ominous foreboding that haunted his thoughts. They were like shadows dancing at the edge of his consciousness, elusive and ambiguous. He grappled with these phantom echoes, unsure of their true message, leaving a nebulous fear within him. It was unsettling, confusing. But what most gnawed at him were the grim images the voices had painted in his mind, each more terrifying than the last. All this made him wary, reluctant to even admit to himself that he had heard anything at all.

"I . . . I might've heard somethin'," he admitted hesitantly. He paused, his fingers unconsciously gripping the ship's railing. "But the words . . . they didn't make no sense. Nothin' more than a jumble of sounds, I'd say."

The morning sun, still low in the sky, spilled golden light across the endless stretch of ocean. Its rays danced on the restless waves, igniting flashes of silver and amber that flickered like scattered jewels. One by one, the crew members emerged from the bowels of the vessel, their faces crisscrossed with lines of sleep but their eyes bright with the promise of a new day. The captain, an imposing figure against the backdrop of the burgeoning sunrise, strode onto the deck soon after, his gaze sweeping over his men with a mixture of pride and expectation.

"Ben," he called out, his voice slicing through the morning quiet. "Take the wheel."

As Ben stood firmly at the wheel, his fingers clenching its burnished handles, a torrent of thoughts and emotions raged within him, each a wave crashing against the shores of his sanity. His eyes fixed on the horizon, yet reflected the storm he fought to master inside. The Dragon's Scale, legendary and elusive, had become the sun around which his world revolved. His every thought was tinged with its iridescent sheen, his every breath filled with its tantalizing promise.

It was time Jim went about his duties on the ship as well. Bella watched him leave before turning her attention to the galley, feeling the need to be useful in some way. With a sense of resolve, she set about helping with meal preparations for the crew, slicing salted beef and pork, and simmering beans and rice.

After their morning meal, the ship hummed with activity as the men went about their tasks, the rhythm of their work punctuated by the creaking of the ship and the rustling of canvas. The sun was climbing higher in the sky, casting a warm glow over the deck. The sails billowed majestically, catching the light and diffusing it into a soft radiance that bathed the ship in a silken glow. Bella slipped away to her cabin, emerging moments later with her lute cradled in her arms. She settled herself on a quiet corner of the deck, positioning the lute comfortably in her lap. As she strummed the first chord, a sweet melody floated into the air, intertwining with the tang of ocean spray. The notes danced on the wind, a harmonious counterpart to the ship's gentle sway. In the serenity of the morning, Bella's music filled the air, her gentle strumming a soothing serenade to the bustling ship, a melody that danced to the rhythm of life at sea.

Each day began with the same routine, as the first light of dawn seeped into the horizon, painting the sky in hues of pink and orange. And each morning, the sailors would rise with the sun, their movements harmonizing naturally with the rhythmic sway of the ship and the rolling of the sea. There were sails to be adjusted, decks to be scrubbed, knots to be tied—a flurry of tasks that kept them occupied. Bella would make herself as useful as a young woman could on a pirate ship, and when tasks were completed, would retreat to a quiet corner with her lute, losing herself in melodies that mingled with the distant cries of seabirds and the soft sigh of the ocean.

Nights were a respite, the darkness providing a blanket of calm, a haven from the uncertainty of their journey that lay ahead. The sailors would gather on the deck, their faces lit by the soft glow of lanterns. And underneath the star-studded sky they would swap boisterous stories and share hearty laughter, their camaraderie echoing warmly along with the gentle lapping of the sea against the ship. Bella would often join with her lute, her fingers strumming a soft melody that served as a backdrop to the tales. The music added another layer to the atmosphere, a soothing rhythm that eased their minds and enveloped the night in a tranquil embrace.

With each passing day, the coast drew nearer, an ever-looming promise that beckoned the Siren's Call from over the horizon. The anticipation was palpable, a silent undercurrent that threaded through every task, every conversation. Sails billowed and snapped against the brisk ocean breeze, while the crew worked diligently, the deck vibrating with the rhythmic thudding of boots. Shouts of commands mingled with the creak of ropes and the hum of the ship as it sliced through the waves. Eyes constantly scanned the distance, eager for the first glimpse of land, while voices buzzed with excitement and speculation about the adventures that awaited.

But along the way, the crew continued to bear witness to subtle changes in Ben. His once steadfast character was slowly crumbling, gradually worn away like rocks succumbing to the relentless tides. His demeanor, previously marked by a strong resolve and unwavering calm, was fraying around the edges. His confident strides, that had carried him across the deck with purpose, were being replaced by a restless pacing. His jovial nature, normally a source of morale for the crew, started to fade. His laughter, once loud and infectious, started to ring hollow. His tolerance dwindled to a mere thread, as he became increasingly irritable, snapping at the slightest provocation. His eyes, which had always sparkled with the thrill of adventure, now held a faraway look. His hands, usually steady as a rock, trembled when anyone even spoke a hint of the Dragon's Scale.

All of the crew of the Siren's Call, especially the captain, were being driven by the same tantalizing promise of the Dragon's Scale. The quest had become their shared dream, a glimmering beacon that united them in purpose and fueled their passion through treacherous waters. Each man aboard envisioned the wealth and glory that would soon be theirs, their hearts stirred by visions of gold coins spilling out from ancient chests. Not to mention, though, the miraculous feat of finally cracking the secret of the Dragon's Scale, with their names, and the name of the ship, the Siren's Call, carved into the annals of pirate legend—the chance to be remembered forever as the crew who solved the greatest mystery of the seas.

For them, the promise of the Dragon's Scale remained a distant, almost ephemeral allure—something to strive for. But they remained grounded in the practicalities of their daily duties and camaraderie. They laughed and joked, their spirits buoyed by their shared goal, even as they labored under the hot sun or battled fierce storms. Their dreams were vivid, but they remained dreams, anchored by the tangible present. However, for Ben, the Dragon's Scale was no mere dream—it was becoming an all-encompassing obsession that gnawed at him day and night, twisting his thoughts and warping his reality. It had become the very lens through which he viewed the world, distorting everything else into insignificance. And when he spoke of it, his voice carried an edge of desperation that sent shivers down the spines of his shipmates, his eyes burning with a wild intensity that bordered on madness.

Nighttime brought no relief. He slept little. Lantern light would spill out from under his cabin door, flickering late into the night. He began to spend long hours poring over old maps and charts, deep lines etched across his forehead, revealing the fierce intensity of a mind wholly absorbed, while his fingers traced imaginary paths to where he deduced the Dragon's Scale might be. Whispers among the crew told of strange sounds—manic laughter one moment, frustrated roars the next.

The changes in Ben were most apparent to Jim. During their days sailing toward the coast, Jim would often watch as Ben stood at the ship's railing, just staring out over the water for hours on end.

Jim was busy fiddling with the rigging on a clear day, as the ship neared land, when he walked over to Ben at the starboard railing.

"Fair winds today, eh Ben?" Jim called out, grinning wide, trying to keep his tone light and casual.

Ben merely grunted in response, his gaze unyielding on the distant horizon.

Jim tried again, hoping to stir some life into Ben. "Ye remember when we as just landlubbers? Even on the smoothest seas we'd get greener'n seaweed."

Again, Ben offered nothing more than an indifferent shrug.

Undaunted, Jim continued, "I remember ye leaning over the side of the ship more often than not."

Ben cracked a small smile. "Ye weren't much better, mate. Every time the ship rocked, ye'd turn whiter than a ghost."

Jim chuckled lightly, attempting to keep the mood light. "Remember how even the smell of hardtack would send us runnin'?"

Finally, exasperated, Ben turned to face Jim, his eyes hard. "What are ye getting at, Jim?" he demanded, his voice gruff.

Jim's smile faltered, but he pressed on. "Nothin' much, mate . . . It's just that ye've been actin' a bit strange lately. Everythin' be alright?"

Ben's eyes narrowed, a flicker of annoyance crossing his face. "I be fine, Jim. No need to worry yer head 'bout it."

"Well, Ben . . . " Jim said, concern seeping into his voice.

"I said, I'm shipshape," Ben interrupted, his tone final.

With that, Ben turned away, dismissing Jim's concerns with a wave of his hand.

His heart heavy, Jim returned to his duties, resolved to keep a closer eye on his friend. The changes in Ben were subtle, but they were there, and Jim couldn't shake the feeling that something was seriously wrong.

Hours passed, and the endless expanse of the ocean began to waver as a faint outline emerged from the edge of the horizon. A subtle murmur rustled through the ship's timbers before it reached the ears of the lookout perched in the crow's nest. Straining his eyes against the glare of the midday sun, he discerned the hazy image solidifying into the unmistakable silhouette of land.

A call of "Land, ho!" rang out across the decks below.

The crew ceased their tasks abruptly. They scampered toward the bow, their boots thudding against the planks. Eyes squinted against the brilliant sunlight, hands shielded brows, and all gazed in unison at the distant sight.

At the sound of the sudden commotion, the captain emerged from his cabin, the door's creak mingling with the excitement from the crew. Stepping onto the deck, his eyes, sharp and calculating, narrowed as they locked onto the faint line of the distant coast.

"Ben!" The captain's voice boomed across the ship, instantly silencing the hum of activity on the deck.

With a quick nod, Ben made his way over. As he approached, Billy crossed his arms over his chest, his eyes never wavering from Ben's face.

Ben halted in front of the captain, but remained composed and steady as he noticed the annoyance in the captain's expression. Billy's face was a storm of barely contained anger, his eyes narrowing into piercing slits that burned with frustration.

"Aye, Captain?" Ben asked, his tone respectful.

Billy looked Ben squarely in the eye, his stare as piercing as a harpoon, his gruff tone leaving no room for argument. "I've been watchin' ye. Ye've been actin' like a loose cannon for some time now, and it be startin' to wear thin. And ye've shown disrespect to yer captain. That I can't abide on me ship." He paused, letting his words sink in before continuing. "So I'm givin' ye fair warnin', lad. Control yer temper and get yer act together, or by Davy Jones, I'll have ye swabbing the decks till yer hands bleed."

"Oh, uh, aye," Ben responded, his tone apologetic. "I hear ye, Captain," he continued, acknowledging the gravity of the warning he had just received. "I didn't mean to ruffle any feathers, nor mean any disrespect."

"Attend to yer duties. We need to navigate along the coast with care, and I be needin' to count on ye." With a final glare, he dismissed Ben, his gaze lingering on him for a moment longer before shifting to the crew.

"Jim! Bella!" Billy called out.

"Now, Jim, me boy," he said, as Jim and Bella made their way to him. "Ye spoke before of other spirits spinnin' riddles in yer head. We be nearin' the coast. It be time we figure out where to go from here. What other strange murmurin's was they tryin' to tell ye?"

Jim's look was distant as he began to recount the words of the spirits. His voice was hushed, as if he was sharing a secret.

"A second spirit... I think was talkin' 'bout Bella. It called itself the Spirit of the Sun. It said it was reborn each day, stirred from slumber by me love's radiant spirit." He paused, turning toward Bella. "It spoke of how her presence has kindled dreams in me of a life flourishing in the warmth of shared sunlight, vibrant and illuminating like the brightest summer day. It said it could see inside me a radiance that pulsates with the rhythm of me heart, a passion as warm and invitin' as mornin's first light." He paused again, brows knitting together as he tried to recall the next part. "Then it talked about how just as the great eagle casts a mighty shadow while soaring under the sun, her love casts a powerful influence over me life." He then looked at Billy. "And lastly, the spirit said to hold firm where the eagle's shadow falls, for it is there that your hearts' desires and destinies will intertwine." As he finished speaking, Jim sighed, his expression a mix of confusion and consternation.

The words of the spirit hung heavy in the air, their meaning as elusive as the morning mist.

Jim scratched his head and shrugged. "I can't make head nor tail of how the spirit's words got anythin' to do with the Dragon's Scale."

The captain scratched his beard, his brow furrowing as he pondered the spirit's words. "Aye, this riddle... Seems to me it talks more of love, and no clue 'bout the Dragon's Scale as I can discern either." Looking at Bella, Billy asked, "What say ye, lass? Can ye find in any of yer priest's wisdom any help in makin' sense of this confounded gibberish?"

Bella paused, her gaze drifting out to the sea, her mind reaching back to the wisdom of Father Ignatius. His voice, gravelly yet soothing, echoed in her ears, as vivid as if he were standing beside her. With a deep breath, Bella closed her eyes, allowing the spirit's words to flow through her. She felt their rhythm, their pulse, alive and resonant. The spirit's language was poetic, filled with metaphors and symbolism, much like the priest's enigmatic riddles.

Then she turned to the captain, her eyes filled with an understanding that ran deeper than the ocean beneath their feet. "The spirit's words hold a great wisdom. These words are not just about love shared between two souls—they speak of a journey, an intertwined destiny that me and Jim are just beginning. They are a prophecy of our future, a hint of how our present path will shape what lies ahead," she explained. "The rebirth that is stirred by 'love's radiant spirit', says love awakens dreams of a shared life. It represents hope, and the promise of a new beginning that each day holds for us."

Jim and Billy leaned in closer, the gentle lapping of the waves against the ship providing a soothing backdrop to Bella's words.

Bella tilted her head back, her eyes lifting to the heavens. The priest's words stirred in her mind, their cadence rising like a distant melody. "A poem Father loved went, 'In the ballet of sun and sky, where does the phantom dancer lie? Invisible in flight, yet etched upon Earth's vast canvas, wide and high. Stand strong where this silent specter sprawls, for it is there that choices mold our lives, shaping where destiny calls.'"

Bella fell silent for a moment, her gaze dropping to the planks beneath her feet. Her fingers grazed the edge of the railing absently, tracing the grooves worn smooth by years of sea air. The faint rustling of the wind and the rhythmic creak of the ship filled the pause, a quiet symphony that seemed to echo her inward thoughts. Her eyes lifted again, her expression soft yet distant, as though she were seeing beyond what was in front of her.

Then, with a voice low and measured, imbued with a deep thoughtfulness, she spoke again. "In his words, Father was speaking of how our lives can take many paths, and our choices affect our destinies. I think the phantom dancer is like the shadow of the eagle as it soars in the sky, always moving, and you never know what path it will take. And love, much like the phantom dancer, is often silent and unseen, but its presence is deeply felt. It leaves a great mark not only on our lives but also in our hearts."

"In the rest of the riddle," Bella continued, "the spirit told Jim to hold firm where the eagle's shadow falls; it is at that point we make our choice, choose our destiny. And when choices resonate with the deepest feelings of love and commitment, they shape a shared destiny. 'Tis a moment where love and fate come together in a beautiful dance."

She paused again, searching for any other meaning buried in the spirit's puzzle. "But if the words have something to do with the Dragon's Scale, I don't see. I think we will know where we must be when we come to it. Father always said, along your journey, you will know when it is time to make choices. You will feel it in your heart."

"Hmmmm . . . ." Billy uttered in a low, drawn-out rumble of disappointment and puzzlement. "That not be helpin' us much, do it?"

Jim also felt a twinge of disappointment. He had placed his hopes in Bella's ability to decipher the riddle, but it seemed their next step in the quest for the Dragon's Scale still remained shrouded in mystery.

"The spirit's riddle certainly be leavin' much to be desired. And love ain't gonna get us no nearer to the Dragon's Scale," Billy said sarcastically. "All we have is some notion that our next call be lyin' at the mouth of a river." He paused, letting his words settle before continuing, "But which river?"

Billy paced the deck, his boots thudding heavily against the salt-streaked boards beneath his feet. His crew watched him intently, waiting for some sign of reassurance and guidance. "We be sailors, not fortune tellers," he grumbled. "We navigate by compass and map, not some specter's peculiar mumblin's."

But with sighs of exasperation and resignation, the captain looked up at Mr. Pew at the wheel. "Mr. Pew!" he called out, his voice echoing across the deck. "Set our course north! We follow the coast! And keep yer eyes peeled for any river's mouth!"

"Aye, Captain," Pew called back.

As the helmsman spun the wheel, the ship, her sails full and billowing, responded with a graceful lean, changing course to hug the rugged coastline. The sea spray misted the air while the wind whistled through the rigging, each creak of the timbers and snap of the canvas echoing the adventurous spirit of the Siren's Call.

It had only been an hour or two when the lookout took a deep breath and bellowed out, "River, ho! River off the port bow!" his voice ringing out clear and loud, cutting through the sounds of the sea and alerting every soul on board.

All eyes turned to the coastline where the river's mouth opened wide, its waters being welcomed by the sea. Jim and Bella found their way to the bow, the wind tugging at their clothes as they watched the shore pass beside the ship. Jim's gaze was steady, his eyes scanning the coastline with great curiosity. The deep crease between his brows spoke volumes of his focus, a silent testament to the intensity with which he took in the unfolding scenery. Beside him, Bella's eyes sparkled with eager excitement as she pointed toward the land, her energy a vivid contrast to his quiet concentration.

Billy stepped out of his cabin, carrying a rolled-up map tucked securely under his arm. He strode toward Jim and Bella at the bow, who were still lost in the mesmerizing view of the coast and approaching river. As he neared them, he unrolled the map, holding it firmly in his hands against the persistent tug of the wind. His gaze flicked between the map and the landscape before them, trying to match reality with the parchment. His eyes then traced the path of the river on the map as it meandered through the landscape, the name Ahuic inked along it, to where it surrendered to the welcoming sea.

Finally, he turned to Jim, his voice gruff and edged with skepticism, yet carrying a whisper of anticipation. "Do you reckon this be the right river, Jim?" he asked, his question hanging in the air amidst the sound of the crashing waves.

The Secret of the Dragon's Scale

With the wind tugging at his clothes and ruffling his hair, Jim remained fixated on the coastline, drinking in the beauty of the approaching river mouth. Then, slowly, he closed his eyes. His features relaxed, the lines of concentration smoothing out. He tipped his face up slightly, letting the sea breeze caress his skin, carrying with it the scent of distant lands. Opening himself up to the world around him, Jim reached out with his senses beyond what his eyes could see—he listened to the rhythmic lullaby of the waves crashing against the hull, and the distant cries of seagulls echoing in his ears; he tasted the salt on the wind as he took a deep breath, feeling the cool air filling his lungs, then slowly leaving his body. Jim was searching for something—a sign, a feeling, anything that would tell him that this was the right place for them to be. But as the minutes ticked by, all he felt was the steady rocking of the ship, the warmth of the sun on his skin, and the constant, comforting presence of the sea.

Jim opened his eyes, a sigh escaping his lips. The landscape before him was like a painting come to life—the wide sweep of golden sand, the dense forest behind it, and the river gleaming under the sun as it emptied into the ocean. But apart from the natural beauty of the scene, there was nothing that stood out to him, nothing that spoke to him on a deeper level.

"No, Captain. I don't feel it. I don't feel this be the right place," Jim said with some disappointment.

Billy gave a solemn nod. "Aye, Jim. Ye've got to feel it in yer bones. If ye say this ain't our river, then it ain't. We'll continue up the coast."

Billy paced back and forth, keeping vigil aboard the ship, but also a careful eye on the coastline. Then, turning on his heel, he made his way toward his cabin, his silhouette a stoic figure against the setting sun. The door creaked open, revealing the dimly lit quarters within. He paused for a moment at the threshold, casting one last glance back at the river that wasn't theirs, before disappearing inside. And with a sigh that was part resignation, part hope, he retreated into his quarters, leaving the ship in the capable hands of the crew.

As the sun gave its final bow and twilight draped itself over the water, the Siren's Call continued its journey, gently cutting through the tranquil ocean. Before it got too dark, it fell upon Ben to issue standard orders.

"All hands," he called out, his tone steady. "Furl sails and drop anchor!" His command echoed across the decks, bouncing off the timbers and ringing out into the encroaching night. Sailing close to shore was dangerous because of the risk of running aground on unseen rocks, reefs, or other hazards. So the crew knew to anchor until morning light made navigation safer.

The men, used to countless nights under starlit skies, sprang into action. The deck came alive with the sound of hurried footsteps and shouted instructions, a well-rehearsed dance of efficiency and discipline. Ropes were hauled, sails were furled, and the heavy anchor chain rattled as it descended into the dark depths, tying the ship to the safety of the seabed. As the anchor hit the water, a splash echoed in the quiet twilight, followed by the low groan of the ship settling into its temporary resting place. The night claimed the sky, and the Siren's Call stood anchored, a solitary silhouette against the vast canvas of stars. The crew then retired for the night, the moon hanging low in the sky, its light spilling like liquid silver, casting a gentle sheen over the seascape below.

The ship swayed gently on the rhythmic rise and fall of the waves, its weathered timbers uttering soft, contented groans. Yet the peace aboard was incomplete. Within this tranquil scene, a lone figure moved with restless energy across the deck. His tall, lean frame cut a stark outline against the shimmer of the silvered water, his pacing a sharp contrast to the steady lull of the sea.

Ben's obsession with the Dragon's Scale had begun as a spark—a flicker of curiosity kindled by the legend. But now, it had grown into a roaring inferno that consumed his every thought, his every waking moment; more and more, he was

The Secret of the Dragon's Scale

becoming a man possessed. His eyes were shadowed, beholding a feverish glint that reflected the turbulent sea of his thoughts. His voice took on a mumbling, obsessive tone. His lips moved in a silent monologue.

"Dragon's Scale . . . Dragon's Scale . . . Riches untold," he muttered, his voice barely audible as the breeze snatched his words away. His boots echoed quietly on the planks as he walked, each step resonating with his growing obsession. His hands clenched and unclenched, mirroring the tumultuous thoughts swirling in his mind. "We've sailed north, south, east, west," he went on, his voice rising with each word, sharper now, more desperate. "Why haven't we found it? It has to be here . . . It has to!"

He turned his sights out to the sea, its surface shimmering under the celestial light. Images played in his mind of it hiding the coveted Dragon's Scale, lurking beneath the waves, just out of reach. He could almost see it glinting—tantalizing him, taunting him, with its promise of chests overflowing with gold. His pacing was relentless, as the wind tugged at his hair and billowed his coat. He paused, staring back out at the dark, boundless water, a haunting eeriness in his eyes.

"It's there . . . laughing at me . . . mocking me!" His fingers clenched into fists, the storm of anger and frustration boiling just beneath the surface.

"And mermaids!" he scoffed, a bitter laugh escaping his lips. "The captain, bless his heart, believin' in fish-tailed maidens that will reveal secrets to us!" he exclaimed, his mocking words hanging heavily in the air. "What next? Will we seek counsel from a talkin' dolphin, or a wise old turtle?" His laughter rang out into the night, a haunting sound that carried with it the echo of a mind spiraling into the abyss.

Meanwhile, in the hushed embrace of the ship's belly, the rest of the crew were in the arms of sleep, their snores low rumblings and gentle wheezes in the otherwise silent ship. Bella as well lay in her hammock, gently rocking with the ship's rhythm. Her eyelashes fluttered against her cheeks, hinting at the vivid dreams playing out behind closed lids. And as she slept, a faint melody began to weave its way into her subconscious. It whispered softly, resonating gently in the tranquil sanctuary of her mind.

With a gasp, Bella jolted awake! Her eyes flew open, her heart pounding against her ribcage, her body drenched in a cold sweat, the remnants of the haunting music still echoing in her ears! She lay there in the dim light, trying to steady her breath, but a knot of unease tightened in her stomach, an icy feeling of dread creeping into her bones. The close confines of the cabin seemed to constrict around her, suffocatingly tight, until the desperate need for air drove her to action.

Compelled by her rising anxiety, Bella jumped off the hammock and flung open the cabin door, the cool night air slamming into her as she hurried up onto the deck. She ran over to the railing, leaning against it as she gulped in lungfuls of fresh air. The breeze playfully danced through her hair, its gentle caresses easing the tension from her body. Closing her eyes, Bella tilted her face to the wind, letting the soothing sounds of the sea drown out the fractured strains of the music from her dreams.

But Bella was still confused, still anxious. She couldn't shake off the lingering sense of foreboding—that the music was not just a melody, but a prophecy. Through it, she felt that the spirits of the ancients were speaking to her; but they weren't just warning her—they were pleading with her, their ancient voices urging her to heed their call. Through each note, they painted visions of ominous shadows looming on the horizon, of a danger that was as real as the pounding of her heart.

As she stood there, leaning against the railing, Bella allowed herself to absorb the peace of the night. The chill of the wind against her skin, the quiet hum of the sea, the soft glow of the moonlight—all of it served to soothe her anxiety, even if only a little. With each passing moment, her mind began to unwind, her thoughts trailing away like leaves caught in a gentle current. With every breath, she drew in the calmness around her, a balm for her frayed nerves.

In the midst of this tranquility, however, a subtle sensation began to creep into her awareness—a gentle sway beneath her feet, the creak of wood, the whisper of the ship cutting through the water. Her eyes sprung open, her heart skipped a beat! The ship was moving! Surprise flooded her senses, momentarily pushing away the calm. She had been so lost in her own thoughts that she hadn't noticed the ship breaking its moorings!

For while Bella was becoming enveloped by the night's quiet reassurance, a swell of music had arisen from the very heart of the ocean, as if the sea itself had found a voice, one that resonated with a depth that transcended the natural realm. The music unfurled across the waves like silken ribbons of moonlight, its melodies a gentle caress upon the night sky; each note cascaded gracefully upon the water, each chord danced upon the wind, captivating and enchanting the soul.

There was no denying it; these were the calls of sirens. Ancient and mesmerizing, they were songs of such exquisite beauty, they whispered secrets of the divine.

And with each enchanting note, the ship seemed to awaken! It groaned and creaked, entranced by the call from the sirens' distant serenade. Suddenly, with a sound like the sigh of a giant, the anchors began to tremble! Chains rattled to life as they ascended from the sandy seabed below!

Ancient legends long spoke of sirens whose mythical songs lured sailors to their doom. With voices as sweet as honey and melodies spun from the very essence of desire, they dwelt upon remote rocky shores, their calls imbued with both sorrow and seduction, drawing seafarers ever closer, enticing them toward menacing shores where jagged rocks lay in wait.

And now unhindered, the ship surged forward under their spell. Her sails billowed out, though there was no wind, and she glided eerily across the water. The sirens' songs filled the air, coaxing the vessel relentlessly toward rocky cliffs thrust into the sea. The melody kept growing louder, more insistent, tugging the ship closer and closer toward the sinister formation that loomed in the distance, their sharp serrated edges glistening menacingly in the glow of the moon.

Mr. Pew, roused from his slumber, lunged for the alarm bell, but its desperate clangor, along with his frantic cries, were nearly drowned in the songs. The other men, jolted awake, stumbled onto the deck, eyes wide with dread, hearts pounding with terror. The ship continued on her course, seemingly bewitched, moving with an ominous inevitability toward the open jaw of a colossal beast, ready to tear into the vessel's mighty wooden hull. The once gentle lap of the waves now was the drumbeat of impending doom, each rhythmic crash against the ship a chilling reminder of the peril they were heading toward! The wind picked up, howling through the ship's rigging, creating a haunting symphony that underscored the threat. Each passing second brought the vessel closer to the deadly embrace of the rocks, the distance between them decreasing at a terrifying pace!

Bella had not noticed Ben pacing in the shadows near the bow when she came up on deck. Ben himself had been oblivious to everything except the maddening thoughts that churned in his mind. But suddenly, he was jolted to his senses, the fog of his obsessive mind abruptly dispelled by the sudden shifting of the ship, the ethereal calling of the sirens, and the clamor of the crew. His gaze darted across the deck, taking in the maelstrom that had erupted—the once tranquil scene had transformed into a tumultuous spectacle of fear and urgency! Ben's pulse quickened as he took in the events, a surge of energy coursing through his veins. His mind was now sharply focused on the reality unfolding before him, as he leapt to the aid of his fellow crew.

The men dashed to and fro, their faces taut with anxiety. Shouts echoed through the night, the captain barking out orders in quick succession, their words blending into a cacophony of noise that reverberated around the deck! The call of the sirens, hauntingly beautiful yet laced with deadly intent, persisted relentlessly, urging the ship ever faster toward the rocks! What was once a serene sea now began to seethe with a growing fury, the icy breath of the wind shrieking through the rigging and snapping the sails.

"Avast there!" Billy bellowed out. "Hands to the braces! Trim the sails to catch the wind just right! We be needin' every bit of control we can muster!"

With danger looming, Mr. Pew, his instinct to be at the helm, sprang into action! He took a deep breath, steeling himself for what needed to be done, and bounded up the steps to the quarterdeck. As he grasped the wheel, a jolt of determination surged through him. He could see the menacing silhouette of the rocks ahead, gleaming treacherously under the pale moonlight, their edges, thrusting up like bared teeth, promising a terrifying destruction!

"Helm! Hard to starboard!" Billy shouted up to Mr. Pew.

Mr. Pew, his face etched with purpose, fought fiercely against the spell of the sirens, his knuckles white as he gripped the wheel, wrestling with the force that threatened to send them all to a watery grave! Every sinew in his body strained under the immense effort, veins bulging like taut cords beneath his sun-scorched skin!

"Not today," he growled under his breath, his voice hoarse and raw with effort, as he tried desperately to steer the ship away from the maw of this treacherous beast.

Amidst all the turmoil, the captain and the rest of the crew fought valiantly! The ropes bit into their flesh, leaving searing grooves on their raw hands as they clung to the rigging, pulling with every ounce of their strength. Their faces were masks of grim determination, their bodies slick with sweat and sea spray, moving with a synchrony born of desperation and hope!

But the relentless tug of war between the sirens and the beleaguered crew caused the ship to tilt dangerously to port, the deck slanting sharply beneath their feet. Men slipped and slid, struggling to find a firm foothold! Chaos reigned as barrels and crates broke free, careening wildly across the deck!

Bella's heart raced as she desperately sought something to anchor herself. Her eyes then locked on the capstan, its sturdy shape standing defiantly in the pandemonium. Determined, she lunged forward, her fingers stretching out desperately. They clasped the rough wood just as a monstrous wave crashed against the ship, tossing it further into a spine-chilling sideways lurch.

The distance closed rapidly, the gap between safety and destruction shrinking with each agonizing second! And then, a shattering impact reverberated through the night as the ship collided with the rocks—a jarring blow that sent the Siren's Call into violent convulsions! The initial impact unleashed a deafening crunch of splintering wood meeting unyielding stone! Then, like the scream of a beast in its death throes, came the rending, tearing sound of wood being ripped apart! Shards, ripped from the side, danced in the air before disappearing into the churning waters below! The ship's hull was now marred by long gashes and cracks.

The ship's precarious tilt also brought a yardarm on a fateful collision course with the looming cliff face. Towering over the ship like a silent titan, the cliff's formidable height matched that of the ship's tallest mast. It was a monolith of raw, unyielding stone, carved by time and weather into a jagged tapestry of sharp edges and sheer faces. And as the gap between yardarm and cliff dwindled, the sailors on board could only watch in helpless horror as the vessel's beam was in a dangerous dance with the land!

Then, with a bone-jarring impact that echoed over the chaos, the yardarm struck the cliff! The impact was devastating, the solid oak yard splintering viciously in half under the raw force, with shards of wood exploding outward like deadly shrapnel, accompanied by the deafening crack of shattering timber, reverberating off the cliff and cascading across the tumultuous sea!

The Secret of the Dragon's Scale

And as if time itself held its breath, there was a chilling moment of stillness. The splintered yard hung suspended in the air, a grim specter silhouetted against the moonlit sky. Then, surrendering to gravity's inexorable pull, it began its fatal descent. Sailors scattered in a frenzy of panic, their cries lost to the wind as they fled from the path of the falling timber! For Mr. Pew at the helm, however, realization came too late. He looked up, his eyes widening in stark terror as he saw the yard hurtling toward him! His body tensed, preparing to leap away! With a thunderous explosion, the broken yard crashed onto the quarterdeck, striking Mr. Pew before he could escape in time, crushing him under its merciless weight!

But with an unstoppable momentum, the yard continued its fall, plunging further onto the deck below!

Suddenly, a monstrous shadow fell over Bella! Her eyes widened in pure terror as she looked up, her heart pounding as she realized the deadly danger only a split second before the yard struck!

A piercing scream tore from her throat, "AAAAAH!"

Just then, from the corner of her eye, Bella saw a figure emerge from the chaos. Jim, his face a mask of grim determination, propelled himself forward, his boots skidding on the wet planks. His eyes were locked onto her, every muscle in his body straining toward the singular goal of saving her! With a roar of effort, he crashed into Bella, sending them both sprawling to the deck! She landed with a painful thud, a sharp cry of agony escaping her lips! The yard then slammed into the very spot where Bella had stood moments before, its impact shaking the ship to its core and showering them with splinters!

Bella gasped, the wind knocked out of her. A sharp pain seared across her arm where the yard had grazed her, drawing a thin line of red against her pale skin. But it was a superficial wound, a lucky escape compared to the crushing weight of the yard that could have been her end. Struggling to sit up, she clutched at her arm, wincing at the sting of her injury. Her breaths were ragged, her body trembling from the adrenaline coursing through her veins. She was saved by the bravery of Jim, who now hovered over her, his chest heaving with exertion and relief.

Despite the brutality of the collision, the ship refused to be claimed by the sea. For although wounded, she was far from surrendering. This stubborn lady bore her scars with a fierce resilience—her damaged hull shuddered and moaned, yet steadfastly held firm. Water gushed into her lower compartments, yet she did not sink. A beacon of defiance amidst the chaos, she had withstood the sirens' deadly lure and powered forward; and driven by her momentum, she skirted past the cliff and navigated through the treacherous rocks. Her sails, though torn and tattered, caught the wind, and propelled the vessel further out of the reach of danger. The rocky menace receded into the distance, gradually swallowed by the misty veil of the sea. So with the peril averted, the sirens thwarted, she sailed on, her journey uninterrupted and her spirit unbroken.

In the aftermath, a wave of shock rippled through the crew, a tangible tremor of grief and horror. The sailors stood motionless, their faces pale in the moon's eerie light, their hearts heavy with the loss of their comrade. The ship was now sailing in calmer waters, but the victory was overshadowed by a heavy loss. Mr. Pew, Elias Pew, a valiant member of the crew, had been struck down during the tumultuous struggle. Elias Pew was not just a fellow shipmate, he was their friend, and a guiding light in the darkest storms.

The captain, though a storm-hardened sailor, stood motionless at the helm, his hands gripping the wheel with a force that turned his knuckles white. His face no longer carried its commanding resolve—it bore the ravages of grief, each line deepened by the weight of loss. He had seen men claimed by the unforgiving waves before—had steeled himself against the hollow ache it brought—but losing Mr. Pew was different. It was as if the sea had ripped away not just a crewmate, but a brother, a part of himself, leaving an unfillable void in its wake.

Billy surveyed the solemn, downturned faces of his crew and drew a deep breath before speaking. "Elias Pew was not just a part of this crew," he began, his voice breaking the silence, burdened with grief yet steady with resolve. "We've lost a good man today, lads. He was a brother to us, a steady anchor in the stormy sea of our lives. His departure leaves our ship poorer, but his spirit sails with us." He paused, his eyes locking with the crew's. "He lived by the sea, and by the sea he's gone."

Billy's words hung in the air, each syllable a tribute to their fallen brother. The crew bowed their heads, their hearts echoing the captain's sentiments.

The next morning, the sky glowed in hues of gold and rose, as the rising sun bid the world awake. The ship, battered and bruised from the sirens' onslaught, sailed forth, doggedly carving its way up the coastline, a testament to its resilience beneath the quiet promise of a new day. The deck transformed into a hive of activity, echoing with the sounds of hammers striking wood and the rasp of saws biting into timber. They toiled under the sun, sweat dotting their brows, their hands moving with practiced expertise to mend what had been broken. Bella helped as best she could, bringing food and water to the men laboriously repairing the ship. Yet, the usual camaraderie, the laughter and bawdy quips that would normally bounce between them, was nowhere to be found. Instead, a somber silence filled the air, as tangible as the scent of salt and timber shavings. The deck, so often a place of raucous life, became a solemn stage for quiet mourning.

After a long day, the sun began its descent toward the horizon, and the men, weary and covered in sweat, downed their tools and sank onto the deck. Bella found Jim sitting alone, his features deeply carved with exhaustion. Placing the tray and jug beside him, she eased herself down, resting her back against a mast.

"Jim," she said, her voice as soft as the evening breeze, "you need to eat."

He took the food and water from her, his movements mechanical. His eyes, rimmed with fatigue, stared out over the ocean, distant and unfocused. There was a heaviness in them, a storm of emotions he couldn't speak aloud.

"Bella . . . " he said, "we all signed up for this voyage, dreamin' of piles of gold and jewels. They spun us tales of the Dragon's Scale and the Admiral Benbow, said it'd make us richer 'an kings. That's what roped us in, that's what's been drivin' the lot of us." He stopped, swallowing hard, his fists balled up tight. "But now . . . now I'm not so sure. Is it worth it? The mates we've lost, the soul's anguish we've seen . . . All for some legendary loot? Does gold weigh more than the lives of our friends? What's the goin' rate for a man's life, Bella?"

His voice wavered a bit as he went on, his feelings raw and out in the open. "I'm feelin' this search ain't for us. Should we keep chasin' the Dragon's Scale? Or should we turn tail and run, while we still have souls to save?" He let out a heavy sigh, raking a hand through his hair. "We've paid a steep price already. And I'm scared it'll only get worse the further we sail." His words lingered in the air, a poignant testament to the inner conflict tearing him apart.

Jim rose, his movements slow and measured. He held a far-off look in his eyes as he moved toward the ship's railing. Leaning forward, he fixed his gaze on the sandy shoreline slowly passing by. The beach was a ribbon of gold, weaving an intricate pattern along the edge of the cerulean sea. It was a sight that had always brought him solace, a reminder of the simple beauty that life offered even in the most challenging times.

Bella then got up and moved to stand beside him. She reached out and took his hand, her fingers enveloping his in a comforting clasp. She didn't need words to express her understanding, her empathy. Her presence was enough, a beacon of comfort amidst the storm of his doubts.

The Siren's Call continued to glide along the coast, her prow cutting smoothly through the gentle waves. Jim and Bella stood together at the railing, their eyes intently following the shoreline as it slipped by. Beyond the sandy stretch, a verdant forest stood tall and proud, a wall of green that seemed to hold secrets of its own. Palm trees punctuated the beach, their fronds dancing gently in the sea breeze; their long, slender leaves fluttered and dipped, arching gracefully like a bird in flight. Sunlight filtered through the gaps in the fronds, casting dappled shadows that danced on the sandy beach below.

The ship's journey soon brought her to the mouth of another river. As it approached, the shifting shadows on the sand began to take form in Jim's mind, his imagination breathing life into them. At first, they were shapeless ripples cast by the gentle sway of the palms above. But as he watched, his tired mind wove shapes from the restless dance of light and shade. Slowly, the shadows began to gather, shifting and merging, transforming into the majestic form of a giant bird, its wings spread wide across the shore. The wings seemed to rise and fall with the swaying of the palms, the bird appearing to soar, tethered to the ground by nothing but shadow and light.

Jim remained motionless, lost within the spell of the illusion. He exhaled softly as he shut his eyes, the world around him fading into the stillness of his own mind. And within that quiet sanctuary, he could hear the voice of the spirit, delicate and resonant, whispering, *hold firm where the eagle's shadow falls.*

Jim's eyes flew open! He turned to Bella and exclaimed, "This be it!"

His heart thundered in his chest, mirroring the pulse of his exhilaration! With a surge of energy, he sprang away from the railing, his boots thudding heavily against the deck as he dashed up to the quarterdeck, Bella in chase, where the captain had taken the wheel.

"Captain! Captain!" he called out. His heart pounded louder, nearly drowning out the sound of his breath. He gripped the railing for balance as he lunged up the stairs two at a time, skidding to a breathless halt in front of the captain.

His chest heaved as he tried to catch his breath, his words tumbling out in a rush. "Captain!" he gasped, his voice filled with an urgency that immediately caught Billy's attention. "This be it! This be the right river!"

Jim pointed toward the spot where the shadows were dancing on the sand, his arm shaking slightly from the adrenaline coursing through his veins. "This be where we should stop. I can feel it! I can feel it! The spirits . . . they told me! Hold firm here!"

Billy looked at him, surprise etched on his face. But there was no doubt in Jim's eyes, no hesitation in his voice. A peculiar sensation crept over Billy—a whisper at the edge of his mind, as though something unseen echoed Jim's certainty, urging him to trust what he couldn't fully understand. Billy knew then, without a shadow of a doubt, that this must be right.

The captain's eyes darted across the chaos of the quarterdeck, with everything strewn about, looking for the map that had been on the bench before the tumult of the rocks. There, among the mess, he spotted it—a parchment, its edges fluttering in the wind, was wedged within a coil of rope that had been thrown askew. Pointing to the map, he asked Jim to retrieve it.

Billy took the map from Jim, his finger tracing lines inked on the damp, worn parchment. His brow knitted in concentration, and for a moment, the only sound was the creak of the ship and the distant cry of seabirds.

"Hmmm," Billy murmured under his breath, his voice weighted with thought. His hand stopped abruptly, hovering over a line that twisted and turned before meeting the coastline. His eyes sharpened. "This," he said, tapping the spot, "this must be the river—the Ilhuan."

A heavy silence followed his words. He stepped forward, looking out across the deck below, and bellowed out to the crew, "Men! Furl the sails and drop anchor! Secure the ship! We stop here!"

The crew scrambled to obey, boots pounding against the planks as ropes were pulled taut and sails folded away. The final drop of the anchor sent a resounding splash that silenced the world for an instant.

Twilight soon cast its cloak over the vessel, softening the edges of the day with hues of gold and violet. Shadows crept up from the jungle, spilling onto the deck like ghostly fingers. The ship swayed gently, her sails rustling in the faint breeze as she settled into her temporary sanctuary at the mouth of the Ilhuan.

Down on deck, Jim leaned on the railing, Bella by his side, his gaze fixed on the darkening river. The air seemed to whisper secrets—old, buried truths waiting to be uncovered. Somewhere in the distance, a faint rustle, almost like a sigh, carried over the water. He shivered despite the warmth of the evening. The captain lingered up on the quarterdeck, still studying the distant, darkened land where the river vanished into uncharted realms. Billy stood tall, one hand gripping the wheel, his face set with determination and a spark of something else—a flicker of hope mingled with unease.

The Ilhuan stretched before them, a winding path carved through the earth that seemed to beckon them deeper into the unknown. Whatever secrets it guarded lay just out of reach, waiting with quiet patience. As the last traces of daylight bled from the sky, the ship drifted into stillness, cradled in the shadow of a river steeped in mysteries far deeper than any could yet fathom.

Steven Eisenberg

Where the Serpent Dons a Feathered Guise

As dawn broke over the horizon the next morning, the Siren's Call sat anchored, a majestic silhouette against the pastel hues of the awakening sky. The ship, regal and silent, was bathed in a soft glow, the first light of day reflecting off her battered hull. On board, the atmosphere was one of quiet anticipation. The crew had begun to stir, their sleep broken by the gentle bobbing of the ship and the distant call of exotic birds from the nearby shore. Murmurs of conversation filled the air, punctuated by the occasional hearty laugh or the clinking of cooking utensils as breakfast was prepared below deck.

The captain emerged from his cabin, his figure imposing against the backdrop of the rising sun. His eyes surveyed the tranquility of the morning with an appreciative glint. He inhaled deeply, the crisp morning air mingling with the salty tang of the sea and the earthy aroma of the riverbanks. As he stood there, lost in his thoughts, a strange sensation tickled at the edge of his consciousness. It was a whisper, as soft as the rustle of leaves in a gentle breeze, of ancient voices—*Seek the land of emerald and jade, where the serpent dons a feathered guise.* The cryptic message, he recalled the spirits speaking, danced in his mind, a tantalizing puzzle that beckoned him toward the unknown. His gaze unconsciously drifted toward the luxuriant expanse of forest beyond the shore. It was a symphony of green, a masterpiece painted by nature's own hand, resplendent in hues of emerald and jade.

Billy's eyes then traced the winding ribbon of the Ilhuan River, snaking its way into the heart of the forest. A realization slowly dawned upon him. The message of the spirits, before shrouded in mystery, was becoming clear—this is where they were being led, into the land of emerald and jade, and the river would be their guide through the veiled depths of the unknown. But the serpent donning a feathered guise? The riddle intrigued him, its symbolism remaining an enigma that beckoned him into the wilderness, to discover for himself.

Ben emerged from his quarters, his sleep-ridden eyes squinting against the bright light. He spotted the captain staring intently at the forest, his eyes tracing the serpentine path of the river that disappeared into the verdant heart of the wilderness. The captain's usual aura of intensity seemed subdued, replaced by an air of quiet contemplation. Ben, too, was calmer, compared to the tumultuous storm of thoughts plaguing his mind the previous night. The terrifying encounters with the sirens and the rocks, the tragic loss of Mr. Pew, and the physically draining task of mending their damaged vessel, had siphoned away much of his obsessive energy, at least for the time being.

But despite the newfound calm that had settled over Ben, his thoughts remained firmly anchored on the Dragon's Scale. Upon reaching Billy, he asked, "Captain, do ye reckon this might be where we find the Dragon's Scale?"

Billy turned to him, his eyes meeting Ben's with a calmness that belied the strain of the hardships they had recently weathered. Just then, the creaking of cabin doors again punctured the morning stillness, drawing their attention toward Jim and Bella. The two of them crossed the deck, their footsteps a soft echo on the worn wood, and joined Ben and the captain. Under the gentle glow of the morning sun, the four of them stood together, their faces softly illuminated by the dawn's light.

"Nay, not this spot, lad," Billy said to Ben. He paused for a moment, looking out toward the vast forest that loomed in front of them. "We be needin' to venture into the heart of that forest. It be there we'll discover the secrets she keeps." Running a hand over his beard, he finished with a determined nod. "I be sure of that. I feel it in me bones."

Jim agreed. "Aye. A spirit said to me there be a time when yer voyage brings ye to new realms, where the rhythm of the sea gives way to the heartbeat of the earth. The spirit's message be guidin' us . . . We've been voyagers of the sea . . . The heartbeat of the earth . . . that's the land. That be callin' us now."

Billy nodded in agreement. He then turned to address his crew, his voice soft but commanding. Gesturing at the longboats roped up at the sides of the ship, he called to the men, "Lower the longboats, lads! We be headin' up river!"

The captain's orders, clear and firm, cut through the morning mist. The ship became a hive of activity as the men hustled to prepare the longboats. The ropes strained against the weight, creaking through the pulleys as the boats were carefully lowered into the gentle swells. Next, they stowed some provisions, and weapons for hunting.

Bella as well moved with quiet purpose. She gathered some clothing, tucking them away in a sack. Then, instinctively, her hand moved toward her lute. The familiar feel of the polished wood brought a small smile to her face. She held it for a moment, strumming a silent melody before grabbing her clothes. It was a part of her, a piece of her soul she carried with her into the unknown.

As the morning sun painted the sky in brilliant hues of orange and gold, the preparations were complete. The longboats, heavy with provisions, bobbed gently on the river's surface. The forest awaited them, its secrets hidden behind its lush, shadowy depths.

The crew of the Siren's Call found themselves enveloped by a world that seemed to exist outside of time as they rowed their longboats up the Ilhuan. The river shimmered as it wound its way into the heart of the forest, the current a playful companion, tugging and teasing at the boats as it guided them onward. Every now and then, the splash of a fish breaking the surface or the soft ripple of a drifting leaf served as gentle reminders of the river's vibrant life. On either side, the forest rose in a grand spectacle of nature's bounty. Towering trees draped in lush foliage reached skyward, their canopies intertwining to create an intricate tapestry of green that arched overhead like the vaulted ceiling of a natural cathedral. Vines hung from branches, and radiant flowers bloomed amidst the foliage, splashing the green canvas with bursts of scarlet, gold, and violet. The air was thick with perfume, the sweet scent of blooming orchids mingling with the tangy aroma of ripe fruits hanging heavily from the branches. Underneath it all was the grounding fragrance of damp earth and the fresh, clean smell of the river. The creaking of the longboats and the rhythmic dip and swish of the oars in the water blended seamlessly with the river's soothing burble. Above, birdsong echoed through the stillness—a chorus of warbles, trills, and calls that filled the air with music, intertwined with the vibrant squawks of parrots. Monkeys chattered and swung from the branches overhead, their curious eyes watching the crew's progress. And the constant drone of insects provided the backdrop against which all other sounds were layered.

Enveloped by this grand wonder, the crew moved as one, their rowing a steady rhythm after hours on the river. Jim and Bella sat together in one of the longboats, their eyes drinking in the sights and sounds of the world around them. After a short time, a soft melody, heard in the distance, began to weave its way into Jim's consciousness, tugging gently at his awareness until he could no longer ignore its presence. It was the beautiful song of a bird, its tune faint yet clear, carried on the gentle wind that stirred the emerald canopy overhead. The melody began as a gentle trill that echoed the rustle of the leaves and the murmur of distant waterfalls; it soon grew bolder, the notes rising and falling in a rhythmic dance, filled with unexpected twists and turns that captivated his ear.

Gradually, as they continued up the river, the bird's song grew louder, and lost in its beauty, he felt a sense of peace wash over him. The world around him seemed to fade away, replaced by the enchanting melody that wrapped itself around his senses.

"Do ye hear that?" Jim asked, his voice a hushed whisper as he leaned closer to Bella.

"Hear what?" she responded, her eyes tracing his line of sight up into the dense jungle canopy.

"The bird," Jim said softly, a hint of awe in his voice. He gestured toward the trees, his fingers tracing the path of an unseen melody. "Its song."

Bella strained her ears, trying to discern the sound he was referring to. The jungle was alive with noise—the squawks of parrots, the distant call of a monkey, the ceaseless hum of insects. But a bird's song? She wasn't sure.

"I don't—" she began, but then paused. There it was, a faint trill that danced on the edge of her awareness. It was a delicate sound, almost drowned out by the surrounding cacophony, but unmistakably there.

"Oh," Bella said, a slow smile spreading across her face. "Yes, I hear it now."

Jim nodded, his eyes still fixed on the canopy above. "Isn't it beautiful?" he murmured.

Bella tilted her head, listening intently until the bird's song came into sharp focus. A smile spread across her face as recognition dawned. "I think . . . I think that's a quetzal! You can see them sometimes outside my village. Oh, they're such beautiful birds!" she exclaimed, turning to Jim with excitement sparkling in her eyes. "They're this beautiful, glittering shade of green. And their chests, they're this fiery red. But the real magic," she said, her eyes wide with wonder, "is when they fly. Their tail feathers catch the light and scatter it in every direction. It's like watching a shower of gold, blue, violet . . . every color you can imagine. You know how jewels catch the light?" Bella asked, her hands gesturing as if she were holding a precious gem between her fingers. "How a ruby or a sapphire seems to glow from within? That's what quetzals do. They catch the sunlight and turn it into a sparkling rainbow of colors, outshining every jewel you've ever seen! That's why we call them the Jewel of the Forest."

Jim's eyes widened in astonishment as Bella's words washed over him, his oar stilled mid-stroke. He felt his heartbeat quicken. "Jewel of the Forest," he repeated, his voice barely above a whisper. The voice of the spirit echoed in his mind—*Let the jewel of the forest be your guide, for her song embodies the spirit of your quest.* In that moment, as they sat in the boat, the world around Jim fell into a profound silence. Like a flower greeting the dawn, the riddle that had been the spirit's words suddenly unfolded, revealing its hidden truth.

His eyes sparkled with eagerness. "Captain!" he called out, his voice filled with urgency and excitement, cutting through the forest sounds around them.

The captain turned. "Aye, lad?"

"Listen! The bird's song!"

There was a moment of silence as they both tuned into the distinctive song in the distance. Puzzlement crossed Billy's face as he strained to hear what Jim was talking about. The song was faint, seeming to blend with the chirps and buzzes and rustling of leaves. Then, after a moment of listening carefully, his eyes widened slightly. "I hear it," he responded, "What of it?"

"The song, Captain! The bird's song!" Jim exclaimed, his eyes bright with excitement. "The spirit told me to let the jewel of the forest be my guide. That be the bird! They call it the Jewel of the Forest! We need to be followin' its song!"

"Ye think these birds be leadin' us somewhere, lad?" he asked, his voice tinged with doubt.

"Aye!" Jim replied.

Billy stroked his beard, deep in thought, then finally sighed and nodded. "Alright," he said. "If it be the bird we're to follow, then so be it. We'll continue up the river."

With each stroke of their oars, the melody of the quetzal's song grew louder. Soon, the vivid canopy overhead began to shimmer with movement. One by one, more radiant quetzals appeared, their brilliant feathers catching the sunlight filtering through the leaves. Their song swelled into a harmonious chorus that echoed through the forest, a symphony of nature that left everyone awestruck.

As they looked up, Bella and the men could see flashes of vibrant color darting through the leafy canopy. The birds moved with a grace and agility that was mesmerizing. Their stunning plumage, a kaleidoscope of emerald greens and fiery reds, painted the air with strokes of brilliance as they darted gracefully between the trees. Each one seemed to carry a piece of the rainbow on its wings, shimmering in the dappled sunlight and scattering it like a prism, transforming the canopy into a dazzling display of light and color. Their long, elegant tail feathers trailed behind them like delicate brushstrokes, adding a fluid elegance to their every movement. Every now and then, one would swoop down closer to the river, captivating the crew as their wings caught the sunlight, erupting in bursts of vibrant reds, blues, and greens. The sight of these beautiful creatures, married with their enchanting song, transformed the forest into a living canvas, a testament to the exquisite artistry of the natural world.

Ahead, a clearing on the river bank, a small patch of grassy land, came into view, bathed in dappled sunlight. The bird song echoed around the clearing from all sides, as if they were saying, "This is the place; this is where you are meant to be."

Billy, perched at the front of the first longboat, surveyed the scene with a discerning eye. "We'll make camp there," he announced, pointing toward the clearing.

After hours of relentless rowing, the crew's exhaustion was etched into their faces, their muscles burning from the day's arduous effort. A surge of relief coursed through them as their boats gently kissed the shore of the clearing. But despite the day's exertions, there was an unspoken eagerness among them to establish a temporary claim on this patch of wilderness. So, with concerted effort, they began the task of unloading their provisions.

The afternoon sun, now mellow, cast a warm glow over the scene, painting everything in hues of gold and green. The men sprawled across the soft earth, their bodies grateful for the solid ground beneath them, their backs against logs or nestled in the mossy beds at the foot of trees. Bella found a spot near the edge, where the light danced through the leaves and played upon her face. Some of the men conversed in low tones, their voices a gentle hum in the tranquility of the afternoon, while others succumbed to their exertion, their eyes closing in blissful sleep.

Jim lay stretched out upon the green carpet of the clearing, choosing one of the large rocks dotting the space as his pillow. It was oddly shaped, encrusted with a mosaic of moss and lichen, and blended seamlessly into the forest floor. As he looked around, his eyes danced with curiosity and awe. He absorbed the sights, sounds, and smells with a reverence born of wonder, each sensation a thread weaving him into the fabric of the forest. Turning his head to the side, Jim's eyes fell upon the surface of the rock. What he saw grabbed his attention immediately. Though weathered by the elements, he could discern marks etched into it. These seemed to be not the random scars of nature's handiwork but the faded inscriptions of a deliberate design.

Propping himself up on one elbow, Jim brushed away some of the clinging growth with his hand, the better to examine the etchings. At first, they were but shadows, mere suggestions of lines and shapes hidden under the cover of nature. Yet, as he looked closer, cleaning off a bit moss here, tracing the edge of a lichen patch there, the rock's secrets began to reveal themselves, its true form slowly coming to light.

For a moment, he simply stared, his mind grappling with the realization. The etchings were faint, their edges softened by the passage of time, yet unmistakably the work of human hands. Lines intersected with curves in patterns that hinted at language, at meaning waiting to be unearthed from the silence of stone. As his fingers followed the paths of the ancient lines, a sense of connection flowed within him, forging a bridge that spanned the chasm of centuries.

"Captain! Ben!" Jim called out with excitement, cutting through the tranquility of the clearing.

Curiosity piqued, the two men made their way over to where Jim kneeled, where they saw his gaze fixed on something just in front of him.

"Take a look at this," he urged.

Jim brushed away more growth to reveal deep grooves carved into the stone. The carvings were unmistakable–intricate shapes, animals, and human faces, their details well preserved.

"Blimey," Ben breathed out, his eyes wide with surprise.

The clearing was littered with such stones that seemed ordinary at first glance. Yet, this discovery had hinted at a story waiting to be unveiled, urging them to delve deeper. They went around to some of the other large stones strewn around the clearing, and with gentle hands, peeled away the layers of nature's camouflage on them. Each stone they cleaned off bore the same unmistakable intricate carvings—a mosaic of symbols, animals, and faces etched into the rock with astounding precision.

Jim's fingers traced the lines of a majestic animal, its form so lifelike he half-expected it to leap off the stone. The captain, with his keen eye for detail, marveled at the symbols, their meanings lost to time yet suggestive of a complex language or system of record-keeping. Ben was drawn to the faces, each one carved with such emotion and depth that it felt like looking into the eyes of the past.

Billy rose to his feet, his eyes sweeping across the array of stones, large and small, scattered haphazardly across the clearing like the pieces of a forgotten puzzle.

"Mark me words, this here must be the remains of an old village," he said.

He studied the clearing, taking in the encroaching forest with its dense underbrush and towering trees that seemed to guard ancient secrets. Billy then addressed the men.

"Listen up, lads," his voice carrying a note of excitement. "This clearin' might be a wee part of somethin' bigger, and I'll wager me last coin there's more hidden amongst these trees. We be headin' into the forest," he ordered, pointing toward the woods. "Spread out, but keep within shoutin' distance."

The men rose from their brief respite, diving into the embracing arms of the forest that bordered the clearing, their knives, glinting as they caught scattered beams of sunlight, slicing through the stubborn undergrowth. Bella quickly joined Jim's side, her curiosity alight with the promise of discovery that lay ahead.

As they ventured deeper, the forest's grip tightened, the air growing heavy with the scent of moist earth and ancient secrets. Suddenly, the oppressive embrace of the jungle gave way to an expansive clearing, revealing a sight that halted them in their tracks. A collective gasp escaped their lips as they took in the scene before them. Their eyes beheld the remains of an ancient village, cradled by the forest itself, where time had gently softened the edges of stone structures. The ruins of homes and a towering temple, ensnared by the relentless grasp of nature, stood as silent witnesses to a time long gone, their stones strewn about like the scattered memories of those who once dwelled within. Vines clung to walls like desperate fingers, and moss painted the stones in hues of green and grey, blurring the lines between manmade and natural. In the background, the remains of the temple stood sentinel over the village, its existence almost swallowed by the voracious growth of the wilderness, its presence both solemn and imposing.

The crew explored further, their gestures and glances speaking volumes of their intrigue. They pointed out details to one another, and shared hushed exclamations of wonder. Their expressions shifted between curiosity and sheer delight, as the rough exteriors of these pirates were momentarily softened by the thrill of discovery, bringing them closer to the people who once called this village home.

Drawn to the heart of the village, Jim walked around the remains of a central plaza. He came to the edge of what appeared to be an area used for communal bonfires. At the center was a large, circular pit, deliberately crafted with stones that had been smoothed and darkened by the heat of many fires. On the ground in it was a mixture of blackened earth and ashes that had lain cold for centuries, witness to the stories shared and the bonds forged in the glow of the flames. Around this central pit, the land had been gently molded to create natural seating areas. Logs and large stones were arranged in concentric circles, offering places for people to gather, sit, and immerse themselves in the warmth and light of the fire. As Jim stepped closer, the marks of countless gatherings etched into the earth and the remnants of coals within the pit told tales of warmth, laughter, and shared joy. Jim imagined the fires that had blazed here, the faces illuminated by the dancing fire, and the stories that had filled the air, weaving through the smoke that rose to the stars. His expression was thoughtful, reflective, as if he could almost see the flicker of flames and hear the echo of laughter and conversation.

Ben made his way toward the nearest ruin. "Oh, bloody hell," he muttered to himself.

The fragmented stones sprawled before him, reminiscent of the ones they had encountered on the exposed seabed before—vast, mysterious, yet seemingly barren of the very prize they sought. With each destination that led nowhere, Ben's patience wore thinner, his obsession with finding the Dragon's Scale tearing further at his sanity. He knelt beside a particularly weathered section of wall, the stones rough and sun-warmed, bearing the scars of time and elements.

As he ran his fingers over the faint inscriptions, he couldn't help but let out a scoff, his voice barely more than a gravelly whisper against the stillness of the ruin. "More old stones, just

The Secret of the Dragon's Scale

like the damned ones before. These cursed piles of rubble better be havin' the Dragon's Scale." He took a step closer, his eyes narrowing as he surveyed the cracks and crevices of the old structure. "I'm warnin' ye," he said quietly, addressing the silent stones as though they could hear his threat, "if ye're playin' me for a fool, if ye're just another dead end . . . there'll be hell to pay. I'll tear down every stone, every blasted piece of this bloody place, 'til there be nothin' left but dust!"

Bella, her heart alight with curiosity, stepped carefully through the remnants of the village, her eyes wide with wonder and reverence. Following closely in Jim's footsteps, she moved with a grace that belied her excitement, her movements deliberate yet filled with an eagerness that seemed to draw her toward each new discovery. Her expression was one of constant marvel; it was as though every stone and every crumbling wall whispered secrets of the past directly to her, and she was intent on listening. Her eyes danced over the intricate carvings on the walls of what might have once been homes, trying to imagine the lives of those who dwelled within. She moved from one point of interest to another, sometimes crouching to get a closer look at the ground, where shards of pottery lay scattered.

Billy, meanwhile, stood still for a moment, taking in the panoramic view of the village before making his way toward the temple. His movements were measured, each step taken with a sense of purpose. The lines of his face were drawn tight, not just with curiosity, but with an evident respect for the craftsmanship and spirituality that the temple represented. As he moved, his eyes scanned the intricate carvings on the walls, a silent testament to the beliefs and traditions of these people.

Silhouetted against the backdrop of the ancient temple's imposing structure, Billy turned to see where Jim, Bella, and Ben were scattered, each lost in their own exploration of the ruins.

"Jim! Bella! Ben! Over here!" his voice boomed across the clearing, reverberating off the stone structures, beckoning them to come. "Feast yer eyes on this," Billy said, as he gestured toward the crumbling edifice.

With heads tilted skyward, they marveled at the imposing structure, tracing its lines with their eyes, taking in the grandeur of its architecture and the mystery that shrouded it. Bella stepped closer to the temple, catching a glimpse of something hidden beneath the dense overgrowth—a hint of intricate carvings on the stone surface. A soft gasp escaped from her lips, the thrill of discovery igniting a spark in her curious spirit. She gently pushed aside the hanging vines, and the tangled thicket gave way under her careful touch, revealing the exquisite craftsmanship of the carvings beneath. Her eyes swept across the details that were revealed—figures entwined in what could be an ancient dance, mythical creatures ready to spring to life, and symbols whose meanings were lost to time.

Noticing Bella's discoveries, Billy stepped closer, his hands reaching out to the cold, damp stones. With a gentle yet firm touch, he began to clear away the layers of growth that had made the temple's walls their home. The vines resisted at first, but soon gave way to reveal more of the intricate carvings beneath—a tapestry of sculpture that spoke of gods and monsters, of heroes and warriors, and the cycles of life and death. Following Billy's lead, Jim and Ben worked to brush away more growth with their hands as well as by carefully scraping it with their knives, each stroke unveiling more of the temple's hidden mysteries.

As the late afternoon sun filtered through the dense canopy of the forest, casting a mesmerizing dance of light and shadow upon the ancient ruins, the temple gradually revealed more of its secrets. The carvings became more visible, depicting scenes of celestial alignments, wild animals, sacrificial rituals, and divine entities, each weaving tales of the people who once revered this sacred ground. The symbols of some unknown language emerged as well—complex, mysterious, and incomprehensible.

"Do ye think this'll tell us anythin' 'bout the Dragon's Scale?" Jim asked.

"Can't rightly say yet," Billy responded. "But in some way, for some reason or 'nother, we've been guided here, pushed by fate's own hand, and not without purpose."

Driven by an inexplicable urge to peer into its mysteries, Billy worked to clear away more of the dense vines and moss that had claimed the ancient temple as their own, until a breathtaking scene began to stir to life beneath his touch. Each layer peeled back was like turning the pages of a sacred tome, revealing the stories of a civilization that danced with the divine. Under Billy's persistent efforts, the dense vegetation was reluctantly giving way when finally, emerging from its verdant shroud, a carving began to take shape—so majestic and profound that it briefly stole the breath from his lungs.

As more and more of the carving was revealed, Billy's eyes widened, a spark of wonder igniting within them. First, the body of a snake, long and sinuous, curved gracefully across the expanse of the wall, etched with scales so finely rendered they seemed to shimmer in the sunlight that filtered through the canopy above. The body then transitioned seamlessly into the resplendent feathers of a bird that fanned out in a vibrant display of plumage. The colors, though faded with time, still hinted at the dazzling greens, blues, and reds that once adorned this divine figure. The bird's wings, carved with meticulous attention to detail, unfolded with a grace that gave the illusion of movement, as if at any moment it might leap from the stone and ascend toward the heavens. Billy's gaze was then drawn to the face, a serene countenance that bore the features of both man and deity. The eyes, deep-set within the carving, beheld a wisdom that transcended time, and stared out at the world with a tranquil authority. A hint of a forked tongue teased at the lips, adding an enigmatic, almost mischievous intrigue to the creature's expression.

Marveling at the chiseled figure, Billy whispered aloud with a mix of awe and incredulity, "Where the serpent dons a feathered guise."

The phrase, once a cryptic riddle tangled in the shadows of his mind, now flared to life, resonating with a clarity that rang through the dense air of the forest. His hands, dirt-streaked from unearthing the figure, trembled as he traced the delicate transition between serpent and bird on the stone.

Drawn by the sound of Billy's voice trembling with awe, and the wonder etched on his face, Ben, Jim, and Bella hurried to his side, their eyes tracing his line of sight to the carving that had been revealed among the vines and moss. Ben and Jim leaned in, their expressions a mixture of curiosity and confusion. The beauty of the carving was undeniable, but its significance eluded them, leaving them to exchange puzzled glances. Bella stepped forward, her eyes widening as the details of the figure came into focus. A gasp escaped her lips, a sound of pure astonishment that drew the attention of her companions.

"That must be Quetzalcoatl!" she said, her voice laced with wonder and reverence. "The Feathered Serpent!"

Ben and Jim's expressions shifted from bewilderment to a deep curiosity at her unexpected recognition of the figure.

"Oh, Father loved to learn about the religions of the natives," Bella explained, her eyes not leaving the carving. "He told me about Quetzalcoatl, a god that is both a quetzal bird and a snake, symbolizing the unity of Earth and the heavens." Her companions listened, captivated by her words, as she shared the fragments of knowledge passed down by the priest.

Time wore on, and the evening sky, painted in deepening hues of blue and purple, was signaling the end of the day's light over the ancient ruins. Billy, his mind still grappling with the revelation of the feathered serpent, suddenly became aware of the encroaching shadows, their silent approach unnoticed during the busyness of the day's exploration. He blinked, looking around at the sprawling ruins that were quickly becoming less visible in the fading light.

"Alright, men!" he bellowed across the ruins to his crew. "Fetch the provisions from by the river. We be settlin' here for the night."

Twilight was enveloping the ancient village, and small campfires began to glow in the shadow of the temple. The crew settled around them, and the ruins became bathed in the warm light of the flames. The night air was filled with the sounds of crackling wood, soft conversations, and the occasional laughter. Logs served as makeshift seats, drawing the crew into a circle of light within the darkness of the forest. Billy, along with Ben, Jim, and Bella, sat around their own fire, the flickering flames casting dancing shadows on their faces.

Billy poked at the fire with a stick, sending sparks swirling into the night. His face, glowing softly, bore a look of contemplation as the conversation shifted toward the ethereal voices that had been haunting them ever since they had stood before the stone that sings to the sky.

"Ye know, mates," Billy began, his voice carrying the timbre of the sea, "I've sailed the seven seas, braved storms that'd turn yer hair white, and faced down beasts that dwell in the deep. This talk of spirits and voices on the wind . . . it doesn't sit right with me." He shifted on his log, the firelight playing across his rugged features. "I'm not one to dismiss the mysteries of this world lightly—the sea has taught me there be more beneath the surface than the eye can see. But spirits? That's a stretch o' the imagination I not be willin' to make."

Billy paused, his gaze shifting from the fire to his shipmates, seeking to gauge their reactions. "We've heard strange things, aye. And there be happenin's to us that'd make even the most steadfast heart quiver. But to say they be the doin's of spirits . . . Well, I've yet to see a ghost hoist a sail or chart a course through starless nights."

He chuckled softly, a sound more of contemplation than amusement. "The sea teaches us to look beyond the horizon, to seek that which is real among the waves and stars. Whatever's happenin' here, I reckon there's an explanation as real as the wood beneath our feet or the sails above our heads."

Bella, who had been listening intently to Billy's skepticism and his wrestling with uncertainty, spoke up, her voice carrying a serene yet confident tone, channeling the wisdom imparted to her by the priest's teachings. "Father taught me that the world is full of mysteries—mysteries that even the most devout or rational mind may never fully understand." She paused, gathering her thoughts. "He used to say that God's creation is vast and intricate, beyond the bounds of our understanding. There are forces at work, seen and unseen, that guide the ebb and flow of all things."

She looked at the fire, her eyes reflecting the dance of flames, her expression thoughtful. "The voices we've heard, the feelings we've experienced on this journey . . . they might well be part of those mysteries. Just because we can't explain them, doesn't mean they're not real or that they don't have meaning." Her voice took on a depth, echoing the reverence with which Father Ignatius spoke of the divine. "It's hard to know what the spirits want or why they choose to speak to us. Perhaps they're guardians of this place, or messengers from beyond, trying to tell us something important for our journey."

Billy found himself in the throes of an internal turmoil, the likes of which he'd never experienced in all his years at sea. He wrestled with the profound discomfort of confronting an unfamiliar realm that defied the rationality upon which he had always prided himself. Voices, as clear as the tolling of a ship's bell in the fog, had spoken to him, urging him toward a land where myths breathed and walked. And yet, despite the guiding star of those voices, he stood at a crossroads between belief and skepticism, unable to step fully onto either path.

He rebelled against the notion of spirits. To him, spirits belonged in the tales spun by old seafarers under the glow of lantern light, not as beacons guiding his own journey. How could he, a man of reason, who had always prided himself on steering clear of superstitions, now embrace such a mystical explanation?

The thought was as alien to him as the idea of land without water, a ship without a compass. And yet, the evidence revealed by the voyage itself—the inexplicable pull toward this place, the alignment of circumstances that defied mere coincidence—loomed large in his thoughts. It was as if an unseen hand had charted their course, guiding them through the mists of uncertainty to this very moment. How could he deny the presence of something beyond his understanding, when it had led them so unerringly? Accepting the guidance of spirits meant acknowledging a world far more vast and mysterious than his maritime maps had ever hinted at. It meant admitting that the horizon he'd always looked to might extend beyond the physical realm, into the dominion of mysticism and the supernatural. Every fiber of his being resisted this surrender to the inexplicable, and yet, the lure of the mystery called to him, a siren song that promised revelations beyond the reach of his maps and charts.

A hush fell upon the four as they lost themselves in contemplation and wonder. The other men, their faces softly illuminated by the gentle glow of campfires, spoke in subdued tones, their laughter a quiet echo in the vastness of the night. In this serene atmosphere, Bella now felt the need for some music and reached for her lute, a companion that had become an extension of her soul on this journey. She tenderly cradled the lute in her arms, her fingers poised to bridge the silence with melody. And as her fingers hovered over the strings, suddenly, the hauntingly beautiful music of the stone that sings to the sky filled her consciousness, a sound that had captivated her beyond words, and which began to flow effortlessly from the strings.

This ethereal music surged through her, demanding expression. Compelled by this inner calling, Bella allowed the melody to guide her fingers, each note a thread in the fabric of a forgotten dream. So with a deep breath, Bella allowed her fingers to dance upon the strings. The sound that emerged was pure and resonant, weaving through the camp with the tenderness of a lover's whisper, yet carrying the weight of untold ages within its song.

Suddenly, the night itself responded. A faint, rhythmic beat came to their ears, surrounding the camp with a presence as ancient as the stars. Drums, their sound barely more than a ghostly thread weaving through the air, pulsed in harmony with Bella's music, a spectral accompaniment that seemed to emerge from the earth beneath their feet.

Surprise etched itself deeply on Bella's face as she abruptly stopped playing, her fingers freezing mid-note. A hush fell over the camp. The men ceased their quiet chatter, eyes widened in wonder, and heads turned; a collective stillness seized them as they looked around, searching the shadows for the source of the mysterious drumbeats.

And as abruptly as they had appeared, the drums fell silent, leaving an echo of their presence hanging in the air like a whispered secret, and a silence that was thick with confusion and unanswered questions.

In the quiet that enveloped the camp after the drums faded, a shared look of collective bewilderment swept over the faces of the men gathered around the flickering campfires. There was a silent exchange of glances, wide eyes meeting wide eyes, as if each person was silently asking the others, "Did you hear that too?" But soon, with the sound, and their confusion, ebbing, thinking they were just hearing things, the men slowly returned to their hushed conversations, their expressions softening as brows relaxed and mouths closed.

Bella's attention returned to her lute, caressing the strings into song once more. But then, like the mysterious drums that had mystified them just moments ago, the air became filled with the faint echoes of joyous laughter. It was light and ephemeral, as though a group of unseen revelers had fleetingly joined the gathering, sharing in a moment of pure delight. The laughter seemed to come from everywhere and nowhere, enveloping the camp in an aura of jubilation and festivity.

The Secret of the Dragon's Scale

Instantly, Bella's fingers stilled on the lute, and a collective gasp rippled through the group. Their eyes, round and gleaming in the flickering firelight, darted from one face to another, then back to the darkness beyond the flames. The laughter, so vividly real, filled them with surprise, and a touch of fear. And again, as with the sound of the drums, the laughter faded as gently as it had arrived.

It was then that the mystical force compelled Bella to continue playing, its call irresistible. The music that emerged under this enchantment was breathtaking in its joyousness and beauty, as though the lute itself was alive, singing its own songs of joy and celebration.

Just then, like a mighty beast awakening, a sudden thunderous roar shattered the serenity!

From the depths of the ancient fire pit—its coals and ashes cold for centuries—an enormous bonfire exploded into vibrant life with such ferocity and magnificence it was as though the very earth sought to challenge the heavens! The fire surged skyward in a spectacular display of raw power and mesmerizing beauty, its flames dancing with wild abandon, painting the dark canvas of the sky with strokes of brilliant gold and deep amber, of fierce crimson and blazing orange! Sparks flew like stars being birthed, spiraling into the cool embrace of the night! The trembling whoosh of the flames reached a dramatic crescendo of crackles, pops, and hisses that reverberated off the ancient stones and resonated through the ruins!

Bella's scream pierced the night, a sharp note of terror that mirrored the shockwave of astonishment rippling through the clearing! Her lute fell silent, her fingers frozen in shock and freight as the inferno roared to life before her eyes!

"What in bloody hell!?" Billy yelled out as the eruption of the flames threw him off his log, landing with a thud on the earth.

Around the campsite, the men were thrown into disarray; some tumbled from their makeshift seats of logs and rocks in a desperate scramble to get away, their movements clumsy and panicked. Others remained petrified, riveted by the terrifying display unfolding in the pit.

Bella, clutching her lute tightly against her chest, could only stare in stunned silence at the enormous fire. The others as well, recovering slowly from their initial shock, found no words to express their astonishment and fear. With eyes wide and hearts pounding a frantic rhythm, everyone just stared in disbelief at the spectacle before them.

As the fire settled into a steady, captivating burn, its flames casting a gentle, flickering light over the clearing, the calm of the moment was interrupted by the return of the sound of beating drums, accompanied by a chorus of festive laughter, all swirling around the crew of the Siren's Call. The sounds started softly, almost imperceptibly, gradually swelling in volume and filling the air with a symphony of celebration that seemed to emanate from the shadows dancing at the edge of the firelight. The silence of the night was awakened by these sounds now reverberating throughout the ruins—a confluence of deep sonorous beats layered with vibrant, pulsating rhythms, each note chasing the other with frenetic urgency! And woven through these drumbeats was a cascade of laughter that floated on the air, resonating with the energy of joy and jubilation! This laughter, ethereal and filled with warmth, spoke directly to the soul, inviting all who heard it to join in the unseen revelries.

It was in this heart of the ancient village, where the rhythmic beating of drums and the jubilant peals of laughter now echoed, that figures began to materialize from the ether, encircling the bonfire where moments before only shadows played; they glowed with a soft, golden light emanating from within, casting their spectral forms in a radiant luminescence. As they appeared, they were already entwined in a rhapsody of music, dance, laughter, and song.

These were the spirits of the ancients, those who had once walked these lands and left their mark upon the stones, called back to the realm of the living to dance once more.

The Secret of the Dragon's Scale

The sight was as mesmerizing as it was terrifying. Bella's heart raced, a gasp of breath catching in her throat as she watched the spirits dance, her eyes sparkling with tears of marvel and fright, reflecting the flickering flames and spectral apparitions. Jim found himself grappling with a sense of awe that bordered on the spiritual. A smile tugged at his lips, a reaction born of the sheer incredulity of the situation. His body trembled slightly from the overwhelming surge of fear, astonishment, and fascination that gripped him. Ben, staring in wonder, felt a chill run down his spine. His obsession with uncovering the mythical Dragon's Scale had already drawn him deep into a labyrinth of fevered dreams and waking nightmares, but the surreal sight of the spirits dancing around the bonfire only served to plunged him further into the depths of his own unraveling psyche. Billy Bones, the hardened pirate captain who had fought many a fierce battle and navigated uncharted waters with nothing but a compass and his wits, found himself adrift in a sea of utter confusion. His eyes widened in sheer disbelief at the ghostly spectacle, their spectral dance reflecting in his gaze. He blinked rapidly, clinging to the hope that this vision was nothing more than a trick of the mind, a hallucination conjured by the fatigue of their journey. And the other men, with faces pale and lips parted, looked at each other, exchanging glances that silently conveyed their shared stupefaction. Some crossed themselves, whispering prayers under their breath, while others simply stared, dumbstruck and unable to articulate their feelings. The mystifying sight of dancing spirits left them in a state of bewilderment that rendered words useless, their voices silenced by the sheer impossibility of the scene.

Under the cloak of night, the ruins of the ancient village were alight with an ethereal glow, as the spirits of the ancients reveled in a timeless celebration. The bonfire at the heart of their festivity crackled and danced, casting shadows and illuminations that brought the forgotten stones to life. Around this fiery heart, the spirits twirled and hopped and swayed to music and song, their bodies shimmering with translucent hues, weaving patterns of joy and community in the cool night air.

And as if attuned to some secret whisper carried on the night breeze, the spirits seemed to know visitors would be there. Some of them paused in their merriment and walked closer, stepping fluidly and gracefully toward Bella and the men, their shimmering forms, with their soft inner light, casting an otherworldly glow that illuminated the path before them. Their eyes sparkled with the light of stars, yet their gaze was warm, enveloping the crew in a comfort that spoke of welcome and friendship. With smiles gracing their lips, their hands reached out with a tender openness, beckoning the visitors to join in the celebration.

One by one, led by the spirits' infectious exuberance, the crew of the Siren's Call stepped forward, their trepidation melting away under the warmth of the spirits' smiles. And as the men surrendered to the rhythm of the music, their bodies began to move in harmony with the spirits, their earlier terror forgotten amidst the revelry.

Jim and Ben found themselves in a moment suspended between their fears of the unknown and the welcoming presence of the specters before them. As the spirits extended their hands in invitation, a transformation began to unfold within the two men, reminiscent of a profound return to the innocence of childhood. Moving among these ghostly beings, an infectious energy began to fill them, a warmth that seeped into their very bones and kindled a lightness in their hearts. The initial nervousness that had clouded their faces gave way to smiles, broad and unguarded, as they found themselves swept up in the festive atmosphere around the fire. Laughter, light and liberating, bubbled up from within, and soon they were mimicking the dance steps of the spirits with joy and abandon.

Bella's eyes sparkled with a childlike wonder, yet her brow furrowed ever so slightly, betraying a hint of apprehension. But then, as the spirits' hands reached out to her, their smiles wide and genuine, she too felt the warmth radiating from them, enveloping her in an undeniable sense of happiness and friendliness, dissolving her fears like mist under the morning sun. Rising to her feet and stepping toward the spirits, she felt the yearning to share in the music, and instinctively reached back to grab her lute. She now found herself at the heart of the celebration, a radiant figure illuminated by the soft, ethereal glow of the spirits that danced around her.

The festivities, alive with laughter and song, resonated within her, awakening a deep, jubilant energy that she could scarcely contain. With a beaming smile lighting up her face, Bella cradled her lute; and as if guided by the hands of fate, her fingers began to dance across the strings, conjuring a melody so profound it seemed to have always existed within her, waiting for this very moment to be born—the beautiful, enchanting music of the stone that sings to the sky flowed forth again, a tune that captured the beauty of the stars and the boundless expanse of the heavens. As Bella played, she began to sway, her body moving instinctively to the rhythm of her music and the primal beat of drums that resonated from the bosom of the earth. Her feet responded with a joyful eagerness, tapping and gliding across the ground in perfect harmony with the notes that flowed from the strings beneath her fingers. The spirits danced with her, their luminous forms weaving around her, their faces alight with smiles, their eyes shining with an appreciation that needed no words. Together, they celebrated beneath the canopy of the forest, a symphony of light and shadow, music and song, spirit and flesh.

But spirits, entities Billy had always dismissed as mere fairy tales and superstition, were now in the midst of revelry before his eyes, their figures aglow with an otherworldly aura that defied all reason. As these apparitions continued their dance, their movements a hypnotic blend of light and shadow, Billy's astonishment and fear slowly gave way to a grudging sense of wonder. Despite himself, despite the terror that gnawed at the edges of his mind, he could not deny the beauty and reality of what he was witnessing. In this moment, caught between the solid ground of certainty and a realm he had never dared to imagine, the steadfast captain was forced to acknowledge that the world was far more mysterious and magical than he had ever allowed himself to believe.

As Billy watched the celebration, the spirits, with a grace that transcended the earthly realm, reached out to him, their movements gentle and coaxing. Billy stood, his gaze locked on the extended hands, creating a bridge across the chasm of centuries. Their hands moved in silent invitation, palms upturned, fingers softly curling in a universal gesture of welcome. With gentle nods of encouragement, their expressions soft and friendly, they beckoned him to be part of their shared joy and timeless jubilation.

In the face of such warmth and friendliness, a gentle awakening in Billy's heart began to unfold. A smile, hesitant at first, then growing in confidence and brightness, broke through the fear and doubt. And with the emergence of that smile, the last vestiges of Billy's apprehensions dissolved into the night air. The skepticism that had been as much a part of him as his own flesh and blood started to wane, eroded by the undeniable reality of the spectacle before him.

So around the bonfire, beneath the watchful gaze of the stars, Billy danced. He danced with the living and the dead, his feet finding the beat of drums that echoed from both the present and the past. Laughter, his own and that of beings whose existence he had once denied, filled the air, intertwining with the crackle of the fire and the whispers of the wind. In those hours, Billy's world expanded, his heart opening to possibilities that stretched beyond the horizon of his former beliefs. He embraced the unknown, danced with the spirits, and listened to the songs of the people.

The night wove its dark tapestry across the sky, the stars tracing elegant arcs through the heavens; and underneath, Bella and the men danced and laughed away the hours. But as the first hints of dawn began to paint the horizon with strokes of pink and orange, the spirits, their forms becoming mere whisps under the growing light, receded into the ether from whence they came. The laughter that had filled the air, echoing off the stone ruins, dwindled into silence, leaving behind only the lingering warmth of shared happiness. The drums, whose beats had pulsed like the heart of the earth, faded away as well, their rhythm lingering in the souls of the crew.

Finally, the bonfire, which had been the heart of the night's enchantment, dimmed. Its flames, which had leaped toward the stars in defiance of the night, now retreated back to the spirit world along with the ancients who had danced around it, its fading embers whispering stories heard only by the stones that stood as silent witnesses to the night's magic.

A soft blanket of exhaustion eventually wrapped itself around the crew of the Siren's Call, a testament to a night spent in merriment and festivity. And so, they lay themselves upon the earth, scattered around the fire pit that again sat as cold and dormant as it had for centuries. Heads rested upon logs, transformed into reluctant pillows, as one by one, they surrendered to sleep. Their faces, illuminated by the gentle kiss of first light, bore smiles of contentment as they drifted off.

The sun soon crested the horizon, and the world around them was awakened by the light of day. Birds took up the melody left by the drums; leaves rustled, stirred by a gentle wind, and monkeys chattered in the canopies. Nestled within this gentle hum of life, the ruins of the ancient village cradled the slumbering adventurers. It was a scene of profound serenity, where the boundaries between the past and the present, the spiritual and the mortal, were blurred into insignificance. Here, under the watchful eyes of the forest, the men and Bella found rest, their dreams undoubtedly filled with images of dragons, ancient spirits, and the magic of the quest that lay ahead.

The morning continued to unfold and the early rays of the sun were gently warming the ruins, weaving through the cracks and crevices of the stones, casting a soft, golden light over the sleeping group. The men began to stir, awakening to the gentle caress of an otherworldly presence that lingered in the morning air. A soft breeze brushed their skin, as if tender hands from beyond were bidding them farewell.

Billy was one of the first to wake, his seasoned instincts attuned to the rhythms of the day, even in this unfamiliar land. A soft grunt escaped him as he shifted, the cold ground beneath offering a stark reminder of the night's merriment. Jim awakened to the slivers of sunlight painting patterns of light and shadow on the ground beside him. For a moment, he lay still, absorbing the serene beauty of the morning, his mind replaying the sounds and sights of the previous night's revelry with spirits long gone. Ben, usually the first to rise at sea, lay sprawled with one arm flung over his eyes, shielding them from the encroaching daylight. Nearby, Bella, whose youthful energy and curiosity often kept her awake into the early hours, slept peacefully, a slight smile playing on her lips as if she were dreaming of music and joyousness.

Rising to his feet, Jim stretched, feeling the readiness and anticipation for the day's exploration settle into his bones. The first thing to fill his senses as he stood was the sight of his crewmates, their bodies slowly stirring to life amidst the ancient village ruins that had been their refuge and witness to the night's ethereal encounters. A sense of the surreal washed over him as he absorbed the scene. The vividness of their shared experience the night before—the music, the dance, the laughter, the communion with spirits of people long departed—seemed too fantastical in the harsh light of day.

He wandered a few steps away from the campsite, his eyes tracing the contours of the ruins, touching the weathered stone with a reverence that belied his inner confusion. The textures under his fingertips, along with the warmth of the rock heated by the sun, grounded him in the reality of the moment. Yet, as tangible as the stones were, so too was the memory of the

The Secret of the Dragon's Scale

festivities beneath the canopy of stars, of the feeling of being part of something far greater than themselves.

Jim's meandering found him back at the temple, its massive structure standing defiantly against the ravages of time. Venturing closer, his gaze fell upon an entrance in the wall, gaping mysteriously open. Jim stood transfixed, his eyes wide with astonishment, for he vividly recalled circling the temple's imposing perimeter with his companions, and not one of them had come across any kind of opening in the wall.

"Captain! Ben! Bella!" Jim called out. His voice, filled with excitement, cut through the tranquil silence of the morning, reverberating off the stones and sending a flock of startled birds flapping into the air.

At the sound of their names called out with such fervor, the captain and Ben jerked fully awake, their senses heightened. Turning in Jim's direction, they saw he was quite animated and pointing toward the temple.

"Over here! Ye must be seein' this!" Jim urged.

Stirred from her dreams by the commotion, Bella blinked her eyes open to see Jim urgently beckoning. Her curiosity piqued, she swiftly rose to her feet, brushing away bits of earth and leaves from her clothes, and joined Billy and Ben as they made their way over to where Jim was standing. As they approached, Jim stepped aside, revealing the reason for his excitement—a grand and unmistakable entrance into the temple.

"Look," Jim said simply, his voice now barely above a whisper.

There, before them, the entrance stood open. Framed by towering columns and adorned with intricate carvings that danced in the shifting light, the majestic portal seemed to beckon them into its depths, a silent promise of untold mysteries and ancient secrets waiting within.

Billy, Ben, and Bella exchanged incredulous glances. Their eyes widened as they processed the sight before them, a mix of curiosity and surprise painting their faces. The impossibility of the situation unfolded between them—this opening, so conspicuously absent just a day ago, now presented itself as though it had always been there, waiting for the right moment to reveal itself.

"It wasn't there yesterday, was it?" Bella asked, her voice low, almost as if she was afraid to disturb the sanctity of the temple.

"No, I'm sure it not be," Ben replied, his mind racing to recall any possible way they could have overlooked it.

The air was thick with the musk of ancient stone and forgotten times as the four of them stood at the threshold of the temple. A shudder coursed through them, as though the temple was reaching out to them, whispering in a language felt rather than heard. They each sensed the same inexplicable pull toward the darkness; it was a strange, almost supernatural compulsion to go inside that wound its way around their hearts, drawing them inexorably into the temple's grasp.

Ben quickly grabbed some sticks and dry grass from the ground nearby. With a few strikes of his flint, he brought a torch to life, its flame casting a warm, golden glow that pushed back the darkness, if only by a few feet. Armed with their makeshift torch, the group took their first tentative steps into the temple.

Behind them, standing back and watching from outside, the other men grouped together, their expressions a mix of curiosity and apprehension.

The air inside was cool and still, untouched by time, and the faint scent of earth and mold filled their nostrils. The walls, illuminated by the flickering torchlight, were covered in intricate carvings and hieroglyphs that spoke of an ancient civilization and its long-forgotten gods.

With the darkness masking any hint of what lay ahead, the narrow passageway opened up into a vast chamber, so abruptly that they nearly stumbled into it. The mustiness of stale air, damp earth, and ancient stone, surrounded them, a tangible reminder of the centuries that had passed since the temple's last use. The high vaulted ceilings were lost in the shadows far beyond the reach of their solitary torch. The scant light, though, revealed a room teeming with pillars that rose like the trunks of ancient trees, supporting the unseen canopy above. In the flicker of the flame, the walls came alive with yet more carvings, more elaborate and detailed than those in the passageway. Scenes of grand processions, sacred offerings, and celebrations of victory, encircled them; it was as if they had stepped into a storybook, where every wall was a page telling of epic legends and mythic tales.

In the profound quiet of the chamber, Ben took the lead, his movements deliberate and careful as he extended the torch further from his body. The small circle of light it cast danced eagerly against the walls, revealing a world that had been shrouded in darkness for so long. His hand guided the torch in a sweeping motion, the shadows retreating before the advancing glow, creating a play of light and darkness that hinted at secrets lurking just out of sight. His heart raced with the thrill of discovery, each step forward fueled by the hope of uncovering something—anything—that might lead them closer to the Dragon's Scale.

"Ye think the Dragon's Scale be in here? Ye think maybe the spirits be wantin' us to find it in here?" Ben asked the others as he peered through the shadows.

His eyes swept over more elaborately carved depictions of mythical scenes—warriors brandishing spears against fearsome beasts, venerable sages deep in contemplation, and majestic birds soaring through skies ablaze with stars. Each image told a fragment of a story lost to time, and Ben couldn't help but wonder if any of these tales held any clues to their quest. Wandering further, his steps echoing in the silence, it felt as though the chamber itself was listening with rapt attention, observing their exploration with unseen eyes. He paused occasionally, lifting his torch to illuminate the lofty vaults of the chamber or to examine a particularly intriguing relief more closely.

Then, quite suddenly, the torchlight fell upon a figure that arrested his attention completely! He gasped and jumped back! His gaze fell in wonder upon the face of a majestic statue of Quetzalcoatl, emerging into view as though conjured by the light itself.

The moment was breathtaking as the transition from shadow to light unveiled the statue in all its intricate splendor! Carved from solid shimmering jade that seemed to absorb and reflect the light all at once, it towered over them with an imposing yet serene presence. The god was depicted in a dynamic pose, its serpentine body coiled, as if ready to spring into motion at any moment. Its scales were meticulously detailed, each one a testament to the artisan's skill and reverence for the deity. Feathers cascaded down its back, each carved with such precision that they appeared almost soft, fluttering in the imaginary breeze of the sacred chamber. Above them, the statue's face held a regal calmness, eyes closed in divine contemplation, lips parted in silent decree.

The four of them stood transfixed, their gazes locked on the dimly lit figure of the ancient god. The shadows cast by the torch made the deity's visage seem to shift subtly, imbuing the statue with a lifelike presence that was both awe-inspiring and slightly unnerving, as though it might awaken at any moment, the eternal guardian of the temple stirring to life before their very eyes.

The late morning sun was climbing higher, and at that moment came to align itself with precision through small holes and crevices crafted into the temple's aged edifice. This celestial alignment, perhaps deliberate, perhaps a serendipitous occurrence across centuries, began to cast beams of light into the darkened chamber. The effect was nothing short of magical, transforming the stone ceiling into a canvas where light painted a vivid imitation of a night sky filled with stars.

Their eyes were irresistibly drawn to the celestial wonder unfurling above. Starlike beams of light pierced through the ancient architecture, scattering across the vaulted ceiling in breathtaking patterns that mimicked constellations. It was as though the artisans of a forgotten age had seized the essence of the night sky itself and meticulously etched it into the stone, waiting for the right moment to reveal this hidden marvel to those who dared to venture into the temple's depths.

Billy stepped back to take in more of the starry panorama. As he did so, he became aware of other light coming from below. He realized light was illuminating the chamber not just from the ceiling, but also from beneath their feet. Glancing down, his eyes widened in wonder, and he quickly motioned for his friends to do the same.

"Stand back," he urged. As they did, what they saw was a breathtaking reflection of the heavens underfoot. In the center of the chamber was a large mosaic inlaid into the floor of black obsidian glass, interspersed with tiles of turquoise. This natural volcanic glass is known for its smooth, reflective surface; and the beautifully polished obsidian, laid meticulously across the chamber's floor, formed an exquisite mirror, becoming the canvas upon which a celestial spectacle was reborn. As sunlight streamed through the holes in the ceiling and met the obsidian, it created a luminous display that mirrored the star pattern overhead.

The thin pencils of sunlight piercing the darkness of the chamber also lit up the particles of dust that danced in the air. The dust scattered the light, casting scintillating reflections on the obsidian surface that mimicked the effect of stars twinkling in the night. The sight was hypnotic. The floor now seemed less solid, more akin to a liquid mirror that held within it the reflected glory of the heavens on the surface of a tranquil, nocturnal sea. As they stood upon the mesmerizing mosaic, a profound sense of awe washed over them. They felt as though they were not standing on solid ground, but were wading through celestial waters, walking among the stars themselves.

In the stillness of the ancient chamber, Billy stood captivated by the play of light reflecting off the obsidian floor, creating the illusion of a celestial guide unfolding at his feet. The shimmering display sparked a memory, a recollection of the woman's words in the village tavern, her voice weaving images as vivid and entrancing as the scene before him. Her tale, he thought then just charming folklore, now resonated with him on a profound level, transforming into a vivid reality under his very feet.

"When the moon is round and full, that's when we cast our nets into the glittering sea. That is our Moonlit Harvest," she had recounted, weaving not just a story but a vibrant painting made of words, of villagers stepping into a nighttime sea, its inky expanse a canvas for the shining stars above, where the boundary between earth and cosmos blurred.

Billy's heart quickened as the realization dawned on him—this could not be mere coincidence.

"Our people," she had said, "stepping into the moon-kissed sea, cast their nets under a canopy of twinkling stars. The waters, quiet as a hushed whisper, mirror the sky above, makin' it seem like we're walkin' among those stars."

The woman's words, that had been just lore of village tradition, now seemed imbued with prophetic significance, painting a picture that aligned too closely with the sight before them in the temple to be ignored.

Billy then remembered the woman ending her tale with, "But the real magic isn't in the harvest itself, it's up there, hidden among the stars. They speak to us, whisperin' secrets, tellin' where the fish are plenty, guidin' our nets. We dance with the sea under a sky ablaze with stars, where the secrets of the heavens are etched in the constellations above, leadin' us to the bounty we seek."

He pondered the idea that perhaps, like the villagers who trusted the stars to lead them to bountiful harvests, they too were meant to follow the guiding light of the heavens to uncover the treasures that awaited them.

He shared his revelation with the other three. Perhaps it was a clue, a celestial signpost, indicating the direction they should head next. Together, they knelt down and pored over the mosaic, tracing the patterns of stars and constellations, seeking any signs, any secrets, that might lead them to the Dragon's Scale.

Jim's attention was soon drawn to the pattern of turquoise under their knees, where the vibrant blue-green hues danced upon the stark blackness of the obsidian. In the theater of Jim's imagination, the obsidian, dark and lustrous, transformed into a boundless sea, cradling the turquoise shapes that hinted at distant lands and hidden shores.

"This . . . this not just be decoration," he thought, the realization dawning on him with the force of a tidal wave. "The glass, black as the deepest night sea, and the turquoise, marking out land surrounded by this darkness . . . It's a map. Of course! It's a map!"

Jim's eyes widened in excitement as the pieces of the puzzle fell into place, an epiphany illuminating his face. He turned to the others, barely containing his excitement.

"Hey, are ye seein' this? This . . . all these stones. It's a map!" Jim exclaimed, his voice echoing slightly in the spacious chamber.

Billy looked up, curiosity piqued. "A map, Jim? How so?"

"The turquoise must mark specific locations, places of importance. The black be water around them. And the constellations—I'm guessin' they be showin' times, seasons maybe, when these places must be visited or when they reveal their secrets," Jim mused, as the puzzle came together in his mind.

Bella, intrigued, leaned in closer. "You mean the green stones could be land and the black is, what . . . the ocean?"

"Aye!" Jim exclaimed. Pointing to the scintillating reflections in the obsidian, he added, "So the stars around them, they must be guidin' us, showin' us the way!"

Billy took a moment, leaning back to absorb as much of the mosaic sprawled beneath them as he could in the dim light. His experienced eyes, accustomed to deciphering the cryptic symbols and lines of countless maps and charts, began to see what Jim had seen. Turning to the others, a smile tugging at the corners of his face, Billy spoke, his voice steady and sure.

"Jim's hit upon the truth." A spark of youthful excitement came to his eyes. "We've been given a gift, mates. A gift from the past that could lead us to the prize we seek. We'll follow this starlit path laid out before us, uncover its meanin', and see where it leads."

"But a map of what? Where?" Ben asked insistently.

Billy paused, his gaze lingering on the mosaic. "Aye, that be the next question," he pondered, a thoughtful frown creasing his brow, not sure yet how they would figure that out.

As they knelt there, contemplating the mysteries laid out before them, the sun continued its inexorable march across the sky. Its rays, which had been perfectly aligned with the openings in the temple's ancient stones, began to shift, changing the pattern of light that illuminated the chamber. Slowly, the vivid starlight scene created by the sun's alignment started to fade, the constellations becoming less distinct, their guidance waning as the stars began to flicker back into darkness.

"Make haste!" Billy implored. "We must be rememberin' as much of this as we can!" Billy's voice carried a note of urgency, tinged with the frustration of losing their ephemeral guide to the shifting sunlight.

As the light faded and the weight of losing their crucial guide pressed heavily on them, Bella's eyes lit up with inspiration. Without hesitation, she scooped up a nearby loose flat stone from the chamber floor. Then, grasping a burnt stick left from Ben's torch, smoldering and blackened at the tip, she knelt beside the mosaic.

The others watched, a collective breath held, as Bella began to draw, her movements swift and sure, copying the points and shapes they all feared would soon be lost to the encroaching shadows. She worked quickly, the burnt stick scratching against the stone, transferring the memory of the starlight scene onto a more permanent record. Billy, Jim, and Ben gathered around her, watching and pointing, helping her make sure she recreated the map, with its star patterns, as accurately as possible. As Bella finished, the last rays of sun slipped away completely, plunging the chamber into near darkness, Ben's simple little torch nearly exhausted. But thanks to her efforts, they now had a version of the mosaic map—crude perhaps, but invaluable.

As the light from the torch began to flicker and dim, Billy turned to his companions, his voice cutting through the encroaching darkness.

"Right. We be headin' back to the ship," he ordered.

Ben, however, was not so easily convinced. His reluctance to heed Billy's order to return to the ship was palpable. The ancient stone walls seemed to whisper of hidden secrets, fueling Ben's belief that the Dragon's Scale must lay somewhere within these sacred confines, his mind consumed by the seductive thought of it lying unseen, perhaps mere steps away, just waiting to be revealed. Despite the captain's command, Ben's obsession surged, refusing the urge to continue on when the promise of discovery hovered tantalizingly close.

With an edge of agitation sharpening his words, he faced Billy. "But what if the Dragon's Scale be here? We should stay and look more."

Billy shook his head, the dim light catching the resolve in his eyes. "Nay," he replied. "It not be here."

But Ben's patience was fraying, worn thin by the tormenting possibility of what they might leave behind.

"But we don't know that, Captain!" His voice rose, echoing off the stone walls, along with his mounting frustration. "Would that not be why the spirits let us in here!? And what if we miss our chance? What if it be right here, hidden in plain sight?"

"I said, it not be here, Ben." Billy's voice carried a steely finality, cutting through the quiet of the chamber. "I feel it in me bones, and they speak clear as day—there's naught to find here. We cannot chase shadows and waste time lingerin' where we ought not."

Ben's patience now wavered on the brink of rebellion.

"Captain, have ye taken leave of yer senses!? We can't simply turn our backs and walk away!" Ben urged, his voice carrying the weight of his conviction. "This here be our chance, and I'll not let it slip through our fingers like sand. The spirits led us here for a reason, and we mustn't be leavin' 'til we've searched every nook and cranny of this cursed place!"

Billy was a leader respected for his open-mindedness, who valued the opinions of his crew as much as the wind in his sails. However, Ben's growing insolence and rebellious tone began to fray the edges of Billy's tolerance, testing his ability to maintain his composure.

Seeing that he wasn't getting through to Billy, Ben squared his shoulders, his voice cutting through the tension with a sharp edge.

"Captain, ye're a fool if ye think we should just walk away. Your stubbornness blinds ye to the answers right under our noses."

Billy snapped! The moment the insult left Ben's lips it ignited an explosive rush of anger! Billy's face darkened instantly, eyes narrowing with a piercing intensity. His fist clenched instinctively, knuckles whitening as the urge to strike Ben coursed through him. With a swift stride, he closed the distance between them, his hand forcefully gripping Ben's arm. Yet, despite the fury boiling within, Billy reined in his emotions, the discipline of a seasoned captain guiding his response. His eyes locked onto Ben's, a fiery intensity burning in them.

"We be goin' back. To. The. Ship," he said with a forceful growl, brooking no argument.

At this tense moment, Bella stepped in, hoping to calm the situation and talk some sense into Ben.

"Look at the map," she urged, pointing to the mosaic on the floor. "It doesn't tell us where we are. It shows us where we need to go. Father spoke of a long journey, and the many places along the way it would lead us. We've not completed the journey. The

Scale wasn't meant to be found here. It's out there, somewhere. We just have to follow the stars."

The tension hung heavy between Ben and his captain. Soon, though, he felt the fight drain out of him. Finally, Ben nodded, albeit reluctantly.

"Aye . . . Captain," he conceded, the fire of his impatience dimming in the face of Billy's threatening insistence.

Billy, Ben, Jim, and Bella emerged from the ancient temple. Waiting outside, the crew of the Siren's Call stood alert, their eyes fixed on the group. Anticipation was written across their faces, each one of them eager to hear of the treasures or secrets uncovered within the temple's stone walls. Billy addressed the men, his voice carrying across the open space.

"Men! There be no sign of the Dragon's Scale in this place," he announced, a hint of disappointment lacing his words. A murmur of dismay rippled through the crew, but Billy raised his hand to still any agitation before it could grow. "Yet," he proclaimed, his tone turning promising, "we've stumbled upon a clue most vital." Interest flared in the eyes of his men, their dismay quickly giving way to bright flickers of hope and intrigue. "This clue," Billy added, with the pause of a seasoned storyteller, ensuring every sailor hung on his next word, "may very well set our course toward the fabled Scale. Our voyage not be near its end, lads."

He then bellowed, "We return to the ship!" his command echoing like a cannon blast. "Prepare yerselves for the morrow's sailin'. We'll be chartin' our path by the stars themselves."

With a rousing chorus of "Aye, Captain!" the crew sprang into action, gathering up their encampment and heading back to the longboats.

Their return to the Siren's Call was abuzz with chatter, the air thick with curiosity and burning questions about the clue and the mysteries it promised to unveil. Under the blazing midday sun they rowed, the river glistening like a serpent of liquid gold, their hearts buoyant with the promise of discovery. The rhythmic dip of oars sliced through the water, a steady cadence that mirrored the unspoken resolve binding them together. With spirits high, they were a crew united in purpose, ready to face whatever mysteries lay ahead in their search for the fabled Dragon's Scale.

Lullabies

After hours of navigating the river's flow, the crew of the Siren's Call, weary yet spirited, found themselves back aboard their ship, just as twilight was descending. The day's end brought a coolness that swept over the deck, a gentle reprieve from the exertions of their downstream row. The ship, nestled in the calm waters just outside the mouth of the Ilhuan, swayed softly with the sea's breath, her sails furled, standing tall and silent against the sky now painted with streaks of orange and indigo.

Lanterns hung from the masts flickered to life, casting a warm, inviting glow across the deck, illuminating the faces of the crew as they went about securing the vessel for the night. Ropes were tied off with practiced ease, equipment stowed with care, and the longboats hoisted and secured along the starboard side. The thumping of boots on wood and the occasional shout or laugh punctuated the evening air, a testament to the camaraderie and well-oiled routine of the crew. The captain, his gaze lingering on the darkening horizon, gave the order to settle in for the night.

"Alright, lads, secure the deck. We dine together tonight, then rest. We've another day ahead," he declared, turning to make his way toward his quarters, his silhouette outlined by the lantern light.

One by one, the crew dispersed, most heading to the galley where a hearty meal of stew and bread awaited them, a welcome reprieve from the day's exertions. The warm aroma filled the ship, mingling with the salty sea air, as the mysteries of their experience with the spirits were exchanged over tankards of ale. The night wore on, and gradually, the ship grew quiet, save for the soft rustle of sails, the gentle creaking of wood, and the occasional call of a seabird. The crew, settled in their hammocks below deck, were rocked gently by the sway of the ship, the rhythm of the waves lulling them into a peaceful slumber.

Dawn's first light broke over the horizon, casting a soft, golden glow across the deck of the Siren's Call. The crew stirred and readied themselves for the new day, a sense of bewilderment hanging palpably in the air. Despite the normalcy of the morning's routine, there was a profound silence among them, each man lost in thought, reflecting on the previous night's ethereal encounter, the surreal remnants of the experience clinging to their consciousness. Their incredulity at what had transpired was profound—glances exchanged over the morning's meal conveyed volumes, their eyes alight with the shared incomprehensibility of it all.

Nestled in his hammock that swayed gently with the rhythm of the sea, Jim stirred from the night's rest. The early morning light filtered through a small porthole, casting a soft glow that danced across his face. He stretched, his bones popping softly, before swinging his legs over the side and planting his feet on the cool wooden floor.

He made his way to the basin, a modest vessel that held water not fresh but sufficient for the rudimentary cleansing rituals of a sailor. With deliberate strokes, Jim splashed his face, the coolness a shock against his skin, banishing the remnants of sleep. A wet cloth, rough against his cheeks, scrubbed away the salt and grime that was the constant companion of life at sea. He looked over to the shelf that held some of his meager belongings—a collection of clothes and personal items typical of a sailor's life. Reaching out, he selected a set of fresh clothes, the fabric worn but clean. It was then that his fingers brushed against something unexpected, hidden beneath the folds.

The seashell necklace lay partially concealed under the pile. He picked it up and held it delicately between his fingers, its shells dangling freely, swaying slightly with the motion of the ship. The early light caught on their surfaces, making them gleam like treasures gifted by the ocean. He turned it slowly, studying each shell, and read again the inscription that had captured his heart—*Where the sun kisses the sea, Where your heart yearns to be.* The words seemed to dance in the light. He traced the letters with the tip of his finger, feeling the grooves and curves of each as if trying to decipher a secret hidden within.

Jim's eyes lingered on the necklace, his gaze introspective. The motion of turning the necklace became almost hypnotic, each rotation bringing new reflections, both literal and figurative. In the shifting patterns of light and color, Jim saw not just the physical beauty of this simple trinket, but the path it represented—the endless quest for a place where peace and longing met on the horizon.

The quietude aboard the Siren's Call in the early morning was abruptly pierced by the commanding bellow of the captain. "Jim! Ben! Bella! To me cabin!" The words reverberated off the wooden planks, carrying the weight of authority and the expectation of immediate compliance. "And lass," he added, a slight softening to his tone, "bring the stone with the map ye made."

Startled from his musings, Jim's thoughts snapped back to the present. Duty called, and without a second thought, he hastened from his quarters. The necklace, still dangling from his grasp, seemed momentarily forgotten in the urgency of the moment.

Hearing the captain's request, Bella, in her quarters, paused. She grabbed the stone upon which she had carefully sketched the map the day before, having wrapped it carefully in a piece of cloth to prevent smudging the markings. She ran out onto the deck, and with Jim and Ben, entered the captain's cabin.

The door creaked open, revealing the captain hunched over his map table. The room was bathed in the soft glow of the morning sun, illuminating the multitude of maps sprawled across the worn surface. Each map told a story of past voyages, of lands explored, of seas conquered. Billy traced his fingers over the maps, lost in thought, his eyes scanning the intricate lines and symbols that represented the vast, unchartered territories of the world.

"Captain," Jim began, breaking the silence. "Have ye found anythin' that makes any sense yet?"

Billy shook his head, still fixed on a particular chart. "Nothin' I've seen yet be helpful," he replied, frustration evident in his voice.

Turning to Bella, he continued, "Lass, put the stone on the table."

Bella nodded and stepped forward, unwrapping the cloth to reveal the stone, covered with her meticulous drawings from the temple floor. Carefully, she moved some of the maps aside, clearing space on the cluttered table, and gently placed the stone to one side of them.

Billy took a deep breath, then slowly exhaled, focusing his attention entirely on the stone. "Let's have a closer look," he said.

He began to shuffle around his maps one by one, trying to align them with the stone's markings. His fingers traced the lines drawn on its surface, comparing them to the maps around it, each apparent alignment bringing a renewed sense of optimism. The others, too, hovered over the table, their eyes darting back and forth between the stone's drawings and the jumble of maps and charts spread before them, hoping for a breakthrough.

Jim's face was a canvas of intense focus, his eyes locked onto the maps with a steely determination, brows knitted and lips a taut line, as he meticulously compared the star patterns and land formations. Suddenly, his eyes widened with realization.

Stretching out his arm, he pointed to one of the maps on the table, a mixture of excitement and uncertainty in his voice.

"Captain, I think I see somethin'. Look here, these land shapes—do they seem to match up with the stone here?"

The Secret of the Dragon's Scale

As he extended his hand toward the map, the necklace that unknowingly was still in his possession slipped from beneath his cuff, dangling conspicuously around his wrist.

Bella's eyes lit up as she caught sight of the necklace. A spark of recognition flared within her.

"Jim," she said, her voice trembling with anticipation, "what's that?" pointing to the necklace. "Can I see it?"

His eyes fell to his wrist, widening in surprise as he saw the necklace dangling there. A sheepish smile tugged at the corners of his mouth. He chuckled softly to himself.

"Oh, heh, forgot about this," he said, realizing he had hurriedly left his quarters without putting it down.

He slipped the necklace off his wrist and handed it to Bella. She raised it to eye level, her gaze intently focused as she examined the shells. She turned the necklace slowly, her brow furrowing, her lips parting, as she traced the shapes with her eyes. The three shells, their familiar contours, stirred something deep within her memory. As she gently turned the large middle shell, to her was revealed the inscription etched into the back.

Where the sun kisses the sea
Where your heart yearns to be

Bella's breath caught in her throat! Her eyes widened and her heart began to race! She read the words again, her mind reeling from disbelief. Her lips quivered as she mouthed the words silently, each syllable resonating with distant memories. A rush of emotions surged through her—nostalgia, shock, and the resurgence of a profound sense of loss that had once seemed insurmountable.

Her hands trembled slightly as she clutched the necklace tighter, her eyes welling up with tears, blurring her vision as she traced the inscription with a trembling finger. The realization hit her with the force of a tidal wave—this was her lost necklace! The necklace had been a cherished gift, a precious connection to a family and home to which she had longed to return. She had lost it so many years ago, believing it gone forever.

"God in Heaven," she whispered, her voice quavering, choked with emotion. A tear escaped, tracing a path down her cheek. She blinked rapidly, trying to clear her vision, as more tears followed. Her other hand clutched at her chest, right above her racing heart. "This . . . this is mine. This . . . I lost this years ago!"

Jim, witnessing her peculiar reaction, stepped closer, concern etched on his face.

"Bella, ye alright?"

Bella looked up, her eyes shimmering with a mixture of astonishment and joy. Another tear slipped down her cheek as she managed a shaky smile.

"Jim, this necklace . . . it's mine."

"Yours!?" Jim exclaimed, a clear note of surprise and curiosity in his voice.

"Yours!?" Ben and Billy uttered in unison, their joint astonishment punctuating the air.

"Yes! I lost it during our sailing to the Americas! My mother, Molly, gave it to me before she died. These words are from my favorite poem! I carved it in the shell when Father told me we would be going west for the Americas. Where on God's Earth did you find it!?"

"Umm . . . I found it on the beach of an island we was anchored at a few months back," Jim answered.

Bella's eyes were glistening with tears as Jim's words sank in. A flicker of recognition crossed her face, her brows knitting together as she delved into her memories. She closed her eyes briefly, allowing the past to resurface. During her voyage to the Americas, her ship had indeed dropped anchor at a small island. They had needed time on dry land to take a break from their arduous voyage, and to stock up on fresh food and water. The memory was vivid now—the lush greenery, the scent of salt and earth mingling in the warm breeze, and the sense of freedom as she walked along the warm sand after many weeks confined to the ship.

It dawned on her—it was there, on that tranquil beach, that she must have dropped the necklace. Back on board the ship, she had searched frantically, not knowing where or when it had gone, but the necklace had seemed to vanish without a trace. She remembered the panic and sorrow she had felt when she realized it was missing. It was the only connection she had to her departed mother.

With sudden clarity she looked at Jim, eyes wide with amazement.

"It must have been there, on that beach, that I lost this necklace! I never knew what happened to it!"

"Can ye show that to me?" Billy asked.

Bella hesitated for a moment, her hands trembling as she handed him the precious keepsake. Billy took it carefully, squinting as he examined the subtle details, turning it over in his rough hands.

At that moment, a sudden spark ignited in Billy's eyes, kindling a blaze of recognition that swept over him. His mind raced back to the island, to when Jim had uncovered the necklace half-buried in the sand. It was there he had felt a nagging sense of familiarity, a fleeting shadow of a memory that now crystalized into vivid clarity.

"Did ye say yer mother's name was . . . Molly?" he asked, his voice barely above a whisper, laced with wonder and incredulity.

Bella nodded. "Yes, Captain, her name was Molly. Molly Cooper."

As Bella uttered her mother's name, a profound transformation swept across Billy's face. His initial curiosity gave way to a dawning realization, followed swiftly by a deep, poignant sorrow. His eyes widened momentarily, then softened, the spark of recognition kindling a glow of tenderness within their depths. His rugged features, hardened by years at sea, melted into a mix of feelings of love and loss. His mouth fell slightly open in silent wonder before pressing into a thin line as he struggled to contain the rush of emotions. The furrows on his brow deepened, etching lines of both heartache and fond remembrance across his forehead.

Billy looked up at Bella. With eyebrows arching and voice wispy and incredulous, he said, "Ye be Molly's . . . daughter?"

A tear began to form at the corner of his eye, catching the light before slowly trailing down his cheek. His lips trembled ever so slightly, caught between a wistful smile and the weight of grief.

For a moment, he looked past Bella, as if seeing a ghost from his past, his gaze distant and filled with unspoken memories.

"I knew yer mother," Billy tells her.

"You knew my mother?" she asked, her voice full of shock and surprise.

"Aye," Billy answered. "Molly Cooper was me first love when I was but a young lad, ye see," his voice soft and gentle, carrying a touch of longing. "She had a spirit like no other, and eyes that sparkled brighter than the stars. I gave this necklace to her as a gift before I left on me first ship, promisin' her I'd return soon, swearin' I'd come back from the sea and make her me wife. But the tides of fate be cruel and unforgivin'."

His expression darkened, shadows passing over his features as he continued.

"I got swept away by the life of the sea. The promise I made to her . . . it became naught but a whisper on the wind. Years passed, and then through the lips of some old mates, I learned the bitter truth. Molly had caught the yellow fever, and passed from this world."

His voice cracked slightly, the weight of regret heavy in his words.

"That news hit me harder than any storm. I never kept me word, never saw her again. This necklace, Bella, it ain't just a trinket. It's a reminder of what was lost, of a love that was taken too soon."

He handed the necklace back to Bella, his eyes glistening with memories and unspoken apologies.

"Keep it close, lass. It carries the heart of a sailor who loved deeply, and lost more than he could ever reckon."

Jim and Ben stood frozen, their faces etched with bewilderment at what they were witnessing, unable to find the words to break the silence that followed.

Bella's heart raced, her emotions swirling like a tempest within her. Tears welled up, blurring her vision as she looked at Billy, the formidable pirate captain known for his gruff exterior and reticent demeanor. Yet, his confession had revealed a tender, hidden part of him—and a connection to her past that she never knew existed.

Without thinking, driven by a deep, inexplicable need for comfort and closeness, and to comfort, Bella stepped toward Billy, hesitating only for an instant before wrapping her arms around his large, burly frame. Slowly, almost tentatively, he raised his massive arms and encircled Bella in a hug. Tears flowed freely down her cheeks, soaking into his shirt, while his chin rested gently on her head. There was a silent exchange happening between them—a communication beyond words, where shared pain and newfound understanding intertwined.

Billy tightened his arms slightly, a gesture laden with meaning. He wasn't a man given to sentimental words or outward displays of affection, but in that embrace, he conveyed all the things he couldn't say. And in that moment, he allowed himself to be vulnerable, to feel the weight of the past and the promise of a future, where old wounds might begin to heal.

In that small, dimly lit cabin, surrounded by the astonished eyes of Jim and Ben, the barriers around Billy's heart began to soften. In his arms, Bella found a fragment of connection to the family she had lost, nestled in the unexpected warmth of a pirate captain's hug. And in her touch, Billy found a chance at redemption and peace.

Just at that moment, a breeze blew through an open porthole of Billy's cabin. The gust, sudden, cool, and charged with a hint of salt air, swept across the room, rustling the maps strewn across Billy's table, sending some fluttering to the floor. Among them lay the Dragon's Scale map, which had been pushed aside and buried beneath the others. Billy had long deemed it no longer of any use, a relic of no consequence, yet never bothered to put it away.

Now, the wind breathed new life into it, nudging it toward the stone bearing the map drawing from the ancient temple.

After Billy and Bella composed themselves, the persistent sound of shuffling parchment, like restless storytellers clamoring for attention, broke the heavy silence. Ben, standing nearest, glanced down, his eyes narrowing as he noticed the Dragon's Scale map lodged against the stone. His gaze fixed on the star patterns drawn on it. Now, his eyes darted back and forth, back and forth, between the stone and the map, tracing the celestial markings with growing intensity. His breath caught as he noticed the pattern of the first few stars matching up between the stone and those that had been dotted across the top of the parchment. A flicker of intrigue sparked in his mind, compelling him to lean in closer. Again, his eyes flitted back and forth, his fingers tracing every point of alignment. As more and more stars matched up, his ember of intrigue ignited into a blazing flame of exhilaration, spreading warmth through his chest! His pulse quickened, each beat resonating with the thrill of discovery! With every star that fell into place, the patterns were becoming clearer, each new alignment feeding his growing excitement!

Then, as though the universe lifted a veil, all the stars aligned in a flawless harmony between the stone and the map. A wave of realization hit Ben with full force—they were exactly the same! The significance of what he was witnessing became overwhelming, leaving him breathless and his heart thundering

The Secret of the Dragon's Scale

in his chest, as a torrent of astonishment, wonder, and disbelief coursed through his veins!

"Look!" Ben shouted, his voice quivering with urgency as he pointed down at the stone and then at the map. "You need be seein' this!"

The others looked at Ben gesturing at the stone and map, their curiosity piqued by Ben's excitement. They gathered around him, looking intently to where he was pointing. Ben's finger traced the star patterns drawn on the ancient stone and then hovered over the corresponding constellations on the map. They all quickly came to see what Ben had discovered, that the patterns on the stone matched perfectly with those on the map.

Billy, Bella, and Jim exchanged looks of surprise, their expressions mirroring the same mix of wonder and disbelief as Ben's. Billy's eyes widened as he leaned closer, his breath growing shallow. He extended a tentative hand, tracing the stars on the stone, careful not to smudge the ancient secret it held.

"By the heavens above . . . They be exactly the same," he said softly, his voice filled with pure amazement.

For a moment, the cabin was enveloped in silence, the only sound being the gentle creaking of the ship as it swayed with the ocean's rhythm. The four of them stood transfixed, their eyes locked onto the incredible revelation that lay before them.

Then Bella broke the silence. "But what does it mean?"

With brow knitted and lips pressed firm, Billy's face bore an expression of intense concentration.

"I can't rightly say, lass," he admits. "This here map was our only connection to the Dragon's Scale, but the only secret it be darin' to reveal was to begin our search in the west. After that, it fell as silent as a sunken ship. But this surely be no happenstance. It be as if the heavens themselves have revealed a riddle, calling us to decipher its hidden truths." Billy scratched his beard, his gaze drifting upward. "But I confess, this confounds me somethin' fierce. There's a meanin' here, somethin' the ancients

183

are tryin' to tell us. Now let's see if we can figure out what that be."

Billy pulled out all the star charts and atlases he could find. He rummaged through collections of antiquated maps from deep in an old chest, their once-vibrant colors faded to ghostly remnants of their former usefulness. Each map, a relic of past explorations and forgotten dreams, told stories of lands and seas that no longer resembled the known world. The crackling parchments, delicate and brittle with age, whispered tales of cartographers who charted the world with quills and ink, guided only by the flight of sea birds and the spirit of adventure that dwelled within their hearts.

He spread all of them around in an organized chaos. His eyes darted between the constellations on the stone, the Dragon's Scale map, and the charts before him. He muttered under his breath, his frustration mounting as he tried to recognize any hint of correlation between them. And if anyone could read the stars, it was Billy Bones. All his life, Billy had sailed the vast, uncharted waters of the world, his soul inextricably linked to the sea. But it was when night fell and the sky transformed into a glittering expanse, that Billy felt truly at home. The night sky became his compass, his confidant, and his guide—a sprawling map of celestial wonders that whispered secrets only he could understand. The constellations were his allies, their positions etched in his memory—Orion, with his mighty belt; the Great Bear, pointing toward Polaris; and Cassiopeia, her regal "W" shape always reassuring. He knew them all, their movements through the seasons, their stories passed down through generations of sailors. Billy flipped through pages of his atlases.

"Orion? Nay, that not be right. Cassiopeia? Not quite."

His fingers traced the familiar shapes of Cygnus and Lyra, but none of them seemed to fit the mysterious patterns. And as he stared at the points dotted on the stone and the Dragon's Scale map, his ever-deepening frustration gnawed at him. The precision with which these designs perfectly mirrored each other surely held a significance, and could be no mere coincidence. Yet, for the life of him, he couldn't recognize them. Nothing in the patterns fit into the familiar dance of the night sky he knew so well.

Standing beside him, Jim and Ben tried their best to be helpful, their eyes darting eagerly over the maps and charts, though their understanding of the night sky was no match for Billy's.

Ben scratched his head, looking puzzled. " I can't see anythin' that matches the stars we know. Are ye sure these even be constellations?"

Jim, squinting at the Dragon's Scale map, chimed in. "Aye, it's like these stars be from some other sky. Maybe we just be lookin' at 'em wrong."

Billy felt a rare sense of helplessness, a weight pressing down on him. If anyone could decipher these star patterns, it should have been him. His mind raced through every piece of celestial lore, every ancient tale and myth, searching for any clue that might lead him to an epiphany, yet none yielded the insight he so desperately sought.

"What about the land?" Bella asked.

"That be another puzzle, lass" Billy responded. "The stars be the same between the maps, but if the turquoise in the temple floor was supposin' to be land, nothin' lookin' like it shows on this map . . . Why the stars would be the same, but the land be nowhere in sight, is a fine question."

"Could the land be shown on another map? Did ye recognize anything on the others, Captain?" Jim asked.

Billy sighed, running a hand through his beard as he glanced at the map.

"Nay," he said, his voice carrying the weight of years spent navigating the seven seas. "I ain't seen these land shapes on any map we got, nor do they ring a bell with any place I know."

The four of them sat hunched over the maps and charts that lay sprawled across the wooden table, the room silent except for the soft rustling of parchment, mingling with the creaking of the Siren's Call as it gently swayed on the waves. But no matter how hard they tried, the patterns remained tauntingly indecipherable. The confounding stars and constellations seemed to mock them, keeping their secrets just out of reach, delighting in their ability to elude understanding.

Billy rubbed his temples. "Lads, lass, we've been at this for hours, and we be no closer to understandin' these blasted stars than we were when we started. I say we should return to it with fresh eyes later."

As Ben, Jim, and Bella left the captain's cabin, returning to their normal routine aboard the ship, Billy remained behind, his eyes transfixed upon the chaotic spread of maps strewn across the table. Like a sailor adrift in a fog-laden sea, he peered intently at the constellations of inked dots, yearning for some hidden revelation that might beckon to him. The frustration of their fruitless search weighed heavily on his mind, as the cryptic designs on the maps refused to yield any useful insight. His hands rested on the table's edge, gripping it tightly as if he wanted to wring answers from the stubborn parchments.

With a heavy sigh, Billy straightened up, his joints aching from long hours spent hunched over the table. He turned away from the maps and charts and walked out of the cabin, the door creaking softly as it closed behind him. Stepping onto the deck, he was greeted by the warmth of the afternoon sun. The gentle sea breeze ruffled his hair and filled his lungs with the crisp scent of brine and the exotic perfumes of tropical flora from the nearby land. He made his way to the bow, seeking solace in the vast expanse of ocean before him.

Leaning against the railing, he stared out at the boundless blue horizon. The rhythmic sound of waves lapping against the hull was a soothing balm to his frayed nerves, and he allowed himself a moment of quiet reflection. He took a deep breath, deliberately emptying his mind of thoughts about the elusive Dragon's Scale.

The Secret of the Dragon's Scale

His thoughts drifted back to their encounter at the stone that sings to the sky. The voices of the spirits had been so clear, carrying messages that spoke directly to Billy and his crew, revealing secrets only they could hear. The experience had been eerie and undeniable, leaving an indelible mark on his consciousness. But so much more profound than anything he had ever experienced were the spirits they had danced with in the ruins of the ancient village, the memory of that spectral waltz still vivid in his mind. He could still see the ghostly figures, moving with a grace that defied earthly bounds, their presence both haunting and beautiful. Deep down, though, Billy was struggling to admit to himself that this had been no mere illusion—they had been real, as real as the deck beneath his feet and the salt air in his lungs, igniting a spark of belief that refused to be extinguished by the shadows of doubt.

Billy wrestled with the vividness of these experiences, struggling to reconcile them with his unwavering skepticism of the supernatural. He had always prided himself on his rational approach to life; he believed only in what he could see, touch, and understand. His voyages across the vast seas had always been guided by a clear-headed pragmatism, dismissing tales of ghosts and spirits as mere superstition, the stuff of old sailors' yarns. But now, those beliefs were being challenged in a profound and unsettling way as never before.

As the memory of the spirits lingered, his thoughts shifted to a more personal revelation. He had only just discovered that Bella was the daughter of his first love, Molly. The realization had been a shock, stirring up a whirlwind of emotions. He remembered Molly's laughter, her fiery spirit, and the dreams they had once shared. Their romance had been a fleeting, beautiful thing, cut short by the unpredictable tides of life. Now, seeing echoes of Molly in Bella's own spirit and unyielding courage, Billy felt a much more powerful connection to the young woman who had become such an integral part of their lives. The knowledge that Bella was Molly's daughter added a new depth to their bond, blending the past with the present in a way that was both bittersweet and heartening.

Leaning against the ship's railing, looking out over the boundless ocean, Billy felt a tug-of-war within him. The gentle rocking of the ship beneath his feet was a familiar comfort, yet his mind was anything but at ease. For as long as he could remember, his life had been defined by the thrill of adventure, the clash of battle, and an insatiable hunger for gold and glory. It was where he felt most alive, where his skills and instincts were honed to the sharp edge of survival. He had carved out a fearsome reputation, his identity intertwined with the fierce, daring exploits that had become legend among seafarers. But now, something deeper was stirring within, challenging the very core of his being. The pirate he had been his whole life clung stubbornly to the desire to continue this way, reluctant to let go. Yet, there was a growing part of him that yearned for something beyond the horizon—a sense of peace and connection to the mysteries of the world that he could neither chart nor control.

Standing there, the salt-laden breeze tousling his hair, his grip tightened on the railing—his knuckles were white with tension. The encounters with the ethereal realm—and a realization that the universe was more mysterious and magical than he dared to admit—had awakened a sense of spirituality that was foreign to him. He found himself contemplating a life less driven by the chaos of adventure and more attuned to the serene rhythms of nature, home, and the simple joys of family and friends. The idea of finding balance, of seeking harmony rather than conflict, was both alluring and unsettling.

He stared out across the water, the horizon blurring into a soft, misty line, as if the world was offering him a glimpse into another life—a life that was calling to him with a silent, irresistible pull. His thoughts drifted to the possibility of a small cottage by the sea, nestled among the dunes and wildflowers. He imagined waking up each morning to the sound of waves gently crashing on the shore, and the scent of blooming flowers carried on the breeze. Instead of plotting courses and commanding men, his days would be filled with the humble tasks of tending to a garden, mending nets, and watching the seasons change. He envisioned a life where the constant clamor of battle and the lure of treasure were replaced by the soft whispers of the wind through the trees and the laughter of children playing nearby. The idea of a home—a true home—where he could return each day to the warmth of a hearth and the comforting presence of loved ones, brought a sense of peace he had never known. He imagined sharing meals with family and friends, their faces lit by candlelight, conversations flowing easily as they recounted stories of the day's simple pleasures.

The ship remained anchored at the mouth of the Ilhuan, its sails furled and its crew growing restless. The cryptic star patterns on the Dragon's Scale map had left them at a standstill, with no clear direction to guide their quest. Billy remained lost in thought, his gaze fixed on the horizon, when Ben approached him from behind.

"Captain," Ben called out, his voice cutting through the silence. "What be your orders? We need to know our heading."

A little startled, Billy turned to face Ben. For a moment, indecision flickered across his face. He knew the crew looked to him for guidance, but without a clear path, he felt uncharacteristically uncertain.

"I . . . I'm not sure, Ben," he admitted, his voice soft and tinged with hesitation.

Billy's hesitation was a stark departure from the self-assured leader Ben had always respected, and it gnawed at Ben's patience, especially as their search for the Dragon's Scale dragged on at a crawl. Every delay felt like an eternity, and each moment lost was another opportunity slipping through their fingers. Upon witnessing Billy's withering decisiveness, Ben's jaw tightened, the muscles tensing as if to hold back an outburst, the madness boiling within him barely contained. He felt if they weren't going to search the temple, continuing their journey would be far better than this maddening stagnation, sitting anchored and with no real sense of direction. He stepped closer, his tone respectful yet insistent.

"Captain, we can't sit here like barnacles on a rock. We need to keep movin', even if it be just followin' the coast. It be better than just sittin' idle."

The tension in Billy eased slightly as he considered Ben's words. The idea of movement, of doing something, sounded better at that moment than standing still. He realized that the true peril lay not in the uncertainty of the waters ahead, but in the quiet death of dreams that came with remaining idle.

He nodded slowly. "Aye, lad. We best be heedin' the call of the sea." With a deep breath, Billy dispelled the fog of uncertainty that had clouded his mind. His voice steady and clear as the sea breeze, he said to Ben, "It be time to hoist the sails and let the winds guide us. Better to chase the horizon than to wither here. Order the crew to weigh anchor. We'll continue up the coast 'til we have a clearer understandin' of our next course of action."

A look of relief crossed Ben's face as he acknowledged the captain's decision.

"Aye, Captain," he responded, his voice firm with renewed purpose. He turned briskly and began issuing orders to the crew.

Billy watched as the men sprang into action, their movements swift and practiced. The anchor was hoisted and the sails were unfurled, billowing out as they caught the eager wind. The ship came alive with the rhythmic creak of the timbers and the snap of the sails, filling the air with a vibrant energy as the ship began to move, breaking free from its temporary mooring.

The sight of his men working with renewed vigor boosted Billy's spirits. Their unwavering trust in his leadership to navigate the uncharted waters ahead strengthened his resolve. The weight of their expectations pressed down on him, but it also fueled his determination.

As the ship glided forward, the endless expanse of the ocean beckoned. Each ripple and swell whispered of the challenges lying in wait, but the promise of discovery, of claiming the legendary Dragon's Scale, burned brightly in the distance. Billy knew in his heart that he was a man inextricably bound to the life of adventure and the open sea—the thrill of battle coursed through his veins, each clash of steel and roar of cannon fire igniting a fierce, primal excitement within him. The uncertainty that had been gnawing at him, the doubts about the pirate life he had always known, began to fade like fog under the morning sun—at least for now.

The sun hung high in the sky, a golden sentinel casting its mid-afternoon radiance over the Siren's Call, bathing the ship in a warm, honeyed glow. The ship cut through the gentle waves with a graceful ease, its sails billowing like majestic wings against the backdrop of the vast blue canvas of the ocean. Ben stood on deck, his stance firm and steady, outwardly exuding a calm authority as he oversaw the flurry of activity around him; his voice rang clear and commanding, guiding the men with an experienced hand. Yet beneath this facade of normalcy, the ever-growing madness roiled within him, dark and consuming. His mind was a maelstrom, swirling with anger and disappointment, the ancient village haunting his thoughts. The captain's decision to leave the ruins without thoroughly searching the temple grated on him—a persistent ache that burrowed deep into his heart, leaving him restless and unsettled. It was another lost opportunity, he felt, just like the when they were at the island where the stone sang to the sky. He replayed the scene over and over in his head—the crumbling stone walls of the temple, the intricate carvings of ancient myths and legends, the gleaming eyes of the god piercing through shadows that whispered secrets he yearned to uncover. The thought that the Dragon's Scale might have been within their grasp, only to slip away due to their hasty departure, tormented him. Now, as they moved farther and farther away from the village, that chance felt irretrievably lost.

There was a wildness in Ben's eyes, a tumult of dark intensity flickering beneath their surface. His gaze darted with a restless energy, haunted and unrelenting, from the men to the horizon and back again. The wind lashed at his face, tangling his hair into wild knots, yet he remained unmoved, a figure both commanding and unsettling. The sounds of the sea—the rhythmic lapping of the waves, the creaking of the timbers, the call of seabirds—became not the soothing sounds of a sailor's life, but a cacophony that only served to heighten his agitation. To the crew, he was a man driven by purpose, but beneath the surface, a tempest raged—a storm far more perilous than any they had encountered at sea.

For Ben, the pursuit of the Dragon's Scale was no longer a journey, but a dark tide that surged within him, its relentless waves battering the once-steady shores of his mind. Every whisper of the wind, each crash of the waves, seemed to carry with them the Scale's siren call, an elusive promise of unimaginable wealth gleaming like gold threads woven into the fabric of dreams.

The line between reality and hallucination now blurred dangerously. Ben began to imagine dragons everywhere. He was seeing them in the clouds, their serpentine bodies coiling and uncoiling, their eyes burning with an otherworldly fire. The sun's reflection on the water became the glint of dragon scales, shimmering with a hypnotic iridescence. Shadows cast by the sails morphed into winged beasts, their forms rippling and shifting as if alive. In the wind, he heard their roars—deep, guttural growls echoing across the vast, empty expanse.

Ben was fighting a war against this encroaching darkness. His thoughts spiraled, tangled in a web of fear and desperation, wreaking havoc on his command. He now stood on the deck a shadow of his former self, his eyes darting wildly as if haunted by phantoms only he could see. His once commanding voice, steady and sure, became a vessel of chaos, delivering orders that twisted logic and defied reason. Commands burst from him like cannon fire, the madness within him spilling into every order.

"Lower the sails and hoist the anchor!" he bellowed, his voice a frenzied mix of authority and delirium that echoed across the deck. "Steer toward the sun, lads—that be where the Scale lies hidden!" His finger jabbed wildly at the burning horizon, eyes gleaming with manic intensity. "Reef the mizzenmast and furl the jib! Prepare to dive below deck and secure the crow's nest!" he barked, his voice cracking under the strain of his hallucinations.

The crew exchanged bewildered glances, their brows furrowed in confusion as they tried to make sense of the contradictory and nonsensical orders. Jim hesitated at the ropes, while John Hawkins scratched his head, glancing nervously up at the captain for guidance. Despite their bafflement, the crew moved to obey, their actions disjointed and uncertain, reflecting the chaos that Ben's madness had unleashed upon the Siren's Call. Each man laid witness to the sweat beading on his brow, the twitch in his muscles, and his cheeks flushed with the fever of mania.

The captain had been up on the quarterdeck, his eyes scanning the horizon, when his attention was drawn to the sound of Ben's sharp and erratic voice, cutting through the usual sounds of the sea. As he overheard Ben's bizarre orders and watched the disarray unfold, Billy's jaw tightened, the muscles in his face twitching with barely restrained anger. The crew's once-fluid movements, orchestrated like a symphony, had devolved into a shamble of aborted efforts and half-executed tasks. His eyes narrowed, the frustration bubbling beneath his stern exterior as he saw the cohesion of his crew unraveling.

His patience exhausted, Billy took a deep breath, the weight of command heavy on his shoulders. He couldn't allow Ben's madness to endanger the ship and confuse the crew any longer. With a resolute expression, he descended the steps from the quarterdeck, his boots thudding against the wooden planks with each determined stride.

Approaching the chaotic scene, Billy's presence commanded attention. The crew fell silent, their eyes shifting from Ben to the captain, sensing the gravity of the moment. Ben, lost in his own frenzied world, continued to shout incoherent orders until Billy's booming voice cut through the din.

"Ben!" he called out. "I've had enough of yer madness. Yer orders be as twisted as a kraken's tentacles, and ye're leadin' us all to ruin!"

Ben turned, his gaze unfocused, struggling to grasp the reality around him. "Captain, I know where the Dragon's Scale lies! Just beyond the . . . "

"Silence!" Billy roared, stepping closer, his face inches from Ben's. "Ye've lost yer mind, and with it, the respect o' this crew. Yer commands endanger us all. Ye're unfit to serve as first mate."

The crew stood rooted to their spots, eyes wide and breaths held. Billy's face loomed close to Ben's, a storm of fury and disappointment etched in every line, as he condemned his first mate's recklessness.

Ben, eyes flickering with a mix of defiance and bewilderment, seemed to shrink under the captain's fierce gaze.

"But Captain," Ben protested, his voice faltering. "I can still . . . "

"Enough!" Billy cut him off, his eyes blazing with anger. "This ship needs clear heads and sound judgment, not the ramblings of a madman. From this moment on, ye're relieved of command. Ye'll no longer serve as first mate aboard this ship. Ye're confined to yer quarters 'til I decide what to do with ye."

Ben's face contorted with a mix of anger and desperation, but he could see the resolve in Billy's eyes. The captain would not be swayed.

"Captain, please. The Scale . . . "

Billy grabbed Ben by the shoulders, shaking him slightly.

"The only thing ye'll be doin' is stayin' out of our way. Men, escort him to his quarters and make sure he stays there."

Two burly sailors stepped forward, their expressions grim but resigned. They took Ben by the arms and led him away, his protests fading into the background noise of the ship's creaking timbers and the relentless sea.

As Ben was marched below deck, Billy turned to face the crew, his voice steady and commanding.

"Let this be a lesson to all. We sail as one, under clear-headed command, or we shan't sail at all. We'll be findin' the Dragon's Scale, mark me words, but we'll do it together, and we'll do it right."

The Siren's Call drifted along the coast, its prow now aimlessly kissing the waves, its directionless journey a stark contrast to the purpose that had once inspired its every voyage. As dusk descended, the horizon blazed with a canvas of fiery hues, the sun dipping low to brush the sky with strokes of amber and crimson. Shadows stretched languidly across the deck, weaving a dance of light and dark, and bathing the ship in a warm, golden glow. At the helm, the captain stood lost in thought, his mind as unanchored as the ship, wrestling with the challenge of charting a new course.

Despite the uncertainty, the crew went about their duties with a quiet diligence. Jim checked the rigging and ensured the sails were properly trimmed—though his mind, much like the captain's, was preoccupied with thoughts of what lay ahead. Bella moved gracefully among the bustling sailors, lending a hand where needed before retreating to a secluded corner of the deck. There, she sat with her lute, the gentle strumming of strings weaving a soothing melody that drifted through the air, offering a momentary respite from the tension that gripped the ship. The notes mingled with the sound of waves lapping against the hull, creating a serene backdrop as the day began its journey into night.

Jim, having completed his tasks for the day, noticed Bella in her quiet corner. Drawn by the music and seeking a break from his own restless thoughts, he walked over to her. Bella looked up and smiled, her fingers never pausing their dance across the strings.

However, amidst the tranquility, a cloud of worry darkened Jim's usually lively face. Bella, sensing his unrest, placed her lute aside and gently took his hand in hers.

"I think Ben's been weighin' on your mind," she said softly, her voice full of warmth, but also concern.

Jim sighed, running a hand through his disheveled hair. "Aye," he said, his voice heavy with frustration. "He's off his bloody block over that Dragon's Scale. It's like he's bewitched. Can't think of nothin' else but that damned thing."

Bella squeezed his hand reassuringly, her eyes reflecting her deep empathy. "Yes, the whole crew's feeling it."

Jim looked down at their intertwined hands, the touch grounding him but failing to ease his troubled thoughts.

"I feel like I'm losin' me best mate," he lamented, his voice breaking slightly. "I got this feelin' . . . a dark cloud's hangin' over us. If Ben gives in to this madness fully, somethin' terrible's gonna happen. I can feel it in me bones."

Bella's eyes sparkled with a reminiscent glow as she spoke, her voice taking on a tone of ancient wisdom.

"Father liked to say, 'The moth that chases the flame may find its wings burnt, yet it is the light that captivates its soul.'" Jim listened intently, his brow furrowing as he tried to grasp the meaning. "Ben's like that moth," she continued, "drawn to the Dragon's Scale as if it were the flame. It dazzles him, blinds him to the dangers. But deep down, he knows it could destroy him."

The worry etched into the corners of his eyes was unmistakable, a testament to the deep bond he shared with Ben and the fear of losing his friend to madness. Yet, beneath the surface of that concern, there was a fierce glint of determination to save him.

"Aye, Ben's a bit of a wild rogue, but he's got a heart as true as the North Star," Jim said, his tone caught between worry and a dash of resolve. "I see madness closin' in, and it rattles me to think he might be lost to it."

Bella nodded with a calm understanding. "I can see how much you worry for Ben. But Father would often say to me, 'It is in the darkest caves that the blind discover new eyes.' Ben may be lost in shadow now, but it's within that darkness he might find a new light. We mustn't lose hope."

Jim found solace in Bella's unwavering support and the promise of their shared resolve. With Bella by his side, he felt ready to face whatever challenges lay ahead, determined to bring Ben back from the brink. The gentle hum of the ocean and the warmth of Bella's embrace made the daunting task ahead seem a bit more bearable.

As the Siren's Call sailed on, the last vestiges of daylight faded into the deepening blues and purples of twilight, while wisps of clouds were painted with the last golden brushstrokes of the setting sun. The sky was punctuated by the first twinkling stars, as it slowly gave way to the deep indigo expanse of night. The air was cool and refreshing, carrying the faint scent of salt and of the thriving vegetation of the distant shore. A gentle breeze whispered through the sails, harmonizing with the rhythmic lapping of waves against the hull.

Billy had withdrawn to his cabin, taking a respite from the day's work. He lay on his cot, the gentle sway of the ship soothing his weary body. The cabin was dimly lit by the soft glow of a single lantern. The day's fatigue soon began to dissipate, and he felt himself drifting into a light slumber. He found his thoughts now drifting, tugged by an unknown force, toward memories of his old friend—the fisherman who had taught him so much about the sea, and with whom he had shared countless tales and adventures.

A flicker of light then began to dance at the corner of his eye. At first, he thought it was merely a trick of the lantern's flame. But as the light grew more distinct, an inexplicable chill ran down his spine. He turned—and there, seated comfortably in the chair, facing him, was the spectral figure of his old friend, the fisherman. Bathed in an otherworldly glow, the spirit looked almost tangible, yet there was an ethereal translucence to him that defied earthly reality. The fisherman was leaning back, calmly smoking his pipe, the smoke curling up in delicate, glowing tendrils that shimmered and vanished into the air. The fisherman's eyes, though ghostly, were filled with the same warmth and wisdom Billy had always found in him. His presence exuded a comforting serenity, despite the undeniable strangeness of the encounter.

Billy sat up, rubbing his eyes in disbelief, expecting the vision to vanish with the next blink.

"Evenin', Billy boy," the spirit began, his voice resonant yet gentle. "It warms my heart to see ya again, though it pains me to tell ya that I have crossed over to the other side. My time in this world has ended."

Billy's eyes widened with shock and sorrow. "Samuel? Ye . . . ye've passed on?" he stammered, his heart aching at the thought of having lost of his old friend.

The old fisherman's spirit smiled gently around the stem of his pipe. "Aye. But do not grieve too deeply, my friend," he said, his voice low and tender, carrying a quiet reassurance that eased the weight of sorrow.

"When?" Billy asked.

"Not too long after we last spoke . . . Somethin' 'bout the Dragon's Scale."

"Why've ye come, Samuel?"

He puffed on his ghostly pipe, the ethereal smoke blending seamlessly with the night air. "I've come to have a word with ya, Billy."

The old fisherman's spirit gazed out at the calm sea, his eyes filled with the wisdom of time. "I've come 'cause I see the tempest brewin' inside ya. Ye've spent many a year roamin' these wild waters, livin' the life of a pirate, chasin' after treasure and adventure. But now, there's a restlessness in ya, a weariness that no amount of plunderin' can soothe."

Billy sighed deeply, the weight of his burdens pressing down on him. "Aye, the sea's been good to me. But I'm tired, Samuel. The thrill of it all don't sit right with me anymore. I feel lost, adrift in these waters with no clear course."

Samuel nodded, his spectral form shimmering slightly. "That's why I'm here, Billy. I've come to help ya see what yer heart's been whisperin'. Ye're searchin' for somethin' different. A quiet life, simple and peaceful. It's a hard truth to face for a man who's known nothin' but the roar of the waves and the clash of swords. But this struggle in yer heart, lad, no one but you can decide which way to turn."

Billy nodded slowly, a flicker of hope mingling with uncertainty in his tired eyes. "But Samuel, how will I know which path be the right one?"

"To find that answer," the old fisherman continued, "you must seek a place veiled in the mist of time, where beauty itself guards the secrets of the sea. Out there, the stars hold the map to safe harbors and the promise of a new dawn. Chart a course for the Cave of Echoing Shadows, Billy. For where light and darkness dance and twirl, you'll find the gate to another world."

Billy looked into the old fisherman's eyes, a mix of confusion and yearning swirling within him. "The Cave of Echoing Shadows? Where be that? What am I to find there, Samuel?"

The old fisherman lowered his pipe, resting his hand on his thigh, and leaned forward. "The journey through the cave is a confrontation with yer own heart, Billy boy. For only when ye've traversed it will yer troubled soul find rest." Samuel smiled warmly, his face creased with lines of kindness and understanding. "Go on then, Billy. The sea will always be here, but now it's time for you to find yer shore."

With those words, Samuel's spirit began to fade. As the last traces of the apparition dissolved into the night, Billy sat alone in silent contemplation, the weight of the old fisherman's message settling deeply within him. He lay back on his cot, the dim light of the lantern casting long shadows that danced with the sway of the ship. But Samuel's wisdom lingered, a guiding star in the vast expanse of Billy's troubled soul.

Jim and Bella had been on deck, absorbing the serene beauty of the transition between day and night on the water.

"Did you hear something?" Bella asked, eyebrows slightly raised, thinking she heard something in the distance. She turned her head, straining to catch the elusive sound again.

At first, the sound was barely more than a whisper, an almost imperceptible hum that seemed to blend seamlessly with the gentle rustling of the sails overhead. It tugged gently at the edges of their awareness, like a distant memory struggling to resurface.

Jim shook his head slowly, his eyes scanning the horizon. "I'm not sure," he replied, his voice tinged with curiosity. "Maybe it's just the wind."

While the Siren's Call continued its steady course, cutting through waters that sparkled with the first twinkling stars, the faint sounds persisted—low, resonant tones that ebbed and flowed with a rhythm all their own. Carried aloft by the evening breeze, the sounds wrapped around Jim and Bella, casting a serene spell over their senses. Gradually, the whispers grew in clarity and strength, evolving into a series of long, sonorous notes that danced across the surface of the waves. The sounds, deep and haunting, resonated through the ship, vibrating through the wooden timbers and into the bones of those aboard. They seemed to rise from the ocean's depths, touching the surface with a gentle caress before slipping away.

"It's not the wind," Bella whispered, her eyes widening as the sounds became more distinct. "It's . . . it's almost musical."

Soon, the sounds became unmistakable. The notes swelled and dipped, weaving a complex and captivating pattern that spoke directly to the soul. All on deck could now discern the distinct, plaintive calls of whales, their voices rising directly from the ocean's heart in a harmonious chorus. The soundscape was a rich blend of moans, cries, and clicks, each phrase imbued with a sense of happiness and belonging.

"Listen," she said, her heart swelling with wonder. "It must be whales . . . They're singing!"

Billy, still lying in his cabin, stirred as the mysterious vibrations reached him. He sat up in his cot, straining to sense what was happening. But the quiet was profound, broken only by the occasional creak of the wooden beams and the rustle of the sails. He stared at the chair where Samuel's spirit had just sat, the memory of their conversation still fresh in his mind, mingling with the dark corners of his thoughts.

The vibrations grew clearer, and focusing more intently, Billy could discern that their origin was unmistakably from the unseen depths below. They pulsed gently through the wooden planks beneath him. But before long, a faint sound began to draw his attention—a deep, primal call that resonated within his bones, as if the very soul of the sea was speaking to him. Slowly, the songs of whales, mournful and beautiful sounds carried through the water, began to fill his cabin.

The whale songs grew louder, filling the night with their poignant, lyrical cadence. The low, soothing tones provided a steady rhythm that echoed the heartbeat of the ocean, while the higher, melodic calls danced in the air, their fluidity reminiscent of the gentle rise and fall of a mother's voice as she hums a lullaby to her child. These calls were tender and nurturing—a mother's whispered assurances that everything would be all right, that sleep would bring peace and dreams would be sweet. The whales' melodies meandered across the surface of the water like the soft caress of a loving hand smoothing a child's hair, each note a gentle promise of safety and comfort.

Bella leaned against the ship's railing, closing her eyes as she let the whale songs envelope her. For as long as she could remember, Bella had been sensitive to music. She heard melodies in everything—the rustle of leaves, the chirping of birds, the whisper of the wind. Tonight, however, she was captivated by an altogether different symphony. Her soul, attuned to the hidden melodies of nature, danced to the rhythm of the deep, as if the ocean itself had become an instrument for the divine. As she listened, an overwhelming sense of comfort and warmth washed over her, akin to the feeling of being wrapped in a soft, loving embrace.

Bella's thoughts drifted back to her childhood, memories of her mother's lullabies coming to the forefront of her mind. Her mother's voice had always been soothing, carrying the warmth of safety and love that could calm even the most restless of nights. To Bella, the whales' melodies were like those lullabies, tender and loving, singing the ocean to rest just as a mother would sing her child to sleep. Tears welled up from a heart overflowing with emotion. For in that moment, Bella felt cradled by the ocean itself, as the ship, like a child nestled safely within its mother's arms, swayed with the rhythm of the waves under the moon's watchful gaze. She smiled softly, feeling a profound sense of connection and peace.

Bella opened her eyes and looked out over the moonlit sea. The water glimmered under the silvery light, while the song of the whales wove itself into the fabric of the night.

"Lullabies," she said softly.

"Hmm?" Jim asked, not sure what she meant.

She turned to him, her eyes still shining with the emotion that the whale songs had stirred within her. "The whale songs," she said, her voice resonating with warmth and tranquility. "They remind me of lullabies mothers sing to their children to put them to sleep. Can't you feel it?"

Jim closed his eyes, letting the cool sea breeze brush against his skin, carrying with it the deep resonant notes of the whale songs. He felt a profound peace washing over him, the kind that comes from feeling truly connected to something greater than oneself. In this serene moment, Father Ignatius' words came rushing back to him, as if the old priest was standing there by his side, illuminating Jim's path with clarity and reassurance, and reminding him to trust in the journey laid before him—*Then, under the moon's silvery disc, to its ears come soft lullabies, putting the world to sleep.*

A deep wellspring of awe and reverence surged through him, intertwined with an overwhelming sense of destiny that electrified his senses. Every fiber of his being told him that this was an important place in his journey, just as Father Ignatius had prophesized. It was as if nature itself was speaking to him, telling him that he was exactly where he needed to be. He was seeing it, hearing it, feeling it, for he was listening with the wisdom of his heart.

Jim took a deep breath, grounding him in this moment of clarity. "This place, Bella, it's a part of me journey yer old padre foretold. His words about how under the moon's silvery disc, to me ears will come soft lullabies, putting the world to sleep . . . They make sense now. This is where I'm meant to be. I feel it, Bella. I feel it."

Billy felt a compulsion to leave his cabin, drawn out by the captivating music. As he emerged onto the deck, the cool night air greeted him, carrying with it the full, enchanting chorus of the whales.

The gentle creak of a cabin door opening drew Jim and Bella's attention. They turned to see Billy stepping onto the deck, his usually restless spirit now very calm. He walked to the railing. He stood very still, the cool breeze brushing against his face, as he listened intently to the graceful lullabies dancing on the breath of the sea.

Jim and Bella exchanged a glance, their hearts swelling with the beauty of the experience, and walked over to Billy, his face awash with wonder. The three of them stood in silence for a moment, united by the magical atmosphere surrounding them.

"Captain," Jim began, his voice soft but filled with conviction. "This place . . . It's where we were meant to be. I can feel it in me bones, like the fire of a thousand stars burnin' within me."

Billy turned to face Jim, his eyes reflecting the moonlight, a mix of curiosity and understanding in his gaze. He nodded slowly, feeling the same profound connection to the world around them.

"The whales," Jim continued, his voice now trembling slightly with emotion, "their songs be the lullabies the old priest spoke of, under the moon's silvery disc, he was sayin'. They be guidin' us, showin' us the way. This place . . . It's more than just a spot on a map. It's a part of our journey, a turnin' point we must be at."

Bella gently added, "The signs, Captain, are all around us. We've heard them in the songs of the whales, felt them on the ocean's breath, seen them in the dance of the moonlight on the waves. Nature itself is telling us we're exactly where we need to be."

The three stood together, side by side, their silhouettes etched against the indigo canvas of the dimming sky, as the whale songs continued to serenade the night. In that moment, the only sounds they could hear were the haunting calls of the ocean's gentle giants, wrapping them in a blanket of calm and contentment. The ocean, the wind, the ship—all were utterly silent, as if the entire universe had paused to listen to the lullabies, putting the world to sleep.

Where Light and Darkness Dance and Twirl

This is where they were meant to be. The captain ordered the trimming of the sales to slow the ship. Its wooden hull sliced through the coastal waters now with barely a whisper, as the gentle songs of the whales ebbed and flowed.

The night was tranquil, bathed in the radiance of a full moon that hung high above like a guardian of the sea, its light cascading down, casting a silvery sparkle across the glittering waves. But as the moon rose yet higher, its mystical pull began to awaken the hidden wonders of the ocean.

Under the moon's watchful eye, the water began to stir with an ethereal glow. From deep below, luminescent plankton and algae, responding to the moon's silent call, drifted upward. Breaking through the surface, their brilliance intensified, each one a minuscule lantern adding its light to the already bewitching scene. They emitted a soft phosphorescence that flickered and danced across the water, creating a dazzling spectacle that bathed the ocean in hues of electric blues and fluorescent greens. The ocean twinkled as if sprinkled with stardust. Entwining with this pulsing life were the moon's silvery beams, creating an enchanting dance of light and shadow that captivated all who beheld it.

All along the shoreline, the water's surface undulated with a rhythmic grace, each gentle rise and fall imbued with a wondrous glow; each crest of the waves was accentuated by the radiant creatures, tracing the contours of the water's edge like delicate strokes of a painter's brush. When the waves broke upon the shore, they did so with a gentle splash, sending ripples of light cascading outward, and when they retreated, the water left behind luminous tendrils, drawing intricate patterns on the beach that shimmered brilliantly before fading away.

A profound sense of wonder enveloped Jim, deeper than anything he had experienced before. He squeezed Bella's hand, feeling her pulse quicken in response. "It's like the sea be full of stars," he said softly, his voice filled with reverence.

Bella's eyes were wide, absorbing every detail of this spectacle of light. "I've never seen anything so beautiful," she whispered. "It's magical."

Billy, feeling the weight of Jim's words that this was an important point in their journey, and equally spellbound by the scene, nodded.

"Hawkins!" he called up to John at the wheel. "Bring 'er about and head toward the land! Let's see this closer."

Mr. Hawkins swung the wheel, guiding the ship as it gracefully pivoted, its prow now set on a course for the distant shore. As the Siren's Call cut through the water, the luminous display grew more vivid, casting delicate, flickering patterns of blue-green light that danced across the entire ship. All on deck watched in awe as these tiny creatures pulsed rhythmically with the sway of the sea, every ripple sending waves of gentle light spreading outward in ever-widening circles, forming intricate patterns that captivated the eye, and illuminating their faces with a gentle, undulating glow.

Below deck, the shift in direction rippled through the hammocks, their gentle sway becoming a pronounced swing. The ropes stretched and relaxed with each arc, producing a soft chorus of creaks. Sailors, who had been nestled in their sleep, stirred, eyes fluttering open as they sensed the change. Some others were still awake, playing cards or whittling, drinking grog, and engaging in their usual banter. The men paused, cards slipping from their fingers as they felt the ship tilt, a silent question passing among them. Curious, they jumped to their feet and spilled onto the deck; the sight that greeted them was nothing short of breathtaking. The waters around them were alive with light, a shimmering spectacle of luminescent life that painted the sea in ethereal colors. The waves seemed to glow from within, casting a gentle radiance that danced and flickered, turning the night into a scene from a dream.

"Blimey, would ye look at that," uttered one of the men, speaking in a soft hush that trembled with a childlike wonder.

Absorbed in the swath of light bathing the beach, Billy noticed that there was a point where the light abruptly faded into the distance, perpendicular to the shoreline. Intrigued, he commanded Mr. Hawkins to steer the ship toward this mysterious sight. It became evident as they drew nearer that the glowing organisms were floating in what at first appeared to be the mouth of another river, flowing from inland into the ocean. However, this was no river. The illumination revealed a hidden continuation of the ocean through a gap in the land—a tidal inlet, which created a stunning corridor of soft blue-green light that stretched into the distance.

With a quiet wonder, Billy's eyes took in the marshy opening of the inlet. The soft glow revealed a waterscape where land and water intertwined seamlessly, forming a luminous pathway bordered by the shadowy outlines of a salt marsh. As the inlet meandered further inland, the marsh gradually surrendered to a dense thicket of mangrove trees, their distinctive stilt-like roots rising from the brackish water.

Billy's gaze fixed on the narrow passageway. Studying the mysterious entrance, he began to feel a peculiar sensation, a tingling at the edge of his awareness. It started as a faint whisper, but with each passing moment, the feeling grew stronger, an insistent compulsion that tugged at his very soul. He felt as if the sea itself was calling to him, its currents reaching out with invisible fingers, urging him to steer the ship into the inlet, promising revelations hidden just beyond the veil of the known.

He turned to Jim and Bella, seeing the same sense of mystery and curiosity reflected in their eyes. Billy knew that this moment was more than mere coincidence; it was a convergence of fate, a crossroads where the prophecy and their journey met.

"We need to take the ship in," he said to them. Feeling it his responsibility to guide the ship carefully through the narrow passageway, he continued, "I must be doin' it meself."

With purposeful strides, Billy made his way up to the quarterdeck. The sensation of being guided continued to grow ever stronger, a strange and compelling force that tugged at him and filled his mind with a singular focus. "John, I'll be takin' the wheel."

Sensing the gravity of the moment, Mr. Hawkins nodded and relinquished the wheel. Billy stepped forward, his fingers closing around the wooden spokes with a determined grip. The ship responded to his touch, every timber and sail perfectly attuned to his intentions.

So, with a steely gaze locked on the mysterious inlet, Billy took control, guiding the Siren's Call through the shadowy waters. The muscles in his face tightened with determination, each line on his brow a testament to the concentration etched deep within. He held tightly onto the wheel with a steady resolve, responding to the subtle shifts in the wind and current. The inlet approached, and Billy's attention sharpened to a fine edge as he prepared to guide the ship into the looming passage.

Ben had been laying in his hammock, having been confined to his quarters by the captain's order. Though sleeping, his mind was a turbulent sea of obsession. His dreams were chaotic, twisted and dark, filled with grotesque images and nightmarish cries that gnawed at his psyche, fueled by his spiraling madness. Yet, as the ship had sailed up the coast, the hauntingly beautiful whale songs seeped into his dreams, their gentle rhythms soothing the jagged edges of his fractured sanity. As with the others, the songs, rich with the serene sounds of nature, wrapped around his thoughts in a comforting embrace. The once tumultuous storm of his mind began to calm, softening to a gentle breeze. Ben tossed and turned, yet as he slept, his movements gradually grew less frantic, his breathing steadied. In this cocoon of sound and serenity, he found a rare moment of respite, the chaos within yielding to the tranquil beauty of the ocean's chorus.

In this moment of fragile peace, Ben had sensed the subtle tilting of the ship as it turned toward the shore, the shift in direction tugging at his unconscious. His eyes fluttered open. For the first time in what felt like an eternity, he felt a semblance of control over the madness that had plagued him. He swung his legs over the side of his cot, his bare feet landing on the cool, rough planks of the floor.

He slowly opened the door of his cabin, feeling the gentle sway of the ship beneath his feet. With measured steps, he walked out, the cool night air greeting him as he emerged onto the deck. He glanced up at the quarterdeck where Billy stood at the wheel, his silhouette stark against the star-studded sky. Summoning his courage, Ben made his way up, his footsteps barely making a sound on the rugged planks.

Billy turned, his eyes narrowing slightly as they locked onto Ben, but the usual fire behind them was tempered.

"Ye were confined to yer quarters," Billy growled. "Why're ye here?"

"Captain," he began, his voice trembling but earnest. "I know I been a right mess lately, losin' me wits an' all. But I beg ye, hear me out."

Billy's gaze bore into him, silent and unmoving, so Ben pressed on.

"I ain't makin' no excuses, sir," Ben continued. "A madness took hold of me. "t's like . . . like there's been a storm inside me head, ragin' and howlin'. I couldn't see straight, couldn't think right. Me own thoughts turned against me, twistin' me head into somethin' dark and hellish."

He paused, taking a shaky breath. "There'd be times I'd see things that weren't there, shadows movin' where there weren't none, hear whispers that made no sense. I couldn't trust what I saw or heard. It was a terror worse than the fiercest of storms."

Billy leaned against the wheel, his gaze unwavering.

Ben paused again, eyes pleading with the captain. "But somethin's changed today, Captain. I don't know why or how, but the madness in me head—it just quieted. It's like the storm passed and left calm waters behind. I can think straight for the first time in what feels like forever. I think I be feelin' like meself again, Captain."

Billy's expression softened, a flicker of understanding in his eyes.

"Please, Captain," Ben beseeched. "I don't care 'bout bein' first mate no more. I just want to be part of the crew again, to show ye I can still be trusted. I know it's hard to believe after everythin', but I swear I be feelin' better now."

Billy had always been the very embodiment of a formidable pirate leader, his personality as rough and unyielding as the seas he commanded. With eyes as sharp as flint and a voice that could thunder over the loudest squall, he tolerated no insubordination or disrespect, and his anger was both quick and unforgiving. But now, Billy's rough edges, once as jagged and hard as the rocks of a storm-tossed shoreline, were being gradually smoothed by the subtle yet unmistakable spiritual and emotional transformation he was undergoing.

The captain studied the young man before him, his eyes no longer filled with the sharp intensity of his wrath, but with a calm depth that spoke of forgiveness and empathy. His recent experiences had woven a serene thread through the fabric of his being, making it increasingly difficult for him to summon the fiery anger and combativeness that once defined him.

Finally, he spoke, his voice gruff but not unkind. "Ben," Billy began, his words measured and steady, "yer behavior's been wilder than a hurricane and as senseless as a fish tryin' to climb a tree. It's caused naught but bedlam aboard this vessel an' shown no respect for me command."

The Secret of the Dragon's Scale

Ben nodded. "I understand, Captain. I beg pardon for me conduct. I meant no disrespect and regret any trouble I've caused. I be wantin' to make things right."

Billy's face took on a fatherly expression, his hard edges smoothing out with a look of care and patience, though his tone remained stern. "Ye'll return as part of the crew, and ye'll be expected to carry out yer duties just like any of the other men. But mark me words, given yer recent folly, ye're right that ye won't be first mate anymore."

"Thank ye, Captain," Ben responded, gratitude evident in his voice.

With a nod of appreciation, he turned and made his way down to the deck below, the worn and weathered planks creaking under his boots as he descended the steps, the sea air whipping around him. As he reached the deck, he spotted Jim and Bella standing together near the ship's railing, their figures outlined against the glow of the life in the water. With an expression of contriteness and a little embarrassment on his face, Ben approached them slowly. They both looked back as Ben approached, their faces brightening with relief that he seemed to be back to his old self.

The captain now returned his attention to the tidal inlet as the ship continued sailing along its winding course. The banks of the inlet grew denser with each passing moment, teeming with a lush tapestry of trees and vegetation that seemed to close in on either side. Vines draped from branches, swaying gently in the humid breeze, while dense underbrush crowded the shoreline. Despite the thickening foliage, the water itself remained a spectacle. It was awash with the luminescent life floating on the surface, casting a soft, delicate glow that danced and shimmered in the gentle current. This trail of light illuminated their path, creating a magical passage through the heart of the wilderness. The captain, ever vigilant, kept a steady hand on the wheel, guiding the ship with practiced ease through the narrowing channel, the soft light reflecting in his eyes as he watched the enchanting display unfold.

As the ship drifted steadily though the inlet, an uneasy tension gripped the crew. The soft rustle of leaves and the occasional cry of a nocturnal bird were the only sounds, the eerie stillness amplifying the tension. Eyes strained through the darkness, trying to decipher the secrets hidden within the reeds and mangroves of the marsh.

Suddenly, like a curtain lifting on a new scene, the light of the moon revealed a towering rock face, looming ominously in the vessel's path! What they had taken for more dense forest concealed the wall of a cliff, its rugged surface expertly camouflaged by the dense growth of trees and vegetation in the dark of the night!

"Captain! Ahead!" a crewman cried, pointing frantically.

Without missing a beat, Billy bellowed out, "All hands! Reef the sails! Slow the ship! Now!"

His voice echoed off the water and reverberated through the night, cutting through the rising panic of the crew. Hands flew to the ropes, pulling with synchronized might as they wrestled the sails into submission; the ship heaved as the sails were swiftly reefed, the canvas billowing less fiercely with each tug and knot secured. The ship now slowing, the clamor of the initial frenzy settled into a steady rhythm of creaking ropes and the gentle swish of water along the sides of the vessel.

A wave of confusion swept over the crew, each sailor casting bewildered glances as the trail of glowing water continued off into the darkness, as though it was flowing into solid rock. Then, inching closer, the outline of an opening in the cliff face, marked by a faint halo of light, became apparent, and it slowly dawned on them that the inlet was flowing into the mouth of a vast cave, large enough to swallow the entire vessel! The rocky entrance had been cleverly masked by the forest and the deceptive play of shadows, invisible until they were nearly upon it.

"By the heavens," the captain breathed, his voice filled with amazement. And as if the cave itself was whispering to him, promising secrets long buried and truths yet to be uncovered, Billy made a split-second decision. "All hands, we be goin' into the cave!" he declared, his voice steady despite his trepidation.

The cave yawned open, barely wide and high enough for the ship to fit through. The Siren's Call came alive as Billy stood at the helm, his hands firmly yet gently guiding her through the narrow entrance. Under his skillful touch, the ship responded with the grace of a dancer, attuned to every subtle coaxing, every minute adjustment that its captain made.

As the ship gently drifted inside, the world transformed into a realm of unparalleled enchantment. The cave was alive with light! The luminous life shone a wondrous display of colors that danced and played across the walls in an endless ballet, where shadows leaped and light pirouetted gracefully, creating a hypnotic spectacle that captivated the senses. The rocky walls became a living canvas for this radiant choreography. Waves of electric blues and fluorescent greens undulated across the surfaces, their movements synchronized with the gentle currents of the water. Each ripple sent cascades of vibrant hues upwards, casting fleeting yet brilliant patterns like stained-glass windows catching the morning sun. Light and shadow echoed off the cave walls, their reflections multiplying and amplifying each other with each rebound. The interplay was spellbinding, drawing the eye into a luminous symphony of movement and color, where every flicker and fade told a story in light.

Suspended from the ceiling, stalactites hung like ancient chandeliers, their crystalline tips adorned with glistening drops of water that glimmered with each captured ray, transforming them into tiny, prismatic explosions of color. Each drop that fell into the tranquil pool created circular ripples that expanded outward, capturing the glow and sending it skittering across the cave walls in a display of iridescent fireworks, made even more dazzling as it was reflected again in the water below.

The Siren's Call continued its silent drift through the mysterious cave, the only sounds being the gentle lap of water against the hull and the distant echo of dripping stalactites. The air in the cave was cool and damp, carrying with it the scent of earth and stone, mingled with the faint, briny aroma of the sea. All on board stood in hushed reverence, captivated by the dance of colors, their faces alight with a childlike curiosity as they marveled at the interplay of light and shadow flickering across the cave walls, and how the water pulsed softly, the light ebbing and flowing in the gentle current. Their eyes followed the glowing brilliance of sapphire and emerald spreading out in the ship's wake as it gently cut through the water, creating rippling waves of light that played across the undulating surface like liquid fireflies.

Jim remained entranced as he watched the luminous life respond to the ship's passage, spreading out in intricate patterns that pulsed with an inner rhythm. He inhaled deeply, feeling the cool, damp air settling in his lungs, and with it a profound sense of clarity and peace. Bella leaned over the railing, feeling the coolness of the air against her skin. Her hair fluttered gracefully, in tune with the gentle sway of the ship and by a gentle breeze weaving through the cave. Her heart danced to the beauty surrounding her, kindling a joy that was pure and unrestrained. Ben stood beside them, his usually stern face softened by the enchanting scene. He closed his eyes for a moment, allowing the cool breeze to wash over him, carrying ghostly voices that seemed to call his name. In this serene moment, he let go of his burdens, replacing them with a profound sense of peace. Billy, at the helm and ever vigilant, felt the faint murmur of long-forgotten tales on the breeze as it brushed against his ear. The cave seemed alive, its secrets palpable in the air, urging him onward. He tightened his grip on the wheel, guiding the Siren's Call carefully through the narrow passage with a deft touch. The crew moved about quietly, their senses heightened by this mysterious cathedral of nature. Every sound was amplified—the creaking of the ship's timbers, the water's gentle touch against the hull, the distant drips from the cave's ceiling.

Then, almost imperceptibly, the weight of the cave began to lift. The air grew less oppressive, the shadows seemed to lighten, and the sound of dripping stalactites faded. Suddenly, the ship glided into an expanse where the cave walls, once vibrant with light, now softened into a dim glow. Pressing onward, an opening began to reveal itself, framed by towering jagged rocks standing like sentinels guarding a grand archway. The ship approached, and the breeze grew stronger, as though the very air was eager to escort them through this ancient gate. And with a final surge of determined energy, it passed through the threshold into the awaiting world beyond.

The crew found themselves in open waters again, glistening under the silvery embrace of a full moon, each ripple catching the moonlight and breaking it into a thousand sparkling fragments that danced on the surface. And like embers of a dying fire scattering into the night, the luminescent life began to disperse and fade, creating a glittering trail before blending seamlessly with the water.

Every crew member's head turned in unison in this mysterious new seascape, their eyes wide with curiosity. Jim leaned forward precariously, his gaze sweeping across the vast expanse of open water that stretched out endlessly before them, his face illuminated with a childlike wonder. Bella's fingers gripped the railing so tightly her knuckles turned white, her eyes flitting from the moonlit waves to the imposing rocky hill behind them through which they'd just emerged.

Ben could not suppress a broad smile, his rugged features softening as he looked about in every direction, trying to absorb this vast stretch of water and the silent grandeur of their newfound world.

"Captain!" Ben called up to Billy excitedly. "It must be an inland sea!"

Billy maintained a steady hand on the wheel as he surveyed their mysterious new surroundings, his curious eyes sparkling with a boyhood excitement. His gaze inevitably drifted upward, and in that moment, confusion gripped him. The star patterns in this sky were completely different from those they had navigated by just hours before.

The stars above were utterly alien to Billy, the unfamiliar constellations defying his vast knowledge of the night sky. These were nothing like the celestial guideposts he had navigated by all his life, leaving him in a state of profound disorientation. What he saw mirrored no chart he ever studied, no map he ever trusted. It was as though he had crossed into another world entirely, one where even the stars conspired to confound his senses. Billy scratched his beard, bewilderment etched on his face.

"Blimey," he muttered, squinting at the foreign sky above. "These stars be all wrong. Not an hour ago, we was seein' Orion, Taurus, and now they're nowhere to be found." His eyes scanned the sky once more, searching for a familiar anchor in this strange sea of stars. "How can this be?"

A sudden thought struck him, piercing through the fog of confusion. His heart quickened as he glanced back at the cave from which they'd just emerged. Could it be? Just then, Samuel's words echoed in his mind—*Chart a course for the Cave of Echoing Shadows, Billy. For where light and darkness dance and twirl, you'll find the gate to another world.*

The realization dawned upon him with a suddenness that pierced his very soul, igniting a storm of emotion within. His breath caught, and his eyes widened in astonishment! *That was it! The Cave of Echoing Shadows!* he thought to himself. *The gate to another world!*

He couldn't fathom why, but somehow, as if the universe had turned a page, they had crossed over into some new realm, revealing a hidden chapter brimming with mysteries yearning to be uncovered.

At that moment, an image, vivid and electrifying, flashed in Billy's mind—a recollection of the Dragon's Scale map surged to the fore. He gasped as he looked back up at the night sky, scanning the bewildering array of stars. "By Neptune's beard," he whispered to himself, his voice quivering with amazement and his pulse a rapid drumbeat in his ears. Billy extended his hand upward, trembling with anticipation. Pointing a finger, he traced some of the stars in the air. His brows arched upward, drawing lines of intrigue across his forehead, while his mouth parted slightly in astonished recognition. He closed his eyes briefly, recalling more details of the map, and then snapped them open to scan the sky again. "Could it be?" he breathed, scarcely believing the unfolding revelation.

Billy leaned over the railing, cupping his hands around his mouth to amplify his voice. "Jim!" he bellowed, urgency threading through his words. "Jim, fetch me the Dragon's Scale map from me cabin! Quick as the wind, lad!"

Jim looked up, then bolted upon hearing Billy's request, his boots thudding against the heavy oak planks. His breath came in quick bursts as he reached Billy's cabin, flung open the door with a forceful clatter, and snatched up the precious map from the table.

With the map secured under his arm, Jim sprinted up to the quarterdeck, his heart pounding with curiosity and excitement. Ben and Bella, their attention seized by the urgency in Billy's voice and the sight of Jim racing through the ship, followed close behind. Their eyes were wide with anticipation, wondering what had set their captain ablaze with such eagerness.

As Jim bounded onto the quarterdeck, breathless but triumphant, Billy's eyes locked onto the rolled parchment. He snatched the map from Jim's hand, and laid it out on the bench in front of the wheel.

"Look, look, look!" he said, his voice brimming with excitement. "Ye need be seein' this with yer own eyes!"

Jim, Ben, and Bella leaned in, their faces illuminated by the faint glow of a lantern hanging nearby. Their eyes followed Billy's finger as it swept across the celestial design along the top of the map.

"Now, look up!" Billy urged. "Feast yer eyes on the heavens above."

Their gazes darted between the stars above and the parchment below, their eyes widening with each pass. As the stars twinkled in perfect mirror with the map's constellations, a profound silence enveloped them. It was a thrilling epiphany, filling the air with a sense of astonishment and wonder. They found themselves in a breathless moment, a moment suspended in time where the universe seemed to whisper its secrets into the ears of those who dared to listen.

Jim, his voice trembling with awe, was the first to break the silence. "God in Heaven!" he exclaimed. "It be the same . . . Exactly the same."

"What does it mean?" Bella asked, the significance of the discovery not quite sinking in yet.

Ben's eyes gleamed with sudden clarity as the revelation struck him; his face lit up with the youthful exuberance of a giddy schoolboy. He bounced slightly on his toes, barely able to contain the bubbling enthusiasm threatening to spill over. Then, with a resolute belief that they were on the brink of an extraordinary discovery, he drew in a sharp breath, his voice trembling on the edge of awe and exhilaration.

"The Dragon's Scale . . . The Dragon's Scale," he repeated, the words escaping him like a prayer and a proclamation all at once. "It must be here. Somewhere. But it must be here."

Billy's eyes met Ben's, reflecting the same profound realization. He nodded slowly, a deep sense of the sublime etched into his weathered features.

"Aye, lad," Billy agreed, his voice resonant with the measured certainty of tides returning to the shore. "The stars be leadin' us true. The Dragon's Scale be here, somewhere in these waters. We've found the right sea."

With a confident stride, Billy descended to the deck, gathering the crew around him.

"Listen up, mates!" he began, his tone rich with the insight of a man who had sailed to the edge of the world and peered into its deepest mysteries. "For many a year, sailors have spun tales of treasures hidden in places that defy our understandin', guarded by the sea herself. The Dragon's Scale be one such prize, bound to the very bones of this world." He paused, letting the moment settle. "I believe the Dragon's Scale be hidin' here, in these very waters, and I'll tell ye why."

Billy's gaze swept over his crew, his eyes carrying the weight of countless horizons seen.

"The stars on the map we hold and the constellations above match up—and I believe that be no mere happenstance. We've heeded the prophecies and heard the wisdom of ancient spirits, their voices singing on wisps of wind. They all be pieces of a grand puzzle. And now, the heavens have whispered their secrets to those willin' to listen, guidin' us to this sacred sea. I feel it in me very bones, lads—this be the right place. Here, we'll uncover the truth that has slipped through the fingers of so many before us."

Steven Eisenberg

A Radiant Tear

The inland sea stretched out beneath the velvet cloak of night, its waters a liquid obsidian, reflecting a canopy of twinkling stars and the radiant glow of a full moon. The Siren's Call glided silently through this mystical realm, her proud hull slicing gently through the ripples of the calm water. Moonlight poured over the surface, painting a shimmering path of silver that wove endlessly into the shadowy horizon, as if inviting the ship toward some unknown destiny. The air was cool and crisp, carrying the faint aroma of salt and the promise of long-forgotten secrets waiting to be unearthed.

The crew had been quietly gathered around their captain on deck as he spoke, their faces lit with the faint glow of lantern light. The significance of the captain's words seeped into the hearts of the men, their spirits were bolstered, and the air was thick with anticipation. But they had sailed tirelessly throughout the day, and now, as night was upon them, they found themselves adrift in uncertainty.

"Now, we've sailed long and hard today," Billy continued, his voice steady yet tinged with the weariness of their relentless journey. "We can't see naught in this darkness, and our maps give us no more clues for now. It be wiser to wait 'til mornin' when the light'll reveal what the night hides. The best thing to do is drop anchor 'til daylight."

Together, they carried out the captain's orders with the steady efficiency of those who had spent countless nights under starlit skies. The heavy clanking of the anchor chain broke the stillness of the night, followed by a deep, resonant splash as it

The Secret of the Dragon's Scale

descended into the placid depths below. The Siren's Call settled into a gentle, comforting sway, held fast by the embrace of the inland sea.

Jim and Bella exchanged glances, their faces etched with determination for the voyage ahead, but also with fatigue. Jim's slow nod conveyed his quiet resolve, while Bella offered a brief, encouraging smile—silent affirmations of their shared purpose. Ben and the rest of the crew scattered quietly, their movements subdued, as if reluctant to disturb the gentle harmony of the evening. Boots shuffled softly against the worn planks, and muted voices rose and fell. Some retreated below deck, shoulders stooped, seeking solace in their hammocks. Others remained topside, taking up their posts for the night watch, their murmured conversations blending with the rhythmic hush of ripples against the hull.

Billy lingered a little longer on deck, the cool breeze playing softly through the sails, and the sounds of the night wrapping around him like a soothing blanket. He felt a calm settle over him, mingled with the anticipation that thrummed through his veins. Each breath he took was filled with the scent of the sea and the promise of discovery. Then, with a final sweep of his eyes across the moonlit deck and the tranquil, undulating sea, Billy turned toward his cabin. His steps were slow and deliberate, each echoing the day's toil and the weight of responsibility he bore. The wooden door creaked softly as he pushed it open, revealing the dim interior that awaited him.

The cabin was bathed in darkness, a snug haven where the outside world's concerns faded into silence. The air inside was thick with the familiar scents of aged wood, salt, rum, and the faint musk of old parchment—a comforting blend that spoke of time-worn adventures and stories waiting to be remembered. It was a warmth that wrapped around Billy like an old friend, grounding him in the present while hinting at past journeys etched into the timbers of the ship. Navigating by touch, Billy's fingers brushed against the smooth surface of his map table, the rumpled edges of well-used charts, and the cold metal of his navigational instruments. He felt for the lantern. Striking a match, he brought the tiny flame to the wick, and the lantern flickered to life.

Warm, golden light blossomed within the cabin, banishing the darkness and illuminating the space with a gentle glow. The soft light revealed the organized chaos of Billy's domain—maps spread out across the table, journals filled with meticulous notes, and an assortment of tools sitting on shelves in readiness for their next use. Shadows danced playfully along the walls, settling into serene corners as if bowing to the light's command. Here, in this quiet calm, Billy could feel the weight of the outside world lift from his shoulders.

He placed the lantern on the table, its golden light spilling outward in soft, flickering waves. For now, in the gentle sway of the Siren's Call, he allowed himself a moment of respite, a fleeting stillness before dawn's first light would call him back to the helm and the endless horizon beyond. He poured himself a small measure of rum, taking a quick sip before setting the mug aside. Though his body longed for rest, his mind buzzed with thoughts of the path ahead. Unrolling an old map, he traced its coastlines, their ink softened by time, searching for any clue that might guide them further.

His eyes drilled into all the maps sprawled across his table. The flicker of the lantern cast a warm glow over the parchments, their faded lines and cryptic markings coming alive in the shifting light. He leaned forward, hands braced on either side of the table, casting long shadows that danced across the walls like restless phantoms. Frustration etched itself into every line of his face. His jaw clenched tight, muscles at its hinge twitching as though wrestling with the unyielding puzzles hidden within the maps. His lips pressed into a hard, thin line, a silent resistance to the agitation threatening to escape.

"Where is this sea?" he asked himself. With each parchment, each atlas, he examined, he found no answers he sought. "Blasted charts," he muttered under his breath, leaning in closer. "Not a single mark, not a whisper of this damned place."

He continued to sift through all his maps, charts, and atlases with care, his movements both deliberate and impatient, his fingers skimming across the them as though willing them to reveal secrets they didn't hold. Each page told the story of known waters and landmasses, meticulously charted by explorers past. But none of them—none—gave even the faintest hint of the open expanse of water they now sailed, beneath the silvered veil of moonlight.

And then, like the first light breaking through storm clouds, it struck. The realization settled heavily on his shoulders, his expression shifting from frustration to deep contemplation.

"This sea . . . It ain't never been found. Never charted. No soul's ever been knowin' 'bout it," he murmured to himself, running a finger along the jagged coastline of a distant land.

He leaned in closer, the lantern's flickering light catching his features, highlighting the faint glimmer of intrigue now etched across his face. His mind raced, piecing together fragments of legends and whispers he'd heard in countless taverns and ports. Was it possible that the very obscurity of this sea was its greatest shield? That its elusiveness protected the treasure more effectively than any secret could?

"Maybe the reason no one's found the Dragon's Scale be 'cause they never knew 'bout this place." A spark of determination igniting within him. "No wonder no one's ever laid eyes upon it!" His eyes brightened, a flicker of hope piercing through the veil of confusion. "An' we've done what no soul before us could—discovered the hidden truth. But now, there's more to this mystery, more still buried, waitin' for us to reveal it."

A slight curl at the corner of his mouth hinted at something between bewilderment and fascination as more questions rushed to Billy's mind, each more confounding than the last. "How in the seven seas could the Dragon's Scale be here then?" he mused,

223

tilting his head slightly, as if seeing the map from a new angle might unlock its riddles. "And if no man's laid eyes upon this sea, then who first spoke of the Dragon's Scale? Where'd the whispers begin?" His gaze turned outward, as though seeking answers directly from the sea itself. "What secrets d'ye hold, ye mysterious waters? What gift—or curse—d'ye keep from our reach?"

He straightened up, his posture firming with a newfound purpose as his focus shifted back to the sprawling parchments. The answers lay not in the charts before him, but in the waters in which they now found themselves—and the secrets it whispered to those who dared to listen.

"We be close," he whispered, a smile tugging at his lips. "So very close."

With that thought, he allowed himself to succumb to the pull of sleep, his dreams filled with visions of treasure, adventure, and the endless possibilities that awaited them with the coming dawn.

A gentle stillness settled over the water as the end of night approached. The moon had gracefully dipped below the horizon, leaving behind a faint trail of its celestial glow. The stars faded one by one, their brilliant points of light surrendering to the soft encroachment of dawn. The dark canvas of the sky began to shift from deep indigo to the softer shades of lavender and rose of the pre-dawn twilight. Wisps of clouds hovered low, their edges tinged with the first hints of silver that heralded the coming day. And as the early sunlight began to blush the sky, a band of ethereal pink and orange painted the horizon. This subtle glow grew steadily, casting a tender light that transformed the tranquil waters into a shimmering mosaic of fiery crimson and molten gold.

With the first tender rays of sunlight spilling over the edge of the world, casting a golden glow over these waters, the crew of the Siren's Call began to stir. The ship, bathed in the warm embrace of dawn, breathed awake, its timbers groaning softly as if stretching alongside its sailors. The crew moved with a sense of shared purpose, and the deck was soon alive with activity.

Jim stepped out onto the deck, silhouetted against the brightening sky. He stretched his arms wide, shaking off the remnants of sleep, and took a deep breath of the crisp morning air. Next came Ben, shielding his eyes from the rising sun with one hand, and squinting at the horizon as if trying to divine what secrets it held. Bella followed closely behind, her steps light but purposeful. She paused at the edge of the deck, taking in the breathtaking panorama of the sunrise over the water. Her chestnut hair caught the morning light, framing her face in a halo of warmth.

Finally, the door to Billy's cabin opened, and he stepped out into the golden glow of morning. Billy's eyes, keen and bright, swept over the scene with a sense of pride and determination. The warm rays of the sun highlighted the deep-set lines etched into his face, underscoring the wisdom and resolve that would continue to guide their journey.

"Mornin', lads and lass," Billy called out, his voice infused with the fresh energy of the new day. "Today, we sail further into these uncharted waters. We've a mystery to unravel and a treasure to claim. Let's make it a day to remember."

A chorus of affirmative responses echoed back, the crew's spirits lifted by their captain's words. With renewed vigor, they returned to their tasks, the excitement of the quest palpable in the air.

Billy took in a deep breath, savoring the crisp morning air, sharp with salt and tinged with the pull of distant, uncharted horizons. The breeze teased through his hair and tugged at the open collar of his shirt, invigorating him as if the sea itself sought to kindle his resolve. With a sense of purpose, he walked to the bow, each step resonating with quiet resolve. Jim, Bella, and Ben followed, their eyes filled with the same mix of curiosity and anticipation.

The four of them stood together, their eyes scanning the vast inland sea. The water stretched out in all directions before them, a seemingly empty canvas painted in shifting shades of blue that deepened toward the horizon. The morning light shimmered on the gentle waves, casting a serene, almost hypnotic pattern. Yet for all its tranquil beauty, there was nothing in view—just the unbroken sea holding its secrets close, as if daring them to uncover its hidden truths.

"Nothin' in sight," Ben muttered.

Billy's eyes swept the horizon, searching for something—anything. But the sea revealed no answers. A quiet unease gnawed at him, a tension he refused to let show. He turned, and with determined steps disappeared into his cabin, returning moments later with his spyglass in hand. With a practiced flick, he extended it and raised it to his eye. The world narrowed to the circular frame of the lens as he began to search, moving along the horizon with slow, deliberate care. But the sea remained obstinate, offering nothing but an infinite stretch of shimmering blue stretching to the edge of the world.

Then, in the distance, something caught his eye. A very thin line of fog, barely perceptible, sat just on the edge of the horizon. His heart quickened as he focused in on the mist, his instincts telling him this meant something.

"Look there," Billy called out, pointing toward the distant line. His voice, filled with a sudden surge of excitement, drew the attention of the others.

Jim, Bella, and Ben leaned against the railing of the ship, their eyes straining as they peered into the distance. The endless blue seemed to taunt them, offering no sign of the elusive line of fog Billy had glimpsed.

"I not be seein' anythin'," Jim remarked, his voice edged with quiet annoyance as he shielded his eyes from the sun's glare.

Billy stood resolute, however, the spyglass clutched firmly in his hand. Turning sharply on his heel, he called out to the crew with firm conviction.

"Men, weigh anchor and set sail! We be headin' dead ahead!"

The deck of the Siren's Call erupted into a whirlwind of activity as Billy's command echoed through the air. Jim rallied the deckhands to the capstan, their synchronized heaves sending the anchor chain rattling up from the depths. Ben leapt into action as well, sprinting across the deck, and with practiced agility, scaled the ratlines, his hands moving swiftly over the ropes. Grabbing hold of a clewline, he expertly loosened it, allowing the sail to unfurl in a dramatic cascade. All sails billowed out like enormous white wings and snapped taut with a satisfying thwack as they caught the wind. Mr. Hawkins reached for the wheel, gripping the polished wood with the certainty of a man married to the sea; he gave it a decisive turn, his entire body leaning into the motion, anchoring the vessel on its forward course. The entire crew moved with a sense of urgency and purpose, their collective energy transforming the ship from a resting giant into a mighty force slicing through the waves in search of the phantom veil draped over the world's edge.

The morning sky stretched out over the sea, its pale blues deepening toward where it kissed the horizon. Delicate wisps of clouds drifted lazily, their edges smudged as though brushed by an unseen hand, adding texture to the serene canvas above. Underneath, the Siren's Call cut through the water with steady determination. Hours of sailing had passed, and the once faint line of fog on the horizon was now a more distinct, looming presence. The crew worked with a mix of routine efficiency and growing anticipation, their eyes occasionally drifting toward the mysterious haze ahead.

High above the deck, the lookout in the crow's nest shielded his eyes from the glare as he peered intently into the distance. Squinting, his heart skipped a beat as he caught sight of something unusual—an indistinct shape peering above the fog.

"Captain! Captain!" he bellowed, his voice raw with excitement. "Something's there!"

Billy immediately snapped to attention. He held his spyglass aloft, bringing it swiftly to his eye as he moved to the edge of the bow. The deck stilled for a moment, the crew pausing in their tasks to listen.

"Where?" Billy yelled back.

"Dead ahead, Captain!" the lookout hollered, pointing toward the mist. "Just above the fog!"

The Siren's Call pressed onward, its prow slicing through the calm waters as the morning sun continued its ascent. Far ahead, a hint of change lingered on the horizon. The sunlight dimmed slightly, as though a thin veil had been lowered. The water seemed darker there, its mirrored surface softly interrupted by the growing presence of haze. It was an indistinct blur at first, but grew steadily as the ship drew closer. Upon approaching the edge of the waiting fog, tendrils of mist began to reach out to greet the ship before retreating, as if they'd changed their mind, only to stretch forward once more.

And then it happened. A single shaft of golden light pierced the veil with sharp clarity, cutting through the mist like a lifeline to the heavens. The crew stilled, watching as the light danced across the deck, shattering the somber gray into radiant, glowing fragments. Another beam followed, and then another, while the fog twisted and parted around the ship, each tendril illuminated in a golden brilliance before dissipating into nothingness.

Slowly, the ghostly shroud began to dissolve in the morning warmth, revealing tantalizing glimpses of a landscape beyond. As the ship glided closer, the shapes rising above the fog began to take on more distinct forms. There, emerging from the haze were the faint outlines of the towering cones of volcanoes—their slender, conical silhouettes stark against the backdrop of the misty haze, each one tapering to a sharp, almost needle-like peak. At first, only the tips of the volcanoes could be seen, their jagged peaks piercing the sky with majesty, as if untethered from the Earth. Gradually, though, the faint but distinct features of an island emerged from the dissipating mist. The crew stood frozen at the railing, eyes wide with wonder, hearts pounding in unison. The first to break the silence was Billy, his face alight with pure wonder. "Look sharp, lads!" he cried, raising his spyglass to his eye. "There be land ahead!"

A ripple of anticipation swept through the crew. Heads tilted and bodies leaned forward, every sailor craning to catch their first glimpse of the mysterious island. Eyes squinted against the thinning mist, sharp with focus, while hands gripped the railings as though steadying themselves against the tide of anticipation surging within them. The sailors exchanged excited glances, their initial awe transforming into a collective sense of determination and adventure. Each one aboard the Siren's Call felt the pull of the unknown, the promise of discovery igniting a fire within their hearts.

Dotting the horizon like ancient sentinels, an array of volcanic peaks stretched as far as the eye could see, each one a majestic monument to nature's raw power. One peak stood tall in the foreground, its rocky slopes cloaked in lush greenery that glittered under the growing light of the morning. Just beyond, another peak rose, slightly taller and wrapped in a mantle of smoke that drifted lazily skyward. Further still, a third peak loomed, its jagged edges blurred by distance and the lingering mist. Beyond these, additional summits emerged, each peak echoing the grandeur of the one before it.

Thick, sprawling forests clung to their slopes, weaving a cloak so lush and unbroken it was as if the land bled seamlessly from one volcano into the next, defying the eye's attempt to discern where one began and another ended. The closer peaks stood bold in their clarity, their ridges carved sharply against the sky, while those farther away blurred into silhouettes of green and gray, blending with the play of mist that coiled along their heights. Adding to the mystery, the fog shifted and swirled, casting fleeting shadows and blurring boundaries. It crept along the ridges, dissolving the sharp edges of the peaks and smudging their outlines into the pale air. Each swirl and drift of mist seemed to conspire with the forests, keeping their secrets close and leaving the crew in a state of wonder, questioning whether they were looking at one continuous land, or many separate islands cloaked in nature's illusions.

Jim tilted his head, squinting hard at the hazy peaks jutting from the sea. His finger traced the air as he pointed, half in awe, half in puzzlement, trying to discern the truth hidden within the layers of land and mist.

"Captain, look at 'em," he said, pointing to each peak. "One peak in front of the other. But are we seein' one island, or many?"

Billy raised his spyglass again. "Aye, it not be clear yet," he answers. "Hawkins!" he called up. "Get us in closer to the land! Then steer her starboard! We'll follow the shoreline and see where she leads!"

The ship turned gracefully, its hull slicing a path through the water as it hugged the curve of the shoreline. At the railing, Jim, Bella, Ben, and Billy leaned forward, their gazes dancing across the landscape ahead with a mix of anticipation and curiosity. The mist-cloaked peaks grew taller with every breath of wind that propelled them, each one a dark, craggy sentinel draped in lush vegetation and dense forests. Shadows shifted across the landscape where the sun pierced the swirling mist, painting the peaks in fleeting patterns of gold and green.

As the Siren's Call rounded the side of the land, the fog gently lifted, unveiling a scene that took their breath away. A wide stretch of sea, shimmering in the sunlight, cut through the land. It became increasingly clear that the peaks they had admired from afar were not part of a single, sprawling island but were instead distinct volcanic islands, each embraced by the sea.

Bella's eyes sparkled with excitement, her gaze tracing the rugged shorelines now clearly separated by narrow straits. "There," she began, pointing at an island emerging from the mist. Jim, Ben, and Billy's eyes followed her outstretched finger as each island revealed itself. "There. And there," she continued, her words shimmering with delight at each peak coming into view. "And, there . . . and . . . there . . . "

Bella's words faltered mid-sentence, her lips parting as if realization had stolen her breath. An image took shape in her mind, vivid and undeniable, sending a shiver down her spine, and when she turned to the others, their faces reflected the same astonishment. Jim gasped, Ben raised a hand as if to steady himself, while Billy's eyebrows shot up. They all realized the same thing at once, a silent agreement passing among them.

Billy broke the hush, his voice steady but charged with urgency. "Uh . . . Bella, lass . . . fetch the stone with yer temple map on it."

Bella turned and dashed to the captain's cabin.

She quickly returned, clutching the stone as if it were treasure. Her breath came in excited bursts, her eyes wide with anticipation. She held out the stone for everyone to see, and they all gathered around, their faces alight with eager anticipation and excitement. The sea breeze carried a palpable sense of discovery, rustling their clothes and hair as they leaned closer to inspect the stone.

Ben, his hand trembling with a mix of exhilaration and disbelief, pointed to the nearest island. "Look," he uttered, his voice barely more than a breath, thick with wonder. His finger moved from one island, back to the stone, then to the next island, and back to the stone.

"And there," he continued, his voice growing stronger with each word. "And there . . . "

The four of them had spent hours in painstaking comparison of Bella's careful sketch of the ancient temple floor to all the maps and charts in Billy's possession, so the image on the stone had been seared into each of their memories—a mental imprint so vivid it haunted their dreams. The turquoise, inlaid in stark relief to the black obsidian of the temple floor, had whispered to their imaginations—these shapes, these patterns, surely, they suspected, represented land. And now, the realization struck with the force of a tidal wave—they were right; the lay of the islands before them was an exact replica of the map's mysterious land pattern.

For a heartbeat, none of them spoke, their breaths caught in a collective gasp as awe rippled through them. This profound recognition bound them together in silent triumph, as they grasped the significance of their discovery with hearts pounding and minds racing.

Then Jim broke the heavy stillness, his voice laced with wonder. "The spirits at the village . . . they led us here, didn't they? They opened the door into the temple for us to find the map. This—" He gestured at the island, trembling from sheer amazement. "This can't be just chance."

"But why?" Ben's voice quivered, caught between disbelief and a yearning to understand. "Why would they be wantin' us to know 'bout the map in the temple?" He paused, his gaze darting between the others, searching for answers that weren't there. "And how could they be knowin' it would lead us to this very spot? Would they be wantin' us to find the Dragon's Scale? How would they even be knowin' 'bout it?"

Billy looked at them with eyes that shone with a clarity that came from a lifetime spent navigating the unknown.

"Aye. The reasons of the spirits be as mysterious as a foggy night on the open sea. Just as we can't always see the stars or know what lies beyond the mist, so too their purposes be hidden from us. We navigate by faith and feel, trustin' that each gust of wind and shift of the waves carries us toward a destiny only they can see."

Bella stood motionless, the morning sun weaving its golden threads through her hair and across her face, catching the depths of her thoughtful gaze. She looked out at the islands with eyes that held both reason and faith, qualities instilled in her by Father Ignatius. Her voice was soft yet carried the depth of her conviction as she began to speak.

"It's all a long thread in the fabric of our destinies, Father would say. He taught me that in God's vast world, there are mysteries beyond human understanding—threads of fate woven into our lives that we cannot always see or understand."

Bella's face carried the weight of quiet reflection, her eyes half-closed as if tracing the spirits' words within her mind. The lines of wisdom etched lightly into her features seemed to deepen, as though each word she spoke came from a place of profound understanding. Her voice steadied with humble reverence as she continued.

"It was the spirits of the stone that sings to the sky that whispered to us—laying bare the virtues and vices in our souls, our loves and our fears, and the paths we must follow. They weren't just telling us tales for the sake of it; they were preparing us for something greater."

She paused, allowing her words to settle like gentle waves.

"Then, it was the spirits of the village that guided us to this place, to these islands, through paths that seem unclear and purposes that remain hidden. The captain's right. It's hard to know what they intended, or why they chose us. But Father would say that this is all part of the divine mystery—part of the way we choose our destinies."

Bella looked back, her eyes now sweeping over the faces of her companions, each reflecting a mix of curiosity and contemplation.

"We stand here, in this mysterious sea, not just by chance but by a design greater than ourselves," she said. "Sometimes we must walk in faith, trusting that each step, each encounter, leads us closer to our true purpose. The spirits have guided us thus far, revealing truths and leading us through trials, and now they have brought us here."

Her gaze dropped briefly as if gathering her thoughts. Then, with a steadying breath, her eyes lifted.

"Though we may not understand their reasons, we must embrace the journey, knowing that our destinies are intertwined with the will of forces beyond our grasp. It is in these moments of uncertainty that we find strength, wisdom, and perhaps, the answers we seek."

Bella's words lingered like the soft echoes of a distant chime. A profound silence followed her thoughtful reflection as each of them was lost in contemplation of the wisdom she offered.

The Siren's Call continued its steady journey, its prow parting the calm water, leaving a faint lacework of ripples in its wake. The islands rose around it, their verdant slopes and craggy brows mirrored in the unbroken surface of the sea. Sounds of the soft hush of the hull brushing the water blended with the gentle flutter of sails overhead, caught by the subtle breath of the wind. Each turn around the undulating curves of the islands revealed new vistas—hidden coves draped in emerald shadows and clusters of jagged rocks breaking the monotony of the shoreline like ancient teeth. Overhead, white birds flew lazily against a clear dome of endless blue, their calls faint yet harmonious with the serenity of the scene. Then, from above, a cry rang out, breaking the quiet.

"Lagoon, ho!" shouted a crewman in the crow's nest, his voice carrying down to the deck with urgency.

Billy's eyes focused sharply as he turned toward the island. "What d'ye see, lad?" he called back.

The crewman, peering through his spyglass, leaned forward. "Aye, a lagoon at the island ahead, Captain—looks to be a safe harbor!"

Jim, Bella, and Ben moved to the railing, their curiosity piqued, eyes straining to catch sight of the lagoon. Then, as the ship rounded a gentle bend, the world opened up before them. A secluded cove unfolded like a secret revealed, cradled within the jagged arms of rocky outcrops and shrouded by a vibrant curtain of foliage.

Billy nodded decisively. "Bring us in slow, lads," he ordered, his voice firm and filled with anticipation. "Let's see what this place be havin' in store for us."

The Secret of the Dragon's Scale

The crew bustled into action—sails shifted in the breeze as hands prepared the anchor. Jim, Bella, and Ben exchanged glances, a mix of excitement and trepidation in their eyes. The spirits had led them here, to this serene and hidden place, and now it was time to discover why.

The sails, now slackening, billowed faintly with just enough wind to nudge the ship forward. Each subtle shift of the rudder sent the vessel into a slow, sweeping curve, its course as smooth as the arc of a brushstroke; the ship moved into the lagoon with the fluidity of a sigh breathed across still water.

The lagoon's entrance was a graceful arch, spacious enough to welcome a proud ship. Beyond the entrance, it blossomed into a shimmering expanse. Billy's sharp eyes scanned this natural harbor, his face a picture of quiet caution. Not knowing the depth of the lagoon, he ordered the crew to halt the ship at a cautious distance from the shore. The men moved with quiet precision, working deftly as the anchor chain unraveled in rhythmic clinks that resonated through the air. With a muted splash, the anchor's iron form slipped beneath the surface, vanishing into the lagoon's mysterious depths as the ship came to rest, becoming a guest in this idyllic sanctuary.

All on board leaned forward, their eyes brimming with keen curiosity as they absorbed the wonders of the lagoon before them. Encircled by vibrant coral reefs and graceful, swaying palms, it felt like a secret unveiled—a masterpiece shaped by nature's hand. Water sparkled in shades of jewel-like turquoise, inviting and seemingly untouched, while the lofty trees whispered in the breeze, their dappled shadows dancing playfully over stretches of pale sand and weathered stone. Overhead, birds of vivid and striking plumage flitted through the foliage, their colors glinting like precious gems in the cascading sunlight.

Jim leaned over the railing, his attention drawn to large ripples disturbing the otherwise placid surface of the water below. The ripples emerged in a random fashion, appearing here and there without a discernible pattern. One moment, the water would be calm, then suddenly a ripple would spread outward from an unseen point, followed by another in a completely different place. Some ripples appeared close to the ship, while others started further out, near the periphery of the lagoon. It was as if the water had its own agenda, sending out these gentle waves whenever and wherever it pleased. The appearance of each ripple felt almost whimsical, adding to the mysterious allure of the waterscape.

Jim followed the appearance of the ripples as they popped up around the ship.

"Ben, Bella," Jim called out softly, not taking his eyes off the water. "Come 'ere and have a look at this."

Jim pointed to the lagoon as they walked over.

"Ye see them ripples?" Jim asked, his voice a mix of curiosity and unease. "They be springin' up all around us, but I ain't seein' what's causin' 'em."

"What do you think it is?" asked Bella.

"Don't know," replied Jim.

"Captain, come 'ere," Jim called out to Billy.

Billy followed Jim's pointing finger to the unusual disturbances, his keen eyes narrowing as he studied the water. But the only thing obvious to him was that the ripples appeared randomly, though each one hinted at something moving just beneath the surface. He stroked his beard thoughtfully before giving a decisive nod.

"Hmm, I see 'em," he said. "Time we get to the bottom of this." Billy turned to face his crew, who were watching him with a mix of curiosity and readiness. His voice rang out clear and commanding over the deck. "Alright, lads! Ready the boats! We're goin' ashore to see what this place be all about!"

With a soft, muted splash, the boats descended into the still water, sending gentle waves across its placid surface. Standing tall and resolute in the lead boat, the captain's keen eyes were fixed unwaveringly on the island ahead.

Ben settled among his fellow crewmates in the second boat, his eyes darting around with palpable curiosity, each ripple and shadow capturing his full attention. In the third boat, Jim and Bella shared a look of exhilaration, their faces alight with anticipation. The other sailors mirrored their excitement, heads turning frequently, their expressions a mix of wonder and eagerness as they scanned the lagoon's surface and the distant island. Each man gripped his oar with a determined hand, their strokes filled with a collective sense of adventure.

From their vantage point in the boats, they beheld a sanctuary of unparalleled beauty. The lagoon, now spread out before them like a painter's masterpiece, displayed its coral reefs bursting with an array of colors—deep purples, vivid oranges, and soft pinks. As they rowed, their eyes wandered over the majestic palm trees lining the sandy shore. Their emerald fronds swayed languidly in the warm, tropical breeze, casting gentle shadows on the pristine white sand. Against the deep greens, bursts of color erupted—vivid cascades of hibiscus glowing in fiery reds and oranges, and wild orchids in soft lilacs and whites clinging to trunks. A floral dance of faint honey and spice wove through the briny freshness of sea water, mingling with a grounding aroma of rich, sun-warmed soil with its undertones of driftwood. The air around them was suffused with the soothing symphony of nature—the delicate hush of gentle waves brushing against the shore then retreating with a soft sigh, the distant cries of seabirds soaring overhead, and the soft whisper of rustling leaves carried by the wind that hinted at the secrets the island held. The scene was one of serene, almost surreal beauty—a sublime paradise untouched by time.

The boats glided forward. Behind them, the Siren's Call stood sentinel-like, a guardian of the lagoon, its image growing smaller and more distant with each stroke. The water had been a placid expanse, the ripples around the ship merely a curious, inconsequential dance upon its surface, and now were of little matter to the crew as they busily rowed toward the island.

Gradually, however, a subtle change began to manifest around them. The once-random ripples started to gather purpose, their movements becoming more deliberate. What had been an innocuous part of the scenery now drew closer, converging on the boats with an uncanny precision, forming serpentine patterns that trailed behind and alongside them. The water shivered with an inexplicable energy, now seeming alive with mysterious intent.

"Look there," Jim said to the others, pointing at the water. "Do ye see that?"

Ben squinted at the water. "Be just fish," he called back to Jim.

"There it be again!" Jim exclaimed, his voice carrying a note of eager curiosity.

Soon, an uncanny sensation began to creep upon the crew—the ripples were not random; they were following the boats with a haunting grace. What began as gentle undulations transformed into complex whorls, tracing mesmerizing designs on the water's surface. The men exchanged uneasy glances, the serene lagoon now infused with an air of foreboding.

As the men rowed, their senses heightened. They could feel a strange energy coursing through the lagoon. Suddenly, the rhythmic ripples on the water were scattered by a new and startling sight! Through the silvery surface, the sleek, curving forms of tail fins began to emerge. They appeared tentatively and gently at first, glistening with an iridescent sheen, catching the light as they broke the surface for fleeting moments before disappearing again beneath the water.

"See? Just fish," Ben remarked smugly.

But the fragile calm was shattered in an instant, replaced by an eruption of chaos as fins now surged upward! Each powerful thrust sent arcs of water skyward, the droplets sparkling in the morning light like shards of crystal before crashing back into the restless water. The fins arched high above the surface, and with each descent, they slammed back down, unleashing a force that sent waves rippling violently outward, slamming against the hulls of the boats! The lagoon came alive, its once placid surface transformed into a seething cauldron of foam and spray! The air was filled with the sounds of the water's protest—splashing, churning, and the deep, resonant thud of the fins striking the surface.

Bella, gripping the edge of the boat, leaned over to get a closer look at the splashing water. Her eyes carried a flicker of childlike wonder, darting back and forth as each tail fin broke the surface.

"Umm, must be very big fish!"

Billy rose cautiously to his feet, the boat rocking beneath him as he leaned forward to catch a better look at the mysterious shapes causing the furious commotion.

"These ain't fish," he said firmly. "Fish tails be up and down. See those fins? They go side to side, like whales and dolphins."

The frenzied chaos of the lagoon ended as abruptly as it had begun. The fierce thrashing of fins fell silent, the wild surges of foam and spray dissipating into nothingness. An eerie calm settled over the water. The boats, their rocking subsiding as the waves dissipated, now floated serenely in the sudden stillness.

A quiet hung in the air, deafening in its contrast, leaving everyone frozen, their breaths shallow and uncertain in the face of such unnerving calm. It was the kind of deep, profound silence that makes the hairs on the back of one's neck stand up. They scanned the water, unsure what to expect next.

Then, all at once, everyone in the boats jolted backwards in astonishment! Gasps tore at their throats, as the faces of women emerged gracefully from the water on each side of the boats, their eyes filled with curiosity as they peered at Bella and the men.

And just as mysteriously as they had appeared, the women vanished back beneath the surface, leaving only a trail of ripples dancing across the water. Eyes, wide and unblinking, stared uncomprehendingly at the now-empty surface where the mysterious women had just been. Brows climbed so high they seemed ready to disappear into the shadow of their hairlines, and mouths hung agape in stunned, slack-jawed bewilderment. The moment seemed to stretch on forever, each one of them transfixed, hearts still pounding from the shock.

Without warning, the water exploded in a cascade of silver spray! With a burst of energy, creatures erupted from the depths, porpoising out of the water, soaring high above the surface before plunging back into the lagoon! The spectacle was both breathtaking and surreal, as women with the elegance of dancers, their lower halves unmistakably like the tails of fish, arced gracefully around the boats!

With each arc and dive, Bella and the men could only stare in amazement as they finally glimpsed the true nature of these creatures. They were not of this world—they were of unparalleled beauty, their upper bodies exuding an almost supernatural allure. Their faces were radiant and flawless, torsos lithe and sculpted, and arms long and delicate. Every curve and contour glistened like mother-of-pearl, each movement casting radiant colors that seemed to pull sunlight from the heavens. Their eyes, wide and hypnotic, sparkled with sapphire blue and seafoam green, with glittering flecks of silver scattered within their irises. Each mermaid's hair flowed like liquid silk, and was a unique reflection of her connection to the sea. Shades of rich teal and deep emerald rippled through their locks. Waves of aquamarine intertwined with streaks of muted rose and sunset amber. Some had threads of opalescent silver and crystalline white woven through, while others had braids that gleamed in pastel pink and soft lavender. Their tails, magnificent and sinuous, cascaded with an iridescence that defied earthly palettes. Scales, as if polished gemstones, glimmered in a dance of brilliant green and lustrous cobalt, while streaks of radiant yellow and vibrant violet flickered like sunlight filtering through crystal. The edges of their powerful fins trailed with translucent fringes, delicate as the wings of dragonflies and embroidered with the faintest gleam, adding an exquisite touch to their already captivating forms.

Billy felt the strength drain from his legs, a weakness creeping up from his feet and spreading through his entire body. The world seemed to spin around him. His breath caught in his throat, and with a low, incredulous gasp, he staggered backward. His knees buckled, and he collapsed into the boat with a thud that reverberated through the wood. The crew, still captivated by the spectacle, barely noticed their captain's fall.

He lay there, his chest heaving in frantic bursts as he stared up at the sky, the light dancing in his eyes.

"Blessed saints preserve us!" he blurted out, his voice crackling with disbelief. "Mermaids!"

Pressing his hand to his chest, Billy tried to steady the rapid shallow gasps that clawed at his throat, but he was overwhelmed by the enormity of the sight he just beheld. Each breath quickened, his pulse thundering in his ears, as the realization set in.

"Mermaids!" he exclaimed again, the word bursting forth between panting breaths, filled with shock and bewilderment.

From the time of his earliest days at sea, Billy had been steeped in the legends of mermaids. All manner of sailor and buccaneer revered these stories, recounting them around flickering lanterns with a mix of awe and fear. Yet, for Billy, these legends had always remained just that—legends, fanciful yarns spun to pass restless nights on endless waters. But now, the fantasies had come to life before his very eyes, bursting forth into his reality, vivid and undeniable, shattering the fortress of skepticism that had always defined his world.

John Hawkins had been sitting alongside the captain in the boat. As Billy lay sprawled on the bottom, Hawkins shifted over and extended his hand to help him up. Billy sat up, still reeling from the shock and breathing quickly, his mind struggling to process the surreal events unfolding around him.

Suddenly, without warning, Hawkins was gone! Billy's eyes darted around in confusion, searching the boat for any sign of his friend. But the moment was shattered by thunderous splashes all around him! Water erupted into the air above the boat, raining cold droplets all over Billy. Mermaids—their faces twisted in raw anger, their once mesmerizing eyes now burning with a hellish intensity—burst forth from the water like avenging spirits and hurled themselves over the boats with terrifying agility, their arms outstretched in a fierce determination to exact their will!

Mermaids came at them from both sides! The water churned and frothed as they erupted from the depths and descended upon the sailors with relentless force! Cries of fear and confusion filled the air, overlapping with the crashing and hissing of splashing water and the sharp, resounding whacks of powerful tails! Billy watched, his chest tightening in dread, as outstretched hands latched onto a crewman, and with a single, brutal motion, wrenched him upward and hurled him into the lagoon! Another mermaid soared over, and with a powerful flick of her tail, slammed into a crewman's chest with a deep, resonant thwack that echoed over the water, launching him into the air, his arms flailing wildly in a desperate attempt to grasp at nothing before crashing into the lagoon! One of the men swung an oar wildly, trying to fend off the attacking creatures, but it was a futile effort. A mermaid lunged at him, her shining tail coiled like a spring. With a jaw-dropping burst of power, she struck the oar clean from his grip! He stumbled backward, eyes wide with shock, before the tail lashed again, sending him hurtling overboard!

One by one, men were cast from their boats as the mermaids flew over, their pleas for help swallowed by the roiling lagoon.

But then, the mermaids vanished back into the lagoon, leaving a deceptive calm in their wake. Along with Billy, Ben, Jim, Bella, and a few of the others were so far spared from the onslaught. Momentarily disoriented, they scanned the now eerily still water, their breaths held in anxious anticipation for what might come next.

    Beneath the surface, though, the mermaids gathered, their bodies taut with purpose, their tails whipping back and forth with a fierce frenzy as they prepared for their next move. The stillness of the lagoon was abruptly shattered as the mermaids erupted from below with a violent surge of fury! Two of the boats were launched skyward, wrenched from the water with a terrific blast and exploding into splinters by the sheer force of the attack! A deafening cacophony of cracking wood and crashing water filled the air as the remnants of the boats scattered in a storm of debris! All on board were hurled high into the air, their cries lost in the ferocious roar of the pandemonium.

    The lagoon became a maelstrom of thrashing limbs and broken wood! Thrown wildly from his boat, Jim barely had time to gasp for breath before he was submerged, the shock of the cold water stealing the air from his lungs. Panic surged as he struggled to orient himself, his arms slicing through the water in frantic sweeps! Summoning every ounce of strength he had left, he kicked frantically, his legs propelling him upward through the swirling madness! At last, his head burst through the surface, inhaling with ragged, frantic gulps, water cascading down his face as he coughed and spluttered.

    Bella was tossed like a ragdoll as the force of the mermaids' strike sent her hurtling through the air! She struck the water with a violent slap! Her body plunged beneath the surface, and for a moment, all was silent but for the muffled roar of the commotion above. Thrashing desperately, she fought her way back up, bursting through with a rasping, guttural gasp tearing from her throat! Her eyes darted around, her legs treading clumsily, as she took in the tumultuous scene. Spotting a jagged piece of the shattered boat bobbing nearby, she lunged for it with trembling hands, knuckles white as she desperately clung to it, her eyes wide with terror as more shards of wood crashed over her.

One moment, Ben was clinging to the side of his boat, and the next, the world was spinning around him in a dizzying blur of sky and sea! His limbs flailed uncontrollably as he was catapulted upward, then hitting the water with a bone-jarring splash, the force knocking the wind from his lungs. By some miracle, he just missed a jagged outcropping of rocks jutting out of the water. Kicking and clawing, he breached the surface with a cascade of spray, his chest heaving violently as salt stung his lips, nose, and eyes.

Then, he saw it—a mermaid, her form cutting through the water with the grace and speed of a predator. Her eyes fixed on him, filled with an eerie intensity that made his blood run cold. Panic surged through Ben. He thrashed in the water, propelling himself toward the rocky outcropping that rose like a sanctuary from the sea. The mermaid drew closer, her presence a dark shadow beneath the water, closing the distance with terrifying speed. Ben's heart pounded in his chest, the sound a deafening drumbeat in his ears. His muscles burned with exertion, but fear lent him a desperate strength. He reached the rocks just as he felt the water stir close behind him. The mermaid's outstretched hand grazed his foot, a fleeting touch that sent a jolt of terror through his body. With a final surge, he scrambled onto the rocky ledge, collapsing in a heap of exhaustion and relief. He lay there, the air tearing into his lungs in heaving, uneven gulps. Blinking through the salty rivulets trailing down his face, he turned toward the water. The mermaid hovered nearby just below the surface, her movements now eerily still. Slowly, her angular features emerged from the depths, her hair floating in dark tendrils around her face. Her bright, magnetic eyes locked onto Ben, pinning him, unblinking, and crackling with a fire that the sea could not extinguish—watching, waiting.

Each wave that slammed into Billy's boat threatened to tear him loose, but his grasp only tightened as it bobbed violently in the now turbulent lagoon, left untouched so far by the mermaids' wrath. From his precarious vantage point, he watched in horror as the two other boats were lifted with brutal force, his face contorting into an expression of sheer disbelief and fright, his eyes wide and unblinking as they tracked the impossible arcs of the splintering wood and flailing limbs spinning through the air. Each splashdown sent ripples of dread through him, the impact resonating in the pit of his stomach.

Bella saw Jim in the water near her, his figure barely visible amidst the roiling water and floating debris. Her heart pounded in her chest, a drumbeat of fear and urgency.

"Jim!" she screamed, her voice raw and edged with panic. "Jim! Over here!"

Without hesitation, she began to swim toward him, her strokes frantic and clumsy yet fueled by panic to reach him. Catching sight of her, Jim pushed himself in her direction. Finally, they reached each other, their hands grasping desperately as if afraid to let go. Bella's fingers clutched at Jim's arms, her nails digging into his skin as she pulled herself closer. Jim encircled her in his arms, and they held onto each other tightly, their fierce grips anchoring each other amidst the chaos.

Billy sat rigid in his boat's curve, his knuckles white as one hand held tightly onto the boat while the other gripped an oar like a lifeline. The lagoon, moments ago a heaving cauldron, had softened again into uneasy ripples, the surface still glimmering with the residue of turmoil. All around him, an eerie quiet began to settle. But the stillness was soon shattered as the surface of the lagoon detonated with a force that sent droplets spraying against Billy's face. A mermaid blasted out of the water, her lithe form slicing through the air like a silver arrow! Billy flinched back, bracing himself for the expected assault, his heart pounding erratically in his chest. But her movement defied his expectations. Instead of an attack, the mermaid arced gracefully and landed right in front of him. The impact was surprisingly soft, the small vessel barely stirring under her weight, its wooden hull responding with no more than a hushed creak as her body met the surface. She sat up almost immediately, her movements fluid and deliberate. Water cascaded down her sleek, silvery hair, glistening under the morning sun; her skin shimmered with an ethereal glow, faintly illuminating the rough planks beneath her. Her presence commanded attention, an unsettling blend of beauty and menace.

The mermaid's piercing eyes, twin emeralds burning with the fury of a thousand storms, locked onto Billy's, the anger in them a raw, seething force that froze him to the spot. Her glare bored into him, as if she could see straight into his soul, judging and condemning him with every second that passed. Every muscle in Billy's body tensed, he felt paralyzed, unable to tear his eyes away from hers.

"Men!" she hissed. "Go back! You are not wanted here!" her words sharp and jagged.

Her gaze, fierce and unblinking, never wavered as she leaned in, her voice becoming a low, menacing growl.

"Men! Evil men! Thieves! Go back to your world!" she commanded, a thunderous decree that left no room for argument. "This place is not yours to conquer or plunder!"

Jim and Bella remained clutching each other, bobbing helplessly as the waters of the lagoon started to calm after the tumultuous rampage of the mermaids. The adrenaline from the encounter still pulsed through their veins, but the immediate threat had passed, leaving them in a state of stunned silence.

With a fluid and silent grace, other mermaids swam over to Jim and Bella. Encircling the pair, they emerged, breaking through the surface to their shoulders. Drops of water cascaded down their glossy skin like scattered pearls, which caught the morning light, making them shimmer with a supernatural brilliance. Each mermaid's flowing hair encircled her in a silken halo, framing faces that bore a beauty and mystery crafted by divine hands.

Their deep, hypnotic eyes, once aflame with fury and mistrust, now softened somewhat as they lingered on the figures before them. Yet it was Bella who held their attention, their gazes carrying a weight that spoke of a profound, almost reverential, curiosity. There was something about Bella that captivated them, a mysterious allure that drew them inexorably toward her, leaving them caught in an enchantment they did not understand.

Bella could feel the weight of their stares, their expressions a mix of wonder and quiet awe. Each mermaid's gaze was penetrating, searching, as though trying to unravel a secret that Bella held within her.

Then, one of the mermaids swam closer. Tilting her head slightly, her eyes locked onto Bella's with an intensity that sent shivers down her spine. It wasn't mere curiosity reflected in that look—it was a recognition of something sacred, as if the mermaid saw a truth in Bella that even Bella herself did not know. She raised a slender hand from the water, stopping just short of touching Bella's cheek. Jim, fearful of their intent, tightened his grip around Bella. But the mermaids showed no hostility, only an earnest fascination that seemed to bridge the gap between their worlds.

The mermaid perched in front of Billy remained fixed on him, her eyes still holding a fierceness that cowed even the likes of a pirate captain. But then, her attention turned toward the lagoon where her sisters encircled Jim and Bella. Through the silent, intuitive communication that bound these creatures together, she felt the sensation that passed through her kin, a shared epiphany that touched the core of their spirits. A subtle change came over her. The ferocity in her eyes dimmed, replaced by a pressing curiosity, though tempered by a lingering shadow of suspicion.

With a slow, deliberate movement, she turned back to Billy. The rage that had fueled her ebbed away, leaving behind a softer, more questioning presence.

"Why are you here?" she asked.

Her eyes searched his face, probing the contours of his expression for truths buried far beneath the surface, trying to discern the deeper motives that had brought him into their realm.

Billy felt as if she could see deep into the marrow of his soul, weighing every word against his true intentions. He swallowed hard, trying to find his voice amidst the overwhelming experience of being so thoroughly scrutinized by such a mystical creature.

"We . . . we be lookin' for somethin'," he stammered, his voice barely above a whisper. The words felt inadequate, almost childlike, against the weight of the moment.

She leaned in further. Her glistening hair cascaded forward, brushing against his arm as she drew close; the faint glow of her skin bathed him in a soft light, while her peering eyes stayed locked on his, drawing him into their spellbinding depths. He couldn't move, couldn't pull his gaze away, as she reached out with a slender, delicate hand.

With a touch as gentle as the brush of a drifting tide, her palm came to rest on Billy's chest. An immediate warmth radiated from her hand, while the steady rhythm of his heart echoed beneath her fingers. She felt herself drawn inward, past the pulse of his blood, past the veil of his flesh, into the vastness of his spirit. And at that moment, she was part of him, witness to the closely guarded truths hidden within his being.

The silence stretched, heavy with anticipation, until the mermaid finally spoke, her words weaving through the air like a spell.

"You speak of a treasure, entrusted to a celestial entity, and guarded by an emerald tempest, its armor shimmering like a thousand falling stars."

Billy's eyes widened, the cryptic revelation sending a shiver down his spine. Her words painted vivid images in his mind— the riches of the Admiral Benbow, shrouded in mystery, its fate tied to the stars, and protected by a guardian of immense strength and breathtaking beauty. His throat tightened, any attempt to speak faltering as the sheer magnitude of it all washed over him. He sat there, frozen, the gravity of her message holding him

The Secret of the Dragon's Scale

captive, unable to form even a single word as he tried to grasp its significance.

Now, her sister in the water, who had been so entranced by Bella, turned her gaze toward Jim, her sea-green eyes reflecting the mysteries of the ocean. As her delicate hand reached out and rested on Jim's chest, a sudden warmth surged through her fingertips. It flowed through her, luminous and alive, revealing layers of the man before her.

Outwardly, Jim was every inch the swashbuckling rogue—a vivid canvas of adventure and audacity, painted with bold strokes of daring and the thrill of the fight. Yet deep within the rough-hewn exterior of Jim's pirate persona lay a heart pulsing with a profound goodness and kindness. It was a quiet, unassuming force, a beacon of light that stood in stark contrast to his outward bravado and daring exploits. This inner goodness radiated a warmth that was both intense and pure, a silent testament to the love and compassion at his core. When the mermaid placed her hand upon his chest, she could feel this radiant essence, like the gentle glow of a hidden gem, untouched by the harshness of the world around it. It transcended his rugged exterior, a quiet yet powerful declaration of his true nature, capable of touching and transforming the hearts of those fortunate enough to cross his path.

The mermaids exchanged glances, their eyes wide with surprise and wonder. They had encountered men before—men whose hearts were shadowed by greed, hardened by malice, their souls an unrelenting storm of selfish desires. But this . . . this was different. The warmth from Jim's heart flowed through her fingers, spreading like a gentle tide, and touched each of her sisters. Tears welled in her eyes, unshed and glistening, heavy with emotions they had never thought possible in the hearts of men. The essence of Jim's soul touched them deeply, a revelation that these men may not be like those who came before.

Billy was clutching the oar with nervous energy, still entranced with the creature before him, sensing the quiet bond forming with her sisters in their shared moment. With a powerful sweep of her tail, she vaulted from the boat and into the water in a burst of glimmering scales, the sunlight dancing across her sleek form. She turned, eyes sharp with determination, and seized the edge of the boat in one fluid motion. With astonishing agility, she set them on a course toward the rocks where Ben sat. When they reached him, Ben's wide eyes met hers, surprise and disbelief flickering into gratitude as she extended her hand. Her fingers, delicate but firm, clasped his, helping him into the boat with unexpected strength, before pulling it steadily toward the shore.

Meanwhile, her sisters reached out and took the hands of Jim and Bella, their cool, silken grip radiating a quiet assurance. The sensation was one of serene trust and newfound gentleness, a stark contrast to the anger and violence at first meeting. With a silent understanding, the mermaids guided them, creating ripples that danced gently across the tranquil lagoon, to the sandy shore of the island.

Here and there across the lagoon, the other men of the Siren's Call, who had been flung wildly by the mermaids' onslaught, were treading water where they had splashed down, their bodies rising and falling with the gentle rhythm of the water, their breaths still uneven from the chaos moments before. They exchanged stunned glances as they now watched the mermaids lead Billy and the others to shore. For a moment, disbelief rippled through the group, their minds fumbling to piece together the confusing scene unfolding before them. But one by one they followed, none the worse for wear, except for still feeling the stings from being whacked by the mermaids' tails.

The afternoon sun bathed the lagoon in a golden glow, its rays spilling over the soft sands, where each tiny grain sparkled like scattered jewels under its gentle warmth. As Billy and Ben stepped out of the boat, they sank gratefully onto the soft, warm sand, feeling the grains shift beneath them, and a collective sigh of relief escaped their lips. Nearby, Jim and Bella crawled onto the shore, their breaths coming in relieved gasps as they lay on the sand, soaking in the serenity of their surroundings. The other men dragged themselves onto the beach as well, dripping and breathless. Their wide-eyed glances darted back to the lagoon, to Billy, Ben, Jim, and Bella, and to the mermaids, their expressions etched with an uneasy mix of relief and bewilderment.

Around them, the beach was a picture of untouched beauty, a pristine stretch of ivory dotted with shells and glistening pebbles, framed by lush greenery that swayed gently in the breeze. The air was filled with the soothing sound of waves gently lapping against the shore, a melody that blended with the distant calls of seabirds soaring overhead. The scent of salt and seaweed lingered in the breeze, mingling with the fresh, earthy aroma of the land. The warmth of the sun enveloped them all, its gentle heat a balm to their weary bodies.

Rocky outcroppings rose up where the sand surrendered to the sea. Their surfaces, weathered and sun-warmed, provided the perfect perch for the mermaids. With effortless grace, they pulled themselves up, catching the light in a rainbow of colors that rippled across the shore. They tilted their heads slightly, looking deceptively delicate against the rugged stone, their luminous faces soft with quiet curiosity as they observed their human visitors.

The salty breeze tugged at their hair as Billy and his crew cast uncertain glances at one another, their expressions a mix of disbelief and guarded curiosity. It was impossible to reconcile what they were seeing with what they had just experienced. Barely moments ago, these same sea maidens had been forces of fury, emerging from the waves with wrath as sharp as the ocean's bite; now, their hostility had melted away, replaced by a strange, disarming kindness that left everyone unmoored. They shifted uncomfortably, their bodies tense as they tried to decipher the mermaids' intent.

Billy sat hunched on the soft sand, grounding him in a moment that felt anything but real, searching the serene faces of the mermaids, as if they held secrets just out of reach. The gentle lapping of the waves seemed to echo the questions swirling in his mind. With a voice thick with confusion, he finally broke the silence, his query as simple as it was profound.

"Why?" was all Billy could muster.

"You are not so much like the others," answered the one who had peered into his soul, her voice carrying the hush of waves beneath a moonlit sky.

Her luminous eyes drifted to Jim and Bella, lingering there with a quiet intensity. "Among you breathes a hidden light—a goodness, a kindness—we have not felt in men before. It is a force, gentle and pure—a spirit radiant enough to pierce even the midnight of our world . . . And she—" her voice caught like a ripple breaking. "She is bound to it, as if together they are a harmony the sea itself has long awaited."

The mermaid tilted her head as though listening to a rhythm only she could hear. Her eyes rested on Bella, profound and searching, drawn to a truth she could feel but not name.

"But more, she carries within her a thread of our world, a breath of the ocean's soul. We feel her presence like the pull of the moon. She is a vessel for something . . . eternal, radiant, transcendent. But what it is, what it means, hides even from the stars."

"What others?" Jim asked.

"Long ago, before the tides wore soft the edges of memory," the mermaid responded, "there came men from beyond the gate, upon a mighty creature of wood, its great wings catching the breath of the wind. Its belly was laden with countless wonders. It overflowed with metals that gleamed like the blazing heart of the sun, stones that sparkled in the colors of dawn's first blush and twilight's final sigh, and objects of such exquisite beauty, as if the heavens had poured their dreams into forms too perfect for mortal hands to hold."

Her tone grew somber, and a shadow passed over her luminous features. "And as these men drew near our islands, we could feel a darkness emanating from within their souls. Their blackened hearts held a monstrous hunger, a dark fire that no wealth, no fortune, could ever extinguish. Their foul greed was like a voracious beast, and the more they fed this beast, the more it demanded, always whispering false promises of satisfaction, yet leaving them always yearning, eternally unfulfilled."

A second mermaid spoke, her voice heavy with sorrow, her hair swirling around her shoulders like restless kelp caught in a tempestuous current, each strand alive with an agitation that mirrored her inner turmoil.

"These men, not content with their earthly treasures, dared to venture into our hidden sanctuary. There, they chanced upon that which the mermaids hold most sacred—the Giant Pearl, shining with the essence of the ocean itself. It holds within it the heart of our Mother, the dreams of the endless depths, the breath that gives life to every creature beneath the surface."

Her words grew heavier, striking like thunder, every syllable vibrating with the weight of her people's grief and rage. "And with callous hands and hearts hardened by avarice, they STOLE IT—tearing it from its ancient cradle!"

A third sat upon the rocks with a regal grace. Her eyes—silver, penetrating, and infinite as the abyss—bore a haunting reflection of her pain, an anguish that darkened their brilliance. And then she spoke. It was a melody laced with disdain and condemnation, layered with the mournful wail of distant winds upon the sea.

"For this desecration, in their righteous fury, the mermaids laid a mighty curse upon the despoilers! The great creature of wood and wind—their proud ocean chariot—was stripped of its grandeur and condemned! We cast it into wretchedness, twisting its form into that of a pitiful dragon!"

Her lips curled into a faint, bitter smile, the scorn in her tone melting into resolute conviction. "These thieving men sought to defile our sacred realm, but they did not escape our justice.

Forever to languish on these islands, a monument to their folly, it would know no release, save for the undoing of their sacrilege."

Another of the sisters sat in stillness, her form wrapped in an air of quiet solemnity. The soft glow of her iridescent scales dimmed, their light dulled by the shadow that had settled over her spirit.

"Then, to seal the curse, so that their hoarded riches could never be in the hands of any undeserving man, the mermaids tore a single scale from the dragon's hide and cast it aloft into the heavens, taking its place among the constellations. They decreed that the only way to break the curse, to change the dragon back into the wooden creature, would be for the scale to be put back in its place, to become one again with the dragon, making it whole."

Ben's eyes widened as his lips formed the soundless beginnings of words that refused to come. Finally, his voice broke free, trembling with the weight of the revelation.

"Wait . . . a scale? Of a . . . a dragon!?" The last word lingered in the air, heavy with incredulity.

Jim's jaw fell open. His eyebrows arched so high they threatened to vanish beneath his tangled hair. His heart pounded and a tremor seized his hands.

"A creature of wood and wind?" He swallowed hard, his throat tight with wonder and incredulity. "She be meanin', a ship? Overflowin' with gleamin' metals, sparklin' stones, and objects of great beauty?" His voice faltered, cracking under the weight of the thought.

He swiveled his head, his frantic gaze darting between his companions as though seeking confirmation, trying to tether his spinning head to reality. He was scarcely able to believe the words forming upon his lips.

"Could that be . . . the Admiral Benbow!? It be here!?"

Bella leaned forward, the warm grains of sunlit sand shifting beneath her fingers as she steadied herself.

"So the Dragon's Scale is . . . something in the sky?" she wondered, her voice unsteady, the words almost catching in her throat as confusion swept across her face.

Billy rose slowly, his legs feeling unsteady beneath him, as though the weight of the moment threatened to pull him back down into the sand. The air around him felt thick, heavy with the impossible reality of what he'd just heard. His broad shoulders held a tension that braced for the unraveling of understanding itself. His chest rose and fell with deep, uneven breaths, each exhale dragged from the depths of a mind struggling to reconcile the tangible with the unreal. His eyes were shadowed with a mix of confusion and incredulity, searching the inscrutable faces of the mermaids for answers he wasn't sure he wanted.

Finally, Billy spoke.

"For untold years—aye, for as long as any seafarer can remember—tales were whispered of the Admiral Benbow," he began, his voice resonating with a reverence for the legends of old.

"A vessel said to be filled with treasures beyond mortal imagination—chests brimmin' with glitterin' jewels and mountains of gold—spoils claimed through many a gallant and bloody battle. Riches so vast, they'd dwarf a king's ransom to naught but a beggar's coin. But the ship had vanished, as if fallin' off the face of the Earth, leavin' behind nary a trace but the faintest echoes of rumor. Men have spent lifetimes searchin' for it ever since."

His face took on a haunted expression, his tone thick with the weariness of the chase.

"But what we sought was never found, eludin' our grasp like the ghostly mist at dawn. We chased shadows and dreams, guided by yarns spun in the dim light of tavern hearths and hushed murmurs spoken 'round flickerin' lanterns. Yet among every story, one thing remained the same—the key to findin' 'er was bound to somethin' known only as the Dragon's Scale; find the

Dragon's Scale, they said, and it will lead ye to the Admiral Benbow."

His voice faltered for a moment, his haunted gaze searching the waves as if still chasing the specter of that elusive dream.

"So as it were, men turned to findin' the Dragon's Scale, chasin' it with the frenzy of demons unchained, as though some dark fire burned in their veins and whispered madness to their souls," Billy continued, each word steeped in the gravity of ageless legends.

"But each man clung to his own vision of what the Scale must be, his mind bendin' to the maddenin' pull of its mystery. Some swore it was a compass, its needle pointing not north, but to the heart of fate itself. Others believed it a fragment of some grand puzzle, its edges begging to complete some unfathomable whole. And still more spoke of a tablet—etched with riddles that held the power to reveal truths no mortal eyes should see."

Billy pressed on, his eyes burning with the lore that held him captive.

"No corner of the world was spared their fervent search. They scoured the bleached sands of desolate shores, where the wind howled like the cries of the damned. They dove into the blackened wrecks of sunken ships, their timbers rottin' in silent graves. They hacked through jungles choked with vines and the menace of unseen eyes, and crossed wastelands where the searin' sun peeled the resolve from lesser souls . . . And yet, the Scale remained elusive, a phantom promise flitting just beyond reach, taunting their every moment."

He shook his head, as if trying to shake off the very idea that now confounded him.

"And now ye stand before me, tellin' me that this object of our relentless searchin' lies not beneath the waves or buried in the sands, but in the sky? How can that be? What manner of sorcery am I missin'!? How does the vast expanse above us—the very stars themselves—hold the key to the Admiral Benbow!?"

His eyes darted from one mermaid to the next, searching their faces for some glimmer of understanding.

"Explain yerselves, I beg of ye. For if the Dragon's Scale truly resides in the heavens, then every tale ever spun, every chart ever followed, has led us astray. This revelation turns our quest all on its head, leavin' us adrift in a sea of newfound perplexity!"

The first mermaid fixed her eyes upon Billy. There was a coldness in their depths, a silent rebuke that held no patience for human folly. Her ethereal beauty was fractured by a look of contempt, her lips tightened into an unforgiving sneer, her brows arched sharply in judgment.

"Foolish men!" she exclaimed, her words dripping with disdain. "You wander this world with such narrow vision, ensnared by your petty earthly desires and bound by the chains of the material. You live your lives in pursuit of what you can grasp and feel, all the while oblivious to the profound mysteries that surround you."

She paused, her gaze piercing, letting the weight of her scorn hang heavy in the air.

"Do you not understand?" she said, her tone, sharp and cutting only moments before, now softened with a touch of sorrow, as though she mourned his blindness more than his ignorance.

"The world you cling to is but a fragment of a grander tapestry, woven with threads of magic and wonder—rich with colors you have not yet imagined. The shore where you stand is not the edge of a map—it is the ink where stories begin, spilling into oceans that cradle the sky's reflection. The heavens are not a ceiling, but a door left ajar, where shooting stars leap like whispers from the mouths of gods . . . Even the midnight sky holds a million tiny songs, but you do not hear them."

She leaned closer, her form shimmering like a dream caught between worlds.

"You bind your gaze to the glint of hollow riches, chasing sunlight trapped in trinkets, but you tread blindly through a world that sings in silence and shines in shadows. To see, to feel, to hear, to truly behold the mysteries that linger at the edge of knowing, you must do only one thing—listen. Not with your ears, but with your heart."

Her expression eased, a tenderness weaving through her words as she spoke again, her tone carrying the weight of both warning and hope.

"And yet," she said, "your quest for earthly rewards, misguided though it may be, is not without meaning. It is a test, not of the strength you bear or the cunning you wield, but of the heart that beats within you. That is why you are here."

Her voice dropped to a reverent whisper, as if revealing a sacred secret.

"In seeking the treasure you so desire, your journey will lead you to the end of one path and the beginning of another. It is there that you must make a profound choice—one that will determine your final destiny. And as you stand at the crossroads of your journey, let your spirit guide you, for it knows the way."

"But these destinies ye speak of," Jim said to the mermaid. "How will we know which to choose?"

"Only when you reach the end of your journey, when it is time to return the scale to the dragon, will all be revealed," she answered.

"But if the Dragon's Scale be in the heavens, how can it be possible to put it back on the dragon?" Ben asked.

"Gaze upon the stars," she began, as her eyes lifted, becoming as glittering as the night sky, her lips parting slightly as if caught in reverence.

"Each constellation was set alight by divine hands, a map of destinies unfurled across the endless black. They are the mirrors of your heart, the keepers of your journeys, the quiet witnesses to your becoming. And each star within is a possibility, a path waiting to be traveled, a potential life waiting to be lived. Some flicker faintly, shy with uncertainty, while others blaze with a ferocity that dares you to follow . . . But remember, while their light may guide us, it is we who must choose our own paths and shape our own destinies."

Slowly, her eyes lowered to meet the gathered souls around her, with a grace that seemed borrowed from the stars themselves.

"The Dragon's Scale is more than just a shape painted upon the night. It is a celestial beacon, meant to guide a noble soul on Earth—a soul that came into this world under its radiant light, carrying the weight of its brilliance."

"To break the curse," another of the sisters said, "the missing scale must be restored to its rightful place. This soul, a mirror of the Dragon's Scale on Earth, must seek out the dragon and lay a hand upon its gleaming hide. In that moment, the soul will surrender its very essence, sacrificing itself to become the missing scale once more. As it merges with the dragon's armor, the void is filled, and the beast is made whole again. The dragon, now complete, will return to its original form; yet the noble soul will be no more, having given everything to restore balance to the world."

There, on the sandy shore of the island, they all sat spellbound, their faces a canvas of raw emotion as the mermaids unveiled the greatest riddle of the seas. Billy's eyes gleamed with unrestrained wonder, reflecting the deep connection he felt with the mystical revelations. Ben's curiosity burned bright. His brow furrowed and lips parted slightly as he hung on every word, eager to grasp the hidden mysteries that had eluded them for so long. Jim's face, usually marked by his carefree and lighthearted spirit, now bore an expression as still and reflective as the moonlit sea. His lips pressed into a thin line, his eyes dark with uncharacteristic intensity, as though the weight of their words anchored him to some far deeper truth. And then there was Bella. She sat as if rooted to the earth itself, her hands clasped in her lap. Her face radiated pure enchantment; her emerald eyes sparkled like the sea under a starry sky, and a serene smile played on her lips, as though the melody of the mermaids' wisdom had entwined itself with her very spirit.

These daughters of the sea had no yearning to say more—only the calm assurance that their words would not simply fade but resonate within the listeners, taking root in human hearts like seeds carried on the currents. And so, they cast a final, lingering glance over the gathered group, their luminous eyes filled with an unspoken farewell. With fluid elegance, they leapt from their rocky perches, their lithe forms arcing through the air with grace and beauty. The sun caught the iridescent shimmer of their tails, scattering a cascade of dazzling light across the lagoon's mirrored surface. And with scarcely a ripple to mark their passage, they broke the lagoon's glassy plane and vanished into its cerulean depths, leaving behind only the faint echo of their parting words and the gentle whisper of the waves.

Billy, Ben, Jim, Bella, and the rest of the crew of the Siren's Call remained motionless, their gazes fixed on the waters that now lay serene and undisturbed. They could only stare in silent awe for the profound truths they just learned.

The secret of the Dragon's Scale had now been laid bare—a revelation as illuminating as it was perplexing. And the Admiral Benbow, that storied vessel said to harbor untold riches, was no longer a mere legend but a cursed truth, transformed by the mermaids' fury into the very dragon that now prowled these mysterious isles, forever imprisoned by their vengeful spell.

Redemption

It was as though the ocean had unburdened itself, surrendering a truth locked beneath waters too deep for prying eyes. The Dragon's Scale—its secret—had been whispered into existence; what had been the greatest riddle of the seas, a tale shrouded in myths and dreams, was now a reality. But this newfound understanding only served to flood their minds with questions that had no easy answers. Paths that once seemed clear now dissolved into mist. Yet they still were not at the end of their journey, and the way forward was as mysterious and elusive as ever. However, the weight of the revelation pressed heavily upon them, demanding a course of action.

In this solemn silence, as he brushed off the sand from his clothes, Billy looked over his companions. His face, etched with the lines of countless journeys, carried an expression of profound, contemplative wisdom.

"Me friends," he said, in a deep and resonant rumble that drew strength from the heartbeat of the sea, "we've journeyed far, driven not just for the gleam of gold or the fleeting taste of glory, but for the pull of something far greater—a fate that calls to each of our souls. The mermaids have torn the veils from our eyes, and revealed the Admiral Benbow's true form as it be now—a dragon, bound by a curse, guardin' not just treasure, but the very essence of our destinies."

He paused with a faraway look as his gaze now drifted toward the lagoon, the glimmering water catching the sun and moving with a rhythm that felt almost alive.

"What we'll find, buried in the heart of this island—or any others we may yet walk—I cannot tell ye, nor how facing this beast will shape the stories we've yet to write. But mark me words, this much I know—we've no choice but to see it through. Our sails are set, and the winds of fate won't abide us turnin' back. So gather yer courage and brace yer hearts, for it be time to press on. And perhaps, when all is done, we'll find we've earned more than treasure—we'll have earned the right to know who we are, and who we've always been truly meant to be."

Ben, Jim, Bella, and the other men stirred from their silent reflection on the shore, its sand pale and fine, glinting faintly like powdered pearl beneath the warmth of the afternoon sun. Driven by their unrelenting desire to see their fate unfold and lay bare whatever truth lingered at the heart of these islands, they headed Billy's words. Ben with his steadfast resolve, Jim with his spirited courage, and Bella with her youthful vigor, rose together. Around them, the rest of the crew readied themselves with quiet determination. The air buzzed with anticipation, the salt wind tangling their hair as they turned toward the mysteries waiting to be unraveled.

"Now, let's see what secrets this island holds for us," Billy remarked.

Casting their eyes forward, they took in the verdant expanse ahead—a forest alive with towering palms, sprawling ferns, and the generous arms of breadfruit trees. The dense canopy wove itself high above, filtering the sunlight into a soft, golden glow that danced over the forest floor. They chose a winding trail that snaked its way through the lush undergrowth. The path was carpeted with soft moss and fallen fronds, muffling their steps as they ventured deeper. The air brimmed with life, carrying the intoxicating perfume of exotic flowers mingled with the sweet aroma of ripe fruit. Orchids and hibiscus bloomed in a riot of colors—vivid reds, blushing pinks, sunny yellows, and regal purples—splashing the forest floor with the hues of a painter's palette.

As they hiked deeper into the forest, wonder filled their eyes, captivated by the vibrant beauty surrounding them. Butterflies with wings like stained glass drifted gracefully from bloom to bloom, their delicate movements painting the air with flashes of color. Agile lizards darted across the path in quick, fluid motions, vanishing into the greenery as swiftly as they appeared. The gentle rustling of leaves hinted at the presence of unseen creatures watching from the shadows, adding an element of mystery to their journey. Overhead, flocks of brilliantly plumed birds darted between the branches, their feathers glinting like jewels in the sunlight, their songs filling the air with a melodic cacophony of trills and whistles. From somewhere ahead, the sound of a babbling brook could be heard, its crystal-clear waters promising refreshment to any who asked. The air was warm and humid, while the rhythmic crashing of distant waves reminded them of the sea's omnipresence.

Despite having no clear idea where they were heading or what awaited them, they trusted in their instincts. Billy led the way, his senses on high alert as he scanned the surroundings for any sign that might serve as a clue to their quest. His eyes, usually sharp and commanding, were now softened by focus and determination. Every flicker of light through the canopy, every peculiar shift in the pattern of leaves or vines, was met with his measured scrutiny, as if at any moment the forest itself might reveal the secrets they sought.

Ben's mind became a canvas alive with the imagery the mermaids had painted, each vision unfolding with surreal brilliance. Each step he took on the forest path seemed to echo with the haunting melody of their voices, resonating in the deepest chambers of his consciousness. His fingers trailed along the rough bark of trees, grounding him momentarily in reality, yet his mind remained ensnared by the mermaids' enchantment. Their words looped endlessly in his mind, each phrase wrapped in a thousand unspoken meanings, as he searched for subtle hints that might lead them closer to their prize.

Jim, usually the group's pillar of joviality and cheerfulness, moved with an unusual quiet. The mermaid's words had cast a shadow over his normally bright spirits, filling him with a thoughtful seriousness. They had spoken of a choice—a moment at the end of their journey where destiny and decision would meet—but they had left its nature cloaked in mystery. Every so often, his gaze wandered skyward or toward the dark spaces between the trees, his eyes clouded with concentration. What decision would he be forced to make, and what would it demand of him? The questions churned in his mind, chasing shadows of answers he could not grasp.

Alongside Jim, Bella walked with heightened awareness, her connection to the natural world making her especially sensitive to the forest's subtleties. The warm, humid air seemed charged with anticipation, every rustle of leaves and distant animal call resonating deeply within her. But the vision of the mermaid's hypnotic stare still lingered in Bella's mind, haunting her thoughts with its unearthly curiosity—as well as something deeper, something that felt like reverence. It left a nagging, elusive feeling that something inexplicable lingered deep within her, as if the mermaid had seen a piece of Bella that even Bella herself could not understand.

The other men of the Siren's Call followed closely behind, their senses attuned to the forest's every nuance, their eyes darting to the glimmers of movement in the undergrowth and the swaying of branches overhead.

It was in this charged silence that Bella began to feel it—a subtle yet insistent tugging at the edges of her consciousness. The sensation was faint at first, an almost imperceptible nudge that she dismissed as a trick her thoughts were playing on her. But with each step, the feeling grew stronger, more distinct, as if invisible hands were reaching out from the depths of the forest, coiling around her with a gentle persistence, and pulling her toward something hidden deep within its embrace.

Her steps began to falter, her sure-footedness replaced by a growing uncertainty. The pull on her awareness became almost tangible, a physical force that seemed to wrap around her being, compelling her forward even as she hesitated, urging her to follow a path only it could see. She stopped abruptly, her breath catching in her throat as the sensation intensified. Her heart pounded in her chest. She stood rigid, eyes wide with a mix of wonder and confusion, as if caught in the throes of a waking dream.

The rest of the crew continued on for a few paces, their attention focused on the winding path ahead, before realizing she was no longer with them. Billy, ever watchful, was the first to notice her absence. His sharp eyes cut through the verdant foliage, finding her standing frozen in place, bathed in the fractured sunlight that filtered through the trees, just staring off into the distance. One by one, the others paused and turned, their determined expressions changing into subtle confusion as they followed Billy's gaze. A quiet curiosity, tinged with growing concern, then flickered across their faces as they saw her, standing transfixed, gripped by some invisible enchantment.

"Bella?" Billy called out, piercing the silence. "What be wrong with ye?"

But Bella barely registered Billy's voice cutting through the forest. Her entire being was consumed by the mysterious force that beckoned her.

Jim stepped closer, his voice low but urgent. "Bella, ye alright?" he asked.

Bella blinked, her head shaking slightly. She struggled to speak, trying to articulate the overwhelming sensations flooding her thoughts. "There's something . . . I . . . I feel something," she whispered, her voice tinged with an anxious uncertainty. "Like something is calling to me."

She turned, following the irresistible pull summoning her deeper into the forest. She pushed through the tangled undergrowth, sharp branches clawing at her arms while leaves brushed against her face like ghostly fingers. Her breaths came in shallow, hurried gasps, mirroring the frantic beating of her heart. The others, sensing her urgency, fell into step behind her.

After what felt like hours, Bella and the others stumbled upon a scene of extraordinary desolation—an expanse where the earth itself appeared to have been rent asunder by some colossal force. The trees, once towering sentinels of the forest, lay scattered across the ground. Their trunks were splintered and torn, with deep, jagged gouges reminiscent of an ancient leviathan's claws, as if it had raged through this heart of the wilderness, leaving a trail of devastation in its wake. Exchanging cautious glances laced with apprehension, the group pressed on, compelled by an eerie compulsion to follow the path of ruin cutting through the forest.

The path twisted and turned, eventually leading them around a bend to where the tangled forest abruptly receded, revealing a wide clearing bathed in an otherworldly light. As they crossed the threshold into this unearthly domain, their eyes were irresistibly drawn upwards—and every thought, every breath, was stolen from them!

Billy stood frozen to the spot, his entire body locked in the grip of overwhelming shock! His face was a vivid portrait of raw astonishment—his mouth hung open, his eyes, unblinking and as wide as the full moon, darted frantically across the impossible sight. The thick muscles in his neck tightened, and veins bulged under the strain of sheer disbelief. His hand trembled uncontrollably, hovering near his mouth as though trying to stifle a sharp gasp that tore from his lips.

Beside him, Ben disintegrated into abject fear. His forehead crinkled with deep furrows, his lips moving soundlessly as though trying to form a prayer or curse. He took a staggered step backward, raising his hands defensively as if to ward off an unseen blow. His trembling fingers, splayed and shaking, betrayed the storm of panic coursing through him. Beads of sweat streaked down his temples, cutting cold paths across his flushed skin as his wide, incredulous eyes remained fixed on the incomprehensible sight before him.

Jim's legs buckled beneath him. He swayed, his normally strong knees giving way as though the earth itself had shifted. With a jagged, choking gasp, he collapsed, hands clawing at the dirt in a futile attempt to anchor himself to some semblance of reality. Each shallow, tremulous breath he drew burned in his throat, laced with a bitter metallic tang that spoke of raw fear. Tears welled—out of pure, unadulterated stupefaction. He rocked back and forth, muttering incoherently, his mind unable to grasp the magnitude of what he was witnessing.

Bella staggered backward, her breath hitching into a sharp gasp that escaped as a choked cry, her eyes wide with a mix of profound awe and utter terror. Her chest heaved, breathing in short, uneven gulps, while her head shook faintly, as if denying the reality of what she saw. A trembling hand flew to her mouth, desperate to muffle the rising whimper of panic, while her other hand clung to Billy's arm with a grip that bordered on frantic, her nails digging into his flesh as if seeking an anchor in a world turned upside down. Her legs quaked violently, threatening to give way beneath her.

The rest of the men, though all toughened sailors who had too often stared down death on the open seas, were gripped by an overwhelming wave of fear and panic. John Hawkins, his face drained of color, fell to his knees, hands clasped together in a desperate prayer. Another stumbled backward, tripping over his own feet and landing hard on the ground, where he lay frozen, his unblinking eyes fixed on the horror with a vacant stare. A third crewmate, his mouth agape in a silent scream, reached out blindly as if seeking something to hold onto, his fingers grasping at the empty air. Their expressions stretched from slack-jawed astonishment to contorted masks of fear, each struggling to comprehend the incomprehensible. Where strength and stoicism once defined them, trembling hands now reached out in desperation, and legs that had stood firm on unsteady decks gave way beneath them, all underscoring the sheer magnitude of their collective terror.

For what they stumbled upon shattered the boundaries of mortal comprehension! In the heart of the clearing loomed a nightmarish vision—the dragon itself!

But this was a dragon unlike anything anyone could imagine. It was not the majestic beast of legend, nor the fearsome, fire-spewing guardian of treasure sung about in tales. There were no shining scales reflecting the sunlight like molten jewels; no powerful wings casting shadows over mountains; no regal serpent that inspired awe alongside fear. No, this was a hideous monstrosity—a grotesque chimera born of the mermaids' curse upon the ill-fated vessel known as the Admiral Benbow.

Its form was an unholy amalgamation of sinewy dragon flesh and shattered shipwreck. The front of the creature towered like a vengeful titan, with the imposing body and head of a dragon, as large and formidable as any sailing ship. The head was a monstrous visage twisted into a cruel snarl, its eyes burning with an infernal glow, its maw brimming with rows of jagged wooden fangs, each one dripping with a vile, black ichor that reeked of decay. The beast's body writhed with the muscular grace of a serpent, its scales glistening—yet, from its hide jutted the splintered remains of masts and yards, piercing through its flesh like grotesque appendages. Frayed shreds of canvas hung like ghostly wings, flapping listlessly in the eerie breeze, while rotting rigging snaked around its limbs, creaking and groaning with each tormented movement.

The back half of the creature was more ship than beast. Its torso resembled a shipwreck's rotting hull, complete with broken beams and warped planks. Deep cracks ran along their surfaces, etched into the grain by the torturous hand of decay. Much of the ironwork that had once held the ship together was corroded, the rust streaking down and staining the wood like the slow tears of time. Its rear legs were a terrifying blend of dragon flesh and

The Secret of the Dragon's Scale

skeletal ship timbers, its massive claws tearing into the soil as splinters of wood protruded from scaly joints.

More horrifying still were the skeletal remains of men, grim reminders of the ship's cursed crew. Their bones, bleached by time and the elements, were entangled in the rigging of the ship, and draped in the ragged remnants of their seafaring attire. These spectral sailors seemed almost alive, their empty eye sockets staring in eternal anguish, their bony hands reaching out as though seeking some forgotten redemption.

This abomination was born of the darkness within their souls. For when the mermaids cast their curse upon the ship, they brought forth in living form all the ugliness in the men of the Admiral Benbow. Their insatiable greed, their boundless avarice, and the festering rot of their desires were dragged from the shadows of their hearts and made flesh. The curse transformed the ship itself into a grotesque reflection of their inner corruption, its every creak and groan seeming to whisper of their sins.

Through this hideous manifestation, the curse embodied in every feature the darkest impulses that had once consumed them. Each scale of this beast shimmered with a deceitful luster, forged from ill-gotten riches that glinted with false promises. Its eyes, ever-watchful and ever-covetous, blazed with a ravenous hunger—windows into an abyss where satisfaction was but a cruel mirage, always within sight yet forever out of reach. Its maw was a chasm that yawned wide like the bottomless pit of human desire, dripping with the venom of rapaciousness, and devouring all in its path, leaving nothing but desolation and despair. The roar of the beast, a thunderous cacophony of sorrow and rage, was a mournful symphony—a dirge for the death of contentment and the birth of eternal yearning. The ship, though intact enough to be recognizable as the once-majestic Admiral Benbow, now lay in a grotesque union with the dragon's body, a haunting testament to decay and ruin, where once vibrant dreams and ambitions had been devoured by an insatiable void—the twisted wood and rusted iron standing as grim reminders of the devastating consequences of hearts enslaved by endless want.

For what had been sculpted from blackened hearts was not merely a revolting beast but a living allegory—a stark warning of the corrosive power of greed and the eternal torment it brings. The mermaids' curse, then, was no mere act of vengeance but a masterpiece of poetic retribution—an elegy for men who had traded their souls for fleeting treasures, now left as ghosts adrift in the wreckage of their own making.

The instinct to flee was palpable, pulsing in every quiver of their legs and every tremor of their hands, yet not a single one of the crew of the Siren's Call moved beyond a feeble step back. Despite the fear coursing through their veins, a glimmer of realization came over them—every one of them—that this thing, this unspeakable horror, was the very prize that had driven their arduous journey, the fateful encounter that the mermaids had foretold would await them at their odyssey's end.

Ben's throat tightened. Hoarse and stammering, he broke the silence first. "Th-this be . . . " He swallowed hard, trying to steady himself. His voice cracked and climbed, a high-pitched, wavering squeal of disbelief that echoed their shared astonishment. "This be . . . the d-d-dragon!?"

Jim's hand trembled violently as he raised it, his fingers barely managing to form a point toward the warped, splintered hull of the ship that formed the back end of the dragon. His chest heaved with shallow, uneven breaths, his voice teetering on the edge of breaking. "And there . . . The Admiral Benbow!?"

"Aye," Billy answered, his voice carrying the weight of profound revelation. "Look well upon this nightmarish beast and know it for what it truly be—the Admiral Benbow, twisted and broken by a curse born from the greatness of the mermaids' wrath. It takes a rage deeper than the ocean's abyss to forge such a monstrosity."

"Captain," Ben began, his face pale but resolute, his voice quivering, caught somewhere between fear and determination,

The Secret of the Dragon's Scale

"we've come this far. Now . . . now we gotta break this damned spell, restore the Admiral Benbow, and get at the treasure she holds."

"But the Dragon's Scale," Jim interjected. "We be needin' the Dragon's Scale. What can it be though? What was it the mermaids said?"

Billy recounted the words of one of the mermaids, his voice low, almost reverent. "Hmmm, one of them said, 'the mermaids tore a single scale from its shimmering hide and cast it aloft into the heavens, taking its place among the constellations.'"

Then Bella spoke. "And one said, 'the Dragon's Scale is more than just a shape painted upon the night, it is a celestial beacon, meant to guide a noble soul on Earth.' Another said this soul was 'a mirror of the Dragon's Scale on Earth.'"

She paused. Slowly, her hand rose to her chest, trembling slightly. Her dawning realization broke across her face like the first light of the rising sun. "A soul . . . " she whispered, her voice barely audible. "A soul, meaning a . . . a person." Her eyes now widened, glistening with a newfound clarity as her look darted from Billy to Jim to Ben and back again.

He saw it—the transformation in her expression as she spoke. A chill raced up Billy's spine, stealing his breath as the truth of her words unraveled in his mind. His chest tightened and his hands instinctively clenched at his sides. Slowly, his own eyes widened with understanding, mirroring Bella's own revelation.

Astonishment tore through every syllable, the words tumbling from his lips as though they did not belong to him. "Then the Dragon's Scale be a . . . p—"

"A person!" Bella gasped. She clasped her hands to her mouth, a giddy, almost childlike laugh escaping amidst the rush of her breath. Her fingertips brushed her cheeks, damp with tears she hadn't even realized had begun to fall. "The Dragon's Scale is not a thing . . . It's a person!"

The other men stood frozen in place, their collective breath caught in their throats. Eyes darted from one face to another, each expression a canvas of astonishment, wonder, and disbelief. Then, like a spark jumping from one to the next, the words began to thread through them.

"A person," John Hawkins breathed.

"A person," another echoed, his voice trembling.

"A person," came the next, filled with bewilderment.

On and on it went, the words ricocheting between them like a chorus building momentum, each repetition drawing them closer to grasping the impossible truth. All around, mouths hung open, eyes were wide with wonder, and hands hovered hesitantly over trembling lips. There was no other sound but their voices weaving together, no movement but the slight incline of heads as they exchanged awed glances, letting the weight of those two simple words settle over them.

Shaking and drenched in cold sweat, Jim had sat up as he fought to steady the storm within. His eyes darted between Billy and Bella, seeing their faces alight with understanding so profound it bordered on otherworldly.

His lips quivered, the faintest breath escaping first.

"So, when the mermaids said the scale took its place among the constellations . . . " He paused, his breath catching, the weight of the revelation sinking in. "They be meanin', there was a new constellation in the sky . . . And they said, 'this soul came into this world under its radiant light' . . . "

His voice trembled with awe and excitement, his heart pounding in his chest.

"This be a person born under the sign of the Dragon's Scale!" he exclaimed, as if the stars above had leaned down to whisper their eternal secrets.

"But who!?" Ben burst out, his voice crackling with an unbearable curiosity that ricocheted through the air.

At that moment, as if awakened from a long slumber, a memory from Bella's childhood flooded forth—her favorite poem, the one her mother used to recite to her when she was young, tucked away in the farthest corners of her mind like a

The Secret of the Dragon's Scale

beloved keepsake hidden in an old chest. Bella's pulse quickened, the gentle melody of each line unfolding in her heart. A delicate gasp escaped her lips as tears again welled up in her eyes. She closed them against the rush of feelings, letting a single tear fall, tracing a slow, silent trail down her cheek.

When her eyes fluttered open again, they glistened with the lingering glow of the rediscovered memory. She looked at the faces around her, her voice quivering yet rich with emotion. "My . . . my favorite poem. My mother read it to me many times when I was a little girl. And now . . . it all just came back to me.

Where the sun kisses the sea,
Where your heart yearns to be.
In twilight's gentle, whispered sigh,
A tale unfolds above the sky.

When Venus, Mars, and Jupiter aligned,
A scale of dragon was designed,
With the star that's always north,
To guide a noble soul of worth.

In the night's expanse up high,
The dragon's mark adorned the sky.
At the hour you took first breath,
Stars aligned, and heavens blessed.

Bound by fate, your path unveiled,
The mystic forces had prevailed.
Where the sun kisses the sea,
You were born, it was meant to be."

As the lines of the poem echoed in her mind, Bella finally understood. The poem spoke of a night when Venus, Mars, and Jupiter perfectly aligned with the North Star, forming a constellation rarely seen, appearing in the western sky. This unique celestial event occurred precisely at the moment of her birth, marking her as the earthly bearer of a heavenly gift.

She remembered her mother's gentle voice, singing her lullabies about how she was born on a night when the stars performed a celestial dance just for her. "This poem is about you, Bella," her mother would whisper softly, tucking the blanket under her chin. She would lean closer, her words a tender secret meant only for Bella. "You were born under a special sign, your destiny blessed by the heavens themselves."

Bella's chest tightened, each breath shallow as emotions surged within her—astonishment, wonder, and a profound sense of humility. The raw intensity painted her features, her cheeks flushed as her lips quivered slightly. Another tear slipped free, catching the soft light as it traced the contours of her cheek. She stood motionless as every thread of her existence wove into this single moment, illuminated by the truth that had suddenly dawned upon her—the constellation the poem spoke of was that of the Dragon's Scale, and that she was its living reflection, the embodiment of its myth brought to earth, making her the key to breaking the mermaids' curse.

"It's me . . ." she said, her voice soft and breathy, as she marveled at the wondrous nature of the revelation. "I am the noble soul . . . I am . . . the Dragon's Scale."

Billy's eyes widened, his mouth agape. He stumbled back as though the ground itself had shifted beneath him. His breath came in shallow gasps, as though his lungs refused to accept what his ears had heard.

"You!?" he blurted, the single word bursting from his lips like a cannon shot, filled with sheer incredulity.

His eyes darted across Bella's face, searching desperately for a crack, a tell, a shred of something false.

But it wasn't just her words that gripped him; it was the way the air around her seemed to shimmer, as though the world itself recognized her every breath. His ears buzzed, drowning out all other sounds save for the steady conviction in her voice.

"You!?" Ben exclaimed.
"You!?" Jim cried.

Shock rippled through the rest of the crew, cold and quick, raising the fine hairs on their skin. Their expressions were a mix of surprise and confusion, faces pale from being drained of certainty. One by one, the exclamation burst forth. "You!?" They stared at her, chests heaving as though the very air around them had turned to glass, shattering with each utterance. "You!?" "You!?" "You!?" The sound broke rhythmically across the silence, pulsing with the force of their astonishment.

Although the air was thick with the incomprehensible, from the time Bella came into their lives, each of them had sensed a uniqueness about her. But it wasn't until they crossed into the mermaids' world that the feeling had crystallized into something deeper. The mermaids had emerged gracefully from the water, their faces turned toward Bella, and their luminous eyes gleamed with wonder. They didn't understand why, but the way they circled her, reached gently out to her, their expressions reverent, told a tale of recognition beyond words. And in that fleeting moment, all knew that Bella bore a destiny none of them yet understood, but one that was undeniable.

In the annals of seafaring lore, few tales could fire the imagination or haunt the soul like that of the Dragon's Scale. It was the treasure of a thousand dreams, a fragment of the impossible that glittered just beyond the horizon. Countless men had journeyed across the seven seas, scouring the edges of the known world, following tattered maps and whispered stories. Entire crews descended into madness, their minds torn asunder by the shadows of their obsession. But the Dragon's Scale eluded all who sought it, leaving behind only the ghosts of ambition and the hollow ache of dreams unfulfilled. The men of the Siren's Call were no different; they, too, had been consumed by the legend. They had stood spellbound by a stone that sings, and danced with the spirits of the ancients; they had been entranced by the haunting lullabies of the ocean's gentle giants, and faced the wrath of mermaids who spoke in riddles and truths. Only now, after months of tireless searching and many sacrifices, did they discover that it had been with them all this time.

Time itself appeared to hold its breath, the moment stretching into eternity, the only sound the distant calls of birds. Ben's thoughts churned wildly, his face awash with the full weight of the epiphany crashing over him. His gaze darted to Bella, then to the dragon, then back to Bella. He took a hesitant step forward, his voice a mere whisper at first, tinged with awe.

"Bella . . . The Dragon's Scale . . . " His words hung in the air, as the magnitude of the truth began to take hold.

All heads turned in unison from Bella, to the dragon, and then to Ben. His fists clenched tightly at his sides in an effort to steady the surge of exhilaration coursing through his veins. He drew a shaky breath, and extending his hand he pointed a trembling finger at Bella, then at the dragon, an almost frantic excitement weaving through every word.

"We've had it all along! We have the Dragon's Scale!"

Ben's voice rang out again, now steady and commanding, and brimming with conviction. His expression bore a mix of calm and fiery determination, his jaw set firm and his eyes alight with purpose.

"It be time to break the curse!" he declared to all the men. He glared at Bella with a piercing intensity. "We must place it back on the dragon and restore the Admiral Benbow."

Jim's face was a canvas of puzzlement as he recalled the words of the mermaids.

"But the mermaids said the soul must lay its hands upon the dragon, sacrificing itself to become the missing scale once more."

A spark of confusion danced in his eyes, a fleeting shadow crossing his expression as he grappled with the mermaids' prophecy. His gaze drifted to the sky, searching the vast expanse as if the answers might be hidden there. Slowly, his lips pressed into a thin line, his jaw tightening subtly as he turned the phrase over in his mind, unaware of the looming horror that was about to crash upon him.

Billy's face slowly paled as he watched Jim's expression shift, the confusion in his friend's eyes melting away, replaced by a creeping dread that spread like frost over glass. His chest tightened as the pieces of the prophecy began to come together in his mind, unfolding with grim clarity. His eyes widened, reflecting the mounting fear that clawed at his thoughts. His mouth became parched, his throat constricting as if the words threatened to choke him.

"And the mermaids said, 'The dragon, now complete, will return to its original form; yet the noble soul will be no more, having given everything to restore balance to the world.'"

He turned to Bella, and in that moment, the crushing enormity of the truth consumed him, sending a cold shudder coursing through his body, leaving an icy knot of terror in its wake.

Bella's eyes darted frantically between Jim and Billy, her heart pounding as she caught the gravity in their voices and the torment etched onto their faces. Her breath quickened, each inhalation sharp and shallow, as if the very air around her had thickened with impending doom. Her face turned ashen, her eyes widened, and pupils dilated in fear and disbelief. Her lips parted in a silent gasp as the horrifying truth struck her with the force of a tidal wave. She felt her knees weaken, threatening to buckle, and she clutched her chest, as if trying to hold her rapidly beating heart in place, the terror within her threatening to tear it apart. Her mind raced, flashing through memories of laughter, hopes, and dreams now overshadowed by the specter of sacrificing her life. The words of the prophecy—"the noble soul will be no more"—rang in her ears, a cruel sentence she never imagined would fall upon her.

Bella's eyes locked onto Jim. Her voice, trembling and small, escaped her lips as a desperate whisper.

"Jim?"

The single word was loaded with a plea for salvation, a desperate cry for the protector she hoped he could be in this moment of despair.

Jim's gaze locked onto Bella, the fear in her eyes a mirror to the turmoil brewing within his heart. He saw the silent plea in her trembling lips, the desperate hope that he could somehow save her from the cruel fate the prophecy demanded. In that moment, the excitement of adventure and the lure of gold that had once defined his life as a young pirate seemed to pale in comparison to the gravity of the sacrifice looming over them.

He had begun as a humble deckhand on a merchant vessel, his young heart pounding with wonder at each new horizon. The open sea spoke to something wild and restless within him, and he quickly found himself craving the freedom it promised. Embracing the pirate's life, Jim felt like he was stepping into a world where his wildest dreams could come true. Those days were filled with boundless adventure. The thrill of the chase electrified his veins, each pursuit a dance of wits and daring. The clash of swords and the roar of cannons became his symphony, every battle a testament to his bravery and skill. Combat was a gamble with fate, and he relished the adrenaline rush that came with each skirmish, the edge-of-your-seat excitement that made him feel truly alive. For Jim, those moments defined him, each scar worn like a badge of honor.

But it was the hunt for treasure that truly ignited his soul. The whispered tales of hidden gold and ancient relics were the fuel that kept his spirit burning bright. Each map he deciphered, each chest he unearthed, sent a jolt of exhilaration through him. The sight of glimmering coins and sparkling jewels was a reward beyond measure, a tangible proof of his daring and cunning. Gold and glory became his obsessions, the twin stars by which he navigated his journey through the perilous waters of piracy.

But now, Jim stood at the crossroads of his soul, a tempest of emotions raging within him. The choice before him loomed like a dark, foreboding storm on the horizon, each path fraught with irrevocable consequences. To break the mermaids' curse, to restore the Admiral Benbow and claim the untold riches it held, he would have to sacrifice the life of Bella—the woman who had become his anchor, his love, his everything. The very thought of losing her, of watching the light fade from her eyes, was like a dagger twisting in his heart, a pain that no amount of gold or glory could ever assuage.

Yet, the other path was equally daunting, a path that demanded he turn his back on the only life he had ever known—a life carved from the rhythm of crashing waves and the roar of the open sea, a life which would fire his soul for decades to come. To forsake the call of the horizon, to abandon the exhilarating chase across the endless blue, to relinquish the promises of riches beyond dreams that had fueled his every adventure—this was no small sacrifice. The idea of a quiet life, one filled with the warmth of family and the simple joys of domesticity, was as foreign to him as the deepest abyss of the ocean. It was a life that promised stability and love but at the cost of the intoxicating freedom and boundless possibilities that had defined his very existence.

And then there was Bella, her eyes filled with fear and desperate hope, her presence a reminder of what truly mattered. More than adventure or fortune, more than stolen jewels and whispered legends, she had become the greatest discovery of his life. The love they shared was a treasure far more precious than any gold, a bond no curse could sever, no prophecy could diminish.

But standing there—torn between two worlds—Jim realized that no matter which path he chose, a part of him would die.

Jim's heart thundered in his chest as he took his place in front of Bella, his body a steadfast shield against the cold inevitability of the prophecy. The air felt thick with tension, a palpable silence hanging over them like a dark shroud. He could feel Bella's trembling breath on him, an unspoken plea that coursed through the space between them. Yet within it, he found his strength, a purpose that blazed brighter than all the treasures he had ever chased.

Slowly, he turned to face Ben, his shoulders square, his stance unyielding, his eyes blazing with a defiant fire.

"No," he said, the single word hanging in the air. It carried no hesitation, no doubt—only the unbreakable conviction of a soul that had made its choice.

"No," he repeated, the word infused with anger at the cruel fates that would dare demand such an impossible sacrifice. It was a declaration, a vow wrapped in fire and steel, that dared the universe itself to challenge him. To protect her, he would defy the prophecy, the curse, and even the gods themselves if he had to.

Ben's eyes widened in stunned disbelief, the sharp edge of Jim's defiance cutting through him like a blade. He blinked, as though trying to convince himself that he had misheard.

Jim's gaze never wavered, his eyes locked onto Ben with an intensity that spoke of a heart ready to fight, to protect, to save.

"Bella will not be sacrificed," he declared, his words echoing like a vow made in blood. His voice dropped to a fierce, guttural growl that resonated with the sheer depth of his love and the unshakable strength of his resolve. "Not for all the gold on God's Earth."

Ben's face twisted with mounting anxiety, a stark contrast to Jim's steely resolve. The color drained from his cheeks, leaving his skin pallid and clammy. His eyes darted between Jim and Bella, wide with desperation and disbelief, as if seeking an escape from the reality bearing down upon him. The dreams that once had once burned so brightly in his mind—the glittering gold, the endless wealth, the intoxicating allure of fortune—all seemed to be slipping through his fingers like grains of sand. The very thought of losing it all sent a shudder down his spine, a cold dread wrapping around his heart.

His breath came in ragged, uneven gasps, each one a struggle against the rising tide of panic clawing at his chest. The air felt stifling, the weight of Jim's defiance pressing down on him, suffocating him. He turned to Billy, his expression a heartbreaking mix of hope and despair, his eyes pleading for an answer, a reprieve from this impossible choice.

"Captain," he said, his voice cracking under the strain of his emotions. "The ship. The treasure. We've come all this way."

Ben's gaze clung to Billy, searching for some semblance of hope, some sign that their quest for the Admiral Benbow's treasures would not end in vain. The desperation in his eyes was palpable, a silent plea that echoed louder than any scream. His heart hammered in his chest, a frantic rhythm that resonated with the urgency of his words.

"Captain," he repeated, his tone trembling with the anguish of dreams slipping away, "the treasure . . . "

Billy Bones, fabled captain of the legendary pirate ship the Siren's Call, stood tall amidst the shadowed forest. Here was a man forged by the sea's restless spirit—a man who thrived in the chaos of battle, where each clash of swords and crack of cannon fire sang the song of his soul. With every voyage, every battle, and every glittering prize uncovered, Billy Bones was not simply alive—he was immortal. To him, the sea was freedom in its purest form, a world without walls or chains, where only the wind and the tides dictated the course of a man's life. This was the only life he had ever known; it was the very essence of his being, the foundation upon which his entire existence was built.

But just as much, his underlying lust for wealth and the allure of gold ran as deeply as the blood that coursed through his veins. From the moment tales of daring pirate escapades reached his ears when just a lad, the promise of great fortune and the glory of conquest became the lifeblood of his ambition, the fire forging the man he would become. To Billy, though, treasure was far more than glittering gold and sparkling jewels. He chased not just the wealth buried beneath the sands or stashed in the holds of doomed ships, but the glory of the quest itself—the salty winds whipping through tattered sails, the clash of steel in the heat of battle, and the breathtaking moment when a treasure sat revealed, gleaming in the light of a victory hard-won.

The fame that accompanied each plunder, however, was the ultimate validation of his life as a pirate. To Billy, the gold itself was fleeting, but the stories woven in its pursuit? They were eternal. He reveled in the tales of his exploits that traveled faster than the winds of a storm, painting his name across the seas—the legends that grew around him were as precious as the gold itself, granting him immortality long after his ship had disappeared into the mist. His name was spoken in hushed respect, in reverent fear, and as a curse spat from the lips of his enemies. He was a man driven by more than just the pursuit of treasure; he was driven by the very essence of what that treasure represented—a life of adventure, the weight of a legacy, and the echo of a name that would outlast the tides themselves.

With Ben's words echoing in his mind—*The ship. The treasure. We've come all this way*—Billy Bones stood on the precipice of what would be the pinnacle of his storied life—a moment that glittered with the promise of the Admiral Benbow's vast fortune. The treasure, though, was more than just the realization of great wealth; it would be the crown jewel of a lifetime filled with peril and plunder. Every scar etched into his flesh, every ghost that haunted his restless nights, every drop of blood spilled by his hand—they all led to this singular moment of triumph, what would be his greatest conquest.

Here stood the fierce pirate captain who would not hesitate to cut the hearts out of a hundred men with his own hands for a fortune such as this. Yet now, he froze; his chest tightened, a vice of anxiety and confusion squeezing the breath from his lungs. He looked back at the dragon, then to Jim and Bella. Jim was standing firm, positioning himself between Ben and Bella, her face partially hidden behind his shoulder, protecting her against the encroaching threat. Bella clung to him, her fingers gripping tightly onto his shirt, trembling yet finding solace in his unwavering presence. Jim's eyes bore into Ben's, a fierce determination radiating from his core—a silent vow that no harm would come to the woman he loved.

Billy had been witness to Jim's love for Bella going back to their days at her village. But in this moment, the true depth of that love struck Billy with the force of a gale. It was a love that was raw, pure, and immeasurably powerful—a love that could move mountains and part seas. And with that realization came a surge of memories of his own first love, Molly, flooding back to him like the tide reclaiming the shore. The fierce devotion in Jim's eyes mirrored the same fervor Billy once saw reflected back at him when he gazed upon Molly. He could almost feel Molly's soft hand in his, the way her fingertips fit perfectly in his palm. Her laughter echoed in his mind, delicate and free, brightening even the shadows of his most restless days. The scent of her favorite lavender perfume filled his senses, transporting him back to those stolen moments under the summer stars, where every whisper and touch felt like an unbreakable promise. But then, the guilt that had always been with him washed over him as well. He had promised Molly, with all the earnestness of young love, that he would soon return from his voyages at sea and make her his wife. Yet that promise had been shattered, and when the news of Molly's death reached him, a tidal wave swallowed his world, leaving only wreckage behind. She had died waiting for him, her life slipping away while he chased the siren call of adventure. The realization of what he had lost was a wound that never fully healed, a scar that throbbed with the pain of regret.

Then, Billy's eyes softened as he looked at Bella, his heart swelling with a tender ache. The revelation that she was Molly's daughter had hit him like a bolt of lightning, yet it also brought a bittersweet sense of solace. Bella's features—the shape of her smile, the curve of her cheek— so reminiscent of Molly's, were a poignant reminder of the love he had lost but never forgotten. Her laughter, her gentle demeanor, even the way she tilted her head when curiosity bloomed in her eyes—all were echoes of Molly's spirit. In Bella, he saw not just a remarkable young woman but a living connection to the past, a bridge to the memories he cherished and the life he had once dreamed of. It was as if Molly had left a piece of herself behind, a legacy that now stood before him, vibrant and full of life. The pain of his loss mingled with a newfound hope, and for the first time in years, Billy felt a weight lift from his soul, knowing that through Bella, a part of Molly still lived on.

With his heart thundering in his chest as he beheld Jim and Bella, a surge of fierce protectiveness welled up within him. He couldn't bear the thought of Jim suffering the same heartbreak that had haunted him across the years. Nor could he stand the idea of any harm befalling Bella, the only living link to the woman who had once been his entire world. Molly would have never forgiven him for allowing harm to come to Bella, for standing idly by while her precious daughter's life was ended. Safeguarding Bella now became a sacred vow etched into the depths of his heart. It was his way of keeping a part of Molly alive, of holding on to a love that left an indelible mark on his soul. The thought of failing Bella, and by so doing failing Molly, was inconceivable.

Now, Billy's eyes locked onto Ben's with an intensity that could shatter stone, his fierce stare brimming with the conviction of a man who had weathered a thousand storms. The world around them seemed to fall away, drowned beneath the relentless pounding of their hearts.

"Ben," he began, his voice low but charged with an undeniable power, "look at me and listen well. Bella's life is sacred, and I will not allow her to be taken from this world. Not now, not ever."

The air shivered with the force of his declaration, his glare remaining as sharp as a cutlass, cutting through any doubt or hesitation.

"Mark me words, Ben," Billy continued, his voice steady and resolute. "No riches, no glory, no cursed treasure buried in the depths of Davy Jones' locker will ever be worth her life."

He took a step closer, his tone rising like a storm gathering strength.

"I'd face the fiery breath of a thousand dragons, the wrath of Neptune himself, to keep her safe."

Ben felt the full force of Billy's words crash over him, a tidal wave of unshakable resolve that left no room for argument. The rest of the crew, standing in tense silence, exchanged brief glances but made no move to speak. The allure of unimaginable wealth lay just within their grasp, a treasure that could change their lives forever, yet to a man they respected their captain's decision. They weren't just men chasing riches—they were Billy's crew, unwavering in their loyalty. And if protecting Bella was Billy's line in the sand, then it was theirs too.

Ben's face became a canvas painted with raw, unfiltered emotion—a storm of panic, horror, and helplessness. His wide, frantic eyes darted between the dragon's looming monstrosity, Jim's steely defiance, Bella's trembling innocence, and Billy's iron-clad resolve. Desperation etched jagged lines across his forehead, his features contorted as if he were teetering on the edge of a scream that refused to escape, his lips trembling as if caught between a cry and a plea. Fear burned in his eyes, his gaze, wild and unfocused, searched for an answer in the faces around him, each look a silent scream for salvation. Every heartbeat seemed to echo louder in his chest, a rumble of impending doom. His breath came in ragged, shallow gasps, each one a testament to the mounting panic that clawed at his throat.

And then, as if all the demons in Hell broke loose, the pent-up madness that had been consuming Ben's soul exploded in a sudden, wild rage!

His face contorted grotesquely, a mask of pure fury, his skin flushing to a molten crimson as if his blood had turned to fire. Veins rose like jagged tributaries across his temples, pulsing with every beat of his pounding heart. His eyes, once darting in frantic desperation, now blazed with an unearthly ferocity, the irises darkening to black pools of wrath. His jaw locked tight, the muscles straining with brutal force, making his neck corded and rigid. His lips curled back, and a feral snarl tore unbidden from his lips, baring his clenched teeth in a flash of raw, animalistic anger. His nostrils flared wide, dragging in great gulps of air with guttural, shuddering breaths that resonated like the growl of an approaching storm.

"BLAGGARD!" tore from Ben's throat like lightning ripping apart the night sky, carrying the weight of his desperation and fury.

In an instant, he lunged toward Bella, trying to grab her arm, his body a storm of desperate energy! His eyes, wide and wild with determination, locked onto her, as predator relentlessly pursues its prey.

With lightning speed, Jim's cutlass flashed from its sheath, a blur of steel slicing through the air as he positioned himself protectively in front of Bella! Ben's response was immediate, his own cutlass flashing out to meet the challenge! The initial clash was a thunderous collision, the metallic ring reverberating around the clearing! Sparks flew as the blades met, each strike a testament to their honed skills and raw determination. Jim's eyes narrowed, the calm precision of a seasoned warrior reflected in his every move, while Ben came at him with a savage intensity, each swing of his cutlass coming harder, faster than the last.

The ensuing battle was a whirlwind of chaos and madness! Their weapons collided with a deafening clang, the force of their strikes sending shockwaves through the charged air. Each movement was a blur, too fast to follow—a dizzying dance of death where every misstep could be fatal. Jim's blade slashed and parried with lightning speed, yet Ben's attacks were wild and relentless—a storm of steel that Jim struggled to deflect. Again and again their blades met. The metallic chorus of their duel rang out, each note sharper, harsher, piercing the tension that hung thick around them.

Billy stood at the edge of the fray, frozen as Ben's eruption of rage thundered through the air. For a single, paralyzing

The Secret of the Dragon's Scale

heartbeat, all Billy could do was stare, blindsided by the sudden ferocity that had overtaken Ben. He could see Ben's eyes burning with a wild, untamed fire, filled with the madness that had utterly consumed him. And in that moment, Billy saw not just a threat, but something summoned from the darkest depths, a demonic spirit clothed in flesh. The contrast between the Ben he had known and the creature before him was stark and jarring, a painful reminder of how far his friend had fallen. The ferocity in Ben's expression was primal—it was a face that spoke of deep, unyielding anger, of a heart consumed by darkness, and of a soul lost to the abyss.

Billy's mind raced, his heart pounding in his chest as he struggled to make sense of the nightmare before him. His eyes beheld in Ben the maddening hunger to claim what he felt was rightfully his, as though the world itself had shrunk to a singular point, the only thing that mattered lying just beyond his grasp. And then, he saw Bella, so small and helpless against the looming threat. She stood frozen, her face pale as moonlight, her trembling form a harrowing picture of fear. It was in that instant, a split-second carved in sharp clarity, that Billy realized what had to be done. His hand moved as if on instinct, gripping the pistol at his side, the weight of the weapon grounding him in the moment. He aimed, his eyes narrowing as he locked onto Ben.

The forest held its breath as Billy's finger tightened on the trigger, the weight of his decision pressing heavily on his soul. Just as the gun cocked, Ben's arm swung back with a ferocious speed, his cutlass slicing through the air in a streak of cold steel. The clang of metal against metal was sharp and jarring as the blade struck Billy's pistol, jerking it violently and redirecting its aim skyward. The gunshot rang out, a deafening crack that shattered the turmoil, its echo ricocheting through the forest like a rolling thunderclap, sending birds scattering from the treetops.

In that fleeting moment of chaotic motion, Jim's eyes caught the sliver of an opening. Time seemed to slow, the world narrowing to the point of his blade and the vulnerable space in

Ben's defenses. With a surge of adrenaline, Jim lunged forward, muscles coiling and releasing like a tightly wound spring. His cutlass drove straight and true, the tip piercing Ben's chest with a sickening ease, the sensation reverberating up through Jim's arm and into the pit of his stomach. The blade sank deep, finding its mark in the heart of the man who he had once called his brother.

Ben's eyes widened in shock and a guttural gasp tore from his throat. Then a wet, choking sound escaped his lips as blood bubbled up, staining his teeth a ghastly crimson.

Bella's scream tore through the forest, her voice raw with horror and heartbreak. She turned away, unable to bear the sight of the gruesome conclusion unfolding before her. Her hands flew to her face, fingers trembling as she tried to shield herself from the brutal reality.

Ben staggered, his grip on the cutlass weakening as his strength ebbed away. He fell to his knees, a pool of blood expanding around him in a dark, morbid halo. His eyes, once ablaze with wild fury, now dimmed, the light within them fading with each weakening heartbeat.

Leaves, moments before shivering in the violence, now hung motionless in the dappled light as a hush fell over the forest, the echo of Bella's scream lingering in the air. The once fierce warrior now lay still, his lifeblood soaking into the earth beneath him. The savage tension that had electrified the clearing dissipated, replaced by a heavy, mournful silence.

Ben's destiny had been fated by the relentless pull of a hunger that consumed so many before him. He had ignored the spirits' whispered warnings, straying deeper and deeper into the labyrinth of his obsession. The chase for the Dragon's Scale had twisted into a ravenous beast—its growls echoing in the hollows of his mind, its eyes gleaming in the shadows of his thoughts—leaving in its wake only the desolate landscape of madness. Yet now, the burden that had haunted him lifted. His features softened, the lines of rage and desperation melting away. Ben departed this world not as the madman he had become, but as the man he had once been. Peace found him at last.

Jim stood motionless, his cutlass dangling loosely in his hand, his head tilted down toward Ben's still body sprawled at his feet. His shoulders sagged as if bearing the weight of a thousand battles, though this one had taken something far greater than any he had fought before. There was no triumph in his eyes—only a quiet, harrowing sorrow that spoke of a cost too steep to measure.

Billy's hands hung limply at his sides, trembling slightly, his eyes fixed on Ben's lifeless form with a hollow stare that spoke of disbelief and haunting regret. Bella's face was streaked with silent tears, her lips quivered, her pale cheeks trembled with barely suppressed sobs. Nearby, the crew stood huddled together, their expressions shadowed by the weight of loss. Ben had been one of them—a brother in arms, a trusted hand, a steady voice in chaotic moments. Now, the air seemed thick with grief that tightened like a knot in each of their chests.

By forsaking the treasure of the Admiral Benbow, once the siren call of their pirate dreams and ambitions, it was here that Jim and Billy made their choice; it was a renunciation that struck deep into their souls like the tolling of a bell marking the death of who they had been, signifying a profound turning point in their destinies. This was no easy decision; it was a reckoning, an unspoken oath to abandon the lives they had once lived—lives steeped in the chaos of life at sea and the lure of gilded aspirations. And yet, in the shadow of that ending, there stirred the quiet, fragile promise of beginning—a step toward uncharted paths illuminated by the steady light of redemption.

For Jim Allardyce, the young sailor whose heart once beat in rhythm with the open sea, the life of a pirate had offered him everything he craved—adventure beyond measure, the intoxicating gamble of battle, and the triumphant ecstasy of unearthing treasures thought long lost to time. The salt-stained wind had whispered to his restless soul, the creak of ship timbers spoke to his boundless dreams, and the gleam of gold had burned as brightly in his imagination as the unending horizon. It was a life that had made him feel invincible, where each scar was a story, each victory a page in a legend yet unwritten.

But in this moment, Jim chose to renounce the call of the horizon, the thrill of the chase, and the promise of riches and glory that once ignited the fire within him. Instead, he now envisioned a future woven with the tender threads of domesticity, of a life shared intimately with Bella. This decision was not merely a departure from the tumultuous life of a pirate but a deliberate embrace of a quieter, more serene existence, where love and family were the true treasures; where he would be a loving and caring husband and doting father, whose days would be filled with the simple joys of home and hearth. The treasures he sought were no longer measured in gold and jewels but in the warmth of Bella's hand in his, the smiles of his children, and the simple, profound moments that define true happiness.

And for Billy, the sea had been more than a home—it was his blood, his breath, the very marrow of his existence. Every tempest weathered and every battle fought beneath the tattered sails of his ship had etched its mark upon his soul, shaping him into the man the world knew as the legendary Captain Billy Bones. Yet now, standing on that fateful threshold, Billy made a choice that even the fiercest storm could not have compelled from him. He relinquished the golden idol of his past—the life of a sailor, a pirate, a captain—the life that had so long defined him, the very essence of who he had been. With that decision, he severed his bond with the relentless, unyielding call of the sea, and with the hunger that had driven him to chase horizons without end.

He now found himself walking toward a horizon not painted with the storms of the high seas, but with the soft hues of dawn's quiet promise. For the first time, Billy could imagine a future less consumed by the chaos of adventure and more in tune with the serene rhythms of nature, where the whisper of the wind through the trees and the gentle murmur of a flowing stream replaced the crash of waves and the roar of cannon fire. His heart now yearned for the simple joys of home, the warmth and laughter shared with family and friends, and the serenity found in quiet moments of reflection. In choosing this new path, Billy embraced a destiny that promised the enduring treasures of connection and inner peace. His decision illuminated the true depth of his character, showing a man who found that true riches were not in conquest and plunder, but in the harmony and tranquility of a life well-lived.

And so, as the sun kissed the sea, the treasure of the Admiral Benbow was left behind, a relic of a life they had outgrown. In its place, they embraced the promise of a future rich with the treasures of wisdom, friendship, love, and a destiny shaped by their noblest aspirations.

It was time to go home—for that was where their hearts truly yearned to be.

About the Author

Steven Eisenberg is an author and educational consultant. Besides pirate adventures, he writes science fiction and nonfiction on the future of AI and society. He has published a novelette inspired as well by the story *Treasure Island* called *Fifteen Men, The Curse of the Aztec Treasure,* and his last book is nonfiction on the concept of robot rights, called *Can You Rape a Robot? Morality, Rights, and the Rise of Conscious Machines.*

He is also President of BTA Cultural and Educational Consulting, and the Princeton Academy of Language and Science. Previously, he had been a college biology/chemistry instructor for over 30 years.

Printed in Dunstable, United Kingdom